Lily-Josephine

Kate Saunders is a journalist and writer. She has written for the *Sunday Times*, the *Sunday Express*, the *Daily Telegraph* and *Cosmopolitan*, and has contributed to Radio 4's Woman's Hour, Start the Week and Kaleidoscope. She lives in London with her son.

Praise for *Lily-Josephine*

'I loved *Lily-Josephine*. Kate Saunders is such a wonderful writer . . .'
Jilly Cooper

'You will be swept along by the sheer force of an unashamedly sentimental saga that will keep you roaring with laughter and weeping buckets in equal proportions . . . *Lily-Josephine* is an armchair-and-cocoa novel of the highest order'
Daily Telegraph

'It's fairytale and thriller, romance and tragedy, everything that a gripping read should be . . . one of those books you won't be able to put down, or forget'
Woman's Realm

'This novel is driven by passion, lust and unrequited love – and it contains all the classic elements that make a good fairy tale'
Express

'Classy, vivid and clever. This epic of relative secrets has echoes of *Snow White*, and is no less scarlet and juicy than the proverbial apple'
She

'In taking Snow White as her template, Saunders pays homage to the power these (fairy) stories have over us. *Lily-Josephine* is a vibrant, unpretentious reworking of timeless themes'
Helen Dunmore, *The Times*

'A hugely addictive saga . . . I lapped it up'
Woman's Journal

'Disgracefully enjoyable . . . beguiling, deftly-written, high-class hocus-pocus'
Val Hennessy, *Daily Mail*

'It's Snow White with sex, and lots of it . . . the whole thing is just the ticket for when you're romance-free'
Red Magazine

'Very enjoyable'
Mail on Sunday

'An absorbing, rollicking story, throbbing with sex and effortlessly controlled by the increasingly assured Kate Saunders'
Good Housekeeping

'A big, engrossing read'
Ideal Home Magazine

'An intriguing, compulsive read . . . she is on top form'
The Bookseller

ALSO BY KATE SAUNDERS

Night Shall Overtake Us
Wild Young Bohemians

Lily-Josephine

Kate Saunders

Thou, queen, art fairest in all this land;
But over the hills, in the greenwood shade,
Where the seven dwarfs their dwelling have
    made,
There Snow-Drop is hiding her head, and she
Is lovelier far, O queen! than thee.

Snow-Drop THE BROTHERS GRIMM

ARROW

Published by Arrow in 1998

3 5 7 9 10 8 6 4 2

First published in the United Kingdom in 1998 by Century

Arrow Books Limited
20 Vauxhall Bridge Road, London SW1V 2SA

Random House Australia (Pty) Limited
20 Alfred Street, Milsons Point, Sydney,
New South Wales 2061, Australia

Random House New Zealand Limited
18 Poland Road, Glenfield, Auckland 10, New Zealand

Random House South Africa (Pty) Limited
Endulini, 5a Jubilee Rd, Parktown 2193, South Africa

Random House UK Limited Reg. No. 954009

A CIP catalogue record for this book
is available from the British Library

Papers used by Random House UK Limited are natural,
recyclable products made from wood grown in sustainable
forests. The manufacturing processes conform to the
environmental regulations of the country of origin

ISBN 0 09 946761 5

Typeset in Bembo by SX Composing DTP, Rayleigh, Essex
Printed and bound in Great Britain by
Mackays of Chatham, PLC, Chatham, Kent

To the memory of a beloved mother,
Betty Saunders

Acknowledgements

Various people have been extremely helpful and sympathetic during the writing of this novel. I owe particular thanks to my father, Basil Saunders, for advice about the Royal Navy, in which he served during the Second World War. Also, as usual, thanks to my esteemed siblings, Bill, Louisa, Etta, Eddie and Charlotte Saunders.

Before she died, our mother, Betty Saunders, gave me some excellent advice about this book. Her advice was always excellent, and we all wonder if we will ever learn to live without it, or her.

I would like to thank Emma Van Laun, Jonathan Lemonsky, Angela Coles, Joanna Briscoe, Amanda Craig, Philip Wells, Jane Hunter and Kate Parkin. Also Felix Wells and Dylan Lemonsky, who helped by simply being beautiful.

PART ONE
The Sisters

Prologue

1980

This time, the dream was beautiful. It was a dream about flowers; a carnival of colour, daubed across a dense tapestry of living green. A hundred shades of green, from palest eau de nil to blackest moss. The leaves were of every possible shape – lances, coins, stars, round shoots, flat fronds, silky filaments.

She had dreamed her way into a walled garden, which was how she had always imagined heaven. An embraced and protected space, holding all nature, boiled down and concentrated into a single acre.

In her dream, with the barnacles of prejudice and self-deception cleared away, she had no protection against the piercing sense of joy. The frets, frauds and sorrows of thirty-five years simply vanished, like breath on a mirror. Here, there was nothing to fear.

Such impossible richness. She was moving weightlessly, studying the plants whose names were symphonies – spike-nard, wake-robin, feverfew, foxglove, betony. They were all medicinal plants, soporific and healing. Also deadly, but in the dream, she knew that Death and Sleep were brothers. Death had never looked so lovely, or so kind.

There was a purpose, a plot, to this dream. Without hearing a voice, or seeing another soul, she was being propelled towards a certain patch of wall. Upon it grew a rambling rose, small and ivory white, veined with threads of scarlet. For some reason, she deliberately wrapped a hand around its thorny stem. It did not hurt. The blood brimmed and dripped from her, in a way that was rather satisfying – a job well done, an important matter dealt with. Where her blood fell, more roses grew. She watched, delighted, as they sprang up at her feet.

Then, suddenly, the delight turned to wrenching, engulfing sadness.

⎯⬦⬦⬦⎯

Primrose woke up. The luminous hands of her alarm clock stood at twenty past three. Her pillow was soaked with tears. Always tears. At first, the dream had seemed so beguiling – but it ended like all the others.

She looked at the pale square in the darkness, where the curtains were, and did her best to be rational. Just another of those bloody awful dreams, which had tormented her since Sidonia's death.

I should tell the doctor, she thought, even if he does write me off as a potty old spinster. I can't bear not knowing what will happen when I close my eyes.

She switched on the bedside lamp, conjuring her bedroom out of the menacing shadows. Here was her pink candlewick dressing gown (so despised by Sidonia), slumped over the foot of the bed, exactly as she had left it. Here, beside the lamp and the clock on the little table, was the mug containing dregs of Horlicks – her latest folk remedy against bad dreams.

Primrose was ashamed of the dreams. People who were practical, who coped and managed, should be able to handle the terrors whipped up by their own minds. She would go downstairs, and make herself some cocoa laced with brandy. That ought to do the trick.

She pulled on her dressing gown and fluffy pink slippers, careful not to wake Bunter, and walked briskly through the great, empty house. But the scent of the dream still clung to her nostrils, and she allowed herself the weakness of switching on all the lights.

Down the shabby bedroom passage, with its bandy-legged Victorian console tables. Across the landing, dominated by a vast and hideous brass urn. Past the gravy-coloured paintings of dead game and victorious horses.

What was she doing in the drawing room? Primrose wondered if she were still dreaming. Her hands shook as they fumbled with the bolts of the French windows, but she could not stop, until she was out on the verandah staring at

4

the rose.

The exact same rose, its flowers so pale and still in the mild night air.

Sweat broke out along her spine. At last, the door in her mind had burst open. She could no longer ignore the pounding and hammering of her own unconscious. She had told nobody about the dreams, she realised, because she already knew exactly what they meant.

These roses. Every day, for thirty-five years, Primrose had tended them, always firmly in the present, with barely a twinge of emotion. And now she was being dragged back to face her young self, crying gently for Guy as she pressed the roots into the soft soil.

Only one other person had known about Guy, and that person had sent the rose-tree when he died. With the sunlit dream-garden still superimposed upon the blackness of the real one, Primrose almost saw her.

Lily-Josephine. Named for the lilies of the Nile, who had turned their faces towards the beauty of Joseph, as to the sun.

She sobbed angrily. Yes, yes, I hear you – but why can't you leave me alone? What can I do? I don't want to look back.

Some peculiar justice was at work, forcing them all to face that unfinished business by plunging into the past. Lily-Josephine, along with so much else, was gone.

If only she could be forgotten.

Chapter One

————◆◆◆————

Before her sisters arrived, Primrose wanted to put the scrap-books in order. She had started her record of Sidonia's public life as a schoolgirl. Now, with a little more snipping and pasting, it would be complete.

'Nothing in the tabloids,' she said out loud, riffling through the pile of cuttings, 'but the posh papers did us proud.'

She was at the kitchen table with her scissors and glue, trimming the obituaries to fit the last pages of the last volume. They were all handsome, double-column affairs. Sidonia had lived all her life in the clamour of wagging tongues. She had done nothing quietly, and could not be expected to make a quiet exit.

The Times had printed the famous Leary portrait, 'Sidonia-in-Emeralds-in-Sidonia', now hanging in the Tate, of Sidonia with emeralds twinkling in her nipples. Primrose had never cared for it, feeling it undignified to have a mother whose naked body was so familiar to students of Twentieth-Century Art. She preferred the Hoppé photograph, repro-duced in the *Guardian*, which merely showed Sidonia's extraordinary, sculpted face.

Primrose studied the picture now, searching for the ruined old woman who had, until a month ago, overwhelmed her life. Once, Sidonia's beauty had inspired and obsessed artists, until it amounted to an artistic movement in itself. She looked like a pagan creature, half-god, half-mortal; caught in some classical glade, before vanishing in a flurry of cloven hoof-prints.

'Artistic Era Ends With Death of Legend'. 'Muse of a Generation Dies'. A fine and fitting climax to the heap of books. Primrose had kept them in apple-pie order. She had

7

appointed herself Keeper of the Flame, to justify her vexing existence caring for the Muse in her old age. It had been rather fun, showing the scrapbooks to the earnest young journalists who had, lately, made the pilgrimage down to Devon. Like being the curator of a museum, with a principal exhibit who guzzled gin all day and told rude stories.

Devotion had become a habit. Primrose had continued her duties as Grand Vizier after the death of the Sultana, because this had been the shape of her life for so many years. The full bitterness of the truth had not yet sunk into her bones.

It ambushed her now, making the scissors tremble in her plump hand. She had no future. Everything she had given to this place counted for less than nothing. God knew, she had not expected gratitude. But she had certainly expected more than humiliation and betrayal. She had made excuse after excuse for that nasty old woman. And at last, she had reached the point where Sidonia's ghastly behaviour could not be dressed up as anything else.

'I'd never have assumed I'd get anything,' she said, again out loud, for she had begun to talk to herself as if addressing an invisible internal jury. 'I did it out of love, always love. She knew that. But she kept telling me it was all mine.'

She stared down at the pile of newsprint, lapping around the plates of food she had prepared for her sisters' lunch. Then she stood, crumpled together all the loose papers and cuttings, and shoved the lot into the boiler.

It had been the final insult flung at boring old Primrose. Apart from anything else, it made her look such a fool. But at least Juana could not laugh at her. Sidonia had made a fool of her, too. Well, ha ha. Primrose was sixty-two, and her memory for smaller things was turning sere – but where Juana was concerned, it was a tender shoot of poison-green. The thing she had done, all those donkey's years ago, had been neither forgotten nor forgiven.

She was sorry for Isobel, limping from one financial crisis to another on her chaotic Irish farm. Mostly, however, she was sorry for herself. As she had done so often during these past weeks, she gazed out of the window above the sink, at her kitchen garden.

In a house of spectacular views, this little domesticated vista of nature trimmed and tamed was her favourite. It was the end of August, and the cycle of tasks was changing – from picking the raspberries to cutting back the canes; from picking salad leaves to planting winter vegetables.

The apples on the dwarf trees were beginning to blush with the sunrise streaks of ripeness. The damsons were plumpening and purpling on their stalks. A good kitchen garden is a perpetual harvest, but she would not be here for the richest harvest of all. Someone else would pluck her pears and plums, carefully swaddled in moth-traps and nets, and sprayed with organic pesticides. Or worse, they would drop off the branches and die neglected in the grass.

So unfair. The picture wavered and distorted in a film of tears. Primrose sniffed them away crossly.

'Come on, Bunter. Show a leg.'

Bunter was a portly, elderly labrador. He lay in his basket beside the Rayburn, surrounded by crocheted blankets and chewed slippers, as dignified as a little Pharaoh in his pyramid. In their declining years, Primrose often thought, she and Bunter were beginning to look rather alike. Grey around the muzzle, and too stout to fit into last year's coats. Both had been golden beauties, who had lost the rich tints of their youth.

She took Bunter's lead from its peg by the door, and clipped it to his collar under the fat, furry folds of his neck. 'You are good about this, darling. Those stupid farmers will insist – even when I tell them the Archbishop of Canterbury is more likely to worry their sheep than you are. You couldn't even make them mildly anxious.'

Side by side, genteelly ignoring the fact of the lead, Primrose and Bunter entered the beloved kitchen garden, walked through the lanes of apple boughs and opened the door in the south wall, framed by Primrose's espaliered peach trees.

At the front of the house, only God could take credit for the view. The Prospect lay, snug as a hazelnut in its shell, at the apex of the small, horseshoe-shaped bay. Lush shrub-beries and smooth lawns rushed down the edge of the cliffs, flinging themselves at the blue vastness of sea and sky. Primrose halted, to survey the kingdom she had lost.

The house itself was a solid mid-Victorian villa in the Italianate style; white stucco with round towers and curving balconies. A deep verandah, furnished with weathered rattan chairs, ran round two sides of the ground floor. The windows above were shaded with green-and-white striped awnings, giving the place an air of continental jollity wholly at odds with its gloomy and inconvenient interior.

The glory of the Prospect was its garden. Everything flourished in the sandy soil, and Primrose had simply filled it with as much colour as possible – searing scarlet gladioli, crown imperials like orange lampshades, bank upon bank of hydrangeas in every hue from shell-pink to purple, salvias from burning red to icy blue. The defiant vulgarity suited it. The bright petals were never still, but continually stirred in the smack and swell and salt tang of the ocean.

She had not loved all this as she had loved her kitchen garden. That was private, and this was the Prospect's public face, where impressions had to be made and appearances kept up. Yet here, too, were markers of her past life, like rings on a tree. Old loves, dead hopes. Primrose was good at burying such things under the prosaic imperatives of everyday life.

Lately, however, the past kept assaulting her, with such clarity of vision that she sometimes wondered if the house were haunted. Swiftly – frighteningly – she dropped back into the atmosphere of her dreams, and the creatures of the past seemed to cluster round her like a troop of ghosts. Sidonia and the sisters. Ralph and Charlie. Guy, of course.

But mostly Lily-Josephine, who now refused to be confined to dreams. Here she was, in broad daylight, demanding to be remembered.

<hr />

Isobel arrived first, fussed and dishevelled, in a taxi. Briefly, the sisters pressed their cheeks together.

'Good, you made it.' Without Sidonia, Primrose felt she had to fumble for a connection. It was like having a huge building torn down outside a window, and being confronted with an unfamiliar view. 'How are you?'

Like all people who never travel, Isobel was full of her journey – the lift from a neighbour to Cork Airport, the plastic carrier she had nearly lost at Gatwick, the connection she had nearly missed at Exeter. Eventually, the recital ended. She subsided into her armchair, sipping sherry and gazing around the well-remembered drawing room with a kind of wary eagerness, as if waiting for a performance to begin.

It was years since she had been here. Sidonia had always seen her youngest daughter in Dublin, at the Shelbourne Hotel. Long ago, Ralph had forbidden her the house, and it had suited Sidonia to extend the ban after his death.

Primrose plumped down on the sofa opposite. This was not going to be too bad. The two of them, though they spoke so seldom, always managed to find safe areas of conversation. You could trust Isobel.

'Only cold grub, I'm afraid,' Primrose said. 'The funeral exhausted all my culinary powers.'

Isobel made a clumsy movement of distress, nearly spilling her sherry. 'Listen, I'm so sorry I couldn't come. But it all happened so quickly, and Marius was ill, and –'

'Perfectly all right,' Primrose assured her. She had not wanted her sisters. The three of them either had nothing to say to each other, or far too much. 'It wasn't a big affair. Just locals, really. I suppose there ought to be a memorial service in town, at some point. But I couldn't have coped with more than a quiet service.'

'Was that what Mummy would have wanted, do you think?'

Primrose lit a cigarette. It was time to experiment with telling the truth. 'I couldn't have given a flying fart what she wanted. A quiet service was jolly well what she got.'

Flushing guiltily, Isobel laughed. Primrose could be quite a hoot, apparently, when she forgot to behave like a Head Prefect. Or was it simply that her assumptions about Primrose were out of date? Without the prism of Sidonia to look through, she realised, she barely recognised Primrose at all.

Impulsively, she blurted out: 'I often think about what

11

you said, that time in Dublin.'

'Oh? What did I say?'

'Don't you remember? Mummy was being filmed at the National Gallery, and you and I went to that bar. And you said she couldn't bear seeing the three of us together. Divide and rule, you said. That was her principle.'

'Hmm. I must have been sozzled, but how right I was.' Primrose decided to change the subject. 'Good grief, I haven't seen you alone since then. Give me the latest family woes.'

'Woeful as ever, thanks. We muddle along, though our house is still falling down, and I still spend my days slopping through the rain with buckets of pigfeed.'

'And Marius? How's his heart?'

'Miles better. You wouldn't know him – he's lost a ton of weight.'

'What about Sophie?'

The messily floundering marriage of Isobel's only child had provided great amusement for Sidonia, in her last year.

'He hasn't exactly left her yet,' Isobel said, 'but he's not exactly living with her, either. He's in an ashram at the moment.'

'Gosh. In India?'

'Basingstoke.' Isobel drained her sherry and twiddled the empty glass in her strong, farmer's fingers. 'So. Was it awful? Her death, I mean.'

Primrose shrugged. 'She conked out in her sleep. I found her next morning, when I took in her tray.'

Awkwardly, Isobel ventured: 'You'll miss her most. It's worse for you.'

Primrose frowned. 'I'll survive.'

From the other side of the house, they heard wheels crunching the gravel of the drive. Rather grimly, Primrose heaved herself out of the soft nest of sofa cushions. 'Juana. Punctual for once, because she smells money.'

Sidonia's favourite child; a fact she had never bothered to hide, and which seemed likely to colour the sisters' relationships until the end of time. It had not been enough for Sidonia to form their opinions of themselves. She had even controlled what they thought of each other.

By the time Primrose reached the door at the top of the porch steps, Juana had swung her elegant, silken legs out of her burgundy Jaguar, and was retrieving her Louis Vuitton handbag from the front seat.

Voraciously, Primrose ran her usual check for signs of age. No amount of money could protect a beauty from the ravages of time but, she had to admit, Juana at sixty was doing better than many at fifty. Her long, slim limbs had kept their feline elasticity. Her hair was still ebony-black – dyed, of course, but terrifically well, and twisted into a becoming French pleat. Juana would as soon have thought of dressing for the moon as for the country, and wore a defiantly urban beige suit, with matching Ferragamo pumps. Primrose, in her sagging blue needlecord dress, felt like a bundle of dirty washing.

And how the hell had she kept the skin around her dark eyes so taut? Primrose was sure she had had plastic surgery, but could never get Sidonia to tell her. Mummy and her favourite child were constantly teasing the others with their secrets.

It still hurt. Primrose felt a stab of mingled annoyance and glee, when she caught the expression of smug expectancy on Juana's face.

'Hello, Prim. Isn't this bizarre? Everything just the same, but no Sidonia. I can't think when I last came here.' The two had always met at Juana's homes in London and Paris. 'Did the funeral go well?'

'I think so.'

'God, you were quick off the mark, bunging her under the sod.' She stretched her polished, meagre skin into a smile. 'Highly appropriate, when she spent her entire life under sods of one kind or another.'

'She was cremated, actually,' Primrose said. 'Sorry you couldn't be there.'

Juana glided along the dark passage, towards the sudden, almost blinding sea-light of the drawing room. 'Oh, I'm glad you got the depressing part over without me – crematoriums, and having to be civil to the doctor and the charlady, and all that. Edgar's organising a proper memorial service in London.'

Edgar was Juana's only child, adored by his mother and Sidonia, and loathed by pretty well everyone else. Before the bombshell of Sidonia's death, Primrose's sole anti-Juana missile had been the fact that Edgar was homosexual, and that his mother pretended he wasn't. Edgar's extravagant queening was explained away as 'artistic temperament'. These had been the only times when Primrose and Sidonia had laughed together about Juana.

In the drawing room, Juana kissed Isobel. 'Poor thing, you look dreadful – all that rain, I suppose.' She took Primrose's place on the sofa. 'Right. We'd better get straight down to business.' From her polished lozenge of a handbag, she produced a morocco-bound notebook and dinky silver pencil. 'I've made a rudimentary list, to start the ball rolling.'

'List?' Isobel echoed stupidly.

'All the things Isobel promised to Edgar and me. Little things, mostly.' She began to reel them off, without taking her eyes from her sisters. 'The Augustus John sketches, the Menendez figure – well, obviously – the pair of Meissen bowls. Oh, and Edgar especially wants the Chinese dragon.'

Isobel cried: 'Not the dragon, surely? Mummy always said it was mine!'

Juana raised two plucked crescents of eyebrows. 'Did she? I'm afraid you must have misunderstood. She told me herself, only last month, when I rang from Paris. After all, Edgar is the only male in the family. I daresay it's all written down somewhere – isn't it, Primmy?'

'Indeed it is.' Primrose, who had intended to be solemn, was enjoying herself.

'Ralphie's snuffboxes,' Juana continued, 'and the silver epergne from the dining room. But not any of the awful Benares brass. That can go with the house. Ralph was a sweetie in his way, but his taste did incline rather tragically towards gongs and tusks.'

Ignoring the notebook, and the tears trembling in Isobel's eyes, Primrose heaved herself to her feet. 'Let's have lunch, before we go into the gory details. I thought we'd eat in the kitchen.'

'Oh, God,' Juana said, 'is that flatulent hound of yours still alive?'

'Very much so, thank you.'

'Sidonia detested him, too. How odd that he should outlast her.'

Primrose could not resist murmuring: 'I know which of the two I'd choose. At least Bunter's an honest character.'

Only Isobel heard her, and looked startled. When had Primrose, of all people, learned to profane the sacred name?

Juana was charging ahead, through the faded, baize-covered door and dank passage which led to the kitchen. There was a narrow shelf above the range, over which hung a large mirror, and a formal photograph of the three sisters, taken in the first year of the war.

In those days, they had all been beauties – Sidonia would never have countenanced a daughter who was not beautiful. Now, as they stood behind the table, they could not avoid comparing the fresh, lovely creatures in the photograph with their aged reflections in the speckled glass.

The young Primrose had been a confection of pink and white and gilt, with golden curls and periwinkle eyes; a girl you could eat with sugar and cream. Juana had been dark and exotic, with wondrous, velvety brown eyes. And Isobel, the baby of the three, had been sweet and bonny; all soft chestnut curls and blue Irish eyes.

Only Juana had any claim to good looks now, and even her lifted face had been marked by the things happening behind it – money, malice, and the inevitable disappointment suffered by people who live by those two totems.

The three sat down. Juana's lips compressed in distaste, as she glanced around the willow pattern plates for something she could eat. A lifetime of slimming had shrunk her stomach to a thimble. It could not possibly accommodate Primmy's hearty triangles of chicken quiche and cold ham.

They sat in awkward silence, grappling for some kind of bond. It was Isobel, usually too crushed by practicalities to express anything abstract, who suddenly said it.

'The trouble is, without Sidonia, we don't know who the hell we are. We're like stage props, for a play that's over.'

Chapter Two

'I have always been at the mercy of the fates,' Sidonia used to say. 'Things just happen to me, and I can't do a thing about it. I'm like a leaf in a storm.' She would open her slanted green eyes wide in bewilderment, giving her pagan face a beguiling vulnerability.

'Can I help it, if people fall in love with me, and want to possess me? I am at the mercy of a dreadfully passionate nature. For me, passion has always been elemental, impossible to deny. Perhaps ordinary people can live without it — what the hell do I know about them?'

Being merely born a beauty was not enough. Sidonia, from early childhood, had the temperament to match. Alternately petal-soft and diamond-hard, she whipped up tempests of passion, and followed wherever they led.

Her parents were respectable, well off and somewhat dull, living blamelessly in Kensington. Mr Venn (later Sir Lionel, knighted for services to the Ministry) trotted away to his office each morning with his rolled umbrella, and trotted home each evening to eat chops and blancmange in his Morris-papered dining room. His wife, Margaret, spent her days paying and receiving calls, ordering (but never cooking) chops and blancmange and playing bridge.

For many years, they were without issue. Then, like the parents of Rapunzel, the Venns were unexpectedly blessed, on the very threshold of middle age. Mrs Venn gave birth to a daughter. She was christened Muriel, provided with silver mugs and teething rings, and given into the care of an excellent nursemaid. For the first year, Mrs Venn saw the infant every day, after tea, and thought motherhood was a simple matter.

It was never simple again. Muriel was a peculiar child,

whose dreamy surface masked a will of iron. She was eccentric and stubborn, and did not always bother to leaven her amazing selfishness with charm. At eleven, she was tall and gawky, with two thin plaits of silvery hair and slanted, knowing green eyes. Mrs Venn would look at her sometimes, and a terrible sense of helplessness would assail her. She had done all the right things, provided the template for a perfect Edwardian childhood, and Muriel could not – would not – conform.

Governesses came and went, each reporting that Muriel was unteachable. Not stupid; simply at odds with the nuts and bolts of ordinary education. Untidy and full of mad fantasies, she tore off her hats in Kensington Gardens and pitched them into trees. When she visited the little daughters of Mrs Venn's bridge partners, she scorned dolls and halma, and initiated weird tableaux, starring herself seminaked in a muslin curtain.

Boarding schools were attempted, but trying to leave Muriel at any respectable school was like trying to leave a bag of orange peel on the train – the less you wanted it, the more people ran after you to give it back. Eventually, against her better judgement, Mrs Venn settled for a 'progressive' school recommended by a friend. Muriel had liked the mixed bathing and self-expression, but still refused to take into her head anything it did not wish to accommodate.

At seventeen, in the last year of the Great War, she returned home with a new name. Muriel was no more. Both parents violently opposed 'Sidonia', but Sidonia won. It was not merely that she refused to answer to anything else – she poured her entire personality into the new identity, becoming Sidonia so utterly that it was soon an effort to remember her as anything else.

And she was beautiful.

Not pretty, as other girls were, with their neat shoes, enamelled faces and smooth ridges of waved hair. Sidonia would not curl her hair, as everyone else did. It hung straight to her shoulders, insubstantial as a mist. She refused to wear a hat, in an era of hats that extinguished the face like huge candle-snuffers. Sidonia wanted to feel the elements, and was not about to hide her light under a flowered bucket.

She would not wear proper clothes, though Madame Violette, the dressmaker, ran her up such lovely copies of the latest models. Sidonia simply held them up against her tatterdemalion figure, laughing. Skirts were getting shorter, almost to the knees. You showed an expanse of silk-covered flesh, or a long, buttoned boot. Breasts and waists were hidden beneath shapeless jackets and the new 'freedom' foundation garments.

Sidonia preferred no foundation garments at all. Her idea of freedom meant emphasising her full breasts and slender waist. She loved old velvets and brocades and embroidered medieval cinctures. Her sleeves trailed, her skirts swept up the Kensington mud. Sometimes, she would see a flower in a front garden, climb over the fence and pluck it. Mrs Venn was mortified to have a daughter who was chased down the street by outraged parlourmaids. But what could one do?

Though the clothes looked – she thought – horrible, she could not deny that they suited the strange creature that had sprung from her decorous, conventional loins. And nobody could deny the fact of Sidonia's beauty. She was unique, undisciplined, almost supernatural; a mermaid, whose green eyes slanted bewitchingly above strong, Tartaric cheekbones.

She was not pretty. Everything about Sidonia – the pale, voluptuous lips, the otherworldly bleached colouring – was too pronounced for vague terms like 'pretty'. She did not even dance like other girls. Sidonia knew nothing of the foxtrot, the lancers, the two-step. Her body could not express itself according to any rules. She put on her father's records of Beethoven and Wagner, and flung herself about the room as if worshipping at some mad rite.

With sinking heart, Mrs Venn prepared for Sidonia's coming-out dance. True to form, Sidonia hated the dress, and elected to wear one of her diaphanous curtains. When her corsage arrived from the florist, she ripped it apart with a cry of delight, and wove the camellias into a coronet. She refused the virginal pearls her mother begged her to wear.

'Give them to the poor,' she said.

And she went leaping down the stairs, to greet the guests who had agreed to come because they liked and pitied the Venns.

Long afterwards, Sidonia would tell her daughters: 'Never assume you know what the fates have in store for you. I had no idea, when I "came out", that I was actually emerging into the daylight of my real life. At the top of the stairs, I was a girl. By the time I got to the bottom, I had seen Clive.'

Clive Rumage, the son of two starchy friends of the Venns, was a young subaltern. He had served gallantly on the Western Front. He had private funds behind him, and a fine army career before him. Sidonia did not care about any of this.

'He was the handsomest man I had ever seen. He stood under the electrolier in his scarlet jacket, with his hair glowing like molten gold. And I just knew. I had that desperate feeling of being shoved and manhandled by Destiny. How could I fight a force of nature? I don't remember anything else about the party, except dancing barefoot in the conservatory – Clive suddenly shouting: "Damn you!" and kissing me – not coming out until the National Anthem . . .'

Sidonia in love was a being of flaming recklessness, who moaned and arched against the body of the poor young soldier, until he knew he must marry her or perish.

'I thought so too,' Sidonia would say. 'What the hell did I know? I was only eighteen.'

Clive's regiment had been posted to India. Neither family was happy about the match, but it was useless to fight Sidonia. Mrs Rumage and Mrs Venn agreed that settling down as an army wife, in a pleasant and salubrious hill station, might very well be the making of her. Privately, Mrs Venn was giddy with relief. Sidonia off her hands, in the keeping of a serious young man. It was the answer to a prayer. Dazed with first love, Sidonia went along with all the arrangements like a lamb.

'If you can picture it, darlings – St Margaret's, Westminster, two spotty bridesmaids – haven't the least idea who they were – me in a hilarious veil, pushed down to my nose and fastened under the chin with a sort of bridle.' Sidonia always sighed at this point. 'Little fools that we were. It was sex that got us to the altar, not love. I often wonder what would have happened, if we had just done it, and got it out of our systems.'

Sex coursed through the systems of the young couple throughout the long voyage to India.

'I thought,' Sidonia said, 'that our minds were as attuned as our bodies. I'm afraid Clive was a disappointment to me. He might have crushed me and broken me, if I'd let him.'

One morning, on the verandah of her suburban-looking bungalow in Poona, it came to her, all at once, that she was not in love with Clive. Far from being her soulmate, he nagged her to conform. All the qualities that had enchanted him at first, and set his slow blood racing, now made him furious. He was horribly afraid that he had saddled himself with the worst liability known to an army officer – the Wrong Wife. Mrs Rumage did not go to the club, watch polo or join the other ladies in their gossips over the teacups.

Sidonia would later claim that she had yearned to immerse herself in the exotic, forbidden culture of the subcontinent, and that this was the reason for her ostracism. There was an element of truth in this, but the reality was simpler. She found herself in the one society where absolutely nobody – except Clive, and he soon joined the majority – found her eccentricities anything but tiresome.

She was six months pregnant, and expected to lead an invisible life, surrounded by other married women of her own class. Women were the key to success in Poona, and Sidonia was always less popular among other women. Why didn't they like her?

'Because,' Clive roared, during one of their frequent rows, 'you don't bloody like them! You won't even try, unless you've got an audience with balls!'

It could not end, until Sidonia had given birth. Weeks after Primrose was born, she swept up baby and ayah and jumped on the nearest steamer home. There were plenty of men on deck, as Sidonia watched the land of her marriage falling away behind her. She took off her wedding ring and pitched it overboard.

'The relief was indescribable, like taking off a corset,' Sidonia said. 'I think Clive was quite grateful. He certainly didn't wait long, before he found himself another memsahib.'

The Venns were heartbroken, furious, despairing, covered in shame. Nobody got divorced, let alone girls of eighteen with new babies. Clive, as a gentleman, had to pretend he had committed adultery, and pay a detective to 'discover' him with another woman in a Calcutta hotel. It cost a great deal, and Mrs Venn felt she could never, never look Mrs Rumage in the eye again. She could not, however, turn her wicked daughter from her door.

Baby Primrose was a major factor in her eventual acceptance. Pink and chubby, with golden curls and an adorable disposition, she was the child Margaret Venn felt she should have had all along. As if turning back the clock, she installed the child in Sidonia's old nurseries, sent the ayah back to India and hired an upright English nursemaid. The perfect upbringing, so rudely interrupted, could now continue.

It was an arrangement that suited everyone. Sidonia liked her baby, but motherhood and Kensington could not contain her. Leaving Primrose with her besotted grandparents, she fled to Paris.

'And there has never, in the history of this world, been anything like Paris in the twenties. One whiff of the air, and I knew I had landed on a star. Mother and Father had found me lodgings, in an apartment with a mean old lady. I didn't even bother to unpack.'

In the still summer night, Sidonia leaned against the open shutter and gazed out over the twinkling lights of the celestial city. The excitement was so potent, it seemed to burn the insides of her nostrils. Her French was poor and the only landmarks that meant anything to her were the Eiffel Tower, Notre Dame and the dome of the Pantheon. But while her respectable landlady slept the sleep of the just, Sidonia escaped, and instinctively followed the siren-call of Montmartre.

Here, among the narrow streets, among the artists and prostitutes and louche, international seekers of freedom, Sidonia discovered Jazz. In the suffocating fug of a smoky cellar, she danced like a bacchante to the wailing music of one of the fashionable Negro bands. And her Destiny watched.

He was an Argentinian sculptor named Diego Menendez, and Sidonia was in his grubby bed, under a filthy skylight full of bleared stars, within hours of meeting his fabulous dark eyes. This time, it was perfect, all-consuming love. Sidonia loved Menendez as she would love only one other man in her long life.

There was no romance here. Never once did he utter a word of love, or even affection. He was a wicked man, as handsome and as ferocious as a snarling panther. Sidonia modelled for him, slept with him, made his coffee and allowed him to rent her out as a model for his friends. When he was not hurling Sidonia's image into stone – growling as he worked, for he did everything violently – Menendez rewarded her with sex that kept her in a trance of adoration.

His tempers, his unreasonable demands, even the black eyes he sometimes dealt out when drunk, did not matter. She was his muse, and he was making her immortal. Crunching chips of stone, coughing in the eternal dust, she simmered and wept as he sculpted her flesh into ecstasy.

Her scent, he said, was civet and musk, and made him crazy. His tongue explored the folds of her vagina and swept rhythmically across her aching, swollen clitoris, until Sidonia could not tell where one orgasm ended and another began. At first, she would buck and moan, clutching his hair and sobbing that she could bear no more. Then she would lie still, almost paralysed. He could make her one giant, pulsing urge, continually shuddering between death-like repletion and painful reawakening.

Sidonia often told her daughters about their great love, but veiled its end, drifting away into dark hints of broken hearts and tragic partings. The truth was too sordid, the fissures in her poor heart too ugly to expose. The humiliation was terrible, and admitting to it would have spoiled the story.

Menendez moved another woman into his studio, and told Sidonia she was no longer required. He did not want a child, and her swelling belly repelled him. She returned to Kensington more dead than alive, stubbornly clinging to the belief that he would change his mind when their baby was born.

Margaret Venn was not surprised. She was beyond horror. The scandal of Sidonia was already so amazing that it could hardly get worse. Things were as they were, and another child in her perfect nursery might be good for Primrose. Sidonia lay eating and sobbing in her bedroom, until the child was born.

Juana (and how Mrs Venn disliked that flaunting, foreign name) was, after Primrose, a disappointment. She was scrawny and angry, with sallow skin and too much feathery black hair. Yet Sidonia fell in love with her, because she was part of Diego Menendez. The baby at her breast acted as cement for her broken heart. She crooned and sang, and would not allow the monthly nurse to take the child away at night.

Mrs Venn surprised herself with an ignoble longing to drive some sense into her with a good, hard slap. Fortunately, Sidonia quickly tired of posing as Madonna when there was nobody – nobody male – to watch and marvel. She left her children with her mother, and settled herself in a flat in Bloomsbury.

'I was wrong, to think my life was over,' Sidonia said later. 'I'm not in the least religious, but I do believe we're all here for a purpose. And after Juana was born, I discovered mine. Daphne was the one who put it into words. "My dear," she said, "you were made to Inspire."'

Daphne Wadsworth was a vigorous, middle-aged lesbian who wrote peculiar plays in blank verse. She also wrote, under the name of 'Phyllis Crewe', overheated romances which were advertised on the sides of buses, and which contained lines like: 'Good God, you little fool – did you think I was made of Stone?' Frail heroines were crushed against tweedy, manly breasts. Sometimes, the hems of their garments were reverently kissed. Her most successful, *Wild*

Wings of Youth, was reportedly inspired by Sidonia.

Women, as well as men, made up Sidonia's giddy circle, but Daphne was the woman who lasted longest. While others mutinied and drifted away, Daphne remained. She adored Sidonia, and felt this gave her the licence to criticise (mildly, and in the guise of praise) her more extravagant behaviour.

'You'll find real love again,' she told Sidonia, 'because a creature like you must be loved – without reason, without limits. You must be young, you must be gay. Can I chide a butterfly for selfishness? Can I reproach an orchid for hardness of heart, when all it says is "gaze upon me"?'

Sidonia appeared in one of Daphne's plays, as St Catherine of Siena. She had nothing to say, but under her long nun's veil she was naked, and her picture was all over the illustrated newspapers. The artists settled around her like a flock of hungry birds. By the time Primrose was a dimpling five-year-old and Juana a three-year-old vixen, Sidonia had been painted more often than the Forth Bridge – clothed and nude, on sofas, in forests; figuratively in elaborate gowns and abstractly with one eye in her forehead. She was, to Mrs Venn's unending embarrassment, famous.

Colm Leary was the most brilliant of the new painters; a good-natured, roistering Irishman with a face like a potato. He made his reputation with a dazzling series of portraits of Sidonia, culminating in the famous 'Sidonia-in-Emeralds-in-Sidonia', where she had emeralds gleaming on her nipples, and wore her own green eyes as a necklace.

Genius could win her. She fell in love with Colm Leary, became pregnant, and married him.

'You can't open a newspaper these days, without being confronted with birth control,' said Margaret Venn. 'So where has Sidonia been? Why hasn't she noticed?'

Little Isobel joined her half-sisters in Kensington. The nursery was complete.

―◇◇◇―

The sisters' lives were ruled and bound together by the presence of Granny. Sidonia was glamorous and thrilling, but she was also chaotic, and not to be relied upon. Granny was constant and unchanging, the same yesterday, today and tomorrow. At any time of day, the girls knew exactly where to find her, and what she would be doing.

They knew, when they kissed her good night, that her cheek would smell of violet powder. She would tell Isobel, as the baby, to dip her fat hand into her cardigan pocket, and they all knew Isobel would find three pieces of barley sugar. When she read to them after tea, Primrose would find her spectacles in exactly the same place each evening, behind the cloisonné vase on the tallboy. Her children and her servants lived to a rigid routine, of which Granny was sternly proud. To say something was 'well run' was her highest compliment.

For years afterwards, the sisters carried round Granny's internal clock as the template for a proper, ordered existence. Lunch, when not served at precisely one o'clock, was not, strictly speaking, lunch. A dinner of less than four courses was not dinner. Primrose liked being in the Wrens when war came, because the routine reminded her of Granny.

Outwardly, Primrose, Juana and Isobel were three nicely brought-up Kensington children, marching round the statue of Peter Pan every afternoon in their blue tweed coats and matching velvet bonnets. Their domain was two large rooms with barred windows, at the top of the tall house. They slept in the night nursery, and played and ate in the day nursery.

Primrose bloomed like a pink in a tidy herbaceous border. She loved Granny and Grandpa with easy, unshowy affection. From a great distance, she shyly worshipped Sidonia. Often, she fantasised about living with her all the time, and leaving wild flowers on her plate at breakfast.

Juana was spry, dark and obstreperous; a child to be squashed and de-cornered, Granny thought. And how was one to address a little girl as 'Hwana', like some heathen deity? Her sisters called her 'Ju', which sounded only slightly better. Sidonia made a silly fuss of her – and it was perfectly true, the child was quite astonishingly pretty. Grandpa, normally so sensible, called her 'Juanita', mesmerised by those huge black eyes. It was a style of beauty Granny distrusted. She knew she was too strict with the little witch, but it was for her own good. She was on her guard, afraid of bringing up another Sidonia.

Isobel, babied by Granny until she was at least four, was simply a happy little butterball, snug and protected in her own innocent world – a creature you could cuddle and kiss, but also ignore. She quickly won herself a shining reputation for being no trouble.

The admirable order of the Kensington nursery was, however, only one side of the picture. Granny could never forget that they were not a normal family. It was impossible to ignore the fact that the three children had three different fathers.

If only, she thought, they had all been like Clive Rumage. A continent away, Clive nevertheless maintained a constant, beautifully correct interest in the daughter he had barely seen. Long letters passed between Granny and himself, concerning Trust Funds, governesses and suitable summer holidays at Cromer.

No matter what Sidonia did, Primrose was never to forget that she was a Rumage. As soon as she was old enough, she was sent to stay with Clive's deaf, invalidish mother, and his jolly maiden sister, Aunt Anthea. It cost Granny a pang to part with her, but she knew she was doing the right thing. Primrose was to attend a decent boarding school, and that was right too. Clive wrote his daughter monthly letters, enclosing photographs of her two half-brothers. Very early on, it was settled that she would sail out to India when she finished her schooling. Granny dreaded parting with her, yet was pleased that her favourite had such a good, conscientious father.

Diego Menendez, on the other hand, made no contact whatever. It was Sidonia who forced him to notice Juana. She had the child photographed by the best portraitists in London. She sent Juana for Spanish lessons, with a snuffy old Señora in Battersea. Juana never saw her father, but Sidonia saw to it that she grew up in his atmosphere. Her delight in the child's likeness to Menendez was extravagant.

26

As for Colm Leary, he claimed to adore his baby, but Granny forbade him the house after the parlourmaid found him, drunk and vomit-stained, on the doorstep. This happened shortly after Sidonia, tiring of marriage, had ejected him from the Bloomsbury flat. He made no awkward claims of his own, but he had a mother. To Granny's vexation, Mrs Agnes Leary – a garrulous, faux-genteel Dubliner – occasionally won permission to snatch Isobel away for holidays in Ireland. Great was Granny's wrath, when the little innocent returned with an accent and a rosary.

Yet what, in the end, could she do? The bitter fact remained. Her three grandchildren were a jigsaw puzzle, with half the pieces missing. She rejoiced to catch gleaming fragments of Clive in her beloved Primrose, but any bits of Menendez and Leary in the other two she utterly deplored.

As the girls grew, Granny became aware of another disunifying force in their lives. Sidonia, who might have been assumed to bind them together, was actually forcing them apart. This was particularly noticeable with Primrose and Juana.

'She makes a fuss of Juana, and ignores the others,' Granny complained to her husband.

'Well, you've always preferred Primmy,' he pointed out.

'If that is the case, at least I try to hide it. I do my duty by them equally. I don't merely use them for cheap effect.'

'You're thinking about the cherries again,' her husband said.

Yes, she was. Granny, whose temper was usually under such perfect control, burned with rage whenever she thought of it.

On Juana's seventh birthday, Sidonia had descended like a bird of paradise, bearing paper crowns wondrously painted by a besotted old Royal Academician. She also brought the old RA himself, and an even more besotted young man in horn-rimmed spectacles. He spoke not a word, and shuddered when offered tea. He had come to watch Sidonia making magic. Granny, who was acquiring a nose for such things, instantly divined that he was her latest lover.

Sidonia and her entourage stayed in the nursery for the

whole afternoon, working all the children up to a dangerous pitch of excitement. Before she left, she gave Juana, who was decidedly vain, a painted box full of theatrical make-up.

Primrose's ninth birthday fell just over a month later. Still reeling from the effects of the last one, the household waited for the next attack. What would she do this time?

Tea was half over when Sidonia tumbled out of her taxi, hatless and with horn-rims in tow.

'Happy birthday, darling! Happy, happy birthday! I have brought you the most beautiful gift in the whole of London!'

Around the birthday tea-table, the atmosphere became electric.

Sidonia, breathing lightly, as if scared of disturbing something very fragile, produced a broken paper bag.

'Cherries!' she exhaled the word prayerfully, gazing round at them all in naive excitement. 'Aren't they perfect? The minute I saw them, I knew I had to have them. Can you think of a more perfect gift? I've brought you nature's riches – summer in a brown bag!'

Primrose was a polite child. Even as the ghastly truth sank in – that her adored mother was giving her nothing but a bag of cherries for her birthday – she gamely swallowed her tears of disappointment. 'Thank you, Mummy.'

Should she eat them, or were they only meant for looking at? She was worried about doing the wrong thing. And she had never cared much for cherries. The stones were tricky to get out, and the juice might stain her best pink silk frock. She put the bag beside her plate, next to the lovely wristwatch from Granny and Grandpa, and went on eating her tea.

It was Granny who made the fuss. She pounced on Sidonia and her lover as they ran away down the stairs. Trembling with rage, she stood above them, wearing a mauve paper fireman's hat which somehow added to her majesty.

'How dare you? All that song and dance over Juana, then you deliberately insult Primmy! A stupid bag of cherries! Is that really all you care about your eldest child? You don't deserve her!'

Sidonia's vivid emerald eyes flooded with tears. She tilted

up her face, brave and defiant. 'You don't see, do you? You might as well be blind. I suppose I should be sorry for you – you live in a world without beauty. I couldn't have given a more precious gift. She'll remember it all her life!'

'She certainly will!'

(She certainly did.)

Cruelly misunderstood, Sidonia fled the house of the Philistines in tears, with her lover's arm around her.

Within days, the tale of Sidonia and the cherries had whirled round every salon in artistic London. Such a perfect illustration, people said, of Sidonia's unique affinity with the natural world. How she must have suffered, at the hands of such a purblind, unimaginative clod of a parent. By rejecting the cherries, she had rejected all that was True and Lovely in Sidonia.

Only one person dared to take the Philistine's view. 'Poor little wretch,' said Daphne Wadsworth. 'If my old mother had palmed me off with a bag of bloody cherries off a barrow, because she was too lazy to get me a proper birthday present, I'd have killed her.'

This was the beginning of the cooling of Daphne's adoration. Under her posturing, she was rich in the unfashionable commodity of common sense, and had a kind heart besides. The cooling was a long process, and ended – much later – in a crackle of frost. There would be a time, in the unseeable future, when Daphne recalled the incident in rage and sorrow.

Granny's rage flared up again in less than a year. The Book of the Month Club sent her an acclaimed new novel, ostentatiously dedicated to Sidonia. Its heroine was a beauty-loving free spirit. The heroine's mother was an unfeeling Philistine, and the story opened with the episode of the cherries. On the back was a large photograph of horn-rims, and Granny pitied the man. He could read meanings into the cherries until he was blue in the face, but Granny knew exactly what they expressed – and it had nothing to do with beauty or art.

Sidonia ignored Primrose and spoiled Juana because she was still in love with Diego Menendez. No other man could hope to be more than a prop in her fantastic saga. Thank God, Granny thought, for Roedean. Her darling Primmy needed to be rooted in the real world; to take her place among normal people who valued Rumages more than Sidonias.

Primrose loved school. She was a fine hockey player, a hard worker and head of everything that required virtue rather than brains. She was a real English schoolgirl; hearty and enthusiastic.

It was a pity about Juana and Isobel, condemned to a dreary convent. Sidonia had insisted Juana must be raised as a Catholic, the faith of the godless Argentinian. Isobel was thrown in after her, as a sop to her interfering Irish grandmother.

After all these years, Sidonia was still trying to persuade Menendez to notice their child. And when Juana was sixteen – a worryingly sinuous and knowing sixteen – he did. Out of the blue, Menendez summoned her to Paris.

'Absolutely not,' Granny snapped. 'She'll have to step over my dead body first.'

'He's her father!' shouted Sidonia. 'We are going to Paris!'

She telegraphed the date of their arrival, and received another telegram in return: 'Not you stop Juana alone'.

Granny simply stood aside, marvelling over Sidonia's inability to take a hint. She was all set to send another telegram, reading 'Do not understand', until Juana scornfully said:

'I'll translate, if you like. He doesn't want to see you. He only wants me.'

She could be a nasty little Madam, thought Granny, but who had made her what she was? It served Sidonia right. Juana went to Paris alone, and returned more knowing and secretive than ever – worlds removed from Primrose, who still liked Bird's toffee and Angela Brazil, and thought 'adventure' meant cycling on the Downs.

Juana's relationship with Sidonia had undergone a subtle shift. The mother seemed almost afraid of her daughter, and almost angry. For some reason, Juana had contracted a habit of speaking Spanish, and some of the words she murmured at her mother made her wince.

'Why send her all the way to Paris, to learn Spanish?' Granny complained. 'Her French is as bad as it ever was — and she won't breathe a word about what she's actually been doing.'

Grandpa had died the previous year, and she now confided in Primrose.

Who said: 'She won't tell Mummy, either. I think she's trying to make her jealous.'

'You have to admire Sidonia, in a way,' was Granny's surprising reply. 'She's never found anyone she loved as she loved that frightful foreigner — not for want of trying, either.'

In 1937, Primrose was eighteen. She was to go to her father in India. This was entirely right, but the prospect of losing her literally broke Granny's heart. She had a bad heart attack, which left her a feeble shadow of herself.

'I'm not going,' Primrose told her. 'I'm staying here. Dr Shaw says you need someone to take care of you.'

'Don't be foolish, child.' Granny was strict, because the tears were making her tired eyes smart. 'The passage is booked. It's all settled.'

'Oh, Granny — as if I could ever leave you! No, I'm to take care of the house and the servants, and you're to rest.'

Primrose's managing skills were very nearly on a level with her grandmother's. Gradually, thankfully, Granny allowed her to take full control.

The war came. And at first, it only affected the lives of the three girls as it affected Sidonia. Colonel Clive Rumage remained in India, in the thick of the bloody run-up to Partition and Independence. Diego Menendez stayed in Paris, ignored by both sides. Colm Leary, as a neutral Irishman, only fought in pubs. Sidonia, however, embraced wartime London with gusto. Throughout the 'phony war', long on patriotic speeches and short on danger, she began to shed her forty years like a phoenix rising.

'She's in love again,' said Juana. 'And this time, it's stupendous. Have you noticed, she hasn't mentioned Menendez for months?'

He was in the Forces, and Sidonia called him 'The Eagle'. Passion swirled around her, scenting the atmosphere of duty and austerity. Her daughters had never seen her in love like this. Juana was fascinated and avid for details, but Primrose and Isobel were rather frightened. Isobel's Irish blood stirred with foreboding, and she said she felt a great change looming, like a storm.

It broke in the aftermath of the Battle of Britain, when the war lost all phoniness and became horribly real. Down came the first bombs. The young parlourmaid joined the ATS, Cook carried her skills away to an Army canteen in Aldershot, and Primrose and the old parlourmaid began to feel the effects of the shortages.

One afternoon, when Primrose was retreating from a long argument with Granny about the Anderson Shelter in the sooty back garden ('It's no use, I'd rather be bombed like a Christian, in my own bed,') she met her mother in the hall.

'Mummy – ?' She looked like a standing corpse, drained of blood.

'He's dead,' Sidonia said. And fainted into her daughter's arms.

The crisis had come, the light had gone out.

Which made them all the more surprised, when she announced – as if announcing a funeral – that she was in love again.

'Of course, she's not in love,' Juana said. 'She's getting old. She needs to snaffle someone rich, before her bosoms hit the floor.'

Even she shared the general astonishment, however, when Sidonia married the man.

Chapter Three

'We'll take our coffee out to the verandah,' Primrose said. 'Shame to waste such a gorgeous afternoon.'

Juana pushed away her untouched plate. 'I'll make it. I refuse to touch the seething grey brew you call coffee.'

'It's the South American in you,' said Isobel. 'Yours has always been lovely.'

Outwardly, lunch had been amiable. This was largely due to Isobel, who could not help enjoying a holiday away from the farm. She could not, however, overcome the insistent tension, tightening with every passing second.

Primrose carried the fragrant cafetière out to the verandah. The sisters arranged themselves on the creaking rattan chairs, their faces half-turned towards the sea and sky, spilling out of the cup of the bay.

I shouldn't tell them here, thought Primrose, on the point of relenting. Then Juana took out the morocco notebook, and her heart hardened to flint. She was only getting what she deserved, after all.

'Yes, how sensible. Time for business.' She tossed a biscuit on the wooden floor for Bunter.

There was a long silence. Juana's dark eyes narrowed. 'You've got bad news for me.'

'Now, what on earth –'

'You're smirking.'

Isobel wrenched her eyes away from the view. 'Don't start!'

'I'm going to make one thing absolutely clear,' Juana's light, conversational tone had always been her preferred medium for conveying threats. 'I know exactly what Sidonia wanted. She told me, categorically, that she intended to leave the lion's share to Edgar, her only male descendant.

33

I've got it in writing, and if there's anything the matter with her will, it's because you've been plotting. Please don't imagine I won't go to court.'

'Oh, for goodness' sake, this is nonsense!' protested Isobel. 'We're not in a film.' She had been exiled in Ireland for so long, she pronounced it 'fillum'.

Primrose was laughing, without mirth. 'I wondered how long we could leave that particular depth unplumbed. Do go to court, if you like. I've had armies of lawyers combing the will, and it's sewn up tighter than Bunter's bottom.'

'I can think of tighter things.' Isobel was desperately trying to lighten the atmosphere. The poison of her sisters' ancient quarrel was seeping into the sweet sea air.

Both ignored her.

'Equal shares,' Primrose said, watching Juana hungrily. 'Sidonia's money, divided neatly into three.'

Up went the plucked eyebrows. 'And the house? Furniture? Paintings?'

'Patience, Ju. Don't you want to know the extent of our wealth?' Primrose left a dramatic pause, then blurted out, with sudden, lashing bitterness: 'We each get two thousand, four hundred and twenty-eight pounds.'

The silence stretched on and on. Not a muscle moved in Juana's tight, immaculate face, but she was at bay, waiting to pounce.

Isobel mumbled: 'That can't be right, surely?'

'And fourteen pence.' Primrose sagged in her chair, old and defeated.

'Now, hang on,' Juana said slowly, 'what happened to the rest of it? The rest of the fortune she's been living on like a queen all these years? If you're going to tell me she left it to some bloody cats' home –'

'What difference does it make?'

'God almighty, the old bitch can't have spent it! No, that's impossible. There was nearly eleven million, all in gilts and stocks as solid as the Rock of Ages.'

'Was there?' gasped Isobel.

Juana nodded. 'Edgar looked into the figures last year.'

'He needn't have bothered,' Primrose said. 'Sidonia

34

didn't spend it. She couldn't, because it wasn't hers.'

Her sisters clamoured: 'What? What?'

Like all bad news, however improbable, this had the doomy ring of truth.

Primrose lit a cigarette. 'She was living on the income. Ralph only left her a lifetime's interest in the estate.'

'I don't believe you!' Juana cried.

Isobel put the screaming question into words. 'So who does it all belong to? Ralph must have left it to someone.'

'Oh my God,' Juana whispered. Her complexion dulled to parchment. She looked ill. 'No.'

'Lily,' Primrose said. 'After Mummy's death, the whole shooting-match was to pass to Lily-Josephine.'

The name, unspoken for years, dropped like a bomb.

Almost to herself, Juana said: 'But she's dead.'

'She died ages ago,' said Isobel. 'Didn't she?' There was a spark of interest, almost of hope, in her shocked eyes.

'She had a son, apparently,' said Primrose. 'And when he's found, everything belongs to him. Money, house, pictures, silver – everything.'

'Found?' Juana snapped. 'Is he lost?'

'Don't get your hopes up, dear. People are easy enough to find, when they're millionaires. He's not Lord Lucan.'

Juana's painted claws tightened on the arm of her chair. 'Did Sidonia know about this?'

'Of course she knew,' Primrose said.

'But she promised –'

'She lied! All right? Have you got that, both of you?' shouted Primrose. 'She promised everything to all of us, to keep us dancing round her, and she was lying.' Her voice rasped and broke. She pulled a shredded piece of tissue from her sleeve, and blew her nose. 'All we ever owned was what came from our fathers. I've got my Trust Fund. You get the Menendez Madonna, and Isobel gets the Leary in the upstairs sitting room.'

'Gosh.' Isobel, well trained in making the most of what was to hand, instantly forgot her dreams and pounced on reality. 'One of his best, too – Sotheby's sold a Leary a few months ago for two hundred thousand pounds. Gosh.' She smiled, and the years dropped from her lined face. 'Bang goes the overdraft, then.'

She turned to Juana, and the smile faded. Juana was shaking. She leapt up clumsily, knocking the table, and dashed indoors.

Isobel and Primrose were left gaping at one another, fumbling for the language of this new country.

'Is she – should we – ?' Isobel began.

Primrose gave a long sniff, as if rousing herself. 'She won't thank you for interfering. And she certainly doesn't want to see me.'

'This is like a fairy story. It was magic gold, which vanished when she died. Why did she tell us all those lies? I'd have loved her just the same, without the money.'

Primrose lit another cigarette, from the stub of the last. 'But she didn't want us to love her. I think she wanted us to hate each other.'

'Here,' Isobel said, 'give me one of those.' She reached for Primrose's packet of Bensons.

'Thought you'd given up.'

'Yes, to encourage Marius, after the heart attack. But by God, I've had a turn.' She lit the cigarette, and inhaled with disarming relish. 'I mean, what a time it's been. There was me on the plane, half wondering if I'd come into a fortune – half worried sick that she'd cut me out altogether. She never did like me as much as you two. And here I am, the owner of a valuable painting. Which I really ought to give to the National Gallery of Ireland, I suppose.'

'You won't, will you?'

'Don't be daft. We're up to our eyes in debt, and so's Sophie. And Marius is going to have a holiday, if I have to chloroform him first.'

Reluctantly, Primrose laughed. 'You only just heard, and you've spent it already.'

'Yes, bugger the Chinese dragon. Hard cash will do me fine. I wish I knew what's got Juana in such a state – she's rolling in money.'

'Greed,' said Primrose. 'Sidonia knew greed was what drove her, and that's what she used to keep her on a string.

With me, it was wanting to be loved. The betrayal was what hurt me most. That and losing my garden.'

'Of course. You'll have to move, when they find the real owner.'

'Her son. I can't imagine him, can you? I wonder if he looks like her.'

Isobel refilled their coffee cups. 'Ju hated her, almost as much as Mummy did. I expect that was a good part of the shock. She'd be mad as hell if she heard this – but I liked Lily-Josephine.'

'Did you?' Primrose laughed again. 'What a day of revelation.'

'She was nice to me.'

The roses were directly in front of Primrose, on the other side of the wooden balustrade. She said: 'I liked her too. Very much, in the end.'

'In a way,' Isobel said, 'I'm sorry for you, losing the house, and all – but in a way, Prim, I'm rather pleased.'

'I suppose I am too. In a way.'

They stared at each other, surprised and curious, as if aware, for the first time, of the secrets that lay between them.

'It seems,' Primrose said, 'we both owe something to Lily-Josephine. She's dead, so she can't have her inheritance. But she can have justice.'

Chapter Four

'I feel as if everything in the world just collapsed like a soufflé,' Juana said, 'the minute the old bitch died.'

Edgar lounged royally on a flimsy Hepplewhite sofa. His arms were stretched along the back, in an attitude of careless arrogance, but his full lips had a peevish drag to them, and one loafered foot twitched irritably.

'I needn't have wasted all that energy being sweet to her,' he said. 'She had the last laugh – whatever the joke was.'

The sofa was in the back room of his current lover's antique shop, in Old Bond Street. Edgar wore faded black Levis and a scrupulously clean, artistically frayed white flannel shirt. He was thirty-six, and still presenting himself in the character of a boy. Mostly, he got away with it. Today, the lines showed round his quick dark eyes. It was suddenly rather obvious, even to his mother, that his stomach was softening and his dark hair showing threads of grey.

She roved distractedly through the shuttered gallery of exquisite objects. 'I'm sure she meant me to be mortified. But you – she absolutely adored you. How could she lie to you like that?'

'I wouldn't be in this fucking mess if she hadn't strung me along about the inheritance,' Edgar said. 'I hope she's sizzling in hell. I hope they're turning her on a spit, and forcing her to wear flared Crimplene slacks.'

'Eddy, we ought to see if we can limit the damage.'

'We can't.'

'Have you talked to Nigel?'

'No, and don't you say a word to him, either. He'll be livid. He was counting on it, too. For pity's sake, why didn't you tell me Lily-Josephine had a son?'

'I didn't know. Sidonia must have, but she had such a

talent for forgetting facts she didn't like. And for making everybody else forget. She loathed Lily-Josephine so much, we got out of the habit of even mentioning her name. Even Ralph. He was a terrible coward.'

'Jesus, what a family,' Edgar snapped. 'It's like a South American dictatorship. You simply let your stepsister disappear – with all that money on her head.'

'I couldn't stand her either,' Juana said, sourly surveying her fingernails. 'She was a scheming little tart. I always understood Sidonia had sorted her out. I mean, out of Ralph's will. That's what she told me.'

Edgar leaned forward, resting his elbows on his knees. 'And who is this lucky little Lord Fauntleroy?'

'I haven't the faintest idea.'

'Well, what's his name?'

'I don't know.'

'Come on! The guy must have a father. Unless the saintly Lily really was a blessed virgin.'

'It could be anyone. After she ran away, she might as well have been dead, for all we heard.'

'Wonderful,' Edgar said furiously. 'What about Primrose and Isobel? Don't they know anything?'

Juana sighed, and lowered herself on to the sofa beside him. 'After I rang you, they turned into the Lily-Josephine Appreciation Society – but they're as much in the dark as anyone.'

'Did you tell them the truth?'

'Darling, do get this into your head. While Lily's son exists, the truth doesn't make the blindest bit of difference. God, I wish I hadn't told Sidonia now. She had a genius for revenge – I simply never imagined she'd turn it on me.'

They sat in silence, in the mausoleum of precious objects, sick and stunned with disappointment.

Eventually, Edgar said: 'Shit.'

'Quite.'

'What's being done, to find this man?'

Juana shrugged. 'Primrose said something about an old servant who was in on the secret.'

'See if you can get his name, at least.'

'What for? I couldn't give a damn about him. Let someone else break the good news.'

'Oh, if I break anything,' Edgar said, 'it won't be news.'

The corners of his mouth tensed ominously, and Juana experienced one of her hateful moments of recognition, when she looked into the adored face of her son, and glimpsed Diego Menendez. Of the three bloodlines Sidonia had spun out into the world, hers was the blackest and the least known.

Chapter Five

◆◆◆

'. . . when they find the son, and the will goes through probate, or whatever, we can have the painting valued, and then we can flog it. Who says money can't buy happiness? Dad looks ten years younger already.'

'That's terrific.' Sophie's desk was in front of the narrow, Georgian upstairs window. As her mother's voice chirped in her ear, down a crackling line from the West of Ireland, she stared, unseeing, over the trim strips of back gardens below. A full ashtray, a brace of dirty mugs and a teetering stack of proofs and manuscripts lay before her.

'I was half-dead when I got back to Ballymunty,' Isobel went on, 'but I had my soundest night's sleep for years. Sidonia couldn't have died at a better moment. You'd have laughed, to hear Dad singing as he went round the pigs' troughs with the whey.'

'Did he? How brilliant.' Sophie loved her parents, but their overwhelming love for each other put a glass wall between themselves and the rest of the world – even their own daughter. She was beginning to realise the oddity of their obsessive silence about the past. It made her misery seem more isolated.

'We'll be able to help you, love. That's the main point. How are you?'

Sophie began to twist a strand of her long, pale hair around one finger. From the pit of her stomach, she summoned a light, breezy voice. 'Fine.'

In the short, crackling pause which followed, she felt Isobel's scepticism. But you couldn't nag at your thirty-year-old child for hiding her feelings. Particularly when you habitually padlocked your own. 'And how's Gus?'

'Come and gone.'

41

'Did he enjoy the ashram?'

Sophie laughed. Her life was dreadful, but she had surprised herself by developing a morbid, maggoty sense of humour. 'Not much. It rained, and he failed to find himself. I only wish I could lose him as easily.'

'Hmmmm.' Another pause in Ireland, while Isobel reeled in her tongue. She was the mildest of women, but the antics of her son-in-law made her furious. 'Where is he now?'

'Spilsby.'

'With her.'

'Don't say "her" like that, Mum.'

'All right. But I don't see why you have to be so bloody civilised.'

Sophie was suddenly terribly weary. If she came out with the usual lines about modern relationships and mutual trust, they would choke her. 'Because it's the only way we can survive.' Unconsciously, she hunched into an attitude of defence, as if the great wave of sadness was a physical force, with the power to knock her down.

'Good God, Soph – can't you take a hint? Stop grovelling. Call it a day. And don't tell me you love him.'

Sophie liked gentle Isobel in one of her abrasive moods, and laughed. 'I can't help it.'

'Try. You're young, you're beautiful, you're clever. You should find someone who appreciates you.'

This time, the breezy voice misfired, and came out almost as a howl. 'Who'd look at me?'

Isobel's voice was full of tender pain for her child. 'It's this baby thing again, isn't it? Oh, God –'

'Actually, these days, I wonder if I want children.'

'Darling, there must be a treatment you can have, and if it costs anything –'

'Look, I should get on.' This was her sorest place, where the lightest touch was agony. Sophie knew that Isobel, not overly religious, nevertheless prayed every night that her daughter would know the joy of cradling her own baby's downy head against her breast. And if she dared to think about it for more than a second, she started imagining the little creature in her arms, and wanting to cry herself to death.

Barren. Unloveable. Unloved.

When it hurt to think about something, Sophie put up the mental shutters. 'Mum, it's lovely to talk, but I've stacks of work.'

Isobel exclaimed: 'It's Saturday!'

'So? You work on Saturdays. Love to Dad. Bye.'

She put down the phone, and sat adjusting her ears to the silence of the empty house.

Come on, she ordered herself. Get a grip.

The stacks of paper on the desk had lost what little charm they ever had. This called for another cup of tea. Homework days were only bearable if you strung them out between little treats and distractions. She collected the dirty mugs, including the three beside her reading-spot on the divan, and ran down the narrow stairs to the kitchen.

Sophie and Gus owned the top two floors of this narrow Georgian house, on the more questionable side of Islington. It was pleasantly proportioned and intelligently furnished, but, like their five-year-old marriage, showing signs of wear and tear. The blue carpeting on the stairs was going bald at the edges. There was a large crack behind the Chagall print on the landing, and all the kitchen appliances were in their toothless dotage.

When Sophie made herself focus on her surroundings she was paralysed by helpless anger. Gus hated the flat these days. When he returned, he complained and criticised and found fault. Gus's hobby was blaming, this was the trouble. She supposed the cycle of blame and guilt was common to all marriages on their last legs.

To be fair, the mess was partly her fault. She was not a tidy person, and owned far too many books, which were constantly tumbling off the top of the fridge, or blocking access to the lavatory-cistern. Even when you loved someone, such things were irritating. When love had flown, they became unbearable.

I've failed him, Sophie thought, filling the kettle. I was never good enough.

Five years before, she had met Gus at the dinner table of a mutual friend, and fancied him instantly. He was tall and self-assured, with a voice like black velvet. Before the first course plates were removed, she had been laying schemes to get into bed with him.

She was not, on the whole, given to losing her heart. She had difficulty understanding friends who messed up their lives for the sake of love. Sophie was a pragmatic young woman, who had been brought up to regard strong emotions as potentially dangerous. She liked sex. Probably because liking sex was in her genes – she had only met her grandmother a handful of times, but Sidonia's history was public property.

Sophie had kept her relationships brief and to the point. Falling in love, as far as she could tell, was an unpredictable, unnecessarily fatiguing business. In that sense, she had been a virgin, totally unprepared for the assault of Gus's passionate and demanding nature. He told her he loved her, and she was lost. You fell all the harder, when you postponed your first falling until the age of twenty-five.

Until that moment, she had thought of nothing except her career. At school, and later at Cambridge, she had been a classic swot. To nobody's surprise, she had bagged a first in English, and won a coveted job in a famous London publishing house.

The Albany Press was a hundred and thirty years old. Oil paintings of Charles Darwin and Herbert Spencer adorned the panelled walls of the offices in Albemarle Street. In the nineteenth century, the firm had specialised in Natural History, and the Albany Nature Series still pulled in most of the income. Over the past fifty years, however, the Press had also built up a magnificent stable of European novelists, including one Nobel Laureate. Much of the European fiction was rather obscure, and did not sell well. But the Press had a vast reputation, as a beacon of cosmopolitan enlightenment in parochial literary London. A tasteful little Albany paperback, of some translated Silesian masterpiece, was an elegant thing to be seen with in public.

Mad old Gerald Albany had employed bright young Sophie Gently because she had good French and fluent German. At the time of meeting Gus, she had been working for Albany for three years, and loving it. She booked translators, pored over manuscripts in the original and oversaw every line of the finished product. She would scribble in margins: 'Question "forsaken" for "*verlassen*" in this context,' and feel she was making a small contribution to literature. For an intellectually inclined young woman, with a tendency to hero-worship authors, it was heaven.

Life had seemed terrific when she married Gus. He was a solicitor, with a firm specialising in corporate law. They were young and in love, and rich enough to buy their two floors in Islington. Sophie assumed they would simply set about living happily ever after, as her parents had done. Weren't all marriages the same?

Gus pointed out, with some justice, that her parents were deep-dyed eccentrics, and that turning into clones of those remote, secretive barkers was the last thing they should aim for. But still Sophie saw nothing wrong with the basic model. She looked forward to a time when Gus would have more money, and she would have their children.

Now, as she so often did in her spare moments, Sophie gnawed over it all again, while waiting for the kettle to boil. When, exactly, had everything turned so sad and sour? There was not much point in wondering, when it could not alter the end result.

Which was that Gus loved someone else, and would have left her like a shot, if their debt-ridden finances had not been so disastrously bound together. Sophie thought their whole story could probably be explained by something as common as Irritable Bowel Syndrome – Irritable Personality Syndrome – but that did not make it any less painful.

He had taken away his love, and the place where it had been felt bald and cold. She wanted it back. She had grovelled and begged for his love, and come to despise herself in the process. She would mentally stand aside, and watch herself begging and cringing and saying 'sorry', until she could hardly blame him for thinking her a pile of crap. By God, she was.

Perhaps she was selfish and boring. Perhaps he really had taken pity on an unattractive, pseudo-intellectual wanker, and she ought to have been more grateful while it lasted. In any case, she was a failure, hopelessly miscast in the role of Woman.

She could not have children. The consultant had told her that her tubes were 'all shot to pieces'. They might try technology, but Sophie was highly unlikely ever to be a mother. This was not Gus's fault. But the loss of her unborn young had thrown Sophie into agonies of mourning.

Sometimes, she felt only the thinnest membrane stretched between herself and total despair. The disintegration of her marriage had brought her face to face with all kinds of hidden monsters. And she had always congratulated herself on her super-sanity, so perhaps it was a punishment.

Her last scraps of self-esteem had been bound up in her job, but even that had not been destined to last. Six months before, Gerald Albany had sold his firm to a huge conglomerate, MacTavish Publishing. The Albany Press left Albemarle Street, and moved to a chrome and glass monolith off the Strand. Kind old souls in cardigans were retired. Impressive foreign writers who made no money were shaved off the list. Sophie and her two remaining colleagues had not been in the monolith a week before the depressing truth sank in. All MacTavish really wanted was the Albany Nature Series.

Sophie, who had given her heart to her European novelists, found herself editing popular works on mushrooms and common garden birds. They bored her until her teeth ached, and the authors were unspeakable – one had actually brought a live ferret into her office. Suddenly, there was less and less time for her novelists.

Just before the takeover, she had bought five books; the fiction list for the coming season. Yet most of her time was hogged by the relaunch of the Albany Nature Series in a new format, with quaint Victorian engravings. She hated every minute. And in absolute spades did she hate her new boss.

Richard 'The Demon' Barber made it clear that the Albany people had only been taken on as a condition of the sale. The moment MacTavish could get rid of them, it would. Sophie was good at keeping her head down, but it is not pleasant to be a chicken whose next-door neighbour is a fox.

I'm being crushed, she thought, between my dead-end, moribund job and my dead-end, moribund marriage.

Naturally tall and rangy, she began to lose weight. The MacTavish secretaries, perpetually on diets, said: 'Aren't you lucky?'

They stopped saying it when she got too thin for all but one of her suits. Protracted bouts of weeping, combined with squinting for hours at a word processor, forced Sophie to get reading glasses. They did not suit her. Isobel, who kept telling her she was beautiful, might have changed her mind if she had seen her now, she thought – a skinny old thing, with a face like a pirate flag.

Barren. Unloveable. Unloved.

So it was all over. The chapter of romance was closed. For ever, as far as she was concerned – she was never going through all that again. In any case, who would want her skinny, whining, deserted carcase? It was just as well she couldn't fancy sex these days.

The kettle boiled. She poured water on her teabag and mashed it aggressively. Come on, woman. Get an attitude. Once upon a time, she had thought herself above self-pity, reasoning that those who could not get their sympathy from other people probably did not deserve it.

She toiled back upstairs, to face the desk, groaning as she thumped down her mug of tea. It made an unattractive ring on a pile of draggy waffle about the life cycle of the wasp. And to her intense vexation, she suddenly remembered that she had one of her nature authors coming in on Monday morning. She could certainly blag her way round the fact that she had not read his manuscript, but the feeling of lost control left her momentarily panic-stricken. She was losing her grip on everything.

Sophie knew she had inherited a family habit of suppressing and denying rage, but she was sure her anger with Gus had truly subsided. A terrible, stifling sense of sadness had taken its place. Gus was a good man, who wished her well. Yet he could not understand, because he had someone who liked him best, who put him first. He had love – the warm, sustaining kind that exists between romantic partners – and she had none.

Half-hidden beneath the drift of papers lay Sophie's private reading, the poems of Christina Rossetti. As she dug the book out, her eye fell upon the words:

'I turn my face in silence to the wall.
My heart is breaking for a little love.'

The wounds opened again, without warning. Sophie laid her head down on the desk, and sobbed.

Chapter Six

<<<<>>>>

Richard popped out like a pantomime demon, while Sophie was still trying to open her door. Her arms were heaped with manuscripts, her bag was slipping off her shoulder, and she had unwisely got herself a plastic cup of coffee from the machine downstairs. Half of this now lay in great splashes and blobs on the pale grey carpet.

'Morning, Richard.'

'Sophie. Could you pop in for a second?'

'Well, I've got an author coming, and –'

'For God's sake.' He pointed down at the coffee stains, glaring through his expensive spectacles. 'Could you be more careful? This carpet costs a fortune to clean.'

'Sorry. I'm rather laden.'

'Let's say ten minutes.' He whisked away, through one of the heavy, metal-clad pairs of swing doors that sliced every corridor in the building. They looked handsome, but were a terrible nuisance if your hands were full – Sophie's shoulder already ached from thumping the things open, and it was only half past nine.

What could the nasty little man want now? He had a perfect genius for upsetting plans. Well, her nature author, whose name escaped her, would have to make do with a few vague compliments and a cup of tea. Perhaps a biscuit. Most, thankfully, were too overawed by their publisher's office to demand more.

She stumbled into her office. At the moment, she had one to herself, because the woman who had once shared it had been made redundant. It was a functional white cube, meanly furnished in black tubular steel. Sophie, in an attempt to enter into the spirit of the Nature Series, had hung up a Dürer drawing of a hare. She liked to remember that the poet Cowper had been saved from nervous collapse by his two pet hares – sometimes, she felt like ordering half a dozen.

The forgotten manuscript lay on her blotter. *Native Woodland Mammals of Southern Britain*, by one O.J. Randall. She tried to arrange it to look as if she had just been reading it, and pulled a mirror from the drawer. Richard was forever sending out memos about the importance of Smartness.

Smartness is a tall order, Sophie thought, but I can at least do tidy.

She brushed specks of lint and droplets of coffee from her black suit and white blouse, and reapplied her neutral pink lipstick. Her long hair, dead straight and the colour of pale butter, was woven neatly into a thick plait.

Sophie – when happy and a stone fatter – was beautiful. But she had always felt slightly apologetic about her looks, because they expressed such difficult points in her family history. She was a living reminder of people her parents did not wish to remember.

Her eyes, blue as the Danube, and her finely sculpted cheekbones, came from her father's hated elder brother. Her full, sensuous mouth and wheaten fairness were pure Sidonia. On her best days, her pale tints flooded with colour, like a stained-glass window with the sun behind it. On days such as this, however, after a weekend of relentless loneliness and weeping, she bleached out to a uniform waxen-white. She was disagreeably aware, as she knocked on the door of Richard's office, of looking like one of the 'starving brides' once displayed, in glass coffins, on Blackpool pier.

Richard was standing at the window with his back to her.

'Ah, yes. Sophie.' He turned to her, as if tearing himself away from affairs of state, to settle a footling chore. 'Sit.'

He was a short man, which explained a lot. His lips were unpleasantly thick, and his receding grey curls decorated the back of his head like a ruff.

Determined to be as obedient and cooperative as possible, Sophie plumped down in the low, low chair opposite, plastering on a smile.

'I thought we should have a tiny word, before this

afternoon's meeting. You've done some excellent work on the Albany Nature Series. Nobody denies that. But I wonder if you're really committed. Time-wise.'

She murmured: 'Sorry?'

'I wonder if you realise how much the Albany Press has changed – must actually change. Gerald Albany may have carried some of his authors out of love, or whatever. But we can't afford to do that.'

Here it came. She bristled defensively, wondering which of her authors she must fight for now. 'Gerald believed they paid for themselves, by giving the firm prestige. They were our prestige.'

Richard snickered condescendingly. 'Yes, but we don't need prestige. We've got quite enough.'

'Well, of course. But I thought MacTavish had a deliberate policy of keeping its imprints separate. Keeping their identities.'

'Sophie, that's exactly what we have done. The identity of the Albany Press is its nature series.'

'Come on, Richard. That was a century ago. Ask anyone what the Albany name means now, and they'll tell you – it's an imprint for serious, challenging, international literature.'

He was eyeing her beadily. 'Which nobody buys.'

'Which a lot more people would buy, if you could be bothered to promote them properly.'

Richard's eyes narrowed to hostile slits in his puffy face. 'Let me tell you something, Sophie. I'm not sure I care for the attitude you've brought with you from Albany. Intellectual snobbery is all very well, if it pays for itself. If it doesn't, it's a luxury. Next season's list –' He tapped a typed sheet of paper, 'Not exactly orgasmic, is it?'

'It depends what turns you on. I think it's brilliant – one of the strongest we've ever had.'

'It's boring,' Richard said.

A surge of fury made Sophie momentarily light-headed. She longed to shout: You stupid little Philistine, you wouldn't know a decent book if it bit you on the bum!

Instead, she cleared her throat, and tried to summon a sweet, reasonable voice. 'Perhaps some of them are a little

51

obscure. Our authors aren't shy about making demands on the reader.'

'Hmm, you can say that again. I never saw such a heap of arrogant, pseudy twaddle. What I want from the Albany Press is popular nature books, about popular subjects – bird-watching, hedgehogs. Gardens. *The Mushroom Picker's Handbook*, for instance – perfect.'

Her voice was icy. 'I take it you'd like me to do a little pruning of the fiction list?'

There was an awful pause. 'May I be honest?'

'Goodness, yes. Be brutal.'

'Your new commissions. Very interesting and all that, but we can't use them.'

Sophie was stunned. Her stomach swooped with shock. 'Not any of them?'

'No.'

'But you haven't even read them!'

'I don't have to. Your descriptions of them were enough. Allegories about totalitarian politics, banned sagas about Kulak families under Stalin – dear God. You didn't have much to do with the Nature Series when you were at the Press, did you?'

'No,' she said, over the tempest of fear and fury inside her head.

'It may be time to take another look at your position with us. Not now, obviously. But I just wanted to give you a little food for thought. I'd be interested to discuss how you see your future here.' His phone bleated. He snatched the receiver, eyes still pinned to Sophie. 'Yes? . . . Who? . . . I'll tell her.'

Sophie's mind had seized up. She knew what he meant, and could not bring herself to believe he had said it.

'There's a Mr Randall coming up in the lift. Your author.'

'Thanks, I'll go and fetch him.' Still automatically polite, she rose.

'Which reminds me,' Richard said. 'It's high time you stopped treating the nature authors like poor relations. Keep a civil tongue in your head, Sophie. Think bread and butter.' The interview was over. He extracted another sheet of paper, and swivelled round in his chair, ostentatiously presenting her with his back.

This, Sophie thought, as she charged blindly towards the lifts, is a disaster. He couldn't have been clearer if he had handed her a P45 on the spot. By dumping her translated geniuses, he had destroyed the last rags of her self-esteem. And the last little dig, about treating the nature-nerds as poor relations, made her absolutely seethe.

Yes, she was arrogant and a snob. She had not burned gallons of midnight oil to end up flattering a collection of bearded wallies in anoraks. Her career was dissolving, and all she felt was a desperate, almost euphoric anger.

There was one man, personable and clean-shaven, waiting outside the lifts. Sophie waited beside him, scanning each set of doors for a bobble-hatted misfit, possibly carrying a ferret.

The young man cleared his throat, and asked: 'Are you Sophie Gently?'

'Yes – how do you do?' Confused, she snatched his hand and forcefully pumped it. 'Don't tell me you're O.J. Randall!'

He was wary. 'Why not?'

'I was expecting someone dressed for a bird-hide. What's the O for?'

'Octavius.'

'Gosh. No wonder you don't want it on the cover. Well, let's get to my office.' She dashed through the metal doors, trusting him to follow her. 'It's a mess, I'm afraid. Please sit down.'

Octavius Randall took the one other chair. For the first time, across the littered desk, they faced each other properly. Sophie was thrown further off balance by the realisation that he was not only young and personable, but positively good-looking.

She drew him into detail piece by piece, as if watching a figure emerge from a mist. First, the obvious. He was tall and thin, dressed in a black leather jacket and a grey jersey. He had very thick, very glossy, curly brown hair – Sophie had reached the age where a man's hairline was the first thing you checked, and Randall had not lost a single thread. Next, she found herself registering his colour and texture; all warm browns shading to dark gold. He made you think of bronze, or butterscotch. Golden skin, brown hair with gold lights, lustrous hazel eyes, gold-veined. As far as Sophie was concerned, the only thing that marked him out as a nature writer was his obvious, prickly shyness. She was making this worse, and she hadn't the compassion left to care. She was as mad as a snake, and could feel an Oscar-winning performance coming on.

'We all enjoyed your book so much.'

'Er – thanks –'

'As you may know,' Sophie went on, 'most of our titles are checked by an expert in the particular field. And the consultant we retain for this area was very impressed.'

A peculiar look – baffled, wary – flitted across the lustrous hazel eyes. 'Was he?'

'Absolutely. You seem to have the woodland world pretty well sewn up, in fact.'

Randall, after a chilly pause, said: 'Thank you.'

'Obviously, we'll need your input on the illustrations.' Something surfaced, in the chaos of Sophie's mind. 'Hang on – Randall. Have we published you before?'

'My grandfather wrote your standard work on European owls.'

'Did he? I mean, yes of course, but that's not – oh, I'm thinking of Sir Bruno Randall. The philosopher, you know.'

'I do indeed. He's my uncle.'

Beneath the barmy clamour in her mind, an alarm bell shrilled. Sir Bruno Randall was a very big name indeed; the jewel in the MacTavish crown. More than a writer, he was an institution. He appeared on grand television programmes and hobnobbed with cabinet ministers. And Richard carried, in his deadly arsenal of unloveable characteristics, an incredible snobbery. If this was Sir Bruno's nephew, she had better find some manners.

'Really? No wonder you can write. Something must have rubbed off.'

Randall said abruptly: 'It surprises people. When you've got an uncle like Bruno, buggering about in bird-hides seems to make you rather a failure.'

This was, Sophie realised, exactly what she had been thinking. 'Perhaps you were rebelling,' she offered, meaning to console.

She did not see her own monumental lack of tact, until he said: 'Perhaps. But if I've disappointed anyone in my family, they've hidden it awfully well.'

'Oh, I didn't mean to imply –'

'Look, Miss Gently –'

'Sophie.'

'We might have our wires crossed. I didn't quite understand what you said about your consultant liking my book.'

It occurred to Sophie that – quite apart from her own reckless anger – there was something distinctly odd about this meeting. She had betrayed her snobbery, but Randall had seemed to grasp at it with a kind of angry masochism, as if he expected to be punished for something. His curt voice had an inward quality; an intensity.

Carefully, she said: 'Well, he did like it.'

'Your consultant in this area is – me, actually.'

'You? Oh God.' She covered her face with her hands. 'Excuse me, I'll just beam myself back to the Mother-Ship. I'm not interfacing with you humans too well today.'

'You haven't read a word of it, have you?'

She emerged, all pretence shed. 'No.'

'I see.'

'Would you like to kill me personally, or shall I get a hit-squad sent up from Reception?'

'It doesn't matter.'

'I'm terribly sorry. I had a very heavy workload.'

'Honestly, I don't mind. But aren't we rather wasting our time?'

For one fleeting moment, Sophie fantasised about simply walking out of the building and never coming back. Maybe this was the limit she had been waiting to hit for so long. If she snapped Randall's head off, however, she would be sacked. This weird, touchy man was, she decided, just the type to complain about her.

'You're right, and I shouldn't keep you. But do have a

look at the illustrations, at least.' She tugged out the folder sent by the picture researcher.

She did not push them over to him. Randall came round to her side of the desk, bent over her shoulder, and spilled the prints out on the blotter. She was overwhelmed by the smell of him, muskily pleasant, with the clean tang of shaving soap. For one, vivid moment, her atrophied sexuality sprang back to life. To her amazement, her forgotten clitoris suddenly reminded her what it was for, by throbbing insistently against the seam of her tights. Only a moment, but when it passed, her entire awareness of Randall had shifted into another key. Unable to risk looking up at him, she focused on the sinewy hand in front of her.

'Charming,' he said.

'Glad you like them. That little whatsit is rather nice, isn't he?'

'*Apodemus flavicollis*. The yellow-necked mouse.' He drew away, and returned to his side of the desk. 'If you'd read the chapter, you'd know all about how it scurries up oak trees, like a tiny Tarzan, and daringly breaks into apple stores.' He smiled suddenly. 'Usually with a length of lead pipe, and a little stocking over its face.'

His smile irradiated his tense face. He was beautiful. Unexpectedly softened, Sophie allowed herself to laugh. The meeting was ending, and the unread author seemed to be offering forgiveness. 'You've been really nice about this. Thanks.'

'May I go now?'

'I'll see you out.' She sprang up, relieved to get rid of Sir Bruno Randall's nephew so painlessly. 'This place is such a maze.'

She led him back down the long grey corridor, absently hefting the doors, while she tried to get her poor brain back into working order. Was it even worth trying to save her job? Anyone with a spark of pride would have torn up the list in Richard's face and stormed from the building.

It was depressing to have to admit she had no pride left. Good grief, she would have got down on her knees and scrubbed the floor to keep that salary coming in. She was doomed to creeping and crawling, biting down her anger until it devoured her.

The unfortunate meeting with Randall was a stern lesson. If she was failing to cope on such a scale, it would be only a matter of time before she gave Richard a beautiful excuse to kick her out. And then what would her bank manager say? Lately, he had sent some very ungracious reminders about the size of her overdraft – as if she could have forgotten it.

'Slow down,' Randall called, behind her.

'Sorry.'

'Could I stop for a pee on the way out?'

'Of course. It's through here –'

Sophie let go of the last set of doors to show him. They swung back with a loud, unnatural thump. Randall yelled.

She pulled it open again, and cried in anguish: 'Hell and damnation!'

He was bent double, groaning, with his hands clamped over his nose. As she watched, in a trance of horror, she saw blood welling through his fingers. It trickled over his wrists, and speckled the expensive grey carpet.

In a fraction of a second, Sophie played through a terrible scenario, in which Sir Bruno Randall's nephew sued MacTavish for millions and charged her with assault. She was suddenly furious with him for being such a trouble-maker.

'Come along.' She slung her arm across his shoulders. The physical contact was startling. 'Look, will you come on! Oh God, what a day!'

Miraculously, a lift was waiting. She steered him into it and – another miracle – found a wad of clean tissue in her handbag. These she thrust into Randall's pain-stunned, astonished face. The third miracle was a vacant taxi, right outside the main door of the building. She had bundled him into it, before the girl on the reception desk had time to do more than gape.

'We're going to – where do you live?'

'Devon,' he said, in a muffled voice.

'Don't be silly. I meant in London.' She was trembling.

'Hampstead. Downshire Hill.'

'Did you hear that?'

The driver was eyeing Randall doubtfully in his mirror.

'Is he all right, dear?'

'Yes, dear,' Sophie snapped. 'I'm a vampire. He's my lunch.'

She banged the window shut and lit a cigarette. She was seething with despair, and no longer gave a damn what she said. For a while, they travelled in silence. Randall watched her over his lump of bloody tissue. He was squinting with pain.

Sophie risked a look at him, and felt kind enough to say: 'Poor you, that must be agony.'

'It is, thanks.'

She sighed, and slumped back into her seat. 'Listen, I could weep and beg, and make you terribly sorry for me, because my troubles are far worse than a bleeding nose. But I'll spare you. It would hardly be fair, after inflicting actual bodily harm, to burden you with my nightmarish marriage or my ghastly job. Just for the record, you cannot imagine how horrible my life is at the moment. I keep thinking I've got someone else's by mistake. I realise I haven't been at all nice to you, and normally, I'd be devastated. But there just isn't anything left.

'I should have stayed in bed this morning. I couldn't even get out of my front door, before the silly old git downstairs pounced on me about the bill for the drains. And then I laddered my tights and had to buy some new ones, because Richard makes such a fuss about neatness. Though I wonder why I bothered. What's a pair of laddered tights, when weighed against killing an author whose uncle is Sir Bruno Randall, upon whom Richard is relying to get him into the Garrick? Not that they'll have a scumbag like him, if they've any sense.'

'You haven't killed me,' he said, when she paused for breath.

'Maybe I should have. Actually, killing an author might have made me a desirable asset for another firm. As it is, I shall have to become a traffic warden, or something.'

'You have all the necessary charm.'

Sophie chuckled. It came out as a fierce witch's cackle. 'Or I could be the person who works the electric stunner at an abattoir. I'd be simply bloody excellent at that.'

'Never mind the electric thing – you could do it with your tongue.'

'Oh, Cornelius, you're such a caution.'

'Octavius.'

'Sorry. Octavius.'

'What are you going to do to me now?'

'Nothing. You can breathe easy. As soon as I've seen you and your nose home, I'm going to bunk off my afternoon meeting, and take a stroll round Keats' house – try to remind myself of the higher side of human nature, and gather inspiration for a letter of resignation in the form of a sonnet.'

Over the tissues, his eyes had a hard, watchful glint of amusement. 'You seem to be getting a laugh out of it, anyway. Your misfortunes must be a wow at dinner parties.'

Sophie's anger suddenly deflated. She remembered her father, seeing her off at Cork Airport after her last visit home.

'I am worried about this attitude of yours,' he had said gravely. 'There is a coarse aggression about you that disturbs me. You will only drive people away, if you behave like a –' he had rooted for the right word, '– a buffoon.'

She had shrugged it off at the time – Dad could be quite amazingly insensitive – but it had hurt, hurt, hurt. Did you only deserve kindness if you were miserable in the right sort of way? Was misery actually only visible when it wore sackcloth? Here was her own father, failing to hear the howls of pain beneath the aggressive barrage. She had felt like an infant crying at night, and nobody coming.

This man, who had the misfortune to be shut in a taxi with her, could not be blamed for thinking exactly the same.

But she could not bear it any longer. Sophie, who had taken such pride in putting on a good face in public, shamingly broke down in tears.

Randall's first reaction, behind his bloodied tissues, was utter dismay, bordering on panic. Then, unexpectedly, he shifted along the seat and put his arm around her shoulders.

'Oh God. You weren't joking, and I was too thick to notice.' He shoved the bloody tissues into his pocket, revealing an ugly, blackening mark on the bridge of his nose. 'I was all you needed this morning, wasn't I?'

Rigid with mortification inside the circle of his arm, Sophie made a desperate effort to regain control. 'This is ridiculous – look, it's not that bad –'

'Yes it is. Whatever's the matter with your life, it's obviously a catastrophe. So cry all you like. Yell and curse. Scream imprecations at the heavens.'

He spoke energetically, and with complete seriousness. It was perversely cheering. Sophie's next sob finished, unexpectedly, in a giggle.

'It could be worse,' she said. 'I mean, nobody's died.'

'There are all sorts of deaths,' Octavius said.

A wall had come down. For the first time, he was speaking to her from his genuine self.

Sophie murmured: 'You shouldn't encourage me.'

'Why not? Nobody gives you a medal for keeping a stiff upper lip.' He smiled, but too late to take away the impression that she had touched something bitterly personal.

'You didn't deserve to get a face-full of my dreary problems,' she said, 'as well as a broken nose.'

'It's not broken. Only bent.'

This time, she could laugh outright. 'I've been horrible to you. Are you honestly all right?'

'Honestly. Dying for a pee, but I can grit my teeth.'

'Hell. I forgot all about that.'

'Oh, I'll last another five minutes or so.' He leaned forward and slid open the driver's window. 'Here, please.'

The taxi halted outside a pretty gem of a Georgian house with gothic windows, sitting like a castellated box at the end of a long strip of front garden. Beside its enamelled neighbours, it was distinctly scuffed and peeling. Sophie had lived in London long enough to recognise the slight dilapidation as a mark of aristocracy. This was Sir Bruno Randall's house, and he was a relic of Old Hampstead, legendary haunt of left-wing intellectuals, before the merely rich took over. She had seen photographs of him here, posed among heaps of books, under standard lamps with orange hessian shades.

While she stared, Octavius paid the taxi. Then, waving down her protests, he said:

'Come in, then.'

'No, no, I'm going –'

'Please. One cup of coffee.'

The embarrassing fit of tears had washed all the fight out of her, and left her limply calm. 'Well, okay. If you're not just being nice.'

Octavius held open the gate for her. 'Suppose I am? What's so bad about just being nice?'

The cramped hall was choked with books. There were bookcases from floor to ceiling, and heaps of volumes lining the stairs. Through a half-open door, Sophie could see the sitting room, complete with the famous hessian lampshades, also barnacled with books. It had a marble fireplace, containing an antique gas fire, and various lumbering, unfashionable chairs. Any space not taken up with books was filled with spotted engravings, or photographs of dim, sepia people in too many clothes.

They went down a steep staircase to the basement, lined with yet more books. Sophie craned avidly at the titles as she passed them, longing for a closer look. This was the library of someone who read everything, from Cicero, Feuerbach and Spinoza in the originals, to 1950s detective stories in old green-backed Penguin editions.

The kitchen, which ran from front to back of the small house, was cheerfully unmatched, and looked out on a leafy well of back garden. The front half was evidently the dining room. A heavy sideboard, covered with framed photographs, nudged the equally heavy table and chairs towards the faded wall. Sophie found the atmosphere of the place intriguingly exotic, yet as familiar as some half-remembered childhood dream.

'Sit down here,' Octavius said, gently pushing her towards a carver's chair with a floppy embroidered cushion. 'Do smoke if you like. Bruno and Gerda are practically kippered. I'll make some coffee in a minute.'

He left her. Sophie listened to his feet thumping up the

stairs, and fading away into the descending peace. It was very quiet. Somehow, the distant sounds of traffic made the silence of the house more pronounced. After glancing round a few more times, Sophie reached for one of the ashtrays – there were enough lying around to start an ashtray museum – and lit a cigarette.

On the sideboard, a mosaic of faces stared at her, from frames of marquetry or silver. She envied the Randalls, for having the kind of family history that was all of a piece, not in fragments. The past and the present lived together here. There were foreign-looking Edwardian portraits, beside colour snaps of modern children. She wondered if these belonged to Octavius. Sophie searched the photographs for clues.

Sir Bruno frowned at her intellectually from behind thick glasses. This picture had been taken in the 1950s, but he had the sort of face that sets at twenty and never changes. His hair, in the picture, was brown instead of grey, but still worn in a floppy, taste-defying Michael Foot bob. Beside him was a young woman with broad cheekbones and brown hair, standing on a mountain, holding an alpenstock. Sophie recalled that Lady Randall was an Austrian. Gerda Wiesel; a psychiatrist who had written books about treating people who had been in concentration camps.

She recognised, amongst the throng of strangers, Octavius at various ages – a curly-headed babe grinning in a pram, a little boy in shorts holding small animals.

The Randall gallery was dominated by two large black and white studies. The first was of a row of men – Sophie counted six young ones, plus a father – crammed together to get into the shot. One was the young Sir Bruno, in a pullover. Three of the others were in uniform; a patriotic selection box. Soldier, Sailor, Airman – it was like counting cherry-stones.

The second was of a young girl. Sophie could have stared at her for hours. She stood waist-high in a corn field, and gazed into the lens with such an air of candour and vivacity that you almost expected her to speak. Sometimes, a photograph really is what it is supposed to be; a moment snatched

62

from time and made eternal.

The girl looked back at Sophie with such warmth, such intensity, that it took her a second or two to notice how pretty she was. No, she was actually beautiful – she had the kind of beauty that is usually never photographed as if it were real. Her black hair curled on her shoulders. She had snapping dark eyes, in a face that might have seemed poignant or ethereal in repose. But there was no repose here – this girl sizzled with life. She was all zest and vitality, poised to move the second after the shutter closed.

Sophie stopped staring, for she heard Octavius returning and did not want to be caught snooping.

He came into the kitchen, behind a strong smell of Savlon. 'My eyes are swelling,' he said. 'I'll have a gorgeous pair of shiners tomorrow, I daresay. Tea or coffee?'

'Coffee, please.' Sophie was shy. She watched him switching on an old electric kettle with a hairy flex, and tossing ground coffee into a wondrous enamel pot, scarred and dented, and painted with flowers and castles.

'Very wise,' he said. 'Gerda's lived here for years, but she still hasn't got the hang of tea.'

Sophie wanted to say that her father was exactly the same, but stopped herself. Instead, she asked: 'Do you swear you're all right now?'

He smiled over his shoulder. 'I swear. Will this be too strong?'

'Not for me. I can never get it strong enough.'

'Good for you.'

He was shy, too – but no longer prickly, and even allowing himself to show reassuring touches of humour. Sophie felt herself, for the first time in ages, relaxing.

'Sorry I ranted at you,' she said. 'I think I'm turning into one of those old ladies who get turfed out of the library for shouting about Martians.'

Octavius smiled. His smile was slow, and made the gold flecks glow in his warm eyes. 'I come from a family of ranters, and that was quite a classic,' he said. 'Having a crappy marriage does that to a person.'

'Is yours crappy too?'

'It was. We divorced three years ago. No children, and it only lasted about five minutes – so don't say you're sorry.'

He joined her at the table, and slid over a cup of coffee. Sophie bathed her face in its vapours, and exclaimed, before she could help herself: 'Oh, the Viennese sort, with cinnamon, that smells of Germolene – my dad moves heaven and earth to get this. Not easy, in the West of Ireland.'

'You don't sound Irish. Or look it.'

Sophie knew what she looked like. Gus, when they first met, had called her 'Strength Through Joy'. This seemed particularly tasteless in Gerda Wiesel's kitchen. 'I got out to university as fast as I could,' she said briskly.

'Where were you at university?'

'Cambridge. I heard your uncle lecture once. He was superb. Do you stay with him a lot?'

'Always, when I'm in London,' Octavius said.

'But you're not in London much, surely.'

'No. I'm based in Devon. I work for a charity that buys and maintains forests.' He chuckled suddenly. 'So you were right – I do have the woodland world pretty well sewn up.'

'Don't remind me. My boss ticked me off for being an intellectual snob this morning, and he's absolutely right.' There was an awkward spell of silence. Sophie put down her mug. 'May I ask you something? I ranted about my marriage, and you understood, because you've been through a divorce. But I still don't see why you should be so nice to me – I mean, apart from the fact that you obviously are rather nice.'

He was self-conscious, but his gaze was level. 'I remembered something,' he said. 'I was very unhappy once, and I thought the loneliness would kill me. My family did their best – but when it's a particular kind of love that's gone, family love only makes things worse. Don't know why.'

'Yes,' Sophie said sadly, 'they mean no harm, but that's worst of all.'

'Well, this sounds wankerish, but I was reading *Jude the Obscure*, and there's this bit where Jude is sitting beside the road, in utter despair. And Hardy says something about how someone might have happened along and comforted him. Then he says –'

'But nobody did,' Sophie finished, 'because nobody does.'

'Oh, you know it. Well, nobody did stop for me, and I swore that if ever I met myself in future, I'd be the person who does stop.'

The tears, still near the surface, rushed painfully to Sophie's sore eyes. This time, she was not ashamed of them.

'I'm glad you did,' she said.

Without warning, they were right up against the barrier, fighting sudden, unmistakable sexual tension. It filled the whole room, like heavy perfume. Sophie felt stifled and panic-stricken. Retreat was impossible, but so was any kind of advance. Octavius looked as edgy and disturbed as she was.

Upstairs, a key grated and the front door slammed. Both started. The net broke.

A woman's voice, faintly accented, called: 'Octavius! Are you back, love?'

A deep male voice, its volume increasing as it advanced down the basement stairs, said: 'How ridiculous they are, all these questions like Are you back? or Are you asleep? Because there can only be one reply. Octavius can't say No, he's not back.'

'What should I ask, then?'

Octavius called out: 'Hi,' and leapt up – defensively, Sophie thought.

In breezed the Randalls, laden with bags and briefcases.

Gerda instantly cried: 'But what has happened to you?'

'Ye Gods,' said Sir Bruno, 'bit old for brawling, aren't you?'

Octavius ducked away from Gerda's plump, beringed hands, which were fluttering round his face. 'This is Sophie.'

Sophie stood, feeling clumsy and gangling, as Sir Bruno and Gerda swivelled round to take her in.

'Sophie Gently,' she said.

The faintest signal, like animals warning one another of possible danger, passed between them. Sir Bruno dropped his ancient briefcase. Being famous, and standing gravely to attention in the middle of the floor, he looked like a waxwork. His green-grey eyes, behind the thick panes of his spectacles, were disconcertingly enormous. Then the lines scored down his thin cheeks ruched into a smile. He came towards her, his hand outstretched.

'Well, hello.'

Sophie tried to work out what was odd, and realised it was the way they were sizing her up. They were being parents – afraid of showing their eagerness, when a beloved child introduced a member of the opposite sex, and also afraid their child might need protection from the unsuitable. She had seen exactly the same look on her own parents' faces as a teenager, when she had brought some shy local youth into the kitchen at home. But Octavius was over thirty.

'Sophie works at MacTavish,' Octavius said. He did not seem to have noticed this mute pantomime of anxiety and hope. 'She's editing my book.'

'How marvellous,' declared Gerda, wrenching open the fridge. 'You're just in time for lunch.'

◆◆◆

Almost before Richard was out of earshot, Sir Bruno leaned across the table towards Sophie, and asked:

'Well? How am I doing?'

She laughed. 'Brilliantly, but I think you're over-egging the pudding somewhat. Perhaps you'd better stop.'

'Hmm. Pity. I was enjoying myself. I don't get many opportunities to use my magic powers. Isn't Barber a prick?'

Sophie, Richard and Sir Bruno were lunching at the Garrick Club, on the day after Sophie had stayed to lunch at the Randalls' and laughed a whole afternoon away around a wooden table in the Hampstead garden.

Sophie had cut her all-important afternoon meeting, and was sure her number was up at last. When Bruno grasped that she wanted to keep her hated job, he had promised to safeguard her position at MacTavish. 'Can't do anything about your marriage, but I can and will disarm that boss of yours – with one wave of my wand.'

And, good grief, he had. Sophie had agreed, because she was full of ripe Camembert and the indigo wine of Cahors, but she did not really take him seriously. By the time she sloped – very late – into the office next day, however, the Wand had done its work. Far from firing her, Richard had greeted her with positive affection, and the news that they were both summoned to break bread with the Wizard.

'I have to hand it to you, Sophie. You seem to have managed the situation incredibly well. The nephew sounds like a bit of a tit – crashing into one of our doors, for godsake. But he won't be making any trouble. Thank gawd Sir Bruno likes brainy young ladies.'

Richard, it turned out, was an absolute breeze to handle, if you just activated his snobbery-gland. During lunch, his delight had been feverish. Bruno had gravely asked his advice and praised his intelligence for employing Sophie, until she was almost ill with suppressed laughter.

'Told you,' Bruno said. 'Have some more wine.'

'No, really. Don't send me back to the office drunk.'

'I flatter myself that you could now get away with virtually anything.' He refilled her glass.

'Bruno,' – it was surprisingly easy, after yesterday, to call him by his first name – 'thank you so much.'

'You don't mind me interfering?'

'No. I can't afford that kind of pride just now. Thank you for saving me from the dole queue.'

'Oh, it would never have come to that.'

'And thanks for yesterday – I've sent a postcard to Gerda, but it doesn't really express what a lovely time I had.'

'We enjoyed it too, you know. And, more to the point, I haven't seen poor old Octavius so animated since that wretched woman left him. He really took to you.'

Sophie felt the heat surging into her face. 'You didn't like his wife, then.'

'Gerda is always telling me that one must never judge a relationship from the outside, let alone start casting heroes and villains. But no, I never much cared for Caroline. And I was bloody furious with her when she upped and left.'

'What happened – do you mind my asking?'

'Not at all. She began by telling Octavius he was sick and needed therapy, and finished by skedaddling with his best friend.'

'Ouch,' Sophie said.

'Quite. There were problems, I'm sure – but he adored her. She should have had more faith in him.'

'Perhaps she didn't love the person he eventually turned out to be. Or perhaps she couldn't stand the kind of person she became, when she was with him.'

'You speak from experience, and very wisely. Gerda would break into applause. But I cannot forgive her for turning my boy into a basket case.'

Sophie was touched. 'You're so fond of him, you and Gerda.'

'Oh God, yes. Some day, when you have four or five hours to spare, I'll tell you why.'

'I didn't think he was a basket case. I was the one dropping my marbles all over the shop.'

'Octavius has a very kind heart – damaged, but kind. And, as I said, he has taken what I believe is called a "shine" to you. Don't you love that expression?'

'Bruno,' Sophie said, 'are you matchmaking?'

'Not matchmaking, precisely. Let's say I'm removing any obstacles I have any right, or power, to remove. The rest is up to you. And none of my business.'

'No, it certainly isn't.'

His eyes, huge and wavering behind thick spectacles, were scanning her face thoughtfully.

'You know,' he announced suddenly, 'you remind me of someone. Your face is curiously familiar. Are you related to anyone I might know?'

'Anyone famous, you mean?' Sophie teased. 'Well, my grandfather was the painter, Colm Leary, and –'

'Yes, of course!' It came out in a startling, triumphant shout. ' "Sidonia-in-Emeralds-in-Sidonia"! Good God!'

Sophie was used to people being impressed by her blood-line to Sidonia. 'She was my grandmother. I do look a little like her, apparently.'

'Good God,' Bruno repeated. 'This is extraordinary. The Montagues and the Capulets.'

'I'm sorry?'

He laughed shakily, plainly rattled. 'So you're Isobel's daughter.'

It was Sophie's turn to be rattled. 'Yes. But you don't know my mother.'

'Not personally. But didn't your grandfather – ? No, of course. He died when you were a baby. And it was complicated, because your grandmother and Octavius's mother were sworn enemies.'

'She did make enemies,' Sophie said. 'And they generally were women.'

'I wonder if this could prove awkward?' It was as if a layer of calcified years had fallen away, allowing her to see a younger Bruno, in whom pain and passion were still fresh and warm. 'Or whether it's a sign that we should let the dead bury their dead?'

There was a spell of silence, during which Sophie felt him retreating into the mysterious past.

'You're being very dramatic,' she said. 'Who was Octavius's mother?'

Bruno snapped back into the present and smiled at her, his magnified eyes glistening. 'You might have seen her photograph yesterday.'

Sophie instantly knew, and wondered if she had always known. 'The girl in the field?'

'Yes. Standing in the corn, with the flowers turning their faces to her, mistaking her for the sun.' He gazed intently into her eyes. 'Her name was Lily-Josephine. And I verily believe she was the great love of my life.'

PART TWO

Chapter One

1922

The library seemed deserted; the only movement being the flames which licked the logs in the stone fireplace, and their reflected gleams in the dull glass eyes of the bearskin rug. Miss Crask, however, was used to Helena's habit of stowing herself away in corners. She spotted, on the other side of the room, a foot sticking out behind the red plush curtains.

'Here you are,' she said.

A thin hand hooked the curtain aside. A pair of eyes, unnaturally large and dark in a peaky, nondescript face, peered out at her. 'Did you want me?'

Helena Vere was curled on the window seat, almost smothered in the folds of a shabby tartan rug. Miss Crask saw that she had been worlds away, and was slowly returning to reality. She had never known such a child for reading.

Except that Helena was not a child. A month before, in the week before Christmas, they had decorously toasted her coming of age in ginger wine. She was twenty-one, and the mistress of the Prospect. Miss Crask knew it was high time Helena grew up, but had no idea how to make her do it. As her former governess, who had gradually taken on the role of housekeeper, she could not address Helena as anything but a child.

'It's a lovely afternoon, dear. I don't like to see you stuffing indoors. Doctor Tressel said you needed fresh air – well, you won't get it this way.'

'I'm sorry.' Helena was always compliant, always polite. 'I didn't realise the time –'

'The light will be quite gone by four,' Miss Crask said briskly. 'And Bruce hasn't had his run yet.'

'Poor old Brucie!' Helena sprang up, her figure as quick and slight as a hummingbird's against the solid furniture.

'Wrap up warmly, dear,' Miss Crask called after her.

She stayed beside the window, looking out at the still, snow-blanketed garden. A moment later, she saw Helena run out into the whiteness behind Bruce, her springer spaniel.

And she thought: I ought to throw those clothes away. It's not seemly for the wealthiest woman in the county to dress like a schoolgirl.

In her darned pleated skirt, reefer coat and red tam-o'-shanter, Helena might still have been the dreamy, delicate little girl Miss Crask had come to take care of ten years before. Surely, it was time for the childhood idyll to end? Helena could not spend the rest of her life shut away in her kingdom by the sea, filling her head with romance.

Miss Crask picked up the volumes Helena had been reading, and sighed. *The Owl and the Nightingale*, *The Song of Roland*. She could hardly object. The poetry of the Middle Ages was her own passion, and she was to blame for feeding the child's imagination on Knights and Ladies.

Lately, she had begun to wonder if so much courtly love was actually healthy. Helena was clever, but not a scholar. She took her medieval romance in the same way that Gladys, the parlourmaid, read the slushy love stories of Florence Barclay and Phyllis Crewe – she had quite a little library of nonsense accumulating on the shelf in the servants' parlour. It wasn't so very different, when you took a practical view, from Helena's shelves of poetry. And this young lady cried out for a strong dose of practicality.

Miss Crask was fond of Helena, but she wanted to leave. The latest letter from her widowed sister, begging her to share the comfortable house in Hatch End, was burning a hole in her cardigan pocket. Yet, absurdly, she could not shake off a feeling of responsibility for this frail orpheline. How could you force someone to grow up against their will?

How could she tell little Helena, who still slept in the night nursery and read her old Nister's Annuals, that she ought to be in London, buying Paris gowns and mixing cocktails? Miss Crask had ordered the *Sphere* and the *Tatler*, in an effort to make Helena admire the smart young belles with their scarlet lips and marcelled bobs. Helena had read of dances and race meetings with obedient detachment, as if studying creatures from another planet.

Stretching her imagination to its limits, Miss Crask tried to visualise Helena having a real, present-day romance, with a knight who wore decent tweeds instead of armour. No, the idea was almost shocking.

She knew no men, unless you counted the elderly doctor, the even more elderly gardener and his two taciturn middle-aged sons. And – money notwithstanding - what man would take on Helena Vere as a wife? The most hardened fortune-hunter would be daunted by her bookishness and peculiarity.

She was no beauty, either. But you could not, Miss Crask decided, call her plain – not with those great dark eyes. The rest of Helena seemed a mere wishy-washy outline to those eyes. Her hair was light mouse, thin and lank. Her complexion was transparently pale, with a tendency to break out in reactive blotches. Her teeth were bluish and brittle, and sloped inwards. Another girl might have made more of herself, perhaps. But Helena was too utterly unworldly.

It occurred to Miss Crask, searching for a way out, that she had done her job far too well.

'She is a delicate child,' the ancient, Victorian solicitor who interviewed her had said. 'She requires shelter and protection – school is not to be thought of. And her late parents wished her to be brought up in an atmosphere of simplicity and propriety.'

My God, Miss Crask thought, she's dying of simplicity and propriety. She must leave the middle of nowhere as quickly as possible, and hurl herself recklessly into the middle of Somewhere – poor, lonely little thing.

If Helena had known Miss Crask felt sorry for her, she would have been amazed. At that moment, tramping through the snow towards the cliff-top, with Bruce cavorting around her, she was almost airborne with happiness.

The snow – a rarity on that tempestuous, blustery coast – filled her with joy. She sympathised with Bruce, yelping and dancing with exultation. There was something wildly exhilarating in the snap of the freezing air. She liked the creak her boots made when they sank into the soft whiteness, the lashing keenness of the wind and the enchanted stillness of the shrubberies and lawns.

The light was on the point of sliding towards dusk, and she always sensed magic, at this time on a winter's day. There was a moment, on the cusp of afternoon and twilight, when everything seemed to hold its breath and wait – when ghosts and spirits might drift out of the trees; when wishes and dreams might come to life.

The phantoms who crowded her imagination almost took flesh at this time. She tramped on, thinking of Roland, dying in the Pass at Roncesvalles. He was the kind of man she would love one day. She did not understand how any woman could settle for less. Miss Crask tried to show her magazine pictures of youths with varnished hair and starched shirts, but Helena had felt for some time that her destiny was a man of a nobler kind – a courtly hero, a soldier, who asked nothing more than the honour of taking her favour into battle.

Ahead of her, Bruce leapt over the edge of the cliff, down the winding, rocky path that dropped to the shore, cutting across the narrow road on its way. Up here, the wind was full of energy, blown straight from the slate-coloured ocean. It sucked the breath out of her lungs and roared in her ears, making her momentarily disorientated.

'Bruce!' she called. She felt the word in her throat, but the sound was snatched away. The cliff path was treacherous at the best of times, and too risky in the snow. 'Bruce! Come back!'

Under the wind came the sound of a car, roaring below her round the hair-raising bends in the cliff-road. It shot across the section of road she could see like a bullet, much too fast. Helena knew what was going to happen, as if she had seen it in a dream, and unconsciously put out her hand to protect herself from the impact.

The crash was unseen, and muted by the sawing wind, but she seemed to feel it in her feet, through the fathoms of rock.

It was followed by a terrible silence.

Helena was picking her way down the path, on trembling legs, before she properly knew what she was doing. Her mouth was dry, crackling with the cold, and her heart hammered. When she stumbled round the bend in the road, it gave a great leap of panic.

The scarlet two-seater lay crazily on its side, against the wall of solid rock. Leather suitcases were scattered around it. Some had come open, strewing the road with clothes. These, flapping in the wind, were the only movement – besides Bruce, who was sniffing around the edge of the road where the cliffs dropped steeply. There was a smell of scorched rubber and petrol.

A man, swaddled in a thick black overcoat, lay in the road. Helena ran towards him, but he was already heaving himself to his feet, shaking his head as if to clear it. He was tall and powerfully built, with a long upper lip and crooked nose. Helena watched helplessly as he staggered about like a drunkard, goggling in amazement at his own grazed, bleeding hands.

She asked: 'Are you – are you all right?'

This woke him. He cried out in sudden anguish, and began staring round. Seeing Bruce, he dropped to his knees beside him, wailed like a banshee, and hauled himself over the rim of the road, to the shelf of cliff below.

Helena felt she watched for ages. The face of the man appeared again, veins standing out with effort. He held another man in his arms.

'Help!' he shouted at Helena. Giddily, she obeyed. By the time she had reached him, however, he had laid the second man in the scorched snow, and was kneeling over him. His hands were over his face, and his body convulsed with dry, breathless sobs.

Helena had never seen a dead body before, and she was very frightened. She was also intensely curious. She dared to look into its face, and her heart lurched.

The face was criss-crossed with ribbons of blood, but it was a beautiful face – woundingly beautiful. She dropped to her knees, like a pilgrim at a shrine.

'I bloody warned him!' his companion sobbed furiously. 'He always knows best –'

It was a face of medieval refinement; lips perfectly incised, dark lashes fanned on his cheeks in perfect repose, one coal-black curl of hair shaken out of its brilliantine across his forehead.

His companion clenched his fists, screwed his eyes shut, and took several deep breaths. Then he reached out and felt behind the young man's ear. His hand was huge, yet his touch was tender.

'He's still alive – bugger knows why . . .' Instantly, he was electrified. 'Where's the nearest house, Miss?'

'The – it's called the Prospect,' Helena stammered.

'Run quick as you can and get a stretcher – no –' He placed his meaty hands on her shoulders. 'Best if I go. Where is it? Where? How far?' He was restraining himself, with difficulty, from shaking her.

'Straight up that path, you'll see the big house. Turn right halfway, there's a cottage through the trees – the gardeners live there –'

He tensed, to spring away, but stayed, tightening his grip on her shoulders, to say:

'You've got to be a brave little girl and wait here with him. Do you understand? Don't run away, don't leave him –'

'I won't.'

He flung himself up the path, skidding blindly on the rocks.

Bruce had begun sniffing the body. Helena put her arm round him, to restrain him. They knelt together, and she thought of the song about the knight slain under his shield – 'His hounds they lie down at his feet, so well they do their master keep.'

She pulled off her glove, and timidly ran her forefinger down his bloody cheek. Then she bent down, and drank a kiss from his cold lips.

<><><>

Ralph Gallant smelled scorched rubber and cordite, and braced himself for the impact. He opened his eyes, saw a wall of flame and closed them again. He was aware of pain – quite incredible pain – but it was a long way off, as if it belonged to someone else.

He opened his eyes again. The flames were behind a high fender. There was a marble fireplace, set with green and blue flowered tiles. With an effort, he raised his eyes and saw a pastel drawing of a galleon in a storm. It seemed familiar. Long ago, he had seen it and associated it with agony.

Tufton walked across his line of vision, carrying a brown glass bottle on a tray. In sudden panic, Ralph called to him. It came out as a hoarse, whispered croak, but Tufton was beside him at once.

'Lie still, sir. Don't you try to move.'

Ralph, who automatically did the opposite of whatever he was told, tried to move. The pain reared up and snapped its jaws at him.

'Didn't I tell you?' Tufton said calmly. 'Don't I always tell you? You've really done it this time, sir. You're lucky to be alive.'

Ralph licked his dry lips with his dry tongue, and tried to remember. They were in a Casualty Clearing Station, a few miles behind the lines. No, they were not. The war had been over for years, and the memory of being carried from the trench was only his old, all-purpose nightmare.

Tufton tugged at the pillow, to raise his head. 'Are you comfortable, sir? Is there anything you need?'

'Don't know,' Ralph mumbled. 'No idea about anything.'

'That'll be the morphia. You're full of it. You won't believe the rubbish you've been talking.'

'Thought we were back at Bethune,' Ralph said. 'We're not – are we?'

'No, as I've told you a hundred times.' Tufton was gentle. 'We're still in Devon. You were showing off in the Bugatti, and you near as dammit pitched us both into the sea. You've got two broken legs, one fractured elbow and one dislocated shoulder. Smashed everything, to smithereens, you did.'

'Dear God – you don't mean my . . .?'

'That's fine, sir. Don't worry.'

'Can't move to feel it.'

'Don't try,' Tufton said drily. 'The rest'll do it good, I

daresay. If it's any consolation, it's been standing to attention these past four days – if it wasn't for the cage, I couldn't have let the ladies in to look at you.'

Ralph had been on the point of tears, but suddenly smiled. 'Ladies?'

'Oh, yes, sir. We've fallen on our feet, into a right soft number. There's Miss Crask – old sort in pince-nez – she's the housekeeper. I thought she was the mistress, the way she rapped out orders when we carried you in. But Miss Vere owns the house, and a fine one it is, too.'

Ralph said: 'There was a little girl, in a red hat. Big dark eyes.'

'No, sir, that's Miss Vere. I took her for a kid, too, at first.'

'I think she stroked my face.'

'Wouldn't be surprised.' Tufton was grinning with relief. This was the first sense he had got out of the Captain since the crash. 'She's taken a fancy to you. She wants to come and read to you.'

'Not the Bible – no, Tufton! Don't let her!'

'Calm down, sir. Only poetry. And she's loaded with money, I gather. I really think you ought to bear our financial situation in mind.'

Ralph sighed fretfully. 'So, I'm to marry that funny little girl, am I?'

'She's better than a lot of rich girls we've met.'

'And altogether better than the bankruptcy court, I suppose you mean.' He sighed again. 'Oh, God. I could be such a nice chap, if I had enough money.'

'All I'm saying is, let her come in and see you. Where's the harm? I'll go down to the kitchen and leave you together – there's a right looker of a parlourmaid, so maybe we'll both be lucky.'

'Fair play to you, Bert. You deserve something out of all this.' Ralph yawned. His eyes slid shut. On the threshold of sleep, he heard Tufton whisper in his ear:

'Glad you're all right, sir.'

⸺◈⸺

As far as Albert Tufton was concerned, this place was the answer to a prayer. Here he was, in a warm kitchen, mopping

80

up the last morsels of an excellent pheasant stew, and feasting his eyes on the ample, comely figure of the prettiest woman he had seen in ages. What a flower, he thought, to find blooming in the middle of nowhere, like a rare orchid under a common hedgerow. In London, a parlourmaid like Gladys would be snapped up by the first tradesman to call at the back door.

They were alone. Tufton was eating while his Captain slept, watched by Miss Crask. Gladys was keeping him company, in the rocking chair beside the range. The warm, yellow light of the oil lamp on the dresser brought out the richness of her colouring – red-gold hair and eyes of vivid blue, which seemed to make a little private summer in this chilly, winter-bound old house.

'Supper all right?' she asked.

Tufton swallowed a belch, and leaned luxuriously back in his chair. 'Delicious. Did you make it?'

'No. Mrs Dove does all the cooking.'

'Well, I've a good mind to propose.'

Gladys smiled. 'Wouldn't your wife mind? Or your girl?'

'Don't have a wife, or a girl. I'm a lonely bachelor. But I'm surprised to find you indoors on a Saturday night. I thought you'd be walking out with your young man.'

She laughed outright at this. 'Get off. We never meet anyone, stuck out here. I've been here two years, and you and Captain Gallant are the first company we've had.'

'What a waste,' Tufton said, wondering how long it would take to get a kiss off her.

'And you wouldn't have come at all, if you hadn't crashed your car.'

'The answer to a maiden's prayer, eh?'

'Get off!'

The colour deepened becomingly in her ripe cheeks. Tufton began to think he might get his kiss in twenty minutes, if the Captain had the decency to stay asleep.

'Mind you,' Gladys continued, after a meaningful pause, 'I'm not complaining about Miss Vere.'

'Yes, she strikes me as a nice young lady.'

'She's a love,' Gladys said warmly. 'It's the people that

make a place, isn't it?'

'Very true. The Captain isn't perfect, heaven knows. But he suits me, and I couldn't work anywhere else.'

There was an edge of curiosity in Gladys's buttery Devonian voice. 'How long have you been with him?'

'Since the war. We were in the army together. I was his batman. He resigned his commission last year, and I stayed on as his valet.'

'Why did he resign?'

Tufton considered, then decided it would be politic to give her at least a portion of the truth. If the Captain ever did make a play for Miss Vere, blatant lies at this stage might ruin everything. 'He left the Guards because he couldn't afford it. To tell the truth, he's up to his ears in debt.'

She pursed her lips disapprovingly. 'He don't look like a person down on his uppers, with that flash car, and gold stoppers on his bottles, and all.'

'The dressing case was a present – he gets a lot of presents.'

'Who from?'

Time to lie. Nobody here needed to know about the married lady who had lavished upon the Captain her treats and tears. 'Oh, he has a lot of old aunties, and they're very generous.'

Gladys had led a sequestered life, but she was not a fool.

'And the car? Was that a present from his auntie too?'

'The car isn't paid for.'

'That'll be awkward, now it's all in pieces.'

'It certainly will,' Tufton said gloomily.

'He shouldn't have got it, if he knew he couldn't pay for it.'

'Maybe not.'

'Almost like stealing.'

'He's not that sort at all.' Tufton did not want to spoil the atmosphere, but could not help defending Ralph. 'I know him, better than any man alive. And I love him. I've loved him since the day I dragged him out of a smashed-up trench, back in 'seventeen. I saved his life, and then he saved mine. He got his MC for saving me.' His voice thickened with emotion, and he cleared his throat. 'He crawled across half a mile of no-man's-land at Cambrai, with shells and bullets bursting around him like fireworks. Then he carried me back to our lines over his shoulder. The Huns could see us, and some of them put up their guns, because it was the bravest thing they ever saw.'

Even now, he could not speak of it without his eyes filling. He dragged out his handkerchief angrily, and blew his nose. Gladys's face had softened into sympathy, and she was leaning towards him.

'Never mind that it was me he saved,' Tufton said. 'I reckon if a man does one thing like that – just one – it makes him all right for the rest of his life.'

<hr>

A second later, Ralph opened his eyes, and found that it was not a second later. The curtains were drawn. A shaded lamp burned on a little table, placed where it would not hurt his eyes. He had slept deeply and dreamlessly, and now felt well enough to flex his muscles, cautiously testing the extent of his imprisonment. His left arm was in plaster. His right arm was strapped across his chest. Both legs were immobilised to the thighs, and the blankets were laid over a metal frame – now he knew what Tufton had meant about the cage.

Tufton was tidying the room. He moved very quietly, for such a large, bull-necked man. When he had hidden all the least aesthetic articles of illness, he put another pillow under Ralph's head, tucked a silk cravat into the neck of his pyjamas, and tugged a comb through his hair.

'You'll do,' he said. 'I'll fetch the ladies.'

The two women came in, and Ralph realised he had seen them before, as part of his pain-crazed delirium. Miss Crask, with her steel-rimmed pince-nez and grey hair coiled in earphones – surely the most unattractive hairstyle ever invented – advanced to the bedside.

'Good evening, Captain Gallant. I hope you're feeling better.'

A cold old trout, Ralph decided, and his most likely enemy, should he decide to pitch for Miss Vere. He summoned up his sweetest smile, and added a hint of patient suffering – not difficult, when his body felt as if it had been pounded with a stone-breaker's mallet. 'Yes, ma'am, thank you.'

'You've had a jolly good sleep.'

'Shall I bring you a chair, Miss Crask?'

'No thank you, Tufton.'

'Very good, Miss. Perhaps for Miss Vere?'

Ralph noted, with amusement, how thoroughly Tufton had worked his way into the household, as if he had been part of it for years.

'Yes,' a soft, shy voice said, 'I'd like to stay, if you think he's up to it.'

Ralph watched her emerge from behind Miss Crask's solid, ironing-board figure. She wore a white frock, like a schoolgirl on Speech Day. He knew her dark eyes – they had lighted his confusion like lamps.

He had taken her for a child because she was so small, and so slight. A reed of a girl, he thought, and plain too, poor kid. Ralph was always especially kind to plain women. Other men were mad to ignore them, in his opinion – the wallflowers were an absolute untapped goldmine of eagerness and gratitude.

Helena did not know where to look, and ducked behind the thick book she was holding. 'I thought you might like me to read to you.'

Ralph said: 'I'd simply love it.'

Miss Crask's train of thought was so obvious, he could almost hear it. She was making a lightning calculation of propriety versus opportunity, and rapidly deciding that in his trussed state, the Captain posed no possible threat to anyone.

'Go downstairs, Tufton, and ask Cook or Gladys for some cocoa,' she said. 'Helena can watch him. Remember, dear, the Captain can't move. Ring the bell at once if he needs anything.'

Respectfully, giving his best imitation of a deferential manservant, Tufton held open the door for her. Before he left the room, he flashed Ralph a brief grin of encouragement.

84

Ralph, however, had already realised that with this girl, flirtation would be impossible. She was the very invalid-food of women, mushy and flavourless as blancmange. But he thrived on the attention of women, and any nourishment was better than none.

With those uncanny eyes pinned to his face, she perched on the chair beside his bed.

'I brought some Wordsworth,' she said, in a rush. 'It's what I usually read, when I'm ill. Will that be all right?'

'Rather.' Ralph cared not a straw for poetry, and if healthy, he would have run a mile. But he was very tired, and full of pain, and there was something immensely soothing about her low, hesitant voice.

> 'So drooped Adonis, bathed in sanguine dew
> Of his death-wound, when he from innocent air
> The gentlest breath of resignation drew;
> While Venus in a passion of despair
> Rent, weeping over him, her golden hair . . .'

Through lowered lashes, Ralph watched her. She was very earnest, and uneven red blotches came and went in her thin white cheeks as she lost herself in the words. Slowly, piece by piece, his tangled memory was unravelling. Another knot loosened. Cutting into her reading, he exclaimed:

'You kissed me!'

Helena flinched, nearly dropping the book, and the red patches deepened painfully. But she spoke evenly.

'I thought you were going to die. I couldn't bear to think of you dying there in the road, with nobody to see you off. You seemed so terribly lonely.'

In the normal way of things, Ralph Gallant was one of the least lonely men on earth. All his life, his natural place had been at the centre of large groups of people who loved him. Now, however, he remembered the dugout at Bethune, and the dreadful isolation of lying there bleeding. He must have felt just the same when he lay half-dead on the road – and this sweet girl had kissed him.

He was too feeble to fight the sudden rush of tears, and

they spilled down his face when he closed his eyes. He could not raise his hands to wipe them away.

Helena cried: 'Oh, don't, don't!'

She took a handkerchief, faintly scented with lavender, from her sleeve, and dabbed the tears away. Then, careful not to hurt him, she reached out to stroke his hair, with a touch as light as a butterfly's wing.

That was the moment at which Ralph decided he would be a fool not to fall in love with her.

<hr>

They were married two months later, beneath a hymeneal arch of blue spring sky. It was the quietest possible wedding, at the small, mildew-smelling village church at the gates of the Prospect. Helena carried a posy of bluebells and wore a white tussore 'costume', ordered from London by Miss Crask. Ralph was starched and shining in morning dress, leaning romantically on a walking stick.

Afterwards, Captain and Mrs Gallant were to depart for Cap Ferrat, attended by Bert and Gladys Tufton, newly returned from their own honeymoon in Weston-super-Mare.

Miss Crask was packed and ready to leave for Hatch End. She was relieved that Helena was off her hands, and determined to think the best of Ralph – not an easy task, for a woman of an automatically suspicious cast of mind. He was very charming, but Miss Crask secretly mistrusted that kind of effortless, undiscriminating charm. Walk round him as you would, only one side of his character was ever on display. Was there another, darker side?

In her worst moments, Miss Crask was afraid she had let her charge fall straight into the hands of the first fortune-hunter who happened along. Not a week after proposing, he had confessed to staggering, hair-raising debts, and offered to call the whole thing off, in the most touching manner. Helena told Miss Crask how he had broken down and sobbed in her arms. By then it had been far too late, since the scene of sobbing and forgiveness had placed Helena on a cloud of bliss.

Mr Venables, the family solicitor, did not much like it

either. But he drew up Helena's new will, leaving everything unconditionally to her husband – because what else could he do? Little Helena was of age, and had suddenly grasped that she was sole mistress of her millions. Ralph had picked up Helena's hand and kissed it, gazing into her enraptured eyes, and Miss Crask and the lawyer had not been able to help exchanging glances of deep scepticism.

Directly after the ceremony, Helena sat on her bed, dreamily inhaling the scent of her bouquet. Miss Crask tried to inject a word of caution then, but had not the heart. Happiness shone from Helena as if she had swallowed the sun. Her old governess could only pity her innocence and frailty, and pray that her handsome young husband would grow to deserve her.

The wedding night was spent in London, at the Savoy Hotel. Helena was afraid of the lights and the noise, and the sleek crowds of jewelled and enamelled people. Many of these seemed to know Ralph, or at least to know of him, and they stared at his new wife rather rudely. Some congratulated, but did it oddly, Helena thought. One beastly man clapped Ralph on the back, and shouted: 'By God, Gallant, you did it! Does this mean I get my two hundred back?'

Ralph, however, made up for everything. He could not have been sweeter, or more considerate. He consummated the marriage with an expert gentleness, which showed that he had studied Helena's courtly, medieval pattern-books. Helena, giddy with love and the honour of his touch, found the courage to give physical expression to some of her pent-up yearnings.

Then there was the thrilling novelty of watching Ralph undress and bathe and comb his hair – small, amazingly intimate acts, which made her feel they lived in the same skin.

Next morning, he laughingly rubbed his unshaven chin against her cheek, and asked: 'Happy, darling?'

'Yes, Ralph – so happy!'

Gladys Tufton, elevated to lady's maid, and wearing a dark suit instead of her black dress and apron, was very happy, too. She sang as she folded Helena's new clothes into the trunk. Tufton smacked her on the bottom and kissed her neck, whenever he thought Helena was not looking.

Happiness carried the four of them to the South of France. To Helena, it was a land of enchantment – the steady power of the sun, the hard blue sky, the lizards darting among the geranium tubs on the terrace. Ralph knew Cap Ferrat, and had arranged everything beautifully. They had a sitting room, a bedroom, two dressing rooms and a deep balcony, all shaded by slatted wooden shutters. The hotel had a terrace and gardens, a swimming pool and a band. Any worries she might have had about the cost were blown away when Ralph laughed, and said: 'Silly, you can afford it.'

He bought her presents – sometimes frocks or jewels, but small things, too. A book, an antique watercolour, a piece of local pottery glowing with the colours of sea and sky. It was Helena's joy to return the compliment. To mark her first fortnight of marriage, she gave Ralph a prodigiously expensive platinum watch-chain for evening, and – like sweet Alice with Ben Bolt – wept with delight when he gave her back one of his heavenly smiles.

Ralph insisted his happiness knew no bounds, though he yawned a great deal, when they spent long evenings together, and kept sneaking glances at his watch.

'Darling,' he said one day, as they lay together in bed, 'I've run into a couple of pals. Would you mind awfully if I asked them to dine with us?'

Helena did not want anyone intruding on her idyll, but could refuse Ralph nothing. 'Of course not. I'd love to meet them.'

They were called Hugh and Madeline Derwent-Sinclair. Hugh was rather old, with a grey moustache and bloodshot eyes. Madeline seemed quite old, too – there were crazed lines, full of powder, in the tanned skin around her blue eyes. But she was very elegant. She wore a shimmering morsel of blue chiffon, which showed a great deal of her meagre brown flesh. A necklace of square-cut sapphires shone with careless splendour on her bony neck.

She seemed to have known Ralph for ages, and the two of them were very confidential over dinner. The band was playing, and Ralph limped round the floor with Madeline. He had to hold her very close, because he had left his walking stick at the table.

Helena, feeling very young and lonely, allowed Hugh to walk her through a foxtrot. He breathed heavily, made no conversation, and smelt powerfully of spirits. Ralph seemed to depress him.

Midnight had come and gone, and Helena was struggling to keep awake, when Ralph declared he wanted to go on to a club he had heard about.

Madeline said: 'Jazz-hot – how too divine! Do let's, Hughie.'

Morosely, Hugh said: 'No fear. I'm for bed.'

Madeline directed a frightening, dazzling smile at Helena. 'Just the three of us, then.'

'Ralph –' Helena timidly touched his sleeve, 'would you mind awfully if we didn't?'

'Dearest, you're exhausted – what must you think of me? You go off to bed. I promise not to disturb you when I come in.'

A weight settled on Helena's chest. He had not heard the 'we', and she could not bring herself to ask him to stay with her. She ended up thanking him humbly, and dragging upstairs with a disturbed feeling of something – God knew what – amiss.

The next morning, she woke to find Ralph dressed for tennis. 'You don't mind, do you, sweet? Only I must have some exercise, and Madeline says she'll make allowances for my limp.' He stooped, to kiss her cheek on the pillow. 'I'm getting so much better, thanks to you.'

He began to spend more and more time with the Derwent-Sinclairs. Helena could not pretend she liked it, but made up her mind to be content. It would have been selfish to complain, she decided – Ralph glowed with health, and had thrown away his stick. She did not have the energy to give him the variety and amusement he needed. He was young and male and full of vitality, and she could not do much more than sit under an umbrella in the garden, with a book and a cup of tea. Truthfully, it suited her far better than gadding about. She was not strong, and her bones were hungry for rest and heat. Besides, when Ralph was with her, he was a perfect darling. She would watch him sometimes, marvelling over his handsomeness, and glancing down at her wedding ring to remind herself that he belonged to her.

His lovemaking was gentle and affectionate. If he thought she looked too tired, he would simply kiss her forehead, and tell Tufton to make up the bed in the dressing room. No, it would not have been fair to keep him tied to her side. She sent a picture-postcard of the Plage to Miss Crask, and wrote: 'Cap Ferrat is very gay. We are having a lovely time. I'll write a proper letter soon.'

One afternoon, Helena was surprised to see Hugh Derwent-Sinclair sipping a drink under a neighbouring umbrella. She disliked Hugh, but he was staring. She was too polite not to go over.

'Hello. I thought you were playing doubles, with Ralph and Madeline.'

'My partner cried off at the last minute.' He let out a bray of angry, mirthless laughter. 'So there you are. Isn't it rum how that keeps happening?'

'Does it?' Helena did not care for the way he was eyeing her, with a kind of gloomy ferocity. 'I'm sorry you didn't get your game.'

'Such rotten luck,' said Hugh. 'Look here, Helena, I'm glad I ran into you. I believe there's a piece of my property in your drawing room.'

'Did you leave something behind, when you came to play bridge?'

'Yes.' His eyes were very miserable, and very cruel. 'My gold cigarette case. It was a present from Madeline, so it obviously has huge sentimental value.'

He was drunk. Helena seized the cigarette case as an excuse to get away from him.

'I'll run up and look for it.'

'Yes. What a good idea.'

The corridors of the hotel were shaded and still in their afternoon slumber. A chambermaid, her arms full of towels, bobbed a curtsey at Helena as she passed. As Helena approached her own door, she halted, her scalp prickling. There were sounds behind it – feral, inhuman sounds, like moans.

In a trance, she pushed open the door of her sitting room. Every emotion had numbed, but at some instinctive level, she had already guessed, for she knew how important it was to be noiseless.

The room was exactly as she had left it, with her books piled on the low table beside the sofa, and the sun making patterns on the carpet through the wooden slats of the shutters. The moans went on, gathering force towards a crescendo. The door to the bedroom stood slightly open.

The world had stopped. Helena moved towards the door, silent as a shadow. Their clothes were tangled in clumps across the polished wooden floor – silks and flannels, ripped off any how. A jewelled watch lay, like a star, in the middle of the rug.

Ralph and Madeline thrashed and wrestled together on the bed. Helena hardly recognised Ralph. He lay on his back, his hands squeezing the flesh around Madeline's waist, grunting aggressively as he slammed her up and down on his shaft. Helena could not take her eyes off this. She had barely seen his penis, and never seen it erect. With her, he slipped under the covers, did something to it with his hand, and pushed it into her – the hardness still startled her. Madeline rode him hungrily, one wanton, varnished finger caressing her vagina.

Helena had never even imagined anything so obscene. Before the disgust hit her fully, her own vagina twitched in shameful response. Ralph had never made love to her like this. His violence, his roaring abandon, spiked her horror with excitement.

Mesmerised, she watched him hurl Madeline onto her back. He knelt over her, and his entire character seemed transformed and overshadowed by the hugeness, the urgency of his erection. Then he forced her knees apart and – no, he wasn't, he couldn't – buried his face in the sparse blonde hairs around her split.

Helena did not know how long she watched this, before

her shudders of disbelief brought her back to some sense of reality. Ralph lapped and sighed, and his tongue was clearly visible, working in the folds of flesh between Madeline's legs.

Suddenly, Helena felt sick. She dashed out into the corridor, closing the door silently, with shaking hands. She wanted to hide somewhere and cry until she died. But she had nowhere to go. Her self-control hanging by a thread, she stumbled through the hotel, and out into the glaring light of the garden.

At last, in the shelter of some dry, sand-dusted shrubs, her sobs erupted with shattering force. The pain was tremendous. Her darling, her perfect knight, was faithless. For the first time in her life, she discovered hate. She hated Madeline, that snake in sapphires. She hated Hugh, the drunken wretch who had purposely destroyed her peace.

But she could not hate Ralph. With the sobs still tearing out of her, Helena discovered a determination to cling to the little she had. She would shame the devil by forgiving her darling. She could not live without Ralph, and she could not live with his anger, if he ever found out she had been spying on him. It was odd, when he had never shown her his anger, that she knew it existed. Yet she did, and sensed it was something to be feared.

In the midst of her ruined dreams, her confusion was worsened by a wicked, pagan desire to touch herself, as Madeline had done, to see how it felt.

No, she could not bear to reproach him, when it might mean losing him. He had not lied, when he said he loved her. His was a reverent, respectful love. She had the best of him. He had married her, and she would always be first. She must hold on to this, if she did not want to go mad.

He loves me – he loves me – he does love me.

—◆◇◆◇◆—

'Ouch!' Ralph yelped. 'Stop sticking those shirt-studs into my bloody chest!'

Frowning, Tufton bundled Ralph into his white dinner jacket. 'It just won't do, sir.'

'What won't do?'

'Glad says she's been crying her eyes out.'

'Well, perhaps she's ill,' Ralph said testily. 'She's always ill.'

'Perhaps she's found out.'

'Don't be ridiculous!'

'Why is that ridiculous?' Tufton demanded. 'You ain't exactly discreet.'

Ralph sighed. 'Do stop acting the heavy father, Bert. You never used to mind.'

'You never used to be married.'

'Oh, God. Look, I couldn't help it. I know I said I'd break it off with Madeline, but when she turned up here–'

'Funny, that.'

'All right, I told her. But dammit, I'm so bored, I could scream.'

'And you couldn't wait until the honeymoon was over. You're behaving like a shit,' Tufton said. And, as an afterthought, 'Sir. She bailed us out of a very nasty mess. A little gratitude wouldn't go amiss. She might be young and innocent, but she's not stupid. I bet she knows what she's not getting from you.'

Ralph met his reflection in the long glass. His curling hair fell across his tanned forehead. The white dinner jacket set off his slender, soldierly figure to admiration. Yet Helena's sweet, plain, boring, anxious face floated between himself and his self-satisfaction.

'You're absolutely right,' he said, still gazing at himself. 'I am a shit. She deserves better.'

Tufton was implacable. 'She does.'

'I try so hard to change, and it all goes wrong. But I will, Tufton – I'll try again. I didn't only marry her for the money, you know. She's the sweetest little thing in the world. She'll never know another moment's doubt.'

The Captain looked very noble as he said this, but Tufton had worked for him a long time. 'Excuse me, sir – does that mean you'll stop fooling around, or that she'll stop finding out?'

'Bert!'

Tufton laid Ralph's clothes over the back of a chair, and

planted his fists on his hips. 'This is the best place I've ever had – nice job, nice wife, big house, lots of tin, not a care in the world. No more bailiffs, no more jealous husbands. Wages up to date and paid regular. We've landed on our feet at last – so why do you want to muck it all up? Isn't it worth keeping your wick dry, at least for a week or two?'

There was a silence. Outside, laughter and the rattle of glasses floated up from the terrace. Ralph bit his lip. His eyes flooded with tears.

'Yes, you're right. I have new duties now. I must simply learn to live with the unutterable loneliness of it, for everyone else's sake. What does my happiness matter?'

Tufton wielded the clothes-brush across Ralph's shoulders with an unnecessarily heavy hand, though the beginnings of a reluctant amusement lurked in his eyes. 'Tears won't work with me this time.'

'Maybe not,' Ralph said, 'but they always do with her. Send our apologies to Mr and Mrs Derwent-Sinclair, and get them to send our dinner upstairs.'

'Very good, sir.'

Ralph blew his nose, careful not to displace the diamond tears on his lashes. 'It was the same on my school reports – could do better, must try harder. Order us a bottle of decent champagne, then you and Gladys make yourselves scarce.'

Chapter Two

The Captain's hard work paid off handsomely. Helena started being sick on the boat home, and spent the next eight months lying on the sofa, stroking her belly in dreamy wonderment.

Ralph's behaviour was exemplary. He sat with her, read to her, brought her posies of the woodland flowers she loved. Every few weeks, he went to London 'on business' and returned fresh and hearty, and laden with totally impractical nursery furnishings.

'He deserves a bloody medal,' Tufton told Gladys. 'You don't know what it costs him, to behave this well.'

Gladys was shaking her head over the latest collection of huge plush animals and Wagnerian music-boxes. 'So he should, when she's so poorly. It's a pity he can't keep it up longer.'

She was fond enough of Ralph, but the fondness was mixed with contempt, and she resented his power to whisk Tufton away from her. Early in her marriage, however, she had understood that the relationship between the two men was sacred – far, far deeper than master and servant. Between them lay the war, and the loyalty they had forged out of their blood. Tufton could complain about Ralph and criticise him, but he could not live without him. Ralph was similarly helpless without Tufton. Gladys wisely chose not to trespass on this forbidden ground, and was careful to welcome her husband home with kisses, rather than reproaches.

He always began by asking: 'How's she been?' For he had a real regard for Helena – and he noticed, long before Ralph did, how frail she was. While her belly swelled, the rest of her seemed to diminish. Her great, haunting dark eyes lit her transparent face with a poignancy all the more affecting because she was so happy.

Eventually, Ralph's visits to London became shorter, then ceased.

'He's not comfortable away from her these days,' Tufton said. 'She'll bring out the best in him yet.'

Gladys said: 'She's got him worried.'

'Yes, love, but it's more than that. The Captain can't be even commonly decent most of the time – but in short bursts, he can be a bloody saint.'

'He's making her happy,' said Gladys. 'I'll always love him for that.'

The winter had set in, and the year was rolling round to the anniversary of their first meeting. Helena, pinned to the sofa under her bulge, lay beside the library fire. Ralph held her feet in his lap, gazing down at her. In the dim light, his eyes were anxious.

He thought she was dozing, but she suddenly asked: 'Do you think it'll be a boy or a girl?'

Ralph chuckled. 'Lord, I hadn't really got round to thinking it'd be either. Why should I bother, when the whole countryside is on the case? Gladys's mother reckons it's a boy, apparently. Whereas the nosey old boiler in the Post Office says it's a girl for sure.'

Helena stroked his arm. 'Poor darling, I'm afraid you find the country maddeningly dull.'

'Rubbish. It's fascinating.'

This made her laugh. 'Never mind. When it's born, we'll all go to London.'

'We'll do nothing of the kind,' Ralph said. 'You'll need rest and this horridly healthy country air, and so will – it.'

'D'you know,' Helena mused, 'I have a feeling it's a girl. Would you mind a girl?'

'Rather not. I adore women.'

'That's because they generally adore you,' Helena teased. 'Well, and so will our daughter. And Ralph – would you terribly mind if I called her Lily-Josephine?'

He was taken aback, then laughed. 'What the hell for? Sounds like a pair of batty old maiden aunts.'

Her eyes left him, and moved dreamily to the fire. 'I read somewhere – can't remember where – how Joseph, in the Bible, was so beautiful that the lilies of the Nile turned their faces towards him, mistaking him for the sun. I want our little daughter to be both the lily and the Joseph – the flower and the sun. I know she'll be beautiful, because she'll look just like you.'

Lily-Josephine Gallant was beautiful, and she did look extraordinarily like Ralph.

'Except for the eyes,' Gladys said fondly. 'I do believe they're beginning to turn. They'll be just like Madam's.'

Poor Helena only saw her daughter once a day, when Gladys or the nurse held her up in the doorway of the bedroom. She had tuberculosis, aggravated by pregnancy, and could not risk infecting the baby. She was wasting away, but Lily-Josephine waxed fat and bonny; a glorious, dimpled, smiling child. Officially, she was in the care of a nursemaid. Gladys, however, was the one who got up for her at night and dressed her in her tiny Chilprufe vests and matinee jackets. Helena seemed happiest with this arrangement, and Gladys often sat with her, talking of Lily-Josephine's many talents and virtues – invisible, except to the eyes that loved her.

Gladys thought it would break her heart, when she saw Helena stretching out her arms from the bed towards her baby, her face alight with love and longing. The lamb-like bleats from Lily-Josephine made the tears cascade from her radiant eyes.

'Oh, nurse – oh, Gladys – isn't she heavenly? Don't cry, precious – Mummy will hold you soon . . .'

The first six months of Lily-Josephine's life were her mother's last, and sadness hung over the Prospect like a pall.

'I wish I could help you more,' Tufton told Gladys, 'but I've got my hands full, keeping the Captain out of the way of the bottle. He's blotting it up like nobody's business.'

Ralph travelled between sickroom and nursery, half-distracted with remorse. He adored the baby, and never tired of cuddling her, or floating celluloid ducks in her bath.

When he played with his daughter, he was almost his old, blithe self. As the months wore on, however, there were times when the sound of her babbling only increased his depression. He would shut himself in the library with the decanters, until Tufton was able to pluck the glass from his nerveless hand and carry him to bed.

On the last night of Helena's life, Gladys could bear it no longer. She took the warm bundle of Lily-Josephine from her cradle, hurried her down to Helena's room, and laid her in her mother's arms.

Helena opened her eyes. They were already glazing over, but she saw the small face inches from her own, and felt the velvet head nestling against her shoulder. With an effort that took all her strength, she kissed the sleeping Lily's cheek, and smiled.

Not an hour later, she was dead.

Ralph sobbed all night, in Tufton's arms.

Gladys had to make do with the jack-towel hanging on the back of the kitchen door. Mrs Dove, the Cook, found her weeping there, and made her a cup of tea laced with gin.

'The doctor can say what he likes to me,' Gladys said. 'I'll never be sorry I did that. She couldn't have gone so peacefully, if she hadn't held her baby in her arms.'

'She'll go to heaven, for sure,' said Mrs Dove. 'But goodness knows what the Captain will do now.'

Ralph's grief was sharp and sincere, but not of very long duration. Two months after the funeral, he took himself and Tufton out of the house of mourning and ran off to London. He was now a very rich man, and easily reverted to the life of a rackety young bachelor.

The country bored him, and the Prospect was full of guilty associations, but he could see that it was a perfect place for a child – and nothing was too good for his curly-headed darling. London could not hold him for long, when Lily-Josephine waited in her kingdom by the sea. Every time he pelted down to Devon, to snatch her in his arms, she was more beautiful. Her hair and eyes were black as ebony against her snow-white skin. Her cheeks were dimpled, her energetic little figure full of grace.

As she got older, Ralph was less able to get along without her. He invited London down to Devon, and filled the house with his elegant, amusing and often somewhat disreputable friends. All considered Lily-Josephine a hoot and a scream and an utter pet – she was a very entertaining child. They vied with Ralph, to load her with expensive presents and impractical treats.

'He treats her like a toy,' Gladys complained. 'If it goes on like this, she'll be thoroughly spoiled.'

She need not have worried, for Lily-Josephine was miraculously immune to spoiling. She grew up as wild as a plover, and as unselfconsciously lovely as the forget-me-nots and scarlet pimpernels that blew in her clifftop garden. The sea was her playground – she swam like a mermaid, and begged Ralph for a boat.

Lily-Josephine in begging-mode could wear down a heart of granite. She used no wiles, she deployed none of her charms. Instead, she attacked with pitiless logic, and the gravity of a cabinet minister.

'Look here, Dad – I've been thinking about this boat. I might be a bit too small for one just now.'

'A bit! Darling, you're five. Nobody sails a boat by themselves when they're only five.'

'That's why you won't get me one, isn't it?'

'It is.'

'Can I have a boat when I'm bigger?'

'Yes, my duck, of course.'

'Then why don't you get a boat for yourself now, and take me out in it?'

The boat was bought, and Ralph taught his determined daughter to sail it. Gladys said the very sight of the thing aged her ten years, and she dreamt at night of her baby drowning.

'I shan't drown,' Lily-Josephine assured her. 'I mean, you'd be bound to cry, wouldn't you? I shan't ever do anything to make you cry, Gladys.'

On the tip of her tongue, Gladys had one of her usual crushing replies about little girls with jammy faces who had been at the store cupboard – but what came out was a murmured:

'Please God, you won't!'

And she suddenly hugged Lily-Josephine tightly, feeling the delicate ribcage under the fisherman's Guernsey, and wishing the little heart inside could beat for ever. She and Tufton had not been 'blessed' themselves, as Gladys put it, and both lavished the love their blessings might have had upon Lily-Josephine.

Every summer, while Ralph was racing or yachting, or visiting a string of country houses, Gladys took the child off for a bracing fortnight in Bude. Here, the sea was tamed and domesticated. They stayed in lodgings, full of hideous ornaments which Lily-Josephine considered the last word in taste and beauty. Every fine morning, they went to the beach. Gladys sat with her knitting, in a row of deck chairs unofficially reserved for nannies, and watched Lily-Josephine playing in the sand with the other children.

The summer Lily-Josephine was five, the nannies were complimentary. 'What a pretty little dear – and such a character! I suppose she'll be off to school soon.'

Gladys said 'yes,' and wondered when Ralph would get round to educating his daughter. It was always difficult to pin him down to acts of fatherly responsibility. Other little girls of Lily-Josephine's age had dancing classes and piano lessons.

Lily-Josephine did not see the point of either. There was a troupe of pierrots on the beach. One of them had a banjo, and this became a passion to rival the boat. She dictated daily postcards to Ralph: 'Dear Daddy, I am having a lovely time. Please get me a banjo. Love from Lily-Josephine.' 'Dear Daddy, it will be nice to see you next Saturday. Don't forget my banjo. Love from Lily-Josephine.'

She asked for surprisingly little, considering Ralph would have bought the moon to please her. When she did want something, however, she was relentless. Gladys wrote privately to Tufton: 'If we're in for a banjo, do tell him to find one the right size, and someone to teach her to play it, or she'll wear us all down to a frazzle.'

Ralph was due to arrive at the Prospect with a party of ten friends. Gladys and the other servants resigned themselves to a frantic week of bells ringing at all hours, beds mysteriously un-slept in, powder spilled across dressing tables, and gentlemen's underwear turning up unexpectedly in ladies' bathrooms.

It was not a suitable atmosphere for a small and curious child. Lily-Josephine, however, loved the bustle and laughter. She was waiting at the top of the steps, dancing with impatience, when the convoy of cars swept into the drive.

'Hello Dad, hello Tufton – where's my banjo?'

There was a woman in the car with them, as there generally was. This time, she was a musical-comedy star named Diana Dare – slim as a whip, with hair like a bright new penny and hard blue eyes ringed with black. Gladys was deeply annoyed to hear Ralph telling the child that he had met Miss Dare when she jumped out of a cake at a charity dinner.

Lily-Josephine was, predictably, fascinated. 'Was she covered in crumbs? Did she have to stay in the cake while they were baking it?'

Miss Dare was an amiable soul. Gladys warmed to her slightly – very slightly - when she taught Lily-Josephine dance-steps in the flower bed and agreed to meet her guinea pigs. But this did not excuse the fact that she draped herself over Ralph at every opportunity, covering his collar with a very tarty shade of lipstick.

'I wish to goodness he'd stop bringing his floozies back with him,' Gladys complained to her husband later. They were in the kitchen. Tufton was eating biscuits and waiting for his summons to dress Ralph for dinner. Gladys was ironing the floozy's pink silk camiknickers. 'It's a different one every time, and Lily-Josie will be asking questions soon. You know how sharp she is.'

'I can promise you,' Tufton said, 'the ones he leaves behind in London are worse. I never thought I'd hear myself saying this – but I wish he'd marry again. To someone suitable, I mean. I keep telling him to grow up, and he always says he's so rich, he doesn't have to. Which is true enough, God knows.'

'If he'd only think of Lily properly for a change,' sighed Gladys, banging the iron aggressively, 'instead of posting her toys whenever he feels sentimental. Do work on him, Bert – it's time he thought about her education, and he listens to you.'

On this occasion, however, it was not Tufton Ralph listened to. One of the house party was a stout, jolly, middle-aged lady, draped in fluttering scarves and strings of amber beads. Her name was Daphne Wadsworth – Ralph called her 'Daph the Saph', and they seemed very fond of each other. She spent her days chain-smoking Turkish cigarettes and typing furiously in her bedroom. Gladys was most impressed when Ralph told her Miss Wadsworth was also Phyllis Crewe, the gifted author of her favourite romances.

Miss Dare tittered, and said: 'Darling, wherever you go, you can always be sure of a welcome below stairs.'

But Miss Wadsworth was very pleased that Gladys liked her books, and presented her with a signed copy of the latest, which had not even arrived at the Boots Library in Bideford.

'Do tell me what you think, my dear – my hero was inspired by the Captain.'

Gladys quickly divined that Miss Wadsworth was the only member of Ralph's party whose interest in Lily-Josephine was genuine. She took real trouble with the child, to the length of teaching her a few simple chords on the little Banjolele which she had helped Ralph choose in London. And the moment she discovered the small enchantress could not read, she ordered Ralph to do something about it.

'She's as ignorant as a savage. There are little ragged children in the East End who know more than your Lily-of-the-Nile.'

Ralph was sitting at her feet on the hearthrug at the time, and he leaned his curly head affectionately against her knee.

'She's too young to be sent away, and too divinely natural to have her head filled with a lot of boring facts.'

'Nonetheless, my darling, her head must be filled with something. And who's talking about sending such a mite away? You must get her a governess.'

He groaned. 'Spare me!'

'No, I won't. I'll keep on at you until you do it. She's an intelligent child – not a baby, or a lapdog, or a doll.'

Something stirred in Ralph's memory. The following day, he asked Gladys if she knew what had become of the dismal old bat who had taught Helena. Egged on by Miss Wadsworth, Gladys wrote a respectful letter to Miss Crask, asking if she could recommend a suitable young woman.

Miss Crask's reply arrived by return. Yes, she could warmly recommend the niece of an old friend, a Miss Dorothy Curtis, educated at Somerville but prepared to care for a small child, because the sea air would be good for her asthma.

The room was prepared, the train fare was sent, the thing was done. Lily-Josephine had a governess. It was right, and Gladys tried not to mind, but could not help feeling depressed. What would happen to her wild, original baby, when the shades of the prison-house closed around her?

Miss Curtis was a whey-faced rail of a woman, with an Eton crop and unbecoming spectacles. She was serious and shy, and the timetable she drew up for her little charge was dry enough to make the heart sink.

Once again, however, Gladys had underestimated Lily-Josephine's capacity for tailoring circumstances to suit herself. While Miss Curtis worked on the child, the child worked on Miss Curtis.

'She's a witch, that Miss Lily,' said Mrs Dove. 'Twists the whole world round her little finger. I'm sorry for her husband.'

Dorothy was musical, and piano lessons had formed part of the original plan. These were amended to banjo lessons. One afternoon, Gladys came into the schoolroom, to find Lily-Josephine playing and singing 'Li'l Liza Jane', accompanied by Dorothy on the comb-and-paper, and saw that the victory was total.

Once the pill was sugared to her liking, Lily-Josephine took very graciously to education. For the next ten years, life at the Prospect went its quiet way. Ralph continued to bring his string of women. Tufton's hair turned grey. Guinea pigs gave way to ponies, the little cockleshell boat was exchanged for a bigger one. Lily-Josephine blossomed and prospered in her sheltered paradise.

When she was sixteen, Dorothy married the friend of a neighbour, and departed, amidst scenes of sorrow, to live in the north of Scotland. Daphne Wadsworth, fonder than ever of her unofficial godchild, volunteered to find a replacement. Lily-Josephine, however, said she had learned enough – from books, at least.

'Well, nobody could accuse her of being idle,' Dorothy said to Gladys, on the eve of her wedding. Lily-Josephine had just had the final fitting for her blue bridesmaid's gown – made by Gladys – and was chasing her pony round the paddock. Gladys and Dorothy watched her, from behind the fence.

'She's clever,' Gladys said. 'I wish she'd get a little more learning.'

Dorothy struggled to put her feeling about Lily into words. It seemed important to do this, now that she was leaving. 'Her cleverness isn't exactly the right sort for passing exams. In a way, it would be a shame to tie her down. She's so free. It will suit her, to set her own timetable.'

Gladys chuckled. 'When has she done anything else? You never managed to set one for her.'

'True.' Dorothy smiled, rather wistfully. 'I'll miss her. I mean, I'll miss you all – you're the only real family I've ever known. But I'll miss Lily-Josephine particularly. What she's given to me –' She was struggling again. 'She's so – special. I think she touches lives, almost like magic. You won't let her change, will you?'

Gladys put this down to wedding nerves. 'I couldn't if I tried.'

'She's not a child any more. She's practically a woman. When she finds love – or love finds her, as it's bound to do – she'll have the power to move mountains. You wait and see.'

Infected by her sense of foreboding, Gladys found herself looking at Lily-Josephine with new eyes. Yes, she had grown and developed. But there was more. A glow in her fabulous dark eyes, an added lustre to her skin. With a shock, Gladys realised her baby was, indeed, shooting away from her into womanhood.

And superimposed upon the laughing child in the paddock, she saw a woman of unsettling, unknowable beauty.

PART THREE

Chapter One

1980

❖❖❖

Primrose and Bunter were waiting out on the front steps, before the car was halfway down the drive. Primrose had been on the phone to Isobel when she heard the car approaching, and had rung off promising to ring back the moment they had gone.

'The very moment,' Isobel had urged. 'And tell me every word. Tell me what he looks like.'

Since the revelation of Sophie's meeting with the Randalls, Primrose and Isobel had run up enormous telephone bills. The magnitude of the coincidence had smashed down the wall between the sisters. Beyond the business of Octavius, they had discovered an urgent backlog of news – years of it, heaped up behind the barrier Sidonia had placed between them.

They talked for hours, to the vexation of Marius, who was inclined to be stingy about phones. He did not care much for Primrose, but it had been his idea to invite her to Ireland, once the Prospect was off her hands:

'If you two are going to gabble, gabble, gabble, you might as well do it for nothing.'

Primrose's sorrow at being ousted from her kingdom had been entirely swallowed by her desperate curiosity to see Lily-Josephine's son. His first visit to the Prospect had been arranged very informally, but she could not shake off a sense of ceremony.

For the first time in years, she had taken trouble with her appearance. The anguish caused by Sidonia's betrayal had had the welcome side-effect of reducing her spare tyre. Her best tweed skirt fitted again. Heartened by this, and by the absence of Sidonia's mockery, she had gone to the length of ironing a cream silk blouse and applying pale pink lipstick.

The Primrose she met in the hall mirror had regained enough colour and gilding to look – in her own eyes, at least – positively reborn.

The car, a muddy Land Rover with a canvas top, halted noisily on the gravel. Two men climbed out. Primrose, in a flutter of anticipation, ran down the steps to meet them. She had not expected two of them. Obviously, the younger one was Octavius. She had been carrying a picture of Lily in her mind, and was disappointed, at first, by the lack of resemblance. She could tell Isobel that he was handsome, but his eyes were hazel instead of black, and his thick hair was brown. More than this, he lacked Lily's indefinable electric sparkle.

If one was searching for a likeness, he looked more like the older man, who had been at the wheel of the Land Rover. His father? While Bunter politely sniffed his knees, Primrose studied him. He was tall and spare, in his mid-to-late fifties; with rough brown hair and a weatherworn, outdoor complexion. He gave her a shy, lopsided smile, and held out his hand.

'Miss Rumage? Patrick Randall. I hope we're not too late.'

His hand was warm. 'It is tricky to find,' Primrose said, trying not to stare at Octavius. 'We share the lane with the farm next door, and I'm afraid he keeps taking down our sign. He has a ridiculous obsession with his sheep and my dog.'

'What, this dog?' Patrick Randall patted Bunter. 'He doesn't look like much of a desperado to me.'

Primrose glowed. 'No, Bunter's a thorough gentleman. And too fat to chase even a stick these days.'

She turned expectantly to Lily's son. He frowned, and stuck out his hand. Primrose just had time to touch it, before he snatched it away.

He said: 'Octavius Randall.'

'How do you do. I knew your mother. I was very fond of her. I'm so very glad we found you.'

Briefly, his eyes flashed the hint of a smile. For a fraction of a second, Lily-Josephine looked out of them.

'Thanks,' he said. 'You're – you're very kind. This can't

110

be easy for you. It certainly isn't for me.'

Both men fell silent. Primrose had an impression of intense shyness, surrounding them like a hedge of thorns.

'Do come inside,' she said. 'Let me get you a drink, or a coffee.'

Abruptly, Octavius said, 'No, thanks.' There was an awkward gap between the 'no' and the 'thanks'. 'Could I wander on my own?'

Primrose was tempted to point out, rather tartly, that since the place belonged to him, he could do what the hell he liked. Seeing the prickling embarrassment of Patrick, she resisted. 'Of course.'

They watched Octavius striding off, head bent, in the direction of the cliffs.

Patrick cleared his throat several times. 'Sorry about that. He – it doesn't mean anything. This whole business has been a shock for him.'

'It must be odd,' Primrose said. 'Suddenly finding you're a millionaire, with a great barn of a house to run. And all because your publisher whacked you on the nose.'

They both laughed, Patrick cautiously. He said: 'I'll come inside. May I?'

'Please do. There's decent coffee, for once. And biscuits, if you can harden your heart and ignore Bunter's scavenging. I'm trying to get some of that lard off him.' Primrose was good at hospitality, especially now there was no danger of Sidonia humiliating her with shrieks for gin, or barbed jokes about spinsters. She brightened as she led Patrick through the passage, to the kitchen.

He glanced curiously at the heavy furnishings and pictures. When she caught him doing it, he mumbled: 'Octavius wants you to keep anything you like. Not that he's in any hurry to chuck you out.'

'That's nice of him, but this isn't the sort of furniture you get to love, even after forty years. All I want is a few cuttings from the garden. Do you think he'd mind?'

Patrick became a shade more animated. 'Absolutely not. Tell me which ones, and I'll give you a hand.'

She had tidied the kitchen into burnished cheeriness.

While she put the kettle on, and tried to recall Isobel's instructions about proper coffee, Patrick stared out of the window at her garden.

He said: 'It caught Octavius at a bad time. The responsibility alarms him. The night he heard about it, he went out and got plastered. Wrapped his car round a tree, and lost his licence for six months. That's why I had to drive him today. I'm his uncle, by the way. In case you were wondering.'

Primrose dropped the vacuum-packed coffee she had been struggling to open. 'Are you the same Patrick Randall who writes the gardening books?'

He smiled. 'Yes.'

She felt her cheeks reddening, as they had not done for at least thirty years. 'I've read every word you've written. Your *Fruit and Vegetable Garden* is my Bible. Oh, this is wonderful –'

'You're the gardener, are you? I was just admiring your spindlebushes.'

This time, she blushed outright, like a teenager. 'You should take the credit for them – I followed your instructions to the letter.'

'Could I take a look?'

'Could you! Poor man, you won't get a drop of coffee until you do.'

She wrenched open the door, and almost dragged him out into the golden September sunlight. 'I divided it into two, as you suggested – vegetables on this side of the low wall, fruit on the other. I do wish the herb patch wasn't looking so scrubby. That rosemary hedge is crying out for a haircut.'

'Lovely sheltered spot, this.'

'Yes, we get all the warmth of the coast, without the winds. It was an old kitchen garden when I came here, but dreadfully neglected. The quinces and medlars . . .'

Forgetting Octavius, Primrose and Patrick launched into an orgy of gardener's shop-talk. She took him round her prized apple trees, and they bandied Worcester Pearmains, Egremont Russets and Beauties of Bath. She was excited, her words tangling on her tongue. His shyness faded, to reveal a professional focus and stillness.

After half an hour, when he had examined everything, and almost reduced Primrose to tears of pride with his compliments, he said:

'But you must hate having to leave all this.'

She sighed. 'Yes, I do. It comforts me slightly, to think that I'll be passing it on to someone who knows how to look after it. The nephew of someone, at any rate.'

'Where will you go? Do you know yet?'

'I suppose I'll buy myself a cottage, and start again. It might be rather fun, designing a new garden from scratch.'

They were moving towards the door in the south wall, and as she said this, it opened on to the magnificent, jubilantly gaudy vista of shrubberies and sloping lawns. Patrick's eyes – hazel, like those of Octavius – narrowed as he took it in.

'Quite a challenge, scaling down from this.'

'Oh, I don't mind so much about this bit. I can never get enough help, and it takes such quantities of work. It's walled gardens that are my particular passion.'

'Really?' His interest sharpened. 'Why?'

'The – the peace, I think. The sense of safety. The way you can gather a lot of richness into a small space.'

'It's a passion I share. I have a walled garden at home. I grow medicinal herbs, mainly.'

Primrose shivered. The memory of her dream loomed up in her mind. They strolled in silence. Distantly, poised on the extreme edge of the cliff, they could see the motionless figure of Octavius.

She asked: 'Was Octavius offended, when I mentioned his mother?'

'I don't think so. It's just that he never knew her.'

'Oh. I see.' She was afraid to pursue the subject of Lily-Josephine's death. She glanced at her watch. 'God, you'd better stay for lunch. I lose all track of time, when I'm showing off my garden.'

Patrick halted suddenly. 'There's something else I'd love to see – if it's still there. Lily-Josephine gave you a rose-tree.'

'How did you know?'

'It was my rose. I bred it, and I helped her send it.'

Wordlessly – with geese absolutely dancing across her

grave, as she told Isobel afterwards – Primrose led him to the bed beneath the verandah.

Patrick stared at the white stars of flowers for a long time. Eventually, he murmured: 'Light Perpetual. Named by Lily. I never expected it to do so well. It's a difficult bugger to manage.'

'Her note said I was to be ruthless about pruning, and not to leave it too late in the season.'

They were standing close together, studiously avoiding each other's faces.

Patrick said: 'I wanted to name it after her. But she insisted. You are Primrose, aren't you?'

'Yes.'

'I've wondered about you for years. She was so certain it would comfort you.'

'I needed comfort then. Lily was the only person in the world who knew how desperately.'

'I'm glad you liked it.'

She did turn to look at him now, her eyes brimming. 'Someone I loved very much had been killed in the war. One forgets what it was like then – how frightening and urgent everything was. I don't think any of the bad things would have happened, if there hadn't been a war. We were far from being a perfect family, heaven knows. But the war absolutely did for us.'

Primrose had almost never had the luxury of someone who wanted to hear her secret thoughts. She checked Patrick's face anxiously, before she ventured:

'My mother's death – you have to understand what she was like. Without her, I can think about the past properly. And I've thought about Lily-Josephine. The war was like what happened when Pandora opened the box. All kinds of horrid things flew out. And Lily –' She reddened again, and forced out, through her fear of being mocked: 'Lily was the hope left behind.'

Patrick nodded gravely. 'For us, too.'

Chapter Two

Spring 1940

———◆◇◆———

Daphne Wadsworth, her portly figure snappily attired in a blue boiler suit, erupted into the tiny kitchen of her Dover Street flat. Her loud voice cut across the zoo-like babble in the drawing room.

'The fat one on the chaise longue is a general, Bert, so give him some Famous Grouse from the castor-oil bottle, but tell everyone else it's finished.'

Tufton was calmly washing glasses, of all shapes and sizes, from a liqueur thimble to a small crystal vase. 'Doesn't say a lot, does he?'

'He's Polish, darling. Nobody can understand a word he says – except other Poles, one hopes.' Halfway out of the baize-covered swing door, she pounced back, to add: 'By the way. I haven't thanked you. I swear, I'd never have dreamt of a cocktail party, if I'd known my bloody maid was going to join the ATS.'

Tufton grinned. 'It makes a nice change from the usual.'

To Ralph's unending amusement, Tufton and Daph the Saph were ARP Wardens on the same post. They had struck up a firm friendship, cemented by the fact that they were both loathed by their neighbours. Tufton had been more than willing to act the butler at Daphne's party. He followed her back into the drawing room, expertly dodging and weaving through the crush with the tray of clean glasses.

The air was thick with cigarette smoke. Bottles and glasses crowded every surface. The war had added an extra flavour to Daphne's circle of well-bred bohemia. Varnished goddesses clung to the arms of uniforms from across the globe. There were Poles, Czechs, Canadians, Romanians – soldiers, sailors, airmen, marines. Nobody wore evening dress, now utterly out of fashion, but the atmosphere of

115

braying jollity was miles removed from any thought of war.

'Tufton,' someone moaned, 'it's boiling hot in here – can't I open the window just a teeny weeny bit?'

'No, Madam. I'm afraid we couldn't do it without showing a light.'

The group around the woman shifted into the eternal, plaintive chorus about the miseries of the blackout.

'– the frightful little man wouldn't let me light a cig, because Baron Von Richthofen or whoever might see it from the air and drop a bomb –'

'Has anyone seen the priceless skit about the blackout in that new revue? All the lights are on, but they act as if it's pitch dark –'

'– someone sidled up and offered her a pound of butter, but she had to say no. Couldn't see for toffee, and it might have been a pound of anything –'

There was a slight eddy in the crowd near the door.

Daphne screamed: 'Ralph, darling!' and fought her way towards him. 'Where have you been?'

Ralph had his arm around the waist of a vivid blonde. 'In Trixie's dressing room. She needs someone to hold her hand on the way home.'

Trixie said: 'I'm hopeless. There's no knowing where I'll end up, when I try to go it alone.'

'Or in whose bed,' murmured someone. There was laughter.

'Yes, they've taken Eros away from Piccadilly Circus,' said Daphne, 'but the little fellow is still very busy everywhere else.'

Trixie smiled at Tufton, as he thrust a glass into her painted claw. He raised his eyebrows briefly at Ralph, and gestured at his collar. Ralph grinned back, and scrubbed at the lipstick on his own collar with his handkerchief. It was only too obvious what he had been up to, in between numbers in Trixie's dressing room.

Ralph was supposed to be 'pulling strings' to find suitable war work, but he was not pulling very hard. So far, his war had been one long party. Tufton reckoned he must have served morning tea to virtually every showgirl in London.

No bombs yet, he thought; knickers are the only articles dropping around here.

Daphne produced a tumbler of her secret Scotch for Ralph, and he rewarded her by saying: 'The Lily telephoned this evening. She sent you her love.'

The mention of Lily-Josephine melted Daphne's social mask into tenderness. 'Bless her. How is she?'

'Rather sorrowful, because the evacuees are leaving. They got fed up with the country, and left Lily with no audience for her George Formby songs.'

'Well, if a little boredom is the worst that befalls her, she's lucky.'

'Oh, the Lily's never bored,' Ralph said, with pride. 'She's learned to make butter, at the farm. She's sending you some.'

'Marie-Antoinette, in her Trianon. What a gorgeous picture to comfort the mind, during a long dull night at the post.'

A British Major elbowed his way over to Ralph. 'Hello, Gallant. How goes it?'

'Doesn't go at all, Watson. My tailor is standing by, but no one else seems to want me back in uniform. Granted, my gammy leg plays up in wet weather – but I could drive a desk, and release some other fellow to get shot. Have a word with the high-ups for me, there's a good chap.'

'With pleasure – but it'd help if you sat outside a few offices before noon.' Major Watson laughed. 'And offered a few of your phone numbers in exchange.'

'He's dying to start doing something,' Daphne cut in eagerly. 'Just as I am, whenever I read a paper.'

'The BEF will settle those bastards,' Ralph said airily. 'I'm just afraid the whole show will be over, before I get my crack at them. I still owe them one for Cambrai.'

'Don't underestimate the Germans.' Reluctantly, Watson had changed gear, and turned serious. He lowered his voice. 'It's not like last time. I see the intelligence reports.'

A space had cleared near the door. Ralph turned his head. A few feet away from him, he saw a tall figure, silver and sea-green.

117

She stood, with perfect ease and assurance, surveying the crush. Despite the prevailing fashion, she wore a long evening gown; a bizarre and formless sheath of eau-de-Nil chiffon, under a cloak of white fox. Every other woman in the room had lips and nails of hard carmine, but hers were naked. Her wide mouth was one shade less pale than her pale face.

The floss of hair which waved carelessly around her shoulders was of an almost inhuman fairness – obviously natural; pure as spun platinum. Her strong, Tartaric cheek-bones made a perfect setting for her slanting green eyes.

When Ralph met those eyes, he was lost. They were clear and moist, and pulled you into depths of fearless, ruthless knowledge. Somehow, her eyes conveyed abandon and carnality, and a royal disdain for the ordinary.

Ralph, not normally given to poetry, felt he had come face to face with the very spirit of a dangerous, primeval Spring. She reached beyond the well-known part of himself that responded to tarts and floozies, squealing totties and knowing ladies with husbands overseas. Though he could never have put the feeling into words, he was aware of the opening of a sealed chamber inside himself, pierced by a single shaft of lethal white light.

He looked helplessly at Daphne, who saw the creature, and bellowed:

'Sidonia!'

◄◦►

'I am reborn, exalted, transformed,' Sidonia said. Her voice was low, with a smoky, husky edge. 'It's the damnedest thing. Is it very selfish of me, to be so insanely happy?'

'Probably,' Daphne said. 'But haven't I always told you, your selfishness is sublime? It's the selfishness of the artist, my dear. Would any of us, if we were honest, hold back our praises of Murillo or El Greco, merely because they had been selfish? No, let them paint, if they have to pawn their mothers to do it.' Daphne was drunk. 'The world cries out for art, and Sidonia must go on creating Sidonia.'

It was four in the morning. Daphne, Sidonia and Ralph lounged in a ruined landscape of lipstick-smeared glasses, brimming ashtrays and empty bottles. Behind the kitchen door, Tufton was attacking the washing-up. Sidonia, miraculously unsullied, lay in a heap of cushions on Daphne's divan. Ralph sat mute, a little distance away, hiding an erection on the point of combustion, but unable to leave.

Sidonia did not seem to mind him listening to her recital. Sometimes, she smiled vaguely at him to include him, like a great actress remembering the cheap seats in the gallery.

'I'm not going to tell you his name. It's all too new, too precious. I call him the Eagle.'

Daphne lit a cigarette. 'From which I deduce he's in the RAF.'

Sidonia smiled. She was older than she seemed at first, but the years added to her mystery. 'Yes, if you must be so prosaic. He flies. And his heart flies, and his soul.'

'Where did you meet him?'

'Does it matter?'

'At one of Barbara's parties, I expect – she knows all the Brylcreem Boys. Or at Franny's.'

'No.'

'You bumped into him at the Berkeley –'

'No.'

'The Café de Paris –'

'No! He isn't ordinary. He wouldn't like those places. There weren't any boring introductions. His arms were round me, before I met him, or even saw him.'

Daphne let out a bray of laughter. 'You bumped into him in the blackout! How priceless! And just like your luck – all I ever get is old ladies who think I'm a bus stop.'

Sidonia shook her head, patient and pitying. 'Please don't cheapen it. I can't joke about destiny.'

'Destiny? Oh God, this must be serious.'

'It is. I have that feeling again – the helplessness, the being dragged along by some tremendous outside force, as if I were a leaf in a storm. I fell against him, and I knew. That's all. He took me into a café. There was light. I turned to see his face.' Her voice deepened. 'And found myself hanging on the arm of an angel.'

'Yes, the uniform is jolly attractive, if you're that way inclined.'

'Please listen, Daphne. I haven't loved like this since Diego.'

This sobered Daphne up a shade. 'Really? Honestly?'

'You were right to tell me to keep faith. He'll come, you said. Keep the lamp burning, and the One will come.'

'God. Does the Gorgon know? Do the girls?' She turned to Ralph. 'Sidonia runs to daughters, too. She has three of them, all raving beauties.'

'I may tell Juana,' Sidonia said. 'She has my temperament, and Diego's. She'll understand. But it's too soon for details. We exist, the Eagle and I, in our own world. I want to keep it private, for as long as possible.'

Tufton emerged, a flowered apron tied over his pinstriped trousers. 'I found some coffee, Miss Daphne. If you're not hiding it, shall I make a pot?'

'I am hiding it, but hell, go ahead, Bert – and don't forget yourself.'

'Very good, Miss.'

'And if you look behind the metal bucket in the cupboard under the sink, you'll find a box of Charbonnel chocs. For you, with my love.'

'Very kind of you, Miss. I'll send them to Glad – she's mad about them.'

He switched off the standard lamp, and opened the curtains. Rosy dawn flooded the room, revealing every mote of dust, every dented cushion, every lipsticked cigarette-end.

Sidonia put up her hand, irritably flinching away from the light of common day.

Chapter Three

◆◆◆

Trixie let out a hoarse moan, and ground her pelvis against Ralph's. He ploughed into her, with increasing desperation. Beads of sweat were forming on his forehead, and dripping down on Trixie's mask of paint. He was dying for the relief of orgasm – perhaps literally, he thought, with his heart straining and his veins standing out like ropes – but he could not get himself there.

Enchanted by the steady and apparently tireless rhythm of his thrusts, Trixie had come twice.

'God, you're a tiger,' she murmured. Giggling, she pushed him away, and wriggled up into a kneeling position.

Ralph wailed: 'No!'

'Shhhh . . .' She held her hands on his shoulders, pinning him on his back. In the moonlight, he saw the smeared gash of her lips, and the brassy glint of her tousled curls. 'Lie still.'

She stamped a line of kisses down his chest and across his flat belly. Her breath was warm on his pubic hair. Her mouth closed round his blocked, bursting shaft. The tip of her tongue flicked expertly at the tenderest part of his glans. Weary, preparing himself to face defeat, he closed his eyes.

He knew exactly what the problem was. In the months since he had met Sidonia, she had haunted him; rising up like a silver phantom, to mock the futility of fucking anyone else. His flesh screamed for her. Nights spent with other women only sharpened the aching sense of deprivation. Nothing like this had ever happened to him before. Tufton said it was the novelty of not getting what he wanted for once, but he knew it was more. Every meeting with Sidonia piled on the agony. At intervals, she would materialise in Daphne's flat, rhapsodising about her young 'Eagle', and

121

often wearing outfits of amazing daftness – once, she had been barefoot, with a wreath of stolen daffodils in her hair. And Ralph, who liked women with several layers of varnish, fell deeper under her spell.

Sometimes, when he could not avoid reading about the state of the world, he despised himself. While cities burned and thousands died, all he could hold in his mind – all that seemed real – was Sidonia.

He summoned a vision of her, to lure himself into coming. It was shattered by loud knocking on the bedroom door.

'Sir! Sir! Captain!'

Ralph opened his mouth to groan, but could make no sound.

'Sir! Can you hear me?'

'No-o-o . . .' With a sudden, terrifying leap of all his senses, Ralph's resistance snapped. The orgasm tore out of his reluctant body, with absolute ferocity.

'Sir!' The pounding at the door was thunderous.

Ralph fell off the bed and dragged on his Sulka dressing gown. Panting and furious, he stumbled across the room and wrenched open the door.

'For God's sake, Tufton, are you trying to kill me?'

'Sorry, sir.' Tufton, in his ARP armband and tin hat, was a statue of disapproval. 'This is important.'

'What's going on? I thought you were at the post–'

'Commander Atkins is on the telephone, sir.'

'Eh?'

'From the Boat Club.'

Tufton propelled Ralph towards the telephone in the drawing room, and forced the receiver into his hand.

'Gallant? That you? Hello?'

Ralph blinked rapidly, to clear his fuddled head, as the voice of the retired naval officer rasped into his ear. 'Yes, Commander.'

'Good man. I'm ringing from the Club House. We should have fuel laid on, by the time you arrive.'

Tufton, still disapproving, placed a large cup of black coffee on the table beside the telephone.

'It's a while since you've been down here,' the

Commander said. 'Your *Lily of the Nile* in order, is she?'

'Yes, but –'

'Excellent. We should put up a fine show. England expects, and all that.'

The conversation was over. Helplessly, Ralph looked at Tufton. He was emerging from the bedroom, wearing his expression of iron discretion and carrying a bundle of Ralph's clothes.

'We heard it on the radio at the post,' he said. 'I guessed the Commander would be on to us, because they've asked for anything that holds water. I left Miss Daphne siphoning her petrol into the two-seater, so we should have enough to get us down to Lymington.'

'Bert,' Ralph said pathetically, 'what the hell is going on?'

Tufton ripped off the dressing gown, and held out the first item of clothing. 'If you can take your mind off fornication for a minute, and think about the international crisis –'

'Keep your voice down, damn you. She's still here.'

'I saw her. I think I've seen her before, but it all gets to be a bit of a blur these days.'

Distractedly, Ralph pulled on one of the rough old jerseys he wore when sailing with Lily down in Devon. 'Spare me the lecture.'

'It'd be different, if you were enjoying yourself.' He threw over a pair of grey flannels. 'But if you ask me –'

'I'm not asking you.'

'–you're getting too old for all this mucking about. It's not dignified. There must be other ways of getting your mind off that Mrs Leary.'

'What's this got to do with her?'

Trixie appeared in the bedroom doorway, her flushed nakedness inadequately covered by a towel. 'Is this a private barney, or can anyone join in?'

Ralph took a gulp at the coffee. 'Sorry, Trix – help yourself to a drink, and let yourself out. We're off to Lymington.'

'Why?'

His face expressionless, Tufton said: 'We're going to fetch the BEF, Miss.'

By the time the two-seater screeched to a halt in the drive outside the Boat Club, Ralph was transformed. The phantom of Sidonia had retreated, as he rediscovered all his old relish for an adventure. He was Captain Gallant again, feeding his determination with memories of the last war. Two armies now waited, helpless, on the beaches of Northern France, with the Germans snapping at their heels. The prospect of doing something real to help them made him feel ten years younger.

And the solid, imperturbable bulk of Tufton, beside him, was oddly inspiring. Unable to talk in the car over the noise of the wind, the two men had had time to forget their quarrel, and adjust to being comrades in arms again. Ralph even forgave Tufton for being right about him – as usual. My conscience, he thought. What an unmitigated shit I'd be, without old Bert.

Behind the Club House blackout, a dozen or so members were gathered around the hastily opened bar. Mrs Atkins, incongruously splendid in a black velvet dinner dress, was dispensing whisky and cocoa. Commander Atkins, in tweed plus-twos and a tin hat, bustled round barking out instructions.

Ralph turned down the whisky, and settled for a cup of the thick cocoa. There was an atmosphere of brisk cheerfulness, almost of jollity, but the laughter overlaid a crackling tension. These were men Ralph had seen at Cowes and Bembridge, and the Club's annual dance; men of pink gin and college blazers. Now, they wore old mackintoshes and sailing-slops. They seemed altogether more substantial. Ralph, still smarting from Tufton's lecture, felt the old strains of unspoken courage and endurance, and was conscious of an immense desire to be their equal.

'It's the cheek of it I love,' he told Tufton, as the two of them loaded supplies from the Club House onto the *Lily of the Nile*. 'They think they've got us beaten. They think they've driven our army into the sea. It never occurred to them that we'd all turn out to fetch them.' He slapped the hull of the boat affectionately. 'Even in tubs like this.'

The *Lily of the Nile* was a handsome little cruiser, bought by Ralph some ten years before, when his boating craze went beyond rough sailing with Lily-Josephine, and took the form of cocktail parties on deck and heavy canoodling in the cushioned cabin. Her paint had faded and her ornamental brassware was turning greenish. But he had never felt so proud of her, as if she had only existed to be matched with this hour.

And so the jaunty pleasure craft chugged out into the moonlit Solent, joining an Armada of small boats – dredgers and tugboats from the docks, ferries and paddle-steamers. Out at sea, they joined small fishing vessels, merchant ships, trawlers and the big destroyers of the Navy. Nearing the French coast, they were joined by Dutch and Belgian fishing crews, turning out in defiance of the armies who had invaded and occupied their countries.

Afterwards, Ralph could never remember the point at which the bombardment started. The days of the retreat from Dunkirk remained with him as a chaos of bombs, shrapnel and planes that seemed to hover just above their heads – the RAF were fighting a desperate battle, to keep the Luftwaffe from destroying the thousands of soldiers on the beaches.

'I'd give the poor bastards three cheers,' Tufton muttered to Ralph, as the first soldiers climbed aboard, 'if I had a bloody minute to spare.'

The men were grey with exhaustion. Many were wounded, in filthy field-dressings, supported – sometimes almost carried – by comrades. Despite the flashes above them, and the bombs sending up great hissing columns of water around them, many of the soldiers fell asleep the moment they hit the deck. Most of the others were unreasonably euphoric, glad to be going home, after the nightmare of their retreat across France.

Some of the troops were French – Churchill had given orders that the two armies were to be treated with strict impartiality. Tufton was especially considerate to these poor, dazed, dispossessed creatures. He gave them extra custard creams, from the large tins of Huntley and Palmer's biscuits Mrs Atkins had requisitioned from the Club stores.

The *Lily* was low in the water, and Ralph was on the point of heading back to the big ships, when two more men scrambled aboard, from a rubber dinghy alongside. They were a serjeant and a private, and between them they carried an officer, covered in dried blood, with a home-made splint strapped around one shattered arm. He was shouting angrily, while room was made for him to lie down on the packed deck.

'I'll have you both court-martialled – leave me on the beach – that was a fucking order – I can't leave before the boys . . .'

The two men, patient with fatigue like a pair of dumb oxen, ignored him. The serjeant said to Ralph:

'Thanks, mate.'

Ralph had pushed through the crush of khaki, to stare into the officer's blackened, agonised face. 'Despard – Charlie Despard!'

The officer stopped shouting. 'Bugger me – Ralph Gallant!'

They were neighbours in Devon, and sometimes ran into each other in town. Despard was a raffish character, devilishly handsome and always game for a jaunt in a sports car with a couple of chorus girls.

He managed a smile. 'I won't ask what you're doing here.'

'Can't stop now, Despard. Hope you'll be all right.'

'And bugger me again, you've brought that man of yours.'

Tufton was working his way amongst the crowd with a stack of paper cups under each arm, and two steaming buckets.

'Good morning, sir. Tea or Bovril?'

Like particles in a maelstrom, shaken together then flung apart, Ralph and Despard lost each other after that one moment of meeting.

But Ralph was to remember it for years; one snapshot in the three mad days of doggedly crossing and recrossing the few perilous miles of the Channel. The bombs, the heart-stopping near misses, the thousands of faces, melted together into one formless adventure – except Charlie Despard.

Of all the men at Dunkirk, he was to think later, why did I have to save him?

Ralph was reeling and barmy with exhaustion when he drove home with Tufton. They had steered the *Lily of the Nile*, bedraggled and pocked with holes, back into her berth. They both had several days' growth of beard, they were stained with sweat and grimed with oil, and England was exactly as they had left it, in a state of peace that now seemed dream-like.

At the flat, Tufton staggered straight into his room, and dropped fully clothed on his bed, like a felled tree. Ralph smiled to hear him snoring, and threw an eiderdown over him. His own head was buzzing. His room smelt of Trixie, and the bed bore witness to the tussle he had found so humiliating.

Impatiently, Ralph ran out of the flat, and went to Daphne's. He had no idea of the time. His watch had stopped, hours before – it was usually Tufton's job to wind it, and he had been otherwise engaged. He guessed it was early. The few people on the streets stared at him, and Ralph realised he was hatless, filthy, unshaven, and dressed like an old fisherman – the reflection he caught, in the window of Fortnum's, belonged on the lid of a cigarette tin.

'Ralph! The conquering hero!' Daphne hugged him glee-fully.

'Get me a drink, Daph, for the love of God.'

'Are you all right? Is Bert all right?'

Ralph said: 'I wouldn't be here if he wasn't. Am I disturbing you?'

'Far from it. I've been up all night, keeping vigil with Sidonia. The Eagle is safely back in his eyrie, you'll be glad to hear.'

'Hmmm. Hope someone chucks him a nice dead rabbit.'

'Naughty,' Daphne said, nudging him. 'She's still here, so you be civil.'

Ralph had been intending to telephone the Prospect, but the presence of Sidonia blasted this from his mind. For the first time, he was conscious of his wild appearance and wilder smell.

She was in the drawing room, as clean and fragrant as a gardenia, sitting bare-legged on the rug. Her slanted emerald eyes sparked with a new interest, as they raked over Ralph.

'Hello,' he said.

Sidonia smiled. 'You're safe. How marvellous.'

'Sorry I'm in such a state.'

'You mustn't be. It suits you.'

Daphne bustled in, huffing slightly under the weight of a loaded wooden tray. On it were crowded cups, glasses, a bottle of brandy, a large pot of tea and a plate of bread and jam.

Ralph murmured, for the sake of something to say: 'I'm glad your chap's all right. The – the RAF put up a terrific show.'

Dew gathered in the green eyes. 'Thank you.'

'On behalf of the Royal Air Force,' Daphne put in drily, 'Sidonia, who graciously takes the credit for all their activities, thanks you.'

Sidonia's lips hardened. 'Don't be such a cat – just because you quarrelled with that boot-faced Wren you're so obsessed with.'

Daphne laughed. 'I haven't the heart to tease you, when you've just heard they haven't made an Icarus of your Eagle.'

Ralph's skin tingled. Sidonia had made an invisible channel between them, and sex poured from her. Perhaps he was seeing things, or dreaming – he was so stretched with tiredness that his head floated and his ears sang. But he had a massive erection.

He gulped brandy and stuffed sandwiches. Daphne interrogated him about Dunkirk, and did not seem to notice that he addressed all his replies to Sidonia. Her smallest movement, the gentlest twitch of her lips, assaulted him like a caress.

I'm a lunatic, he thought. And still the dream went on.

The telephone rang. Daphne left the room, to answer it. Her absence stretched into minutes. Sidonia stood up. She wore a curious dress of ochre silk, with a long, full skirt, and a plain bodice. Her bare feet were pushed into flat, pointed slippers.

'I haven't slept,' she said. 'But I'm keyed up beyond tiredness. I feel – immortal.'

128

Daphne shoved her head round the door. 'Sorry, I have to rush – the Fleet's in!'

She fled. Ralph and Sidonia listened to her sensible shoes clumping down the stairs. The front door slammed.

Ralph asked: 'Where has she gone?'

'I expect she's just made it up with boot-face,' Sidonia said, without interest. 'Audrey must have come off her shift at the Admiralty full of the urge. London is so passionate, nowadays. Morality withers in the face of spiritual need. People make love as naturally as birds. It's rather beautiful.'

Ralph, sleepwalking with desire, got out of his chair, crossed the room and roughly seized her in his arms. Sidonia tensed irritably, then suddenly relaxed.

'My God,' she whispered, startled, 'My God, how you smell. You stink. My God, it's divine!'

She made him take her on the floor, the pad of his thumb against her clitoris. With his free hand, he plucked desperately at her covered breasts. Neither had undressed. At first, she was maddening. Ralph could barely stay inside her, as she rocked and bucked against his thumb.

She came, with a growl of pleasure that ripped away Ralph's last shred of control. He grabbed her buttocks and bashed into her, until his own orgasm poured out, in a series of violent, blissfully relieving shudders.

They lay in silence, breathing heavily. With a sigh, Sidonia disentangled herself. She stood before the mirror on the overmantel, and smoothed her dandelion-clock of hair.

Ralph was still sprawled across the rug, beached and gasping. His limbs were leaden. He spat out fragments of grit and hair.

'Sidonia –'

'Mmm?'

'What – what did that mean?'

'We had gifts to offer one another,' Sidonia said solemnly. 'A need to commune and exchange. If you're looking for meaning, this is what it meant.' Absently, she searched the floor for her slippers. 'That my heart belongs to the Eagle, and my body belongs to – myself.'

129

Chapter Four

Summer 1940

Lily-Josephine was singing in the drawing room. Not tenderly and poignantly, as young things were supposed to sing, when their sweet voices drifted out on the summer air. She carried a tune with more volume than artistry, and accompanied herself vigorously on the banjolele.

Ralph, his skin tingling with salt and sunshine, paused on the verandah to listen. He could not help smiling grimly over her choice of song – 'Hard-hearted Hannah'. His obsession with hard-hearted Sidonia was eating into him like an infection. Here was a gal who definitely liked to see men suffer. He had come home hoping to forget her, and his spellbound brain burned the image of Sidonia everywhere he looked. Men were supposed to get over this helpless, lunatic brand of love at around the age of seventeen. It had come to Ralph too late, and the bitter taste spoiled the flavour of everything else.

He kicked off the boots he wore for sailing, and stepped through the open window. Lily sat in the window seat, clutching the idiotic banjolele he had bought her as a child against her faded flannel shirt. To Ralph, she was still a child, with her scratched brown legs and long plaits. He had to keep reminding himself that she was eighteen. Even then, it did not seem real.

There was someone else in the room. A tall man, carrying an invisible, aggressive atmosphere of youth, struggled to his feet from the sofa. He wore a jacket of heathery tweed, with one empty sleeve. His right arm was in a sling, tightly strapped across his chest. His hair was soft light brown, his complexion was pinkly tanned. He had blue, blue eyes. His patrician profile made Ralph think, with obscure irritation, of Robert Taylor in some Hollywood romance.

'Hello, Gallant.'

'Good God. Charlie Despard.'

'I did telephone first, to see if you were in. Lily invited me over to tea.'

On coming in, Ralph had caught (or thought he had) an expression of puppyish eagerness on Despard's matinee-idol face. He saw now, to his relief, that Lily-Josephine had stuck in Charlie's limited consciousness as a little girl.

In the absence of Tufton, she had prepared one of her awful, sloppy tea trays. He relaxed into a laugh.

'Oh, darling. Doorstep sandwiches, and rock-cakes that contain actual rock.'

Charlie laughed too. 'Is he always this mean about your cooking, Lily-girl?'

'Yes, always,' Lily said. 'But it's Mrs Dove's day off, and he simply won't learn that beggars can't be choosers. Doesn't he know there's a war on? I'm the only source of rock-cakes for miles around.'

The pair of them had been getting on famously. Ralph swallowed an almost unconscious, hair's-breadth awareness that he had broken up the party. He dropped into the window seat and put his arm round Lily's waist. 'It's good to see you looking so well, Despard. How are you?'

'The holes are closing up, thanks. Lily thinks I'm in fine form, and wants me to devote my one arm to the Home Guard.'

Ralph gave a theatrical groan. 'You too, eh? She won't leave me alone, either.'

'Well, why not?' Lily demanded. 'If they won't let you back in uniform, at least you'd be in the front line when the invasion comes.'

'I'm sure I seem tremendously old to you, but I am actually only forty-five, and –'

'Forty-six,' said Lily.

'All right, forty-six. With all my own teeth and a full head of hair. I'm far too young to go square-bashing with a lot of old farts.'

This made her laugh, but she would not drop it. 'You go on and on about hating the Nazis, but you won't do a thing

131

about it. Whereas if it was me – if I were a man . . .'

'I served under a CO like you, in the last show,' Ralph said. 'He was always dreaming up new ways to kill us.'

Lily-Josephine gave him a rough hug, and ran her hand over his windblown, grey-streaked curls. 'I'm not trying to get you killed, Daddy. I'd murder anyone who hurt you.'

This was more like it. The reproachful blue gaze had worked, for the moment. Lily-Josephine had her mother's troubling dark eyes, but there the resemblance ended. She was far less easy to manage. He kissed her soft cheek.

'Rustle up some more tea, will you, poppet?'

'Right-ho.'

Ralph followed her to the door, and whispered: 'Leave us together for a minute. I'd like to talk to Charlie.'

He had spotted a bottle of whisky on the floor, half hidden by the chintz skirt of the sofa. His daughter, acting under Tufton's strict orders, was rationing his booze. The minute she had gone, he whipped two crystal tumblers out of the sideboard.

Despard sat back down on the sofa, crossing his long legs with easy elegance. 'I really came by to thank you for Dunkirk.' He liberated the bottle, and handed it to Ralph. 'If I'd missed your boat, I'd have been a goner.'

'I take no credit – but I'm not about to turn down a bottle of Scotch.' Ralph poured two handsome measures, gave one to Despard, and sank into the opposite armchair, with a homecoming sigh. 'Your health.'

'Where is everyone?'

'You mean, where's Tufton? On holiday with his Missus, until Saturday.'

Despard chuckled. 'Splendid. Let's get plastered.'

Ralph poured again. The alcohol swept through his body, a liquid blessing. He leaned back to survey his guest, wondering why he found his presence so unsettling.

It might have been his looks. Charlie was very handsome; handsome beyond argument. Ralph, long used to being the best-looking man in any gathering, instinctively mistrusted possible rivals.

But there was something else. He took another gulp of

whisky, to numb his depression. The bugger was young. Ralph was forty-six, and beginning to show it. Charlie was at least twenty years younger. No one of forty-six could pass as youthful, let alone boyish, with this genuine article in the same room.

'I should have been in touch after Dunkirk,' Ralph said. 'But I kept putting it off. Didn't want to hear that you'd died.'

'It was close.'

'When do you go back?'

'I don't.' Charlie's tone was as light as ever, but a fixity in his smile betrayed how he hated it. 'They've invalided me out. When my arm's recovered, it'll be about an inch shorter, and pretty well useless.'

'Bad luck.'

Charlie shrugged. 'So here I am. Young, free and bored, rusticating on my acres. How about you?'

'Eh?'

'Are you really going back in uniform?'

Ralph refilled his glass. There was no need to give Charlie the official version, as broadcast to Tufton and Lily-Josephine. 'In theory, I'm being held back by my age and my bad leg. In practice, too many people remember that I left my old regiment in the absolute nick of time, before I was cashiered. I was up to my ears in debt, and the chap whose wife I fucked at the 1920 Christmas dance is now a General. He's put out the word that he'd rather see Adolf Hitler in his mess than Ralph Gallant.'

Charlie laughed. 'No go, then. Unless you fuck the wife of someone higher up.'

The blanket of alcohol was not warm enough to soothe away the perpetual ache of Sidonia. Ralph could not risk going through any doorway that might lead to her. She had never touched him again, since their mad coupling after Dunkirk. And once he had felt the heat of her desire, the world was miserably cold without it.

'I'm getting too old for grappling in taxis,' he said.

'Then I've a good mind to take back my Scotch. I came with very high hopes.' Charlie lowered his voice. 'You've got

133

to help me, Ralphie. I haven't been to bed with anything except a hot water bottle for months. If I don't get some totty soon, I'll go crazy.'

'You won't find anything round here, old darling. I've looked.'

Charlie said: 'I'm off to London, the minute my doc lets me. I'm relying on you to let me have some of your famous phone numbers.'

Ralph found that he had reached an agreeable state on the threshold of drunkenness; a sort of pre-intoxication. He suddenly felt very fond of Charlie.

'Blonde or brunette?' he asked.

'Blonde, please.'

'Yes, they generally are more fun – even the dyed ones. Tits or legs?'

'Either. With a slight bias in favour of legs.'

They roared with laughter. Ralph's mind flashed an image of the Eagle, helmeted and goggled and being a hero in his Spitfire, and resolutely drowned the bastard in another shot of whisky.

<hr />

'You're doing it again,' Gladys said, with an edge of impatience. 'You're looking at your watch.'

'I know he's drinking. I can feel it.'

'Oh, nonsense. You just can't bear the thought that he can manage without you.'

'He can't.'

Gladys laid down her knife and fork. They were having dinner, in the gloomy dining room of their seaside lodgings. 'Bert, couldn't we have just one evening when you don't talk about the Captain? It's like having him in bed with us.'

'Sorry, love.'

'I want you to myself, for once.'

Tufton grinned at her. 'You certainly had me last night.'

'Stop it!' Gladys stifled a giggle in her napkin. 'Mrs Small will hear you – if she didn't hear last night.'

Tufton salted the morsel of fish nestling in a grove of potatoes on his plate. 'Well, what does she think we're doing, when we're tucked up in bed? We're married.'

'People aren't meant to do it at our age.'

'Not from behind,' said Tufton.

'I said stop it!'

'And what d'you mean, at our age?' Tufton reached across the darned cloth, and squeezed Gladys's hand. 'Two days since you turned forty, and you act like you've got one foot in the grave.'

She sighed. 'Well, there's something about forty, isn't there? It makes you think about time passing, and things changing. Or not.' She gave extra weight to the last two words.

Tufton, shovelling in potatoes, asked: 'What do you mean? What's up?'

'Oh, nothing. I don't know. It's just that neither of us are getting any younger – me forty, you fifty-two. And we never get any nearer settling down. I never see you.'

She gazed at him imploringly, willing him to understand.

Slowly, testing the ground, he said: 'Well, it's the petrol, love. We can't run down as we used to.'

Gladys wanted to groan. 'And you're always going to be tied to the Captain.'

'That was my life, when you met me. Has it been so hard?' He was bristling defensively, as he always did when Gladys threatened to come between himself and Ralph.

'Of course not.' She made a great effort to sound reasonable. 'Of course not. When you two crashed into the Prospect, it was the best thing that ever happened to me. If there wasn't a Captain, there'd be no Lily. But Bert, I didn't think it was going to be for ever. I thought we'd get to live together properly some day – just you and me.'

This was mean of her, she knew. She wasn't going to be mean enough to make him choose between them – but she had to introduce the idea, at least.

Unhappily, he chewed through his dreary, wartime food, weighing up the rival demands on him. Gladys was sure of his love for her. He was a wonderful husband, as her family were always telling her. But in exchange for this, she had to accept that he loved Ralph, too. Seeing the pain dragging at his face, she relented.

'Some day. Not this minute. There'll be a cottage going on Arthur's farm soon.' Arthur was her brother. 'I said I'd mention it.'

Tufton shook his head. 'There's part of me would love to settle down with you, Glad. Maybe turn my hand to a spot of market gardening, before I get too old. But I can't leave him. Specially not now.'

'No, I suppose not.' Gladys lowered her eyes to her plate, so he would not see her expression of scorn, and be wounded. That bloody Ralph Gallant didn't know he was born, she thought. It'd do him a world of good, to learn to control his own drinking and wipe his own nose, at long last.

'And there's Lily.' Tufton knew this would put the lid on the whole argument. 'I can't see you getting far, without her.'

'She's growing up so fast,' Gladys blurted out. 'Soon, I'll need her more than she needs me.'

'She'll always need you. And don't you think I'm not considering her, as well as the Captain. He'd have been married a dozen times, and to right little cows, if it hadn't been for me.'

Gladys had to admit, this was true. Tufton's protection of Ralph from the floozies also amounted to blessed protection for her darling. To see Lily-Josephine submitting to some awful stepmother would have broken both their hearts.

She attempted a smile. 'I know. I'm just all upset about being forty,' she said. 'Take no notice.'

Sensing the crisis was over, Tufton chuckled, and the years fell away from him. 'Gladys Mary Tufton, you are every bit as beautiful as the day I first saw you.'

'Oh, get off.' She was smiling properly now.

'Do you know, even while that doctor bloke was strapping up the Captain, I couldn't take my eyes off you? You're still gorgeous, and I'm still mad about you.' Under the table, his foot brushed her ankle. 'You finish that square inch of haddock and come upstairs – and I'll prove it.'

136

Chapter Five

Autumn 1940

❖❖❖

On the low stage, bathed in a chiaroscuro of cigarette smoke, the ugliest girl Ralph had ever seen danced barefoot, in a hessian sack.

'Brilliant, so elemental,' Sidonia purred earnestly. 'Ralph, I think we need another bottle.'

Scowling, Ralph rose. None of the other people around their table was taking the slightest notice of him, except to ask him for drinks or cigarettes. Nobody looked up when he left, to fight through the badly dressed crowd around the bar.

The Chrome Yellow Club was a long, low-ceilinged basement, allegedly bomb-proof, near Sidonia's flat in Bloomsbury. Ralph, rich enough and unpatriotic enough to ignore rationing, wondered why on earth he was drinking disgusting red wine in this hell-hole, when he could afford decent whisky and the Café de Paris.

Because Sidonia had summoned him, of course. He had obeyed, hungry for a sight of her. Since his summer in Devon, he had hardly seen her. The days were shortening now, and crisping with the first edge of cold weather.

After that summer of breathless suspense, watching Britain's struggle for survival in the skies, London was at war in good earnest. Night after night, the German bombers droned across the Southern counties, to drop the bombs that were turning the East End into a wasteland of blackened, blazing ruins. There was a jittery awareness of standing alone in a hostile world. People had started to say 'London can take it', meaning that London had no choice. Tufton, braced for the invasion that seemed only days away, was agitating for a return to the Prospect – and Ralph could not bear to remove himself from the aura of Sidonia.

He knew he was crazy. He caught himself on the very threshold of wishing the Eagle, one of the 'few' to whom so many owed so much, would hurry up and die. The heroes of the RAF had been going down like grouse on the Glorious Twelfth, yet Sidonia's beloved was still pranging German Stukas in his Spitfire, apparently immortal.

God, what a shit I am, Ralph thought. He leaned against the bar and lit a cigarette, waiting to catch the eye of the dreadful, bearded Conscientious Objector who was serving. Glancing around the room, he decided it was a pity the place was bomb-proof. If the Nazis had dropped one on this nest of conchies, lefties and queers, they would have been doing Britain a real favour. For ten bob, he'd have done the job himself.

What was she playing at, bringing him here? She must have known his loathing of spectacles and sandals, and all things improving. Under the babble of voices, a solo flute hooted. The dancer was writhing on the stage, showing too much bare, mottled thigh. Ralph's lip curled in distaste.

Beside him, a deep, slow voice, with a thick Irish accent, murmured: 'Jesus, will you look at her. Don't know which is worse – the face or the fanny.'

The man was shabby and thickset, with a blunt, genial face. Ralph grinned at him, thinking this was the first sensible remark he had heard all evening.

'No, she's not exactly a Tiller-girl.'

'And what have we to do, to get a drink in this place? I'm as dry as the Saharry.'

'I should have brought my own,' Ralph said gloomily.

'Well, you can afford it,' the Irishman said. 'Sidonia generally attaches herself to someone with a few bob under the mattress.'

Ralph knew he should have been offended. But the man was right. The lovely Sidonia, who could not bear to think about mere money, was airily entertaining half a dozen friends at his expense. He was humbled beyond offence.

'You know Sidonia, then?' he asked.

The Irishman nodded cheerfully. 'She married me once.' He stuck out a muscular, workman's hand. 'Colm Leary.'

'Ralph Gallant.' They shook hands. 'I've heard of you – you're the painter.'

'I am. Sidonia was my muse. She's very good at it.' Suddenly, without warning, he lunged over the bar, and grabbed the Beardie by his batik tie. 'Are we invisible? Two more bottles of that evil Red Biddy you call wine. He's paying.'

Sulkily, the man at the bar produced two more bottles of the sinister fluid. Leary filled a tumbler, sprawled against the bar, and became vinously friendly. 'Magnificent –' nodding towards Sidonia, '–isn't she? The most truly beautiful creature I ever painted. God, she practically painted herself. And the morals of an animal.' He said this with smacking relish. 'A pagan hedge-creature, that never spoils its innocence by fretting over others.'

'I'd rather you didn't –' Ralph began indignantly.

'Ah, you're in love with her. Have you fucked her yet?'

'I beg your par–'

'Or is that pleasure still to come?' He nudged Ralph's waistcoat with his elbow, friendlier than ever. 'You can't really know Sidonia, until you've fucked her.'

There was applause. The dancer bowed, unsmiling, and dived off the stage, through the crush. At the bar, she halted beside Leary, just long enough to mutter:

'I'm going home to feed the baby. Don't be late.'

She vanished behind a door. Leary smiled proudly. 'The current Mrs Leary, bless her.'

Ralph, mortified by his remark about Tiller-girls, decided he would never learn the bizarre codes of this world.

'Leary, my darling.' Sidonia parted the crowd, fell into the painter's arms, and kissed him on the lips. 'Divine to see you.'

'Hello, Sid. How's that daughter of mine?'

Sidonia laughed. 'How many children have you got now? I bet you don't even know. Ralphie, they're shrieking for booze. Do hurry.' She was off again, to exchange greetings and accept worship at another table.

'Well, you have your orders,' Leary said. As Ralph was moving away, he laid a hand briefly on his sleeve. 'Knowing

Sidonia has its rewards. But take the advice of the chewed-and-spat. If you value your family silver, whatever you do don't marry the owld bitch.'

The words scurried around Ralph's mind, as he drove his Bentley home through the dark, deserted streets. He was furious with Leary – bloody impertinence – but not because the man was wrong. Sidonia was unreachable. Hankering after her was pointless, and it was destroying him.

It was only ten o'clock. He had left the Chrome Yellow Club, without even bothering to say goodbye. Let Sidonia miss him when she wanted another drink. He turned into Bruton Street and parked his car, mentally going through his contacts for petrol. Could he get enough, without Tufton finding out that he was dealing with the black market? Might he forget his disapproval, when he knew what the petrol was for?

Tufton was at the kitchen table, sewing buttons onto one of Ralph's Savile Row shirts, his glasses low on his nose. It was his night off. Normally, he would have been pacing the streets in his tin hat, blasting on his whistle and roaring: 'Put that bloody light out!' Tufton was a tiger for duty, but Ralph suspected he rather enjoyed his taste of power.

'You're back early,' he said.

Ralph had brought in a bottle of whisky from the drawing room. He poured them each a tumbler, and sat down. Tufton eyed his whisky gravely, obviously wondering what was in the wind.

'It was ghastly. I decided I'd rather have an early night.'

Tufton grinned. 'Bad as that, eh?'

'Don't gloat.'

'Shouldn't dream of it, sir. Is Mrs Leary well?'

'Bert, how long would it take you, to get out of your duties at the post? Only I've been thinking. It's time we went down to Devon.'

There was a silence.

Ralph felt himself squirming under Tufton's scrutiny. 'Well?' he demanded irritably. 'I thought you'd be delighted.'

'What's brought this on, then?'

'For God's sake. London's being bombed to buggery, and the Germans might stroll across the Channel at any moment. I don't fancy being here, when the bastards goose-step along Whitehall. Will that do?'

Tufton chose his words carefully. 'And will we be taking anyone with us?'

'No.'

'That's a relief.' He folded the shirt carefully, and stood up. 'For one awful moment, I thought she'd finally agreed to marry you.'

Even in his anguish of unfulfilled desire, Ralph could not help laughing dismally at this. 'Fear not, I said. For mighty dread had seized his troubled mind.' He knocked back his whisky, glad he had steered clear of the wine at the Chrome Yellow. 'Bert –'

'Hmm?' Tufton had put the kettle on, and was reaching into the cupboard for the tea-caddy.

'Would you mind telling me exactly why you're so down on Sidonia?'

'Not my place, sir.'

'Go on!'

Tufton banged down the caddy, and turned to face him. 'I mean, it's really none of my business. You shouldn't expect me to do it.'

'Let's have it, Bert.' Ralph refilled his glass. 'Your meaningful looks have been driving me mad for months.'

'All right. It's not that she's a tart – you've been out with tarts before, God knows. But most of them have been quite nice little tarts. And this one's a right –' Tufton hesitated, then drove on, '– cow.'

A silence.

Pettishly, Ralph said: 'That's it, is it?'

'No. She's the type who uses people. She doesn't give a damn about you. What she likes is your money.'

Ralph winced. He had expected something like this, and had asked because he felt ready to hear it. But the truth was intensely painful, nonetheless.

'And you don't seem to have thought about Lily-

141

Josephine. That woman hasn't a feeling bone in her body. Let alone a moral one. You shouldn't even be thinking of letting her loose on your daughter.'

'She has daughters of her own –'

'Yes, all with different fathers.' Tufton sat down again. Almost with tenderness, he said: 'Look. I haven't said anything to Glad. But if that woman ever comes into your household, I go out of it.'

Ralph stared, stunned. In twenty-five years, Tufton had never once threatened to leave him. He had been punched by debt-collectors and harangued by furious husbands. He had lied to tearful women, and bailed Ralph out of the cells with his own money. But the bond between them, forged in blood and war, had always been invincible.

And now he was being forced to choose between them.

The silence stretched into minutes.

Two roads were before him: life without Sidonia; a dreary monochrome. And life without Tufton – simply unthinkable.

'Don't leave me, Bert,' he murmured. 'I'll never look at Sidonia again, if you feel that strongly. I didn't realise.'

'I'm sorry, sir.' Tufton was aware of what he was doing, and his heart was full of compassion. His face plainly said what he could not put into words, that he was acting out of love. 'But there it is.'

'Oh, well.' Ralph lit a cigarette, and attempted a shaky laugh. 'I daresay you're right. I've never been a judge of women, have I?'

'No.' The kettle boiled. Tufton made a pot of tea, with exaggerated bustle.

Ralph sighed, but was slightly comforted. Tufton's unwavering constancy was healing balm, after the wounds Sidonia had ploughed into his ego. 'You know, I've often wished you were a woman, Bert. I'd marry you like a shot. We suit each other so well.'

Tufton chuckled. 'If I was a woman, I hope I'd have the sense not to get mixed up with a type like you. Have a cup of tea.'

'Thanks.'

142

The long, escalating howl of the air-raid siren sounded outside. Both men groaned softly.

'Typical,' said Tufton. 'They always come the minute you make tea, or sit down with the paper.'

'I wonder who's getting it tonight?'

'Come on.' Tufton took a gulp of tea, and reached for their gas masks, hanging on the back of the door. 'Let's get down to the shelter.'

There was an Anderson shelter, in the scrubby patch of garden belonging to the house, which they shared with the deaf old dowager downstairs, and her equally deaf old maid.

'Must we?' Ralph asked plaintively.

'Yes, we must. I'll go and wake up Lady Bathgate.'

'By the time you get the batty old crone out of her flat, it'll all be over. I almost wish I'd stayed at that club.'

'I'll bring the biscuit tin, and the whisky bottle. Come on, sir.'

'All right, all right.' Ralph stood up, stretching. 'I'll go and have a pee.'

'Don't forget –'

'– to leave the light off, because there's no blackout in the bathroom. I know.' Ralph smacked Tufton's shoulder affectionately. 'I won't ruin your reputation.'

He had pulled the chain, and was fastening his trousers, when he heard the bluebottle drone of the planes overhead.

There was one fraction of a second, in which time stopped and seemed to hold its breath. Then a massive explosion, which burst the sky apart, and brought it crashing down around them.

━━◈◈◈━━

'This one's still alive,' the fireman said. 'Tell the ambulance.'

The man on the stretcher was a crushed statue of white plaster-dust, vividly striped scarlet with fresh blood. He moved his lips painfully.

The fireman, pushing his helmet back from his soot-streaked face, knelt down beside him. 'Take it easy, mate.'

The statue choked. The fireman bent his ear down to the

dry white lips, and made out the words 'dugout' and 'shelling'.

He shouted: 'Hurry up with that fucking ambulance!'

'Bert,' Ralph mouthed, 'Bert . . .'

On the shattered pavement, three more figures lay, motionless, under tarpaulins. The fireman adjusted the tarpaulin of the longest figure, to cover its incongruously neat grey hair.

Chapter Six

Winter 1940

A rough west wind stormed across the Prospect's garden, coating the battered shrubs with fine salt spray. The sky was a sheet of lead, hanging low over a boiling sea.

Lily-Josephine leaned her forehead against the cold glass of Ralph's dressing room window, to watch her father's slow progress across the lawn. She had begged him to stay indoors, but the doctor had ordered a daily constitutional, and Ralph obeyed orders these days. He walked like a captured beast, dragging its length of chain. Damp leaves whirled around his hair; cropped short, and iron-grey after six weeks of sharp suffering.

Her heart bled for him. Without Tufton, he was pitifully forlorn and rudderless. Even Gladys, devastated by the loss of her husband, felt sorry for him.

'I miss the old Captain,' she had told Lily-Josephine, 'almost as much as I miss Bert. It's as if they'd both gone.'

Ralph was lucky to be alive – though Lily-Josephine doubted 'lucky' was the word he would have used himself. The bathroom ceiling had flattened his ribcage, and a fragment of broken bone had punctured one of his lungs. He had nearly died of pneumonia.

When the telegram arrived, Lily-Josephine had been all set to dash to London. Daphne Wadsworth, however, had put the lid on this scheme. With characteristic energy, she had got a telephone connection to Devon, and delivered a bracing lecture. 'Don't you dare come here – we can't risk your neck too. Poor Gladys has enough on her plate, without worrying about you.' She knew Lily-Josephine's talent for acting first and thinking later. 'Trust me to look after your father.'

Daph the Saph had proved herself a true friend. As soon

145

as Ralph could be made to understand that he was no longer in the dugout at Bethune, she had been the one to break the news that Tufton was dead. She had hired a private nurse and ambulance to bring Ralph home. And she had come with him, to soften Lily-Josephine's shock when she saw his haunted, hollow face.

The Indian summer of his youth was over. His wasted features gave him an air of otherworldly fragility. His eyes were set deeper in their sockets; his hair had turned grey. The beauty of his bones, lately dimmed and coarsened by too much roistering, had been thrown into startling relief. In a way, Lily-Josephine thought, he was handsomer now than he had ever been. But every last vestige of his fabled boyishness was gone. Peter Pan had lost the way to Never-Never Land, and fallen into sad middle age.

Sometimes, the longing to comfort him, to heal him, was an actual physical pain. Lily-Josephine dropped the blue paper parcel of clean laundry on Ralph's bureau, and ran downstairs. She was wearing a thick jersey, but the wind was cold enough to make her catch her breath. She ran across the lawn, to take Ralph's arm.

'Come in now, Daddy. It's nearly time for tea.'

He said, as he often did: 'It should have been me.'

This was his obsession; a corrosive, guilty conviction of unworthiness. He could barely speak to Gladys. If she looked at him, he averted his eyes in shame. Gladys never reproached Ralph, but she held herself aloof, and silently made a point of not reassuring him. Lily-Josephine hated this distance between the two people she loved best. They were grieving for the same man, and should have been doing it together.

'Don't. It might have been both of you.' The child in her, sternly kept down, wanted to cry. Ralph leaned on her arm as he toiled up the steps of the verandah – the dashing young father who had sailed with her and ridden with her, only months before.

She settled him in the armchair beside the fire and put a rug over his knees. When she ministered to him like this, their unspoken longing for Tufton rose up between them, like a ghost. Filling the void left by him was impossible, but Lily-Josephine had to try. Ralph was weak and helpless, servants were not to be had, and Gladys was already over-burdened.

In the kitchen, Mrs Dove was at the table, very slowly peeling potatoes with her swollen, rheumaticky hands. Poor old thing, she was turning into another burden. Lily-Josephine and Gladys were constantly repairing the damage caused by her startling episodes of forgetfulness – the day before, she had tipped a perfectly good cottage pie into the hen-bucket, and put the scraps for the mash into the larder.

'The laundry van's been,' she said, without looking up, as Lily-Josephine came in.

'I know. I've taken Daddy's things upstairs, and I paid the man.' She began banging about in the cupboards, assembling Ralph's tea tray with more zeal than efficiency.

'Don't know how long we'll see that van,' Mrs Dove said. 'Mr Davis told me he can't get the petrol, and young Sid's gone and joined the Navy. Where did you say Gladys was?'

'Bideford. She's at the doctor's.'

'Oh, yes. That's right.'

Lily-Josephine hauled the heavy kettle onto the range. 'I wanted to go with her. She's so po-faced, I'm sure she won't tell him properly.'

'In our day, young lady,' said Mrs Dove, 'you didn't tell the whole world about your troubles down below. You just carried on. My Auntie Sarah had a growth the size of a foot-ball, before she could bring herself to bother the doctor.'

Lily-Josephine made a face to herself. Mrs Dove had a lugubrious relish for horrible illnesses. 'Your Auntie Sarah was very silly, then. And for the last time, Gladys has not got a growth. She's run down, because of Tufton.'

'All this began long before Bert was killed, God rest his soul. She's been under the weather for months. Off her food, pale as death, turning faint. And she's been having trouble with her –' Mrs Dove's voice dropped to a sepulchral whisper '– monthlies.'

The death of Bert had been a catastrophe, but the idea of anything happening to Gladys was the world turned upside down. 'For God's sake,' snapped Lily, 'hasn't she got enough to depress her, without you hovering over her like a buzzard?'

Mrs Dove wagged the potato-peeler reprovingly. 'There's nothing wrong with looking trouble squarely in the eye, Miss Madam. If you young folk did a little more of it, this country would be –'

The back door slammed. Gladys came in, breathless, with a shopping basket. 'Hello, love. Sorry I was so long. Arthur got a flat tyre.'

She was as measured and as matter-of-fact as ever, but there were pouches of exhaustion under her eyes. Lily-Josephine hugged her, hungrily inhaling her familiar sweet, pastryish scent. Something was wrong.

'Sit down, Glad. I'm making tea.'

Gladys looked bewildered, as she had done in the first days after Tufton's death. She dropped into the rocking chair, and made a visible effort to stick herself back into the groove of the present. 'I should object, but I haven't the strength. Don't use up the whole ration in one pot this time.'

'I won't.'

'And pop this in the larder, there's a good girl.' She held out her basket. 'Arthur's wife sent us some pork chops.'

Mrs Dove snorted. 'I can't believe she's brought herself to kill one of her blessed pigs. I daresay it died of old age.'

Lily-Josephine darted to the larder, threw the parcel of chops into the meat-safe, and darted back. 'What did the doctor say?'

Gladys sniffed. 'Something's burning.'

Before she could move, Lily-Josephine had wrenched open the oven. Acrid smoke bellowed out, around a tray of porous black rock-cakes like volcanic lava.

'Drat,' said Mrs Dove. 'They went right out of my mind, what with Gladys's growth and all.'

'You beastly old ghoul!' shouted Lily-Josephine.

Gladys had snapped out of her bewilderment. Some of the high colour surged back into her cheeks. She startled Lily-Josephine by suddenly laughing.

'What did he say, Glad?' Lily-Josephine dropped to her knees beside her. 'You haven't got a growth, have you?'

Gladys stroked her head. 'No, no, my duck. I'm quite well, never you fear.' She was still smiling, but her eyes were wet. 'It's funny, you know. I felt so peculiar, I was all set for him to tell me I'd soon be joining Bert. And what he did tell me was such a shock, he had to give me a glass of water.' The tears spilled out. She leaned forward, wrapped her arms around Lily-Josephine, and whispered: 'I'm going to have a baby.'

<hr />

Ralph grabbed at the astonishing news with wild relief, as if some stern, heavenly judge had relented at the eleventh hour, to lighten his sentence of remorse.

'When?'

'Next May, sir.'

'Isn't it thrilling?' Lily-Josephine demanded, perching on the arm of her father's chair. 'I really will learn to knit now.'

She had marched Gladys straight into the drawing room to tell him, and was rewarded by his giddy, stammering delight.

'It's wonderful – marvellous – God, how I wish Bert had known about this.'

Shyly, Gladys said: 'Well, it's odd, sir. Somehow, I think he does know.'

They looked each other squarely in the eye, and smiled. Lily-Josephine had a sense of tension evaporating from the atmosphere, as if an ancient injury had been forgiven. A few years ago, she would have run from one to the other like a little mad thing, hugging them both fiercely. These days, she was learning restraint, but her beautiful eyes were stars of joy.

'I'll be godmother, naturally.'

Ralph and Gladys laughed, in the way they had laughed together when Lily was small – she had always been their main channel of communication.

Ralph tugged at one of her long plaits. 'That's up to Gladys, not you.'

'Oh, Glad will ask me. She knows I'll stump up for one

hell of a silver christening mug.'

Distractedly, Gladys smoothed her hair away from her forehead. 'I can't think that far ahead – I haven't thought about anything. It won't sink in.'

The issue of the future, dramatically revised, was suddenly between them.

Ralph threw the rug off his knees, with something approaching his old energy. 'We must make some plans, then, toute suite. The tooter-the-sweeter, as Bert would say.'

'I'll go and fetch the tea,' Gladys said.

'No, you won't. Bert would never have let you run around with trays.'

'Oh, but I'm fine, and –'

'He'd have wrapped you in cotton wool. And so will we – won't we, darling?'

'You bet. Sit down, Glad. I'll fetch the tea.'

Behind the baize door to the kitchen, Lily let out a yodel of triumph which nearly startled Mrs Dove into a heart attack. The house felt right again. It was still a house of mourning, but the bitterness had gone. Her father and Gladys, strangely delicate with one another, were finally grasping the connecting thread of their love for Tufton.

Much later, Gladys came to find Lily in the library, where she was attempting to build a fire with damp logs and no kindling. Perching on the arm of the big old sofa, she told her about the plans she had barely digested herself. Ralph was giving her the money he had intended to leave Tufton in his will. After Christmas, she would move to the vacant cottage on her brother's farm.

'I'll be near you, lovey,' Gladys said. 'I can't carry on here, with a baby on the way. I owe it to Bert to take care of myself. But I promised your mother I'd never leave you, and I never will.' Her voice faltered, and she scrabbled in her sleeve for a handkerchief. 'This baby's a gift, and I'll love it to bits – but never more than I love you, my Lily-girl.'

Lily leaned back on her haunches, wiping her sooty hands on her jersey. She was determined not to let Gladys get maudlin. They had all been sick with grieving, and now she

150

was sick of grief.

'Why are you crying? Gladys, I forbid you to cry. You're going to have a lovely little baby to knit for. A tiny replica of Tufton, in a khaki matinee jacket.'

Gladys smiled damply. 'I suppose I'm frightened of so many changes. I've lived in this house since I was fifteen –'

'– and your dad drove you here in the old pony and trap, weeping like a waterspout.' Lily knew Gladys's history as well as she knew her own. 'And Mrs Dove knew how to make a parlourmaid's life a Holy Hell. You thought you wouldn't last a week.'

Gladys giggled. 'You're right, I was always scared of changes. And they're never as bad as you think.'

Lily leapt off the rug, and wrapped her skinny arms around Gladys's plump shoulders. 'Personally, I'd love a bit of a change.'

'Yes, I know. But don't you go looking for it while my back's turned. I know you, young lady. Change will come and find you, soon enough.'

It found her a month later, when a telegram arrived for Ralph:

EAGLE KILLED STOP COME COME COME STOP SIDONIA

Chapter Seven

❦

The omens were not good. On the eve of Sidonia's third wedding, Mrs Venn had a bad attack of angina, and Primrose stayed at home to take care of her. Daphne Wadsworth erupted in late, hungover and broken-hearted. The registrar at Kensington Town Hall had married Sidonia before, and unthinkingly said he looked forward to seeing her again.

'You should give her a season ticket,' said Daphne.

Afterwards, when the party had moved to the happy couple's rather cramped suite at Claridges, she hauled Ralph aside, to say:

'I can't wish you joy. You won't get any.'

Ralph laughed. 'You're jealous.'

'Of course. Madly jealous. Howling at the heavens, like a flayed Laocoon, because I can't marry her myself.' She looked despairingly at Sidonia, in leaf-green velvet, flanked by her two younger daughters. 'She's my great passion. I've adored her for years. But I also adore you and Lily-Josephine, and in an altogether more edifying way. It's you I worry for.'

'Well, don't. I couldn't be happier.'

'She doesn't love you.'

Testily, Ralph said: 'I know she's still getting over that Eagle of hers. I'm not a complete fool.'

'You are.' Daphne took another pull at her champagne. 'She usually marries for love. This time, she's running for cover.'

'What if she is? I want to look after her. For the first time in years, my life has some meaning.'

Daphne shrugged off her soggy self-pity, and made Ralph face her properly. 'What about Lily?'

'What about her?'

'Where is she? Why isn't she here?'

'Sidonia thought it would be too much of a disruption. Such a long distance.'

'Has she ever seen Lily?'

'Not yet – long distance, and all that. She wrote her a very sweet letter–'

'Oh, I'll bet.' Daphne looked at Sidonia now with the helpless dislike a chained captive feels for a jailer. 'She's going around telling people you've got a dear little girl, as if the Lily was a kid who could be packed off to boarding school. I wouldn't care to be around, when she finds out the dear little girl is a full-grown stunner.'

Ralph only chuckled over this description of his innocent Lily. 'Now, Daph, stop being so dramatic.'

'I know Sidonia, and I'm warning you – the one thing she cannot cope with is a woman more beautiful than she is.'

'But Lily's not –'

'You wait, my lad. The minute she stands beside your Lily of the Nile, Sidonia will find out what it's like to be utterly in the shade.' She hiccupped, and gloomily added: 'Without a paddle.'

Ralph decided that Daphne was soured by unrequited love, and did not report the conversation to Sidonia. Two months later, he managed to entice Sidonia down to the Prospect for a long weekend, and confronted Daphne afterwards with his triumph.

'You were utterly wrong. Sidonia was divine, and she's been singing the Lily's praises like an angel.'

Sidonia's version, imparted to Daphne halfway down a bottle of black market gin, was somewhat different.

'You old bitch. Why didn't you tell me?'

'Darling, I've told you heaps about the Lily. Isn't she wonderful?'

'God, it was ghastly. She sails boats and milks cows, and tinkers about with cars. She plays the banjo, and strums the wretched thing after dinner. She's a great, overgrown Girl Guide, who digs for victory, and goes round the village collecting old saucepans to make Spitfires. Never once did I see her out of her breeches. I can't think why you make such a fuss about her.'

'Why do I?' Daphne's face softened. 'I suppose I idealise her. The fact is, it's easy to make a saint of someone who is both beautiful and good. We want beautiful people to be good, but we don't really believe it's possible – mostly, they're monsters.'

Sidonia knew Daphne's theory of beauty off by heart, and sighed impatiently. 'Like me.'

'Yes, but Lily's different. She's not trapped in her own reflection. She's a desperate criminal, of course. How dare she be so much younger than you are?'

Sidonia rolled her green eyes. 'Age doesn't mean a thing to me. You know that.'

'She's also very beautiful.'

'Quite pretty, I suppose. Once she passes the gawky stage – if she ever does. Daphne, why are you laughing?'

'You don't like it, so you simply refuse to see it. But for once, you can't blind the rest of the world.'

'What are you talking about? She's not half as pretty as Juana. Or Primrose.'

'No, darling. She's exactly twice as pretty as the pair of them put together.'

'Hmm. Thank God I shan't have to live with her, anyway.'

'Yes,' Daphne said. 'Thank God.'

The year moved on. Bombs rained down on London, and the parties moved underground. Sidonia and Ralph lived in a state of glassy-eyed revelry, picking their way over streets covered with rubble and broken glass. Sidonia thought the war effort was a bore, and Ralph soon stopped talking about getting back into uniform. He salved his conscience by giving to war charities, and obtained his unobtainable luxuries on the black market.

Sometimes, dealing with the worst of the spivs, he would think of Tufton, and hope he was not turning in his grave. Mostly, he could think of nothing except Sidonia. She was not materialistic, exactly, but she had a great appetite for luxuries and seemed to think they grew on trees. She had never understood that rationing was not voluntary.

154

Summer approached. Lily sent an ecstatic letter proclaiming the birth of Peter Albert Tufton, and Daphne paid a fortune for one of the last teddy bears in London to send to Gladys. The Royal Navy sank the *Bismarck*; Germany invaded Russia and Crete.

Isobel left her convent school, and waited patiently for Sidonia to admit that she was no longer a child. Juana embarked on a shameless affair with a married industrialist, and shimmered around the devastated streets in silk stockings and furs.

Primrose continued to run the Kensington house, rising splendidly to the extinction of servants and the challenges of rationing. She was also a zealous firewatcher, tea-maker for the WVS, packer of Red Cross parcels and knitter - as Sidonia remarked, quite half the British Fleet were wearing her balaclavas.

To the deep satisfaction of her grandmother, she spent her spare time being introduced to suitable, Rumage-ish people by her half-brother, Guy. She had not seen Guy since his schooldays at Haileybury, and was delighted by his reappearance in her life as a handsome young officer of nineteen. With him, she could be someone other than the daughter of Sidonia; appreciated for all the dull, sterling qualities Sidonia so despised.

'If it wasn't Primrose,' Juana said to Sidonia, 'I'd swear she was in love. She's looking frightfully pretty, in a milk-fed sort of way. Soon, she'll have shaken you off altogether.'

Sidonia shrugged. 'I wish she would. What am I meant to do with a daughter who doesn't like sex?'

Fate, however, had a way of altering Primrose's plans. First, Mrs Venn died. Then, two weeks later, a large bomb fell on the Kensington house – fortunately, when Primrose and Isobel were in the shelter, and Juana was out on the tiles elsewhere.

'Fuck, fuck, fuck,' Sidonia said. 'Where can I put them now?'

'They can't come here, I'm afraid,' said Ralph. 'Every decent hotel in London is bursting at the seams.'

'Fuck. We'll have to take a house.'

'We've already got a house, my sweet.' Ralph had been waiting for a chance like this. He was beginning to feel his wife would be easier to contain outside London. 'Bring the girls down to Devon.'

He saw the appraising glance Sidonia shot at him, out of the corner of her eye. She never defied him too strenuously, though God knew how long that would last. 'Well, we all have to make sacrifices,' she said. 'At least we'll get away from the bombs.'

'And the cellar's full,' said Ralph. 'It mightn't be so bad.' For the first time in his life, he was looking forward to the dullness and predictability of the country.

Primrose, Juana and Isobel, camping in a grim ladies' hostel in Fulham, packed the remains of their bomb-damaged possessions, and prepared for the novel experience of living with Sidonia.

Isobel, who loved the country, was delighted. Primrose was pleased, too. Guy did not join his unit for another six weeks, and had promised to come with her. Juana was openly furious. Her married lover had refused to get her a little flat, and was evidently using the move as an excuse to get rid of her. That Juana did not love him – was, in fact, bored stupid by him – was not the point. How was she to replace him, stuck out in the middle of nowhere?

'It'll be the sheerest hell,' she said. 'We'll have to be civil to Ralphie's bloody daughter.'

Primrose said: 'It is her house. And she might be nice.'

'Sidonia says she's a pill.'

'I've got a feeling about Ralph's daughter,' Isobel announced.

Juana groaned. 'Oh, spare us your Irish soothsaying. You never predict anything useful.'

Isobel said huffily: 'All I'm saying is, this time, Mummy shouldn't expect to have things all her own way.'

Juana stubbed out her cigarette, and reapplied her scarlet lipstick. 'Rubbish. She always gets her way. They should drop that woman behind enemy lines.'

Primrose looked pained. 'I wish you wouldn't speak about her in that horrid, scornful way.'

'My dear Prim, when will you learn? I adore Sidonia, but she's the completest cow that ever drew breath. I'd back her against the entire Wehrmacht. That little country girl doesn't stand a chance.'

Chapter Eight

All Primrose's feelings for the Prospect were shaped and coloured by the fact that she walked into the place on the arm of Guy. His optimism was catching, and made her determined not to let him down. She would stop fretting for Granny and her old life, and put her energy into building a new one.

Guy had been her amulet all day, warding off the evils of the long, crowded journey, and the tempers of her sisters. He had a gift for smoothing the path, and had wangled them a taxi at Barnstaple, with his combination of soldierly authority and sweetness of nature. She was fiercely proud of him.

The tiled hall, with its gloomy paintings and pointless brass ornaments, was empty. Without Guy beside her, Primrose's wavering courage might have failed her.

Juana complained: 'Where is everyone?'

They halted uncertainly before the empty fireplace. Primrose was anxious to make a good impression, and her kingfisher colouring shone out of tweeds and a Burberry. Guy was in uniform, and Isobel wore her school gaberdine and felt hat. Juana, unfortunately, rather spoiled the picture, in a clinging black dress, and wicked little saucer of a hat. She was pouting at herself, in the mirror of her compact.

'Perhaps I'd better –' Guy began.

A door banged, and an extraordinary figure ran out into the hall. A slender, dark-eyed Atalanta, in shorts, with a streak of grime across one cheek.

'I'm terribly sorry – I wanted to meet you, but we're all in an uproar – something blew up inside the range, and the fish-man was late.' She drew a breath, and smiled. 'I'm Lily-Josephine, by the way.'

Sidonia had prepared them for the shorts and the long plaits. But she had not prepared them for the fact that Lily was beautiful. She was so decidedly, unarguably beautiful that Primrose felt they must emphasise their superiority at once. Start off on the wrong foot, she thought, and we'll be poor relations in a trice, helping that creature with the potatoes.

In her best Head Girl manner, she said: 'How do you do. I'm Primrose Rumage, and this is my brother, Lieutenant Guy Rumage. My sisters, Juana Menendez and Isobel Leary.' It seemed particularly important to separate their names.

'My stepsisters,' Lily said, smiling. Then, turning to Guy: 'I don't know what that makes you.'

Guy saluted solemnly, and shook her hand. 'Hello. It's jolly decent of you, to let me tag along.'

'You're very welcome.' She looked from Guy to Primrose, with naked curiosity. 'Anyone can tell you're brother and sister – don't you look alike?'

Normally, Primrose would have been pleased, but she had begun to worry about the general air of chaos. Sidonia would be in such a mood, if none of her comforts was prepared for her arrival. Primrose dreaded her mother's attacks of foulness. Guy must never be allowed to see one.

'Could you tell the servants we're here, please?'

'God, there aren't any servants. Except Mrs Dove, and she's nearly eighty.'

Juana groaned, and rolled her eyes heavenwards.

Primrose frowned unhappily. 'I don't understand. How can you possibly run a house like this without staff?'

Lily threw one of her heavy black plaits over her shoulder. 'We just have to. It's the same for everyone else – there's no help to be had anywhere. So Mrs Dove and I do the cooking, and the gardener's wife comes in to clean most mornings, and we manage.'

'Oh, I see. But Ralph and Sidonia will be here any minute, and I do want to be ready. I suppose the beds will need airing?'

'Oh, no. I made them up myself.'

'How – how kind of you.' Primrose smarted under the sense of obligation. It was going to be difficult, living in a house she did not run herself.

'I can't do it every day,' Lily said, 'but I thought you'd all be tired.'

'Thank you. Could I discuss dinner with the cook? Sidonia's so fussy.'

'I'm afraid there's nothing to discuss,' Lily said. 'Except that it's fish pie. Followed by raspberries from the garden.'

'Oh.' What the hell would Sidonia say about that? 'Well, Mummy will need a hot bath, before we dress for dinner.'

The dark eyes widened. 'We never dress for dinner here.'

'We always do, and I don't want to shock Mummy with too many changes all at once.' In an attempt to be kind, Primrose added: 'But please don't worry if you've nothing to wear.'

'I've plenty to wear,' Lily said, with just a hint of freshness. They stared at one another.

Guy cleared his throat. 'Shall I come and look at your range? I'm rather good with boiler-type things.'

Juana said: 'I need a drink-type thing.'

⸻◈⸻

'They're awfully elegant, and they're all pretty. Primrose – that's the oldest – is the prettiest, but she's incredibly bossy. She made Mrs Dove furious, barging into the kitchen and poking about in the larder. The young officer is her brother. He's not related to the others. They all have different fathers.'

Gladys clicked her tongue disapprovingly. 'There's a husband or two missing, somewhere along the line.'

'The middle one is the smartest, and is obviously awful. The youngest stands around gaping, with her mouth open.'

'You were welcoming, though, weren't you?'

'Oh, yes. It must be ghastly being bombed out. But I fled before the descent of Sidonia. I wasn't up to the huge effort of trying to like her. May I hold Peter?'

'Not half. He hasn't let me put him down all day.'

Peter Albert was now two months old. Lily, who had never known a baby, thought him lovely. She never tired of

160

watching his squashed face, as his windy emotions blew across it. She laughed with pleasure, when the squirming bundle was placed in her arms. 'I swear, he's just like Tufton. He has the same disapproving look.'

Gladys sighed and stretched, then began snatching nappies and small garments off the fender and dropping them into her laundry basket. 'It's nice to have myself back for a minute. I'm sure you were never such a bother, but maybe I've just forgotten. Arthur and Iris say you forget ever so quickly.'

'Are you all right, Glad?'

Gladys smiled wearily over her shoulder. 'Oh, I'm not complaining. Lady Violet Despard says he's the best-looking baby for twenty miles. Well, you know what a nosey parker she is. I'm sure she's seen all the babies. And I believe her, because she's the type who prides herself on telling the truth. If she'd just been trying to be nice, she wouldn't have lectured me for being fat.'

'I wish Charlie would come back,' Lily said, with a wist-fulness that made Gladys turn round sharply. 'It's much more fun when he's here.'

Gladys moved the kettle onto the fire. 'I'll make a pot of tea, and you can tell me the real reason you cycled over here like a maniac.'

Lily laughed. 'How terrible, to be known so well. Yes, I was working up to something.' She dropped a kiss on Peter's velvet crown. 'Sidonia and her daughters dress for dinner. If that's the way they're going to play it, I must have some decent clothes.'

'If you're after coupons, you can think again.' Gladys spoke crossly, because it hurt her to think of her girl feeling dowdy beside her usurping stepsisters. Lily had never cared about clothes, and now it was too late.

'The thing is, I've had one of my ideas.' From her basket, she pulled a tattered, pre-war *Vogue*. 'I provide some material, and you run it up into something like this.' She flipped it open, and pushed it under Gladys's nose.

It was a drawing of a woman, all lips and lashes and improbable scrolled hair, clad in a long black robe which left her arms and shoulders bare. Gladys stared at it, not knowing whether to laugh or cry. Even if the gown had not been completely unsuitable, how was she supposed to 'run up' such an extravagance?

Lily had something else in the basket; a musty lump of black fabric, streaked with dust. Gladys was about to tell her not to be ridiculous, when her attention was snared by a black button. There were several exactly like it, rolling round at the bottom of her mending basket. A small button, which had the power to reel back Time. She took the fabric reverently.

'Good grief. Miss Helena's boudoir-gown. It was part of her trousseau.' She laughed shakily. 'She wanted to give it to me, bless her, but I was too fat. Where on earth did you find it?'

'In one of the old trunks, in the attic.'

Gladys shook out the folds of the gown. 'Swan and Edgar. Miss Crask knew quality when she saw it.'

'Was it wrong of me, to take something belonging to my mother?' Gladys's dewy rhapsodising made Lily feel guilty, as if she had robbed a tomb.

'Indeed not. Your mother loved doing things for you.' Having Peter had given her painful insight into the anguish Helena must have felt, at being parted from her child. By God, Lily would have a new dress, if she had to conjure it out of thin air. She smiled encouragement. 'The velvet's still good, see – I'll put it in Iris's copper, and bring the nap up with a kettle.' She stood up. 'I'll take His Majesty. You try it on.'

'Now?'

'I need a proper view.'

Lily surrendered the baby, and put on Helena's gown. The elaborate cuffs flopped over her hands. Her grass-stained sand shoes stuck out underneath the hem. She trailed her draggled finery around the room, with exaggerated, Sidonia-inspired hauteur. Gladys laughed, though with a painful stab of loss. In her mind's eye, she could see Helena's slight figure and timid face. Time slipped by so fast.

Then she said: 'Stand still,' and studied her, narrowing her eyes.

Concentration settled around her. Lily recognised the hush of Gladys's genius at work, and kept quiet. The only sounds in the room were the complaining snuffles of Peter, and the scratchings of the Drivers' hens outside the open door.

Thoughtfully, almost to herself, Gladys said: 'It wouldn't be much like the picture, but that style's too old for you, anyway. You want the bodice cut right down. A short sleeve, and one of those new sweetheart necklines. A little bit of padding in the shoulders, a big piece cut out of the skirt –'

'Well?' Lily demanded. 'Can you do it?'

Gladys was a famous dressmaker, and took the question as an insult. 'Of course I can. I'll get Iris to give me a hand, and when we've finished, you'll be the best-dressed woman in that house.'

And the best-looking, she thought. Lily-Josephine had been a child for too long. When the idiotic Charlie Despard came home, he must see the funny little girl transformed into a woman. Lily, though she hardly knew it herself, liked him. Gladys did not think there was a man in the world who truly deserved the Lily, but she had a traditional awe of the local squirearchy. Their estates lay side by side, and here were the raw materials for a splendid match. It was time to bring her up to date. She made herself scrutinise her, with the critical eyes of a stranger. 'You know, love, you ought to lose those plaits.'

Lily picked up one of the heavy ropes of hair, and surveyed it dispassionately. 'Really?'

'Nobody has long hair any more.' Gladys took a feeding bottle from the fender, and tested the temperature on the back of her hand. 'Sit down on the stool. You can give Peter his tea, while I cut it.'

She positioned the stool in the middle of the floor, handed baby and bottle to Lily, and set about unravelling the thick plaits. She was glad Lily could not see her face as she did it – the hair was so abundant and so lovely, she could not help feeling sentimental, as the warm masses fell over her fingers.

Lily, however, was immersed in the pleasure of feeding Peter. She loved the greedy way he gulped at the teat, his whole body shuddering with each swallow.

Hardening her heart, Gladys made the first cut with the kitchen scissors. The blades crunched, and the severed hair sprang into tough curls. She snipped and combed, until the hair was worked into a bob around Lily's shoulders.

This would not do. It billowed across her face, and stood out like a haystack. In a white heat of artistry, Gladys pinned back two smooth wings at the front.

A miracle. She gazed at her handiwork for so long that Lily said: 'What's the matter? Does it look silly?'

Her shorn black hair lay in shining heaps on the faded lino. The pinning had freed a new face. A broad forehead balanced the delicate nose and chin which had been over-shadowed by that ton of hair. The tips of her ears were visible now, rather shockingly perfect and vulnerable.

'Well?'

Peter was nosing away his bottle, and working towards a volley of mighty belches. Gladys took him, and put him over her shoulder.

'You'll do.' She felt she could have wept with pride, as she watched Lily rushing to the mirror on the door, and meeting a stranger. For a moment, she was silent and stunned. Then her lips curved into a smile of amazed delight. 'Glad, you're brilliant. Don't I look lovely? Wait till Daddy sees.'

Yes, wait, Gladys thought grimly. Ralph would probably be furious with her, for spoiling his unspoilt Lily of the Nile. But he needn't imagine he could keep her frozen in countri-fied artlessness, just because it happened to suit him. Gladys had a powerful sense that she had done her duty – not to Ralph, but to the phantom of Helena. Lily was now armed for the battle of the women.

Afterwards, when Lily had cycled away and Peter lay, sated, in his basket, she bundled up the discarded hair, tied it with cotton, and laid it carefully in her mending basket. She had given expression to her secret fury with Ralph, that was the truth.

How could he let that woman and her brood swarm all

over her Lily's home? It was like leaving a child alone with matches – straight into a stupid marriage, the minute Bert was under the daisies.

If only Lily had not been so beautiful. Gladys did not know Sidonia – but what Queen could live alongside a Princess who looked like that? No good could come of it, she was sure.

⸻◆⸻

Sidonia halted in the dim bedroom passage, to adjust the waist of her mustard-coloured chiffon. Damn, the hooks were tight. And where on earth was she to find a decent dressmaker, among these bumpkins? War was hell.

She already found living in the same house as her daughters oddly depressing and claustrophobic. That red-faced brother of Primrose's didn't help – he was so eerily like his father. And Ralph seemed to think that being on his own territory gave him the right to unlimited sex. Sidonia found sex with Ralph very boring.

She went into the large bedroom allotted to Primrose, in which her girls were preening.

'Darlings, I implore you to come down. Ralphie is rumbling tiresomely about regular hours and burnt food.'

Juana said: 'It's only half past seven, for Pete's sake.'

'What are you drinking? Where did you get that bottle?'

All the sisters were drinking pink gin from tooth-glasses.

'Not from Ralphie's precious cabinet, never fear. It was a farewell gift, from an acquaintance.' Juana raised her eyebrows briefly, to indicate to Sidonia that the bottle of Tanqueray's came from her married lover. 'Want some?'

'No. You mustn't make the others tight. We're up against the daughter, and we'll never get the upper hand unless we make a reasonable impression.'

Primrose giggled, and said, with unwonted gaiety, 'Don't fuss, Mummy.'

'I thought she seemed quite nice,' offered Isobel.

'You've been shut up too long with nuns. She's no fool – she's waiting for an excuse to turn you all out.'

Sidonia inspected her daughters. As her belongings, they must set her off, in a way that solidified her position. She was

165

Ralph's wife, and the girls must neither usurp nor undermine this power. Isobel wore her blue dinner-frock from the convent. It was too tight, and looked most incongruous beside a glass of gin. But Sidonia wanted to keep her embedded in childhood, and was glad to note that the frock neutralised a prettiness that was threatening to turn voluptuous – she really could not cope with too much sex washing about in the atmosphere.

There was, regrettably, no way of neutralising Juana. That little Madam was flaunting the abbreviated sequinned thing Diego had bought her in Paris. Sidonia's mind returned obsessively to the old wound. Diego had never bought her so much as a cup of coffee. He was the meanest of men. How had Juana weaselled her way into his wallet?

She focused on dear, predictable Primrose instead. And was surprised to find that she, of all people, disturbed her most. What had she done to herself? Sidonia rarely paid much attention to her eldest child. Doing so now was a shock. She actually looked beautiful. Sidonia tried to pinpoint the change.

Not the rather dowdy white dress, which she had seen a thousand times. Not the bubbling blonde curls, combed into smooth waves. Good grief, she was even wearing lipstick. At last, she had started taking trouble with her appearance. With a warm sense of relief, Sidonia realised Primrose had simply decided to grow up. Now that Granny was out of the way, she was free to become a real woman. For the very first time, Sidonia realised what a brilliant thing it would be, to marry her off to some dull man.

'Primmy, you look scrumptious.'

'Thanks.' Primrose met her mother's eyes in the mirror. She was polishing her white neck with powder. Her smile was knowing and complicit.

'Far too lovely to bustle around doing domestic things. See if you can spend one evening above stairs.'

'I ought to help. They're very short-handed.'

'Nonsense. The daughter is managing perfectly. And if you disappear, your brother won't say a word. I can't tell you how it gets on my nerves.'

Primrose laughed. 'He's terrified of you.'

'Does he think I'll bite him? Well, I do bite, of course. But never boys like him.'

Downstairs, a gong clanged frantically. Ralph's voice rose above the tattoo. 'Sidonia! Girls! Get the bloody hell down here!'

Primrose and Isobel hurried out immediately. Juana stayed where she was, sipping pink gin on the bed.

Sidonia regarded her with apprehension. 'You really ought to make an effort, darling. This is our first evening.'

Juana's Hispanic eyes had a combative gleam. 'I hate the country. I hate this frightful house. What are we doing here?'

'Darling, you know perfectly –'

'You've made a mistake, Sidonia. You should never have married him – even though he's miles better than you deserve, and divinely rich.'

'And handsome. And he adores me. Ralphie is my refuge.'

'It's a shame about the daughter, though.'

Sidonia shrugged impatiently. 'Oh, she doesn't count.'

'Doesn't count? That depends. You ought to find out how much of this concern she owns. And what she could do to you, if Ralphie suddenly dropped dead.'

'I didn't marry him as an investment.'

Juana's soft drawl was relentless. 'Of course you married him for his money. It was quite sensible of you. But I'm waiting for the next great passion.'

'After the Eagle? My God, do you think I have no heart?'

'You're over the Eagle,' Juana said. 'Now, you're only in love with the idea of yourself in love – I know all the signs.'

'Ralph knows I could only bring him a broken heart.'

'Phooey. Why did I bother to unpack, I wonder? You'll be madly in love in about five minutes.' Juana slid sinuously off the bed. 'And then don't be surprised if Ralphie looks for comfort elsewhere.'

Chapter Nine

Primrose lay in bed with the curtains open, waiting for the silver dawn to become broad day. The quiet had woken her. After months of sirens, fire-watches and nursing Granny, she had forgotten how to sleep. She was glad when the birds shattered that eerie blanket of silence.

As anyone who knew her would have guessed, she was passing the time by worrying over domestic details. Someone had to, and she had always been the Martha of the family. Nobody would have guessed, however, that she was only worrying about these details now in relation to Guy.

His toast. His tea. The scrambling of his egg as he liked it. The possibility or otherwise of obtaining a rasher. Thinking about him gave her an exquisite, suffocating pleasure; very like pain.

If only Granny had not died. If only their house had not been blitzed. If only they had not been forced to come here, where nobody wanted them, and Primrose had no power. She had loved it when Sidonia had said she was too gorgeous to fuss below stairs, but last night's dinner had been a disaster which a little fussing might have averted. Guy and Sidonia, and all those belonging to her, should not have to eat burnt fish pie and overripe raspberries. She ought to have faced down the nasty old woman in the kitchen, and cooked something else. They seemed to have limitless eggs here, and Sidonia dearly loved an omelette.

To make last night's meal worse, the dreadful Lily-Josephine had put Ralph into a horrid mood, by appearing minus her plaits. She had looked prettier than ever, and that had brought Sidonia dangerously close to a horrid mood of her own. Guy had stared at Lily, too, and that had been worst of all.

Sighing, Primrose sat up in bed. It had taken such a short time for Guy to become vital to her happiness. She told herself it was because he represented her Rumage side; her lost birthright of decency and normality. But there was more to it than that. Every time she replayed their mutual history, she dared to circle a little closer to the truth.

She had first met her two half-brothers when they were little yellow-headed boys. Daddy and his second wife – a kind, colourless person named Maureen – had come home on leave, to settle Guy and Julian at boarding school. After this, she had been aware of Guy, as an inky schoolboy, at various family gatherings in the hols.

The bridge to something else had been crossed three Christmases ago. They had both gone to stay with Grandmama and Aunt Anthea, in Sussex. The inky schoolboy had swelled into a strapping member of the Haileybury First XV. There had been a party for local children, at which they had played sardines.

Guy had found Primrose in the linen cupboard on the upstairs landing. He had squashed into the dark space beside her, and she had heard his rapid breathing over the distant cries and shouts, and sounds of feet pounding along passages. Warmth had radiated from his shadowed bulk. She had smelt his sweat, over the scents of linen and lavender.

And he had kissed her. A clumsy, impulsive kiss; desperate and fearful. It had been her first kiss. Fortunately – unfortunately – the cupboard door burst open in the middle, and Aunt Anthea plumped herself down between them. Guy and Primrose were very shy with each other for the rest of the visit. Their faces had been scarlet for hours afterwards. When he came back into her life, the previous summer, there had never been a right moment to mention the incident.

Lately, it had absolutely haunted Primrose. She dreaded it happening again – their comradeship, she told herself, must not be spoiled. The second she felt herself approaching the realisation that she wanted more than comradeship, she shied away in terror.

She looked at her travelling clock, a present from Granny

when it was assumed she would be sailing out to India. It was time to go downstairs, and tackle the fearsome Mrs Dove. The family ration books must be handed over. Primrose, naturally, was in charge of these. She was just getting out of bed when she heard a peculiar, lowing sound in the garden, echoing with the dewy ring of early morning.

The night had been full of peculiar sounds. Primrose went to the window, with a vague idea that some farmyard beast had wandered onto the lawn. Before she got there, however, the sound resolved itself into a wordless cascade of song, hideously out of tune.

Oh, God. Sidonia's pagan love-rite. Primrose adored her mother, and did her best to see her absurdities as artistic and enchanting – but with Guy in the house, she saw through his eyes and was mortified.

Sidonia, clad in what looked like a sheet, swayed and keened in the slanting spears of the rising sun, her floss of platinum hair lifting in the breeze. Ten years before, she had enjoyed enormous success doing this in one of Daphne Wadsworth's dotty plays. It expressed her oneness with nature, she said. It also expressed restlessness and discontent. Primrose had not seen the pagan rite since the advent of the Eagle. She watched, full of foreboding, as Sidonia hurled her body into an extravagant dance of worship.

'Isis! Goddess! Mother!'

She bowed to the horizon and ran, all fluttering grace, towards the verandah. The grace was marred, at the last minute, by the hem of her sheet. She tripped, nearly overbalanced and retired cursing.

Primrose's eyes stung with tears. A door banged nearby. To add the final flourish to her shame, she heard the unmistakable sounds of Sidonia and Ralph making love. The more bored Sidonia became with her husband, the louder and more elaborate were the efforts she made to endure him.

Primrose listened, shuddering, until the two of them yelled out their noisy climax. Because of Sidonia, Primrose had always assumed she could not possibly like sex. She had always hated the fact that she knew so much about it, because Sidonia seldom talked about anything else. Now, she could not help thinking – before she strangled the thought at birth – that sex with Guy would not be like any act performed by Sidonia.

<hr>

Eggs and milk from the farm had arrived at the back door. Lily, seeing them, was relieved. This would look like abundance to the bombed-out Londoners. They might even be pleased, and stop gazing around them as if they had landed in a leper colony.

'Mrs D, you should have called me. You must have been up for hours.'

Mrs Dove had hauled out the silver breakfast service – brown with tarnish – from the old days of limitless help. She was placing curls of parsley on a chafing-dish of kedgeree. 'I don't need my sleep like you young things.'

Lily recognised this as a gruff statement of allegiance, and was touched. 'What can I do?'

'Nothing, except have a cup of tea. Plenty in the pot.'

'That smells delicious.' Lily poured herself tea. 'Where did you find the fish? I thought we used it all last night.'

Mrs Dove let out a hoarse, rusty chuckle. 'The hen-bucket, that's where. They'll never know what I had to scrape off it.'

Lily laughed. 'Very economical. You could teach Lord Woolton a thing or two.'

'They complained because it was burnt. It was burnt because they kept it waiting.'

'May I make some toast? I'll only take from the old loaf.'

'You'll do nothing of the kind,' snapped Mrs Dove. 'I made this 'un yesterday, and I won't have you eating stale. You want to stand up for your rights, young lady.'

'My rights?'

Mrs Dove sternly wagged a stalk of parsley. 'Don't you let them eat you out of house and home.'

'They're welcome to my stale bread and rotten fish.'

'I mean it, Miss Lily. Treat them as guests, and you'll end up as their servant. Make them muck in and do their share. It wouldn't hurt that Madam Fancy-Pants, for a start.'

Lily, smiling at this obvious reference to Primrose, cut

herself a thick slice of new bread and liberally slathered it with butter. 'I'm sure she'll step in, if we do things badly enough. I saw the face she pulled, when she tasted my coffee.'

'I won't have her treating you like the in-between maid. Or your poor mother would turn in her grave.'

Mrs Dove was always imagining what people got up to in their graves – turning, shuddering, uttering reproaches. It added an interesting dash of melodrama, but was seldom productive.

'I don't mind helping out at first, till things settle down.' Lily made for the back door. 'I'll be back to carry out the dishes – nobody will be up for hours.'

In the kitchen garden, she ate her bread. It was very sweet to her, to have cross old Mrs Dove on her side. She did not enjoy being invaded by a gang of superior strangers. But she thought of her besotted, foolish father – so unwisely shackled to that silly old bag who danced in a sheet. Her love for Ralph would have melted her into a desire for harmony, even if harmony had not been the only practical option. God knew how long they would all have to live as a parody of a family.

She strolled out onto the lawn at the front of the house. The morning was clear, promising heat later. Lily's bare feet made a ghostly trail across the dew-soaked grass. Shading her eyes against the new, white light, she watched a pair of gulls circling above her in the infinite blue.

The Prospect had been her life, and she had taken the beauty of the gardens and the bay for granted. Now, she had to stop herself seeing it with the eyes of an exile. The coming of Sidonia and her daughters should not have made her feel excluded in her own kingdom. Why did it?

'Lily! Lily-Josephine!'

She turned, and delightedly shouted: 'Charlie!'

Charlie Despard loped across the grass towards her, and stooped briefly to kiss her cheek. 'My God. You've lost your plaits.'

'Do you like it?'

He checked her, a little suspiciously. 'I don't know. I don't like finding changes.'

'I'm afraid I would insist on growing up.' They had instantly resumed their old, teasing friendship. 'Admit it suits me.'

'It suits you.'

'Now, are you home for good, or do you have to go back? And how on earth did you get here? And what made you think we'd want to see you, at this hour?'

He smiled down into her face. 'Yes, home for good. Hitched a lift on the milk-van – and positively knew you'd be thrilled, because it's so dull without me.'

'Dull? Oh, you wait. How's your arm?'

The bad arm was no longer bound, but hung, heavy and useless, with the hand tucked into the pocket of his tweed jacket.

His smile did not waver, but his eyes dulled. 'Presentable. At least young ladies won't scream, when I take my clothes off.'

'No nice girl would scream at you, Charlie-boy.'

'I'm not interested in nice girls.'

'Can I be your chauffeur again? I've missed our excursions.'

Charlie, who had once terrorised the countryside in a series of snappy roadsters, could no longer drive. Before he left, for his final stay in hospital, Lily had driven him to the cinema in Barnstaple once a week. She loved the pictures, and Charlie, without the influence of Ralph, simmered down into a very good companion. It certainly beat going to the pictures with Gladys, who fell asleep and snored.

'Right-ho. I'll watch anything.'

Lily – though she would never have admitted it to him – decided Charlie was handsomer than ever. Surely, nobody in the world had such blue eyes. What a shame, she thought, that they should belong to such a shallow and bounderish young article. She was impatient to experience falling in love, and would gladly have tried it out on Charlie, if he had made the smallest effort to earn her respect.

He asked: 'How's Ralph? I heard he'd come back.'

'Not half he has. With the new Mrs Gallant, and her three daughters.'

'Three? My God.'

'Such nice girls – you wouldn't be interested.'

'And what about your wicked stepmother?' The previous Christmas, they had driven out to see Walt Disney's *Snow White*. It had been a child's outing – how old did the idiot think she was? – but he had amused her, by sniffing loudly through the affecting parts. 'Has she sold you any apples yet? Or prepared a dinky little box to put your heart in?'

'You'll see her at breakfast, so you can judge for yourself.'

'Seriously, Lily, I'm sorry to crash in so early.'

'I'm glad you did. How is your arm, truly?'

Once again, he kept smiling, but with a bitter drag to his mouth. 'They tell me this is as good as it'll get. I'm supposed to be grateful they didn't cut it off. But I've given a limb for my country, just as surely as if they had.'

Lily felt a surge of fondness for him. In his own fashion, he was being brave. 'Come inside. Nobody's up yet, but Mrs Dove will look after you. You know how she adores you.'

As if she had touched a switch, he snapped back into his usual, one-dimensional cheerfulness. 'Yes, I do seem to have found the soft spot under that hard old pinny.'

'Because you're the lord of the manor, Charlie-boy.' She tucked her hand into the crook of his good arm. 'Now, I'd better fill you in on the news. Did you hear about Gladys Tufton's baby?'

'Mother wrote to me,' Charlie said. 'A fine little chap, she reckons.'

'He's divine. I'm his godmother.'

'Nice for Mrs Tufton, after losing her husband. I say, how the hell does Ralphie manage without him?'

'Not at all. Well, you'll see.' She led him through the raspberry-canes, into the kitchen. 'Mrs D, look who's turned up.'

A pale figure, silhouetted against the monstrous black range, raised its shining head. Sidonia, bare-legged in a linen tunic of smoky grey, trapped Charlie in her emerald gaze.

'Morning, Lily. Who's this?'

'Isis! Ow-ooh! Goddess! Mother!' Lily swooped and fluttered round the kitchen table, billowing out the tablecloth on her shoulders. Gladys, Mrs Dove, and Mrs Neck, the gardener's wife, were howling with laughter.

Mrs Dove kept repeating: 'She'll be the death of me!'

Lily bowed in adoration to the dresser. 'Oh, tea-caddy! Cream-jug! Ow-ooh! Souvenir-cruet-from-Bude!'

The laughter abruptly ceased. She raised her head, to see the three faces around the table frozen in rictuses of embarrassment. Framed in the doorway stood Primrose, Guy and Isobel. Primrose looked murderous.

Biting the insides of her cheeks, to stop herself giggling, Lily scrambled to her feet. Did she imagine it, or did she catch a flash of guilty mirth, hastily stifled, on the timid face of Isobel?

'I don't think you've met Mrs Tufton. Gladys, this is Primrose Leary, and –'

'Rumage!' spat Primrose. 'Leary is Isobel's name.'

'Sorry.' Lily removed the tablecloth. 'Primrose Rumage, Guy Rumage, Isobel Leary.'

Gladys was on her feet. 'How do you do.'

The pink heat of Primrose's cheeks turned her eyes to glaring chips of blue glass. 'I was so sorry to hear about your husband, Mrs Tufton.'

'Thank you, Miss.'

Lily stared at Primrose and Guy, fascinated by the likeness between them. They were a perfect matching pair in pink-and-gold; tall, healthy and very slightly antiseptic. Primrose, despite her sparkling, crackling anger, looked very lovely.

A motor-horn tooted outside. The sound raised a bleat from the basket on the table.

Isobel stepped forward, and exclaimed: 'Oh, Prim – look!' Since her arrival at the Prospect, she had uttered only gulped monosyllables. This was the first time Lily had heard her voice properly, and its fresh sweetness took her by surprise.

'This is Peter.' She beckoned Isobel closer. 'My godson.'

'Isn't he gorgeous?' Isobel's shy pleasure drew her soft

175

features into focus. Lily smiled boldly into her eyes, and the two girls bent over the baby.

'That's Arthur, with the van,' Gladys said. 'We should be off.'

Lily said: 'Can I bring Isobel, next time I cycle over to see Peter?'

Gladys tried not to laugh – this was such a typical Lily impulse – and eyed Primrose cautiously. 'Yes, of course, if Miss Leary would like to.'

With surprising firmness, Isobel said: 'I'd love to.'

'Settled,' declared Lily. 'We'll come tomorrow. Isobel can borrow Neck's bike, I'm sure.'

Gladys kissed her. 'See you tomorrow, then.'

Mrs Neck, withering in the heat of Primrose's fury, took the opportunity to scuttle out after her. Mrs Dove tottered out to the garden, in search of lettuces.

After a pungent spell of silence, Lily said: 'I'm sorry you saw me fooling about just now.'

Isobel helped herself to one of the biscuits on the table. 'I'm sorry you saw Mummy fooling about this morning.'

Both girls laughed. Lily was delighted to hear the first rustlings of sense from the invading army. 'What was she doing?'

'Her pagan worship.'

'Isobel, I don't think Lily-Josephine needs to hear about our mother's private life.' Primrose, very conscious of Guy beside her, spoke through clenched teeth. 'Our mother is an artist. Only very shallow people fail to understand that.'

Lily coolly took a biscuit. 'Oh yes, she told me, last time she came here. Beauty! One must be surrounded by beauty! Everything one touches, everything one tastes –'

It was a perfect imitation of Sidonia. Primrose, Isobel and Guy were thunderstruck.

Enjoying herself, Lily dropped her voice another octave. 'How very lucky you are, not to be pierced and made wretched by beauty, as I am.'

Isobel and Guy exploded into screams of pent-up laughter. Primrose saw, very plainly, that Guy had been dying to laugh for days. She was deeply hurt. She stood, a statue of humiliation, while Lily made a fresh pot of tea and liberally dispensed biscuits. Guy and Isobel settled themselves chummily at the table. Guy was ignoring her. Stiffly, she perched on the chair beside him, guarding him.

Nobody noticed, as they laughed and chatted, that she was shivering. When Guy's attention moved away from her, it left a physical chill. He is crushing my heart to pieces, she thought. He is torturing me.

And then she was amazed at herself. Sisters did not think in such terms about their brothers. When had she ever suffered like this, for anyone? Finally, she faced the appalling fact. This illness was called love – she was in love with Guy. She was a sinner, and she deserved her pain.

She lingered in the kitchen, after Guy and Isobel had gone, to hiss desperately at Lily: 'If you laugh at my mother again, I'll kill you!'

Chapter Ten

❖❖❖

Primrose and Guy picked their way cautiously down the steep cliff path, maintaining a distance that seemed unbearably significant. They did not speak. Primrose, exquisitely miserable, took in the useless perfection of the day.

A breeze snaked between her skin and the heavy glare of the sun. Without looking directly, she was overwhelmed by the immense blue dazzle of the sea, spread out before them as if they were clinging to the very rim of the earth. Drowsy in the heat, the waves slapped against the rocky shore in lazy, sighing rhythm. Fat bees hummed drunkenly in the clumps of coarse grass and scarlet pimpernel. But none of it was worth a damn, while this deadening awkwardness lay between them.

More than two weeks had passed, since Primrose's great and (she could never forget) forbidden realisation. The day of giving Guy up to the war came nearer, and she could not reach him. She could not help being shy and formal with him, and he seemed to know that something essential had changed. He avoided being alone with her – horribly easy, in a house so stuffed with people. He's guessed, she thought, and he's obviously horrified.

He said: 'Shall I take the basket now?'

'I can manage.' It was heavy, but she wanted him to see that she was angry.

Guy jumped down in front of her, and held out his hand, to help her down the shelf of rock. She did not take it, and would not look him in the eye. They stood very still, listening to the cawing of the gulls. She dropped the wretched basket.

'Prim, what's the matter? What've I done?'

'Oh, nothing. I'm just sorry you're disappointed.'

'Why am I disappointed?'

'That Lily wouldn't come with us, in spite of all your begging and pleading.'

'I didn't beg. I only asked.'

'You didn't bother to ask Isobel or Juana.'

'Well, Isobel spends all her time on the farm these days, and Juana isn't much of a one for the great outdoors. Why are you always so hard on Lily?'

'I'm amazed you can ask, when you've seen her attitude to my mother.'

'God, you're not still going on about that! It was only a jape.'

Primrose's voice was tight and mean with unhappiness. 'I don't happen to find that sort of jape amusing.'

Another spell of silence.

Then Guy said, with disarming gentleness: 'You've been awfully odd with me for ages. I know you're trying to keep out of my way. And the thing is, I don't blame you.'

'Me? What are you talking about?' She looked at him now, and saw that his face was a mirror of her own unhappiness.

'I ask you what I've done,' he said. 'And I know perfectly well. I'm trying very hard not to – spoil things.'

Primrose felt her heart expanding with hope. She wanted to laugh. 'We're so alike, it's ridiculous.' She had either gone out of her senses, or come into them. Suddenly, there was no more shame. With the solid wall of cliff behind them and the sea rolling at their feet, nothing mattered but the declaration of love. Their mirrored faces were blushing in identical patches.

'I've been meaning to ask you for months,' he said, 'if you ever think of – of – sardines.'

She did laugh this time, on the point of crying. 'On toast?'

'At Grandmama's –'

'Silly, I'm teasing. I think about it all the time.'

'Were you angry?'

'No.'

'You should have been,' Guy said. 'It was wrong.' Desperately, he added, in a rush: 'And I'd give almost anything to do it again. That's why I don't trust myself.'

'I thought it was me you didn't trust.'

She took his hand. His fingers tightened around hers. Primrose printed the moment on her mind, knowing she would remember it, and long to return to it, all her life. The sea, the breeze, Guy's fair face in the sun. The unspoken shift, which meant they had made up their minds, in a most anti-Rumage fashion, to be joyous and unrepentant sinners.

Primrose had never imagined such happiness. She was crying with the relief of surrender. Guy held her, stroking the back of her head, and she sobbed into his shoulder. They drew apart, and she saw that he was crying too.

They laughed shakily, tried to wipe one another's eyes, and began again as two new people.

'I'll take that bloody basket now,' said Guy.

They scrambled down the last few yards to the shore. Guy found a flat table of rock, half-hidden from the beach, and baking in the heat. Primrose blew her nose, and poured them both cups of mouldy-tasting Thermos tea. They sat down, very close together.

Slowly, slowly, against the sun-warmed stones, their mouths fused. They kissed, in perfect, seamless sequence. Guy, no longer a grappling schoolboy, eased his tongue between her lips. Primrose felt as if her heart had dropped between her legs. His hand brushed the silk of her dress there, and her body surprised her, with a sudden, racking throb of longing.

Guy rolled on top of her, the outline of his erection bruising her thigh. His face was scarlet with the effort of restraint. Primrose, not knowing or caring what she did, opened her legs, so that his body lay between her knees. They were both trembling.

He pushed up her dress, and hooked his clumsy fingers into the top of her stocking. He groaned, and began to grind his pelvis into hers, through the layers of their clothes. His back tensed, his eyes widened helplessly.

He cried out: 'No – no!' and burst against her.

Sobbing, he collapsed into her arms. Primrose felt the powerful drumming of her heart. Inexperienced as she was, she realised what had happened. Sidonia often told the story of doing exactly the same thing to his poor father, when they were alone in the car after their wedding – 'he went off like a rocket,' was how she always put it, 'in full dress uniform, gloves and a sword; and all I did was lick his ear a little.' Primrose, once deeply disgusted by this story, felt a twinge of excitement remembering it now.

'Sorry,' Guy said, his voice muffled in her shoulder, 'I've never done this before.'

'Neither have I.'

'All I know is, I'll die, if we don't – I'll die, that's all. It's got to the stage where I don't dare to be alone with you.'

She understood him perfectly. Consummation was more than desirable; it was imperative. Love had blasted her open. She was no longer correct, prudish, well-behaved, or even decent. Aching with tender anticipation, she began – shamelessly – to plan.

◆◆◆

It was nowhere near time for a drink, but Ralph mentally apologised to Tufton, and poured himself one anyway; the one comforter that never let him down. Poor old Bert, at least he had been spared the spectacle of his Captain's decline.

There were one or two rags of decency still clinging to Ralph's rudderless soul – enough to remind him, very occasionally, about the hash he had made of absolutely everything. Tufton would say he had betrayed Lily. He did sometimes feel uneasy about this. Mostly, however, he watched her suspiciously, for signs of disrespect to Sidonia.

Any fool could see the animosity between them. And if Lily didn't bloody well make an effort, he would be forced into the cheapness of choosing his wife over his daughter. Oh, Lily, Lily – don't make me do it! When it came to that, his ruin would be complete.

He had fondly imagined life in the country being simple and manageable, and it was a nightmare. Far from being more controllable, Sidonia was slipping away. Recently, the ravening, erotic beauty, dimmed by the death of the Eagle, had come rushing back. And as it did, he was forced into all sorts of mental contortions, in order not to notice that none of it was aimed at him.

Sex – when he got any – was a maddeningly one-sided business. Sidonia said she wasn't in the mood for sex, and she reeked of it. He hoped to God she had the sense not to make him confront the truth, because he couldn't bear it, and had no idea what he would do.

Where was she now? Sidonia was always vanishing these days. He had a mad, feverish instinct that she was near – he was sure he caught her scent sometimes, in unexpected corners of the house – but he could never find her. Three days before, she had suddenly appeared with a black eye. She said she had got it when she fell down and broke her heel. Ralph wished someone would doubt this out loud, so he could punch them. If he refused to doubt his wife, how dare anyone?

If only he had someone to talk to. Sidonia's girls, and his own Lily, always seemed to be out. Funny little Isobel, child of the rude Irishman he had met on the night of Bert's death, had developed a mania for farm work. She hared off at dawn, to milk cows on the home farm, or help out at Arthur Driver's.

Primrose usually scuttled out with her tongue-tied brother – a relief, since Ralph found the pair's relentless wholesomeness rather wearing. Lily, apart from weekly drives to the pictures with Charlie, spent every spare moment with Gladys and her baby. And heaven alone knew what the mysterious Juana got up to, when her mother's mistrustful eyes were turned elsewhere.

At one time, Ralph had hoped the girls would make themselves scarce. Now, he was lonely. Charlie turned up fairly often, but was not enough of a fixture to make much difference. And in any case, he tended to be rather boorish and insolent to Sidonia. She never complained, but Ralph felt it as an affront to his own dignity. He supposed Charlie had been recruited by the opposite camp – the idiot was evidently rather sweet on Lily. God, if only he'd marry her. What problems it would solve.

Ralph did not see how he was to get through the rest of this war, on such short rations of love. He refilled his glass, and wandered to the window. Disconsolately, he stared out at the hot summer afternoon. He was in the library, and (no matter how determined he was to ignore them) the room was packed with markers of his history.

And it had all boiled down to this. Ralph looked at his life – blitzed, defeated and occupied – and was dimly glad his feelings never went deep enough for real despair.

He jumped guiltily, as the door clicked behind him. 'Oh – hello.'

It was Juana, with her dark eyes and her dark red lips. Her bare legs were tanned and slender, under the short hem of her printed silk dress. 'Only me, I'm afraid. You hoped I'd be Sidonia.'

'Yes, I did, actually. Haven't seen her since breakfast.'

Juana smiled, and came towards him. Ralph noticed, with the unoccupied part of himself, that her smile was delightful. For once, she was in a good mood, and it lifted a veil from her face. He saw again – as he had seen before, but freshly – that she was very pretty. Also very sexy, which Ralph noticed now, and decided he had better not notice again.

'Poor old Ralphie, you're too dignified to ask me if I know where she is. But I haven't seen her either. She shimmied off in a kind of yokel's smock, with a ludicrous bee-keeper's hat covering her black eye.'

'She never looks like other people,' Ralph said automatically. 'It's part of her charm.'

'Is it? I wouldn't know. My father used to give her black eyes.'

'She broke her heel –'

'Oh, darling, I wasn't for a minute suggesting you'd walloped her. Though you'd be well within your rights. She's unbearable when she's restless.'

'Is she restless?'

'Madly. It's being in the country. I sympathise, because it makes me restless, too.'

Ralph said: 'We didn't have much choice. But I hoped you'd like it here.'

She helped herself to a glass of the precious Scotch. He watched her red mouth kiss the rim of the crystal tumbler. 'I do like life to be just a tad more – thrilling.'

She narrowed her eyes, with such comic meaning that Ralph laughed. Juana, in this incarnation, was like a wicked and beguiling cat, daring him to admire her wickedness.

'You were seeing a chap in London,' he said. 'I'm surprised he let you go.'

'He was a thundering bore.'

'You'll – you'll have to look out for a replacement.'

She chuckled, and arched her black brows. 'All suggestions gratefully received.'

'Well, I don't know. Charlie Despard.'

She laughed outright at this. 'He's only a boy. And he's off-limits.'

'You mean, because he's got his eye on Lily,' Ralph said. 'It wouldn't be a bad thing, but he's not doing much about it. Lily wants men to be heroes. Just like her mother.'

He had not meant to say so much, but there was something receptive in Juana's manner. She listened intently, with a faint air of scepticism.

She said: 'Her mother was impressed with you.'

'Yes, poor kid. She died before I disappointed her.'

'Oh, Ralphie, men like you never disappoint. Men like Charlie Despard usually do – but frankly, he's not my type anyway.'

Ralph, as the alcohol stole into his bloodstream, was conscious of a sensation that had deserted him for too long. It wound through the air towards him, like a delicious fragrance – the balmy warmth of female sexual attention. For a fraction of a second, he felt his power returning, and the years falling away.

'Go on,' he said, smiling, 'tell me about your type.'

'Young men are tiresome. I prefer them older, and more experienced.' Keeping her gaze boldly locked into his, she held out her glass. 'May I have another?'

Chapter Eleven

━━◆◆◆◆◆━━

Mickey Mouse's rival was an abominable rodent; flashy, brutal and occasionally cruel. Minnie Mouse, his old flame, insisted that he was 'a scream'. Lily decided he reminded her of Charlie, and Charlie – delighted – had played up to it all the way home from the cinema.

He was still doing the squeaky voice when he climbed out of his mother's serviceable Austin, in the stableyard of Despard Court: 'Sa-a-ay! If it ain't my old sweetie, Minnie Mouse!' The joke was as thin as a cigarette paper by now, but he seemed to be relishing it for entirely private reasons.

Lily retrieved her bicycle from the empty stable. 'Thanks, Charlie. See you next week?'

'Okay. It's a musical – some Eleanor Powell thing.'

'Lovely.'

'Wasn't it priceless, when Mickey got the doughnut stuck on his nose?'

'Hilarious.'

'I'm sorry for the Yanks sometimes. Holes in their dough-nuts, instead of jam - bad show.'

'Charlie, you're an idiot.' She kissed his cheek. 'I'd really hate to get lost in the wide open spaces of your brain.'

'I keep wanting to tug your plaits,' he said. 'I miss them.'

'I don't.'

His handsome, fatuous face suddenly became serious. 'You mustn't change too much, you know.'

'I wasn't planning to.'

'Sometimes, I feel as if I hardly know you any more. I have to make up my mind to start all over again.'

'Look, I must go – Daddy fusses if I cut dinner. He says it's rude to Sidonia.'

His smile flashed back. 'Just tell her you were with me.'

They had seen, besides the cartoon, a newsreel of the Germans invading Russia, and Deanna Durbin in *Three Smart Girls*. The outing had taken longer than she expected. Charlie had made her stop the car three times on the way back - twice for him to pee, once to buy cornets. He was often demanding, but this afternoon he had been as fidgety as a ferret. She slightly wondered what was the matter with him. Come to that, what was the matter with everyone? The atmosphere at the Prospect was pregnant with mystery, and crackling with tension. Lily - after waving to the vigilant figure of Lady Violet, in the drawing room window - pedalled off furiously, determined not to make things worse by being late.

A mile or so along the road, a motor-horn tooted, and Arthur Driver's battered old disgrace of a van spluttered up beside her. He was a few years older than Gladys, with the same high colour and plump solidity. 'Sling your bike in the back, duck, and I'll take you home.'

'Thanks.'

'Been out with Mr Charlie, have you? Poor chap, he takes it very hard, that arm of his.' When Lily had climbed into the front seat, he started the van, with ominous clashings and grindings of the gears. 'Damned old banger. For the chop, she is.'

'What - are you getting a new van, at long last?'

'Yup. Don't know anyone who might fancy this 'un, do you?'

'Frankly, no. How much are you asking?'

His laugh was a masculine version of Gladys's. 'How much d'you reckon I can get?'

'You'll have to give someone a fiver to take her away.'

Arthur had known Lily since babyhood, and thought her a card. He chuckled again. Then he said: 'Glad was hoping I'd catch you. She says your dress is ready.'

'Tell her I'll come over tomorrow.' Lily found herself thinking of Charlie, and what he had said about her 'changing'. When she appeared before him in a black velvet gown, her transformation would be complete. Would he like her, or would she lose him? And if she lost him, would she care?

Thanks to Arthur, she was in plenty of time for the awful ceremony of dinner. She went to the kitchen, where Mrs Dove was grumbling over a pan of watercress soup.

'Thank goodness it's only you, dear. I was afraid it'd be Madam again, looking for raw steak to put on her shiner. Steak, indeed! Doesn't seem to know there's a war on. Get us some apples, would you?'

'Righto.'

Lily went out again, into the crimson and gold sunset. The apples were kept in a hayloft, above one of the empty outbuildings. It was full of silver and gold motes of hay-dust, and smelled of cidery sweetness. She ran nimbly up the wooden ladder – then froze with shock, her hand clamped across her mouth.

Pillowed in a bale of hay, a bare rump moved with frantic energy. A pair of stockinged legs were clamped above it. Almost indistinguishable from the sunlit hay were the fair heads of Guy and Primrose – wantonly locked together, groaning through sealed lips with the rhythm of Guy's thrusts.

Lily had to clutch the top of the ladder, to stop herself falling. After the first shock, she waited to feel angry, or disgusted, and was assaulted by an overwhelming sense of their beauty. They ought to have looked ridiculous, and they were as beautiful as angels. In the few seconds of watching, Lily felt a sympathetic, dissolving shudder in the very pit of her stomach, and her mind flashed up a picture of Charlie, similarly translated and transformed.

Primrose turned her head, and her eyes widened in horror. Lily hurled herself down the ladder, and ran back to the house in flames of embarrassment. Deaf to Mrs Dove's shouts about apples, she hared up to her room, and leaned against the door, cooling her burning cheeks between her palms.

She almost did not believe what she had seen – starchy, disapproving Primrose, abandoned and inflamed in the act of love with her brother. But if you accepted them as lovers,

187

the ghastly behaviour of Primrose could be explained, if not excused. What agonies of guilt she must be suffering; what tortures of secrecy and fevers of jealousy. She was at her horridest when Lily was friendly to Guy. Lily now saw why, and the first nugget of sympathy formed in her soul.

It grew when they all assembled for dinner. Primrose and Guy were unnaturally tidy, as if they had each scrubbed away a layer of skin in an effort to remove the evidence of the hayloft. They looked very young, and very pale. Both avoided Lily's eyes, with a shame and fear she found heart-rending.

'You're quiet, Prim,' Sidonia commented. 'My God, it brings back memories – Clive used to go all quiet, generally when I'd done something awful. Does he still do it, Guy? Dinners used to be perfect seances.' Fortunately, her drag-onfly attention darted across to Isobel. 'Darling, if you must spend your days shovelling cows' Number Twos, I wish you'd wash it off afterwards. You pong to heaven.'

'Oh, leave her alone,' Ralph said. 'I can't smell anything except hay.' He smiled down the table. 'Rather pleasant.'

Ralph was jauntier than he had been for weeks – months, even – but Lily sensed a grating undertow of sourness. And Sidonia was in a dreadful mood. So dreadful, you could almost taste it in the food. She wore her black eye as if black eyes were all the rage. When Ralph decided to pay attention to his daughter, the emerald embedded in the puffy bruise shot pure poison.

'Well, my Lily-girl, what have you been up to?' He looked at Lily, but was playing to Sidonia. 'Cooing over your godson?'

'No, actually. I drove Charlie to Barnstaple. It's our day for the pictures.'

Sidonia's shoulders tensed angrily. 'Poor Charlie. He sits through hours of drear, with some confused notion of being kind to children. You really must make him see you're not a kid any more, and let him off the hook.'

'It was his idea,' Lily said stiffly. 'You know he never does anything he dislikes.'

'Funny sort of kid, who drives a car,' Ralph said. 'Even

188

Charlie must have worked that one out.'

'Of course, Lady Violet loves to dream up suitable, harmless outings for him,' Sidonia said. 'She thinks boredom will improve him.'

'He wasn't bored,' Lily said. Though it occurred to her that boredom might have been the reason for his restlessness.

Ralph laughed. 'If there's a kid around, it's Charlie. Before the war, he was always dragging his girlfriends out to zoos and pantomimes. Let's hope he finds a wife who likes Walt Disney.'

'A wife? That's the last thing he needs,' Sidonia said. 'It's his mother who wants to get him to the altar. Interfering old bat.'

'Lady Vi's not such a bad sort,' Ralph said. 'She won't give me the time of day, but she's always been tremendously nice to Lily.' He said it with smiling aggression, which made Lily wince.

Sidonia pushed away her plate, and lit a cigarette. 'Yes, and he knows it will please Mummy, if he trots off to the cinema with a sweet young thing. But anyone who held him to duty-outings would be rather selfish, don't you think? And frankly, rather vain. People assume having only one arm makes him enjoy anything.'

Lily stood up. The malicious sparring between her father and Sidonia frightened her. They were batting her to and fro between them like a shuttlecock. She had not thought Ralph capable of using her to score points. She was trying not to discover that his surface shabbiness covered something still more shabby. And naturally, she blamed Sidonia for the change in him. Gladys would say 'six of one, half a dozen of the other', but she refused to stop believing in the essential, sweet Ralph of her childhood. He had existed once. She was still hoping to get him back.

She piled up the dirty plates, fighting off a feeling that a toxic cloud of wickedness was spreading through her home. Guy, studiously avoiding her eyes, got up to open the door.

In the empty kitchen, Lily dropped the plates on the draining board, and watched her tears splash into the sink.

Sidonia was a bitch. Ralph had forgotten his love for his child. Charlie thought she was a nuisance. Gladys was miles away; Tufton was dead. She felt alone and painfully vulnerable; a soft thing among flints.

'Lily –'

Angrily wiping her eyes on a dish-towel, Lily turned to see Primrose and Guy, framed in the open doorway.

'What?'

Primrose clutched Guy's hand. 'Has Mrs Dove gone to bed?'

'Yes.'

Guy softly closed the door. The three looked at each other, then dropped their gazes to the floor, blushing furiously.

Stiffly, Primrose said: 'You saw, of course.'

'I'm terribly sorry –'

'I didn't come here expecting an apology. You can't accuse me of that much cheek, I hope.'

'I'm still sorry, though.'

Primrose and Lily stared at each other levelly now; both on the defensive, with damp lashes.

'And when are you going to tell?' Primrose snapped.

'Why should I tell?'

'Perhaps you'd rather keep it hanging over our heads. A useful bargaining tool – you know we'd do anything.'

'Prim,' Guy murmured unhappily, 'shut up.'

Neither heard him.

'You've been dying for an excuse to throw us out. Well, here it is. I expect you're overjoyed.'

Lily said: 'Unlike your family, I don't enjoy making trouble. I won't tell Daddy, and I certainly won't tell Sidonia – my God, I wouldn't tell her if the house was on fire. I'm not a sneak, so you can rest easy and leave me alone.'

Primrose's lower lip buckled pathetically. Still clinging to Guy's hand, she broke down into wrenching, anguished sobs. Guy, suddenly seeming far less boyish, swept his arm around her protectively.

'She doesn't mean it. We didn't come here to call you a sneak. We both know we're doing something very wrong. If you did tell on us, it would probably serve us right.'

'We can't help it.' Primrose's voice was muffled in his shoulder. 'We love each other so much – oh, Lily, please, please – if you'd just let us have the rest of Guy's leave!'

Guy said: 'After that, we'll have the whole war to be sorry in.'

He was in uniform, and Lily could not help being aware of what he had not said – that poor Primrose might be sorry for the rest of her life. Primrose was aware of it, too. Her sobs became whoops and howls, as if a dam had burst inside her, releasing months of hidden pain.

Lily was appalled by so much naked passion, and intensely sorry for both of them. Of course she thinks I'm going to squeal, she thought. She's the soul of duty, and her beastly mother has ordered her to hate me. But I'll make her know me properly now.

She filled the kettle. 'Guy, you have a way with the range. Stoke the bloody thing up, and I'll make us some tea.'

This was not what Guy had expected, but he was too polite to argue. After tenderly settling Primrose in the carver's chair, he knelt down to stoke the kitchen fire. While the kettle boiled, and Lily dashed about assembling cups and saucers, he soothed Primrose.

Her sobs subsided. She raised her head; a crushed, meek, unrecognisable Primrose. Guy gave her his handkerchief and a cigarette. Lily gave her a cup of tea. She whispered: 'Thanks.' Crushed as she was, it was still an effort to be grateful to the enemy.

'You can't keep up a tragedy in the face of tea,' Lily said. 'So let's not have any more. I don't think real love is ever tragic. Or wrong.'

'It is when you're brother and sister,' Primrose said. 'You're very naive. I suppose because you've spent all your life out here, in the middle of nowhere. In the real world, we're unnatural. We're freaks. I can't tell you how horrid it is, to love someone and know you can never belong together in a normal way. I hate not being normal.'

'But if the two of you are happy, you should enjoy it while you can.' Lily could not resist adding: 'Make hay while the sun shines.'

Guy let out a nervous bray of laughter, then flushed puce and glanced aside at Primrose. 'I daresay we were – quite a sight.'

'Guy, don't.' Primrose was vehement. 'I'll never live it down.'

'My darling –' he took her hand. 'It's going to be all right. She's not going to tell on us.'

'Why should she be so kind?'

'Because I am kind,' Lily said. 'I shan't ask for anything in return, either. Though a little civility might be fun.'

Primrose's face reddened, in the same places as Guy's. 'I know I've been a cat to you. I'm – I'm – sorry. Sidonia was so sure you'd be against us all.'

'I am rather against her.'

'She'd be furious, if she caught me being friendly. And I absolutely can't live with her when she's furious.'

Lily saw what it cost her to be humble, and how deeply she was in thrall to her mother. She relented. 'We'll be friendly in secret, then. Or declare a truce.'

'You really won't tell?'

'Never ever, or I hope to die.'

Primrose attempted a watery smile. 'Thank you.'

Lily went to bed with a lighter heart than she had carried for weeks. She was no longer excluded or alone. There was still a little warmth left in the house, beneath the shadow of the bat's leathery wing. She had nothing but sympathy for bossy Primrose now. And she was sure she was right to sympathise. When the world lay in ruins, surely no kind of love could be sinful. One day, love might be the only hope left. It was far too rare and precious to spoil with shame.

Chapter Twelve

The truce with Primrose outlasted Guy's return to his unit. Primrose surprised herself, by achieving a certain intimacy with her stepsister. It was a secret, underground intimacy – only Lily knew why she wandered about with draggled hair and red-rimmed eyes. In a house where everyone was caught up in their own dramas, only Lily noticed.

After a week of fretting for Guy, Primrose made a noble effort to pull herself together. The Prospect cried out for proper management, and household management was her great solace.

'It's the one thing I'm really good at,' she explained, after Lily had found her dismantling the linen cupboard. 'I slipped in here to have a good cry, and decided to tidy it instead. Would anyone mind, if I used the old sewing machine in the pantry?'

'Course not. Go ahead.'

'We get through so many sheets – well, Mummy's so obsessed with clean sheets. I thought we could eke them out, by turning the worn ones sides-to-middle.'

'Good God. Do you know how?'

'Oh, yes. Granny taught me. And I've had a little word with Mrs Neck. Now that the laundryman's in the Navy, we're going to get the old copper going and wash them here.'

'But it'll be such a lot of work,' Lily said. 'Won't you hate it? I should.'

Primrose smiled, for almost the first time since Guy's departure. 'Work stops me feeling miserable. There's no satisfaction in the world like making order out of chaos. Do you think it's very cheeky of me, barging in to take charge?'

'I think it's wonderful of you, if slightly mad.'

'The kitchen garden is crying out for attention, too. I

don't know much about gardening, but I do know it could yield more than knobbly carrots and wormy apples. I mean, there is a war on, and we are supposed to be digging for victory.'

Mrs Dove, though she grumbled, was happier under Primrose's new regime. She acknowledged she was in the presence of high competence, and meals immediately got better. Lily surprised herself, by finding Primrose's energy rather comforting. Once she was properly in charge, her bossiness had an outlet.

Juana never did anything which might endanger her fingernails. Isobel thought only of joining the Land Army. In the meantime, she astonished everyone, by persuading Arthur Driver to take her on as a farm-hand. This left only Lily to help Primrose. And helping her was less oppressive than she had feared. She even learned a thing or two – for which she soon had reason to be most devoutly grateful.

'It is getting better,' she assured Gladys. 'Except for Sidonia.'

Sidonia never lost a chance to snipe and carp; to mock Lily's hair and clothes; to snub her and squash her. Sadly, Lily accepted that Primrose and Isobel, though they furtively allowed themselves to like her, would never defend her. Sidonia cowed them with unpredictable bursts of charm, until they were helpless and mesmerised. Primrose, in particular, absolutely lived for her approval – her mother's crumbs of affection could reduce her to tears. She was, like Ralph, besotted.

And Ralph's desertion hurt Lily most cruelly. He might be angry with Sidonia - might even hate her – but was thoroughly netted in her fascination. Lily realised how long it was, since anyone in her house had treated her with open warmth. Ralph's marriage had ripped away the comfortable wadding of affection she had taken for granted all her life. Primrose's covert spasms of cordiality were painful, because they intensified her craving for love. She felt like a plant in a dark cellar, desperately sending spindly green shoots towards any speck of light.

Gladys bled for her, and privately wondered if Charlie

Despard might be the answer. Lily was very fond of him. He only had the narrowest bridge to cross, Gladys thought, to make her fall in love with him. And a love of her own might be the child's salvation.

She knew it was a serious possibility, because Lady Violet Despard had starting buzzing round her. Charlie did nothing without her approval. When she took to 'dropping in' on Gladys, to interrogate her about Lily's suitability, Gladys made huge efforts to open the woman's critical heart to her darling.

It irritated her, to have the nosey old so-and-so sitting in a chair on her scrap of lawn by the hour, criticising her care of Peter and guzzling her tea ration. But for Lily's sake, she bore it.

One afternoon, the day before Charlie was expected at the Prospect for dinner, Lady Violet said: 'Mrs Tufton, I want to ask you something. A rather delicate matter, I'm afraid.'

That's never stopped you before, Gladys thought. 'Yes, Lady Violet?'

'Just what is Lily-Josephine's financial situation?'

Gladys was staggered by her impertinence. 'You mean, how much money has she got? Well, the Captain gives her an allowance, which she hardly ever spends, and –'

'I mean, how much of the Vere estate will she own outright, when she's twenty-one?'

'I don't know –'

'All of it? Some of it? An income, until the Captain's death?'

In spite of her indignation, Gladys was interested. 'It's funny, I've no idea. I witnessed Miss Helena's will when she got married. It left everything to the Captain.'

'Everything? Were there no trusts set up for the child?'

'My husband would have known. I just assumed Lily would get it all in the end, because there's no one else.'

'Was no one else,' Lady Violet said, with unpleasant emphasis. 'Suppose he has a son?'

Gladys wrestled down a laugh. 'Oh no, Madam. The new Mrs Gallant is much too old.'

'You weren't too old.'

'She's older than I was, when I fell for Peter,' Gladys said furiously.

'Still, one hopes some provision was made. Or it might be awkward when she marries.' Lady Violet sighed gustily, and helped herself to another biscuit, as if sugar-points did not exist. 'Forgive me, Mrs Tufton. You know what it is, to be the mother of a beloved son. I have to keep my head, when Charlie decides to lose his heart.'

Did Charlie have a heart? Gladys marvelled at his density. Would he ever take a proper look at Lily, and realise how much she had changed? Or did the poor girl need to hang a sign round her neck?

'I never see him these days,' Lady Violet said lugubriously. 'I assume he's at the Prospect. And though I never cared for Captain Gallant, Lily-Josephine strikes me as a sweet girl. Perhaps you could speak to her. Tell her to be kind to my dreadful boy – his bad arm makes him so shy with women.'

If he's shy, Gladys thought, I'm Carmen Miranda. But she did encourage Lily to wear her new velvet gown, when Charlie came to dinner. 'It'll be out of fashion, by the time you get round to it.'

'I'd feel silly, in the depths of the country, with a war on.'

'I bet that won't stop Sidonia.'

As Gladys had guessed, that clinched it. And the new dress would be the one, decisive shove Lily and Charlie needed, to bring them together. Some men could not recognise beauty, unless it was clearly labelled.

But things had come to a pretty pass, Gladys thought, when marriage seemed the only way to save Lily from her home.

The memory of Bert was not enough, these days, to stop Gladys wishing Ralph would fry in hell. When she stood before the bar of heaven, she would have something to say to God – the bomb that had killed Bert had left more than one child fatherless.

⬥

Lily wore the dress. It was like removing the shade from a candle, or wiping a clouded sheet of glass. She stood at the

196

drawing room window, against a splendid backdrop of blood-red sunset, a miracle in ebony and ivory. Her beauty, polished and combed, and sheathed in a soft black velvet, was a fact beyond question.

The transformation filled Charlie with obvious and comical confusion. He was clumsy and distracted; visibly struggling between enchantment and alarm. Ralph and Juana were laughing at him. To them, it looked like the touching dawn of youthful romance.

To Sidonia, it looked like the Seventh Circle of Hell. Mere prettiness she could have endured. Lily had that extra quality; the indefinable vitality and magnetism that could turn a plain woman into a siren, and make a pretty one invincible.

It was no longer possible to wrap herself in self-delusion. Her beautiful stepdaughter had committed the ultimate act of war. She had revealed herself as the creature Sidonia had dreaded for years; the woman whose beauty was destined to surpass her own.

'Lovely evening, isn't it?'

'So you keep saying. What has got into you?'

Charlie laughed. 'I don't know.'

'You never notice the weather.'

'Perhaps I feel more poetic than usual.'

'Poetic? Don't be an ape,' Lily said. 'The only poems you know begin "There was a young lady of -".'

'It's you. You're different. You look like the scent of a flower would look, if you could see it.' His face was red. He ran a finger round the inside of his collar. 'I'm rather tight, I'm afraid. Ralph must be getting through that cellar at a rate of knots.'

They were strolling across the dusky sweep of lawn, half-hypnotised by the rhythm of the sea, both aware of a pressing need to redefine their friendship. Sidonia had sent Primrose out with them, but she had slipped away to write to Guy. They had been left to work out the steps of the unfamiliar dance themselves. Lily knew she was about to make an enormous discovery. Charlie had lost his rattle, and was disturbingly quiet. He did not look at her often, but when he did, there was a new intensity – as if he were trying to fathom some deep mystery.

'What flying fiends Daddy and Sidonia will be in the morning,' Lily said, 'when they wake up to massive hang-overs and no more drink.'

'The story of the whole war, in a nutshell,' Charlie said. 'You blow everything you've got, because it might be your last hurrah. You don't want to die, without having lived.' He shot her a cautious, appraising glance. 'It reminds me of running for the coast, in France. The poor old frogs poured their booze down us, to stop the Germans getting it.'

'How close were the Germans?'

'We could practically feel their hot breath on the backs of our necks,' Charlie said. 'I made my chaps leave our heavy guns behind, simply standing in the road. If I hadn't, I wouldn't be here now.'

'I'm glad you are.' Lily felt tender towards Charlie, when he let her catch a rare glimpse of his former, soldierly self. He became miles less silly, and she wished he would do it more often.

'The high-ups wouldn't necessarily agree,' he said. 'Given a choice, they might have decided to save fewer men and more artillery. Men are cheaper.'

'Oh, Charlie – nobody thinks like that!'

He laughed again, but in a new, rueful way. 'Oh, Lily. It's exactly how everybody thinks now. We're not even trying to win any more. Just trying not to lose too soon.'

'Is it really as bad as that?'

'The new Germans aren't like Ralph's Germans. They're too below-the-belt for words. If you'd seen –' he made a curious grimace, to force back his smile. 'Long may your innocence remain.'

The twilight was white and grey, and full of strange, floating shadows. As the colours of the flowers faded, their scents were almost shockingly vivid. The assorted rose-trees under the verandah, lately taken in hand by Primrose, poured sweetness into the warm, ghostly evening.

Charlie, without the usual daft leer and endless stream of

inanities, made Lily feel she was being led away into a new country.

She wanted to hold the mood. 'How soon after you left the guns were you wounded?'

'I didn't get hit till we were on the beach. If I'd got it on the road, I'd have made my boys leave me behind too. I had it all worked out.'

'Really?'

His voice had entirely lost its tiresome, bantering tone. 'Absolutely. I know such self-sacrifice doesn't sound much like Charles Despard. But he was an officer in those days. And that's what officers are for.'

'I didn't mean –'

He grinned at her, with genuine affection. 'Yes, you did. And you're perfectly right. I don't speak that language any more. The only good thing about a war is the way it can make a fearful shit into something like a gentleman.'

She put her hand into the crook of his bad arm. She had never touched it before. It had an unnatural heaviness and flaccidity. 'You sound like Daddy.'

'I daresay. Ralph and I come out of the same factory. We can't do decency, unless there's a large and bloody conflict.'

'Do you miss it?'

He noticed her hand on his sleeve, and frowned down at it, as if afraid of frightening it away. 'That question isn't quite as loopy as it sounds. There are things I miss, as a matter of fact. Apart from my arm, I mean.'

'Such as?'

'My own better nature, I suppose. The sort of – surprised feeling you get, when you do a thing out of pure instinct, and it's a good thing.'

'Your heroic side?'

Charlie chuckled savagely. 'Steady on. I'm talking about the kind of decency I can't seem to do out of uniform. Well, there never seems to be any point. Perhaps I'd find it again, if the Germans overran Despard Court, and started taking liberties with my mother.'

Lily said: 'Don't.'

'Don't what, my sweet?'

'You were going to make a crack about being sorry for any German who tried it.'

'Oh, God. I was, too.'

They climbed the steps up to the verandah. Someone – probably Primrose – had blacked out the drawing room. Behind the thick curtains, the radio could be heard. Henry Hall's orchestra were playing 'When You Wish Upon a Star'. Charlie steered Lily towards the unlit library.

'Let's not go in yet.'

'Charlie-boy, you're not a bad sort. I don't know why you go to such trouble to hide it.'

'That's what Mother says. She thinks the Charlie with the ass's head is the false one.'

'So do I.'

'She thinks all my naughty behaviour is a sort of tantrum, because I'm so furious about my arm.' His expression did not change, but Lily was acutely aware of the pain and outrage in his voice. Being crippled had brought him to the edge of despair. I'll never let him irritate me again, she thought.

She asked: 'Would you become good, if it suddenly got better?'

This made him laugh. Hearing him, she was more than ever conscious of a darkness in him, which the idiocy normally masked. 'I expect I'd be a very bad boy indeed. But I'd have an excuse, because I'd be in uniform. It makes such a difference to the way people look at you.'

They stood in expectant silence for a minute or two, listening to the muffled music.

Charlie said: 'Let go of my arm.'

'Am I hurting you? I'm sorry –'

'I want you on my other side. So I can put my good arm around you.'

'Are you making a pass?'

He laughed properly this time. 'For God's sake, give me a chance! I mean, of course I'm making a bit of a pass. You look so smashingly pretty in that dress.'

'Thanks.'

'But it's all so peculiar. Don't rush me.' He ducked round

to her other side. His good arm folded firmly around her ribs, under her breasts. Its strength came as a shock. She felt her heart galloping against it, and became very still.

His grip on her tightened. 'Lily, tell me honestly. Does my rotten arm make me disgusting?'

'No. Your rotten manners do that.'

'Seriously.' His voice was very low. He turned her to face him, bending his head towards her upturned face. 'I can't look at it myself. Sometimes, when I catch my reflection, I feel absolutely sick.'

'But that's so silly!'

'You've never seen it. I only ever leave it uncovered in the bath. When a woman falls for what she thinks is me, she – I daren't show her what a freak I am underneath.'

Lily, wary of rushing in too far, chose her words carefully. 'Any woman who loves you properly will just love all of you. She won't give a damn about your arm.'

He was smiling. 'You know so much about it, of course.'

'I promise you, if she really loved you, all sorts of bits could drop off and she wouldn't care.'

'How strange, to hear little Lily talking about love. Have you ever been in love?'

The nearness of his blue eyes made her slightly giddy. 'Of course not. How about you?'

His eyes chilled – the question did not please him. 'Me? Either dozens of times, or never.'

'Never, then, if you don't know.'

'Lily, darling,' he placed his good hand on her shoulder. 'Tell me – would you like me just the same, if another bit dropped off?'

'Depends on the bit.'

'Would you? Would you?'

She longed to comfort him. 'Yes. Of course.'

He took a step back and lifted his dead left hand – upon which he still stubbornly wore his watch – out of his pocket. The arm bumped and dangled awkwardly. The hand was unnaturally smooth and newborn, like a waxy new bud on a gardenia. The whole dead limb was a grotesque contrast to the sinewy energy of the rest of him.

'Revolting, isn't it?' He said it with a boastful leer, which did not reach his eyes.

Lily had never felt so fond of him. 'It's fine. No girl in the world would turn you down because of it.'

'Liar.' He slipped the bad hand back into his pocket, then lit a cigarette. He used his good arm with lightning dexterity. 'I'm sick of being told it's nothing, and not to make a fuss. People think a left arm doesn't matter. It's not a right arm. Or a leg, or an eye. But they haven't been saddled with their own dead flesh – it's like carrying a part of your own corpse.'

'Charlie –'

'I can't swim. Can't drive my own car. Can't ride a horse. I have to learn all the cripple's dodges. And it doesn't get any easier. I'll never get used to not being a whole man.'

As if he could suck wholeness from her, he kissed her frenziedly on the lips, thrusting his tongue into her mouth.

Behind them, in the library window, there was a juddering, rheumy gasp, which escalated into an eldritch screech of fury.

'You shit! You lying, cheating shit!'

They sprang apart. Sidonia bounced into the space between them, and dealt them each a ringing slap on the cheek. She looked bleached and haggard. Her swollen eye, faded to olive and mauve, seemed to throb painfully.

Lily held her stinging cheek. Sidonia had been too angry to hurt her, but the shock made her faint and giddy. Nobody had ever hit her before. She clutched at the railing of the verandah, frozen by the unreality of it all.

The new, sweet Charlie simply vanished. His face closed and coarsened. He grabbed Sidonia's wrist. 'Go away.'

'Like hell I will. How dare you let that little bitch eat your face off?'

'She doesn't find my arm disgusting. She touched it. She says no nice girl would turn away from me – wasn't it sweet of her? If you'd spied just a little bit longer, you'd have heard me propose to her.'

'You're lying!'

'She'd make a perfect wife. She's not a filthy old whore like you.'

202

'Try living without me – you'll be begging for it after a day. And Ralph – poor Ralph – I shall have to confess, if you're about to marry his daughter – ow!'

Charlie shook her violently. His voice was a whisper, strained through layers of anger. 'Breathe one word to Ralph and I'll black your other eye!'

He hurled her away, so hard that she staggered back against the wall. He shot one glance – unrecognisably corrosive and calculating – at Lily, and stumbled back into the house.

Sidonia, massaging her wrist, stared after him. Then she went absolutely still, and focused narrowly on Lily.

For a moment, not throwing up in front of her stepmother took all Lily's concentration.

Eventually, she said – in a voice that came out in a humiliating croak – 'I don't know why I'm surprised. I must look pretty stupid.'

Sidonia arched her eyebrows. She was horribly calm, and nakedly, brazenly hostile. 'You do. I'm sure your father's guessed.'

'He can't – he doesn't – I'm sure he doesn't know.'

'Are you? Charlie on heat is hard to overlook. Remember the day you first brought him into the kitchen? We didn't need words. He took me into the downstairs lav, and fucked me sublimely, standing up against the basin.'

Lily whipped round, just in time to save the front of her dress. A jet of vomit hit the roses, with a disgusting wet splatter. Sidonia watched, beady as a cobra, while she wiped a drizzle of rancid sweat from her upper lip.

'You're disgusted,' she observed unnecessarily. 'Why? You didn't get up to anything with Charlie, but you were dying for it. God knows how you've managed to hold on to your virginity all this time.'

Sidonia lit a cigarette. She was bizarrely matter-of-fact; even conversational. 'I was beastly to you about those little jaunts to the pictures, wasn't I?'

'Yes.'

'It was because I couldn't believe you weren't out screwing Charlie on the sly.' This was not an apology. 'I

203

should have known you're the type who thinks love is a delicate bloom, needing nurture for years. It isn't. If you're not doing it as soon as you clap eyes on each other, it's not love. You'll learn - though not on Charlie.'

Lily stared at her, willing herself to beat off a feeling that she was drowning in unreality. She could not explain to Sidonia – would have died first – that what had really sickened her was the flash of the Charlie Despard beneath the layers of crassness and misery. The real Charlie, she now saw, was the warped, nasty creature who dealt out black eyes and coupled standing up in the downstairs lav. She was angry with herself, falling for skin-deep, throwaway decency because it had come with a pair of fine blue eyes.

Sidonia's views on love, however, did not surprise her at all. Ralph must be made to see exactly what he had married. Since his marriage, he had plummeted disastrously in Lily's estimation. She had to work hard, to excuse his amazing silliness, but she still clung to a stubborn belief in his essential goodness. The sweet, dashing, indulgent young father of her childhood lived on in her memory. Once his life was purged of Sidonia, she was sure he would return.

Sidonia said, in a voice curiously expressionless, 'It can't go on, you know. Let us both be practical and honest, Lily. You are spoiling my life. I don't want you in this house.'

The sheer impertinence of this gave Lily courage. 'I'm going to tell my father.'

Sidonia shrugged. 'Suit yourself.'

'I hate telling tales, but I won't stand by while you make him look ridiculous.'

'Oh, God. I suppose I ought to be sorry for you.'

'Don't bother.' Lily had seen her stepmother with the hard rind of artifice torn away. One sight of the monster underneath would surely be enough to shock Ralph back into his depleted senses. She marched into the house.

I've been sparing his feelings for far too long, she thought.

In the hall, she caught the back of Charlie, making a stormy exit. He slammed the door behind him, and she wondered, fleetingly, how he proposed to get home.

Primrose and Isobel were in the drawing room. Primrose was knitting something khaki, Isobel was reading the *Radio Times*. They both glanced up, but Lily was already turning wordlessly away.

She went upstairs, acutely aware of the transformation of her house, since the Enemy Occupation. The taste and smell of nausea seemed to hang over the whole place. Outside the door of Ralph's room, she paused, to dredge up a morsel of compassion for him, then walked in without knocking.

Ralph was standing in front of the curtained window. His trousers were round his ankles. Juana knelt at his feet, holding a glass of something in one hand, and sucking vigorously at his groin.

⧫◈⧫

Primrose was worried. Not usually sensitive to fine changes of atmosphere, she could not miss this one. Isobel said her blood was creeping with foreboding and, for once, Primrose understood what she meant. Charlie had left, in a theatrical rage. Sidonia had drifted in from the house barefoot and trailing flowers; always a bad sign. Where was Lily?

'There you are,' Sidonia said, when Juana came into the room and turned up the wireless.

'Where did you think I'd be?'

'Have you seen Ralphie?'

'No.'

Primrose hurried out, ready with an excuse about making coffee if anyone asked. No one did. The feeling of general wrongness intensified. Hesitantly, she climbed the stairs.

At the end of the passage, light spilled from the open door of Lily's room. Primrose crept towards it, and blurted out:

'Oh, God!'

'Come in,' Lily said. 'Shut the door.'

Shaking, Primrose obeyed.

A suitcase gaped on the bed, spewing a tangle of vests and stockings. Lily was very pale, her dark eyes huge in her chalky skin. She was also very angry – at the still stage of anger, absorbed right into the marrow, so that the surface had a ghastly calm.

'What're you doing?'

'Oh, Primrose, honestly. What does it bloody well look like?'

'Is it – Mummy?'

The question was pathetic. For a second, the black eyes snapped out a spark of humour. 'I know you'd love me to say it's not because of Sidonia. It's not directly, but all the horrible things that happen in this house come from her. If you start defending her, I'll sock you.'

'But what did she do?'

'I'm not going to tell you. It's my father, too. I've seen what he really is –' her lips trembled with disgust, 'and I can't stay here.'

'Please –'

'He doesn't want me,' Lily said.

'No, I'm sure –'

'He told me. All right? I gave him a choice between her or me, and he chose her. So I'm leaving. I should have done it months ago, only I've been too dumb to see what's going on.'

'What?' Primrose begged tearfully.

Lily checked herself, remembering that Primrose was even dumber. 'I can't live in this place,' she said. 'It's wrong, and wicked, and hard-hearted – and if you've any sense, you'll escape too.'

Primrose stared helplessly, while Lily marched about the room, snatching books and photographs, apparently at random, and hurling them into the case. She had never seen Lily's room before. It was the domain of a cherished child, with painted furniture, cheerful chintz and pictures of boats and horses.

Lily picked up a photograph, in a silver frame, of herself as a little girl, beside her handsome young father. 'I loved him such a lot,' she said. 'I thought he was just marvellous, the bloody cat's pyjamas.' She dropped the photograph. 'I wish I could cry, but this doesn't seem like my house any more. It looks the same, and it's not.'

'It is your house.' Primrose was frightened. 'We're the ones who should leave.'

'It's my father's house,' Lily said, her voice hot and hard with contempt. 'I never want to see it, or him, again.'

She selected two of the photographs; a snap of herself, between Tufton and Gladys, and a wistful, sepia portrait of a young girl. Lily briefly tilted this towards Primrose, before stowing it in her suitcase. 'My mother.'

'Oh.'

'It's odd – I'm thinking about her as if she were real, and I've never done that before. She's always seemed like someone in a story.'

'Lily –'

'Don't ask me!'

'Can't something be done?'

'I've made up my mind,' Lily said. 'There isn't any other way. And if you run to my father or your mother, they won't lift a finger to keep me here.'

Not daring to ask again, Primrose whispered: 'I just wish I understood.'

'I hope you never do.' Lily closed the shabby leather case, with its gaudy, faded stickers of Cap Ferrat, and snapped the clasps. Over her velvet dress, she pulled on a light raincoat. She picked up the case, wincing slightly at its weight. Then she put it down on the floor beside her, and looked levelly at Primrose.

'None of this is your fault. Or Isobel's. In case you think it is.'

'Thank you.' Primrose's eyes filled with tears.

'When I know where I'm going, I'll probably tell Gladys. And she'll assure any interested party I'm safe – if I am.'

'But where will you go?'

'No idea,' Lily said.

'Aren't you terrified?'

Lily considered this. 'I don't think so. I expect I'll find a job pretty easily – maybe in a factory. Or maybe I'll join the Forces.'

Two tears slipped down Primrose's pink cheeks. 'I wish I could make you stay. I – we'll miss you.'

'So long, Primrose. I think I'll miss you, too. Send my best to Guy.'

Impulsively, Primrose kissed Lily's cheek. 'Good luck.'

For the first time, Lily's righteous determination

207

wavered. Tears rushed to her eyes. She threw her arms around Primrose. They embraced. Lily drew away, and hefted her suitcase out of the room.

At the door to the back staircase, she turned once, smiled and waved, and was gone.

Primrose was left, long after her footsteps had died away down the uncarpeted stairs, gazing at the space where Lily had been, as if expecting to see a picture of her printed on the air.

Chapter Thirteen

And that was how Lily-Josephine rode away into the realm of myths and shadows, never to be seen at the Prospect again. Primrose and Isobel, frozen by Sidonia's fury, had no idea where she had gone and did not dare to ask.

Gladys, at first, was no wiser. She was roused, in the dawn of the next morning, by Arthur. Red and agitated, he pushed an envelope into her hand.

'She's pinched it – my van – I told her I was selling the bloody thing, and she ups and pinches it!'

Peter was teething, and had kept Gladys awake into the small hours. Reeling and stupid from lack of sleep, she had to read the note several times, before she could take it in.

'Dear Gladys, I have run away. Please don't ask why, but I am never going back. When I am settled, I will let you know. The money is for Arthur, I hope it's enough. All my love, Lily.'

Enclosed was a cheque for twenty pounds. Gladys handed it to Arthur. 'Well, you've got yourself a bargain.'

'I think we should call the police.'

'Certainly not,' Gladys said sharply. 'It won't do a bit of good, if she's made up her mind – you know her. She says she'll be in touch, so we'll just wait.'

'But where will she go? Aren't you worried?'

'I'm worried sick! But I tell you, Arthur, she'll have her reasons. I don't know what's been happening up at the house, but if you ask me, she's well out of it. I'm almost glad.'

The petrol ran out, after Lily had charged through silent lanes, hell-for-leather, for nearly an hour. Arthur's moul-dering Wolsely wheezed to a halt on a rutted, unmade road between high hedgerows.

Lily listened to the engine whispering away into profound rural quiet. Reality began to drip into her ecstasy of outrage. She had thought only of putting as many miles as possible between herself and that final, ghastly betrayal. Now she was alone, in the middle of nowhere. It was a quarter past ten – early, if you felt you had lived a dozen lives since dressing for dinner, but too late to find proper shelter.

A place to lay my head, she thought. A barn, or a byre. She could not remember having passed any human habitation for ages. And even if she found a cottage, she was not sure she could simply knock on the door and demand a bed, as fleeing Princesses did in fairy tales. This, as she was rapidly admitting to herself, was unvarnished real life.

For one moment, the courage oozed out of her, and she was acutely conscious of her loneliness and vulnerability. But this was no way to begin an adventure. The rest of her life lay before her. She was young and strong, and one night in a ditch would not kill her. Tomorrow, she would find petrol, a town, a telephone. Perhaps a job. She could sleep in the van.

Except that she was too energised and excited to sleep. Afterwards, Lily would say that fate, or providence, had guided her to this exact place. And she would wonder, had she known, even then, that she had come home?

There was no doubt that she was remarkably calm, and remarkably certain about what to do next. She recalled a signpost, a little way back, and climbed down from the van. The night was beautifully mild, with a soft, velvet breeze. The high hedges were full of wild lime, mallow and dog roses. Through the first opening, she felt rather than saw that the surrounding fields were wilder than the fat country she had left behind.

There was a full moon, low-hanging and veined with orange. By its light, she read the single word on the dilapidated post: RANDALLS.

A long path, fringed with harebells and poppies, sloped down into a hollow. And in the hollow, at the edge of a black copse, lay the jumbled outline of the house. Her heart thudding, almost with anticipation – but of what? – she made her way round to the side of the house. She trod on stones now, pushed awry by roots of trees and bursting oozes of moss.

When all of England was supposed to lie in darkness, one dim light burned, in a small window near the ground. The wood of the back door was warped and veined with age; its iron bands scabbed with centuries of paint.

Lily thumped the iron knocker, with an absurd desire to call something like: 'I'm here!', as if the people inside had been expecting her. But the sound echoed flatly inside the house, and died away into nothing. No voices or footsteps, or even the special kind of living silence that comes from people asleep. The only noises were the callings and rustlings of night animals, busy in the lapping vegetation.

She lifted the latch and pushed open the door. A smell rushed out to greet her. Lily knew that houses have smells, as people have souls. This was the scent of a very old house – a compound of woodsmoke, mould, lavender and damp, underlaid with something rank and feral. Like a musty game-larder, crossed with an unswept stable, and faintly tinged with carbolic. Not a pleasant smell, exactly. But familiar, in a way Lily could not define.

Dirty yellow light bled from an open door ahead of her, onto worn stone flags. She was in a hall. At her left hand, a grandfather clock – very old, its face scarred and faded, but with a stubborn, querulous tick. At her right hand, a tall gun cabinet, squeezed up against the low ceiling as if bearing the weight of the entire house. In the moonlight, which stole in beside her like a friend, she saw a heap of boots on the floor. Some of leather, some of rubber. Some with new red mud on them, barely dried; some draped in cobwebs, as if taken from a Pharaoh's tomb. There were nets, too, and a bundle of tweed and mackintosh which smelt of tobacco, sweat, moths, and wet soil.

And Men. Lily did not have to be Sherlock Holmes to know she had come to a house of men. Her skin felt alien here, as if her femininity was an invasion, displacing the atmosphere. She went to the open door, and saw a grubby oil lamp standing in a deeply recessed window.

In a matter of seconds, she took in the features of a sprawling, shadowed kitchen, its low ceiling criss-crossed with blackened beams.

Then something flew at her out of the shadows, with a long, hissing screech, swooped over her head and dived to the floor behind her.

The shock and terror seemed to make the floor fall away under her feet. Hearing hideous scutterings and gulpings, Lily whisked round – and saw a huge owl.

'Oh God! She could have cried with relief. 'God!'

Its head revolved, to take her in. From its ivory bill, curved like a scimitar, protruded the struggling legs and tail of a tiny brown mouse. The eyes of the owl, black and beady in its pale, heart-shaped face, surveyed her critically. A snap, an irritable jerk of the head, and the mouse was gone.

Lily had only begun to get over the turn it had given her, when something whirred down to the floor, and ran close to her foot. Another owl – a little one, with a comical, determined set to its head, scurrying as if on casters.

Amazement and intrigue taking the place of fear, Lily turned up the oil lamp, and found that the kitchen was full of bloody owls. Eyes gleamed at her, sleepy and disapproving, from the chimneypiece, from the shelves of the dresser, from the disused bread oven beside the range. From the scullery, which opened out of the kitchen. From the sill of the scullery window.

The unidentifiable part of the smell was now explained – owls. A house of men and owls. Lily placed the lamp in the middle of the huge kitchen table. She had started to enjoy herself. Never having met owls at close quarters, or in such numbers, she had not been given much time to make up her mind about them – but she decided she liked them. She liked the scholarly primness of their faces, and their air of crabbed experience. Evidently well used to the company of humans, they accepted her with sober cordiality.

Lily now took a proper look around the room. It was the strangest room she had ever seen, outside a dream. And God, it was untidy. You could blame the owls for the shiny pellets, with regurgitated scraps of feather or bone horridly visible, that littered the stone floor.

But those innocent creatures could not be held responsible for the ragged underwear drying on the range. Or the teetering piles of filthy saucepans, or the grey haze of cobwebs around the pewter candlesticks on the chimneypiece. She saw that anything not in constant use here was lashed down with cobwebs, and everything in constant use was dirty.

In the scullery sink, she found dirty plates, knives and forks. Also chipped teacups (no saucers) and bleared glass tumblers. There were seven chairs grouped round the table, and a row of pewter tankards on the top shelf of the dresser.

Of course, she thought of Snow White, and of course, she smiled. But her amusement had an edge of bitterness. She had seen the film of *Snow White* with Charlie – once very nearly her handsome Prince. Her Bonnie Prince Charlie, whose love turned out to be worth so little.

As she automatically grappled in the scullery for sink-soap, bucket and toothless broom, she found herself wondering about Snow White's father. He was the King. Didn't he object to the Queen's treatment of his daughter? Did he notice she was no longer in the castle? Did he mourn, when his evil but beautiful wife told him Snow White was dead?

The rage returned. Two small owls rose in alarm, when Lily whipped up a tempest of dust with the broom. Snow White's father was obviously as besotted and enslaved as Ralph. Weak, self-indulgent, disgusting. The goody-goody cartoon Snow White probably forgave the King – well, there was the difference between art and life. Lily would never forgive Ralph. She could not stop herself loving him, and that love gave her terrible pain. But she despised him. He had shown her that he had sunk to Sidonia's level, and that this was his true level. He was as happy with his new position as a pig in muck.

Lily cleaned like a fury, crying as she swept and scrubbed and scoured. Eventually, the hard labour and the owls brought her back to something like cheerfulness. The two small owls were uncannily tame, and perched companionably on the edge of the bucket when she washed the floor. To her delight, she found a nest of owlets – little grey balls of down – inside the old bread oven.

The atmosphere of the house embraced her; benign and safe. She dusted the chimneypiece, washed the crockery, wrestled the heap of shabby male garments into a folded pile. She trimmed the lamp (like the wise virgin she was), stoked the embers in the range, and sat down at the table to wait. Nobody came. Slowly, she collapsed with her head upon her folded arms and fell asleep.

She dreamed of the seven dwarfs, singing as they trudged home. They crashed into their clean kitchen, and growled at her in deep, threatening voices. She tried to explain that she was not a monster – they must see this, or they would kill her by mistake, and be sorry.

A hand was shaking her shoulder. Lily snapped back to consciousness. A bandaged face, with burning, vengeful eyes, stared down at her. Through a slit in the bandages, it shouted: 'Who the hell are you?'

PART FOUR

Chapter One

1980

◆◇◆

Gatwick was teeming with the youth of Ireland, away home for Christmas. They skidded across the vast expanses of shiny floor, eyes unfocused with seasonal cheer, bags clinking with duty-frees. Sophie envied them. She was dreading the week ahead. It was mean of her, when they had so much to celebrate. Isobel's inheritance, the Leary painting, had been valued at nearly half a million pounds. Primrose had found her dream cottage, on the edge of Exmoor, and the great Patrick Randall was helping her design the garden. But these were not the headlines.

The main topic for discussion would be Sophie. She and Gus had now dragged themselves to the point of a legal separation. They had sold the Islington place very profitably, and Sophie had bought a flat in Crouch End with her share. She had not seen her parents since the upheaval. They were obviously dying to make long funeral orations over the corpse of her marriage.

She glanced at her watch. Her plane – a superannuated Sopwith Camel full of nuns – did not depart for another hour. It was the cheapest flight to Cork you could get, short of them actually paying you. Sophie was skint again. The bath salts (Mum and Primrose) and socks (Dad) she had just purchased had made a serious dent in her cash. One coffee and one croissant would have to last her a long time.

She settled at one of the inadequate round tables by the coffee stall, thinking that not being married made her feel suddenly years younger. It was rather like being a student again – living alone, eating rubbish, always skint. She was rediscovering the hormonal illiteracy of adolescence, too – not knowing the difference between sexual desire and love. Thinking that if this was sex, you were a wanton slut; and if it was love, you were dying of it.

Until that wretched dinner last Wednesday, her crush on Octavius had been perfectly manageable. They had been friends, slowly and cautiously progressing towards something deeper. Or so she had assumed. Sophie moodily spooned up the froth of her cappuccino, mulling over the oddness of Octavius. He hated his good fortune. The business of Sidonia's will had thrown him into a savage depression, and he became intensely prickly when she tried to find out the reason. Questions about his family were met with stubborn muteness.

Bruno and Gerda, at least, seemed to be acceptable. Octavius had taken refuge with them after trashing his car. He spent most of his time in his room, working on a book about forestry. He emerged to take Sophie out to lunch. She had eaten so many elegant London lunches, at his expense, that she had put on enough weight to stay inside her best clothes.

It had always been clear to Sophie that Octavius fancied her. Let's be frank, she thought; we want each other so desperately, we can barely swallow.

Even allowing for the fact that they were both damaged relics of failed marriages, they ought to have made more progress by now. When they met or parted, she got one grave kiss on the cheek. It would set them both quaking for twenty minutes afterwards. Once, their lips had accidentally brushed, and thrown the pair of them into scarlet-faced, stammering turmoil.

Then the die had been cast and the Rubicon crossed, when Octavius blurted out his invitation to dinner. At last, after all those simmering lunches, a compromising dinner which could mean only One Thing.

Sophie tidied her bare flat, picked the tampons off her dressing table and put new sheets on her bed. She spent money she did not have on a clinging dress of dark red velvet. They dined at L'Escargot, in Greek Street. They shared a taxi to Sophie's flat, silent and trembling with anticipation.

Octavius folded her into a long kiss, the moment they

were through the door. He kissed and kissed her. Sophie's knees turned to water; her vagina swelled and moistened. His tongue parted her lips, and she felt it as a dagger-thrust. She was faint with the longing to have him inside her.

He pulled away, breathing hard. 'Sorry, I can't. Sorry. I've got to go.'

And to her utter amazement, he had dashed out of the flat. With a highly noticeable erection, which puzzled her more than ever. What was he fighting? The next day, he had sent a dozen roses to her office, with a dreadful florist's 'Sorry' card attached.

Sophie had felt humiliated, and somehow responsible. Obviously, he found her physically attractive. Perhaps there was something in her personality, which made his mind recoil.

She looked at her watch again. Still ages to wait. She joined the long, noisy queue at the stall, to squander the last of her cash on another cup of coffee.

'Sophie! Thank God – I thought I'd missed you.'

She dropped her handbag, scattering her money. Octavius was beside her. He kissed her cheek, then dived for the dancing, spinning coins. Some had rolled a surprising distance, and while he chased them, Sophie had time to collect herself.

'Octavius, what on earth are you doing here? Where are you going?'

He put the pile of money into her hand. 'Going?'

'I mean, where are you flying to?'

'Ah.' He was solemn. 'I see. Well, I'm not flying anywhere.'

'But this is an airport.'

He pulled her out of the queue. 'I came to fetch you. I don't want you to go to Ireland.'

Sophie felt as if a hot water bottle had been placed inside her ribcage, making her glow all over. Oh please, God, don't let me cry. This was the most wonderfully romantic thing anyone had ever done for her. 'I have to. I promised my parents.'

'I know. I promised my family, too. I'm supposed to be on

219

a train to Exeter. We'll just have to phone home and say we're not coming.'

'Don't be silly.'

'Do you want to go to Ireland? I won't stop you if you really want to.'

She smiled. 'You know I don't.'

'I've booked us into a hotel near Oxford. I'm afraid it's one of those special Christmas breaks, and there'll be a certain amount of unavoidable business with funny hats and carols. But we can hide. Will you come?'

Sophie was suddenly light and giddy with happiness. 'Like a shot.'

Briefly, he squeezed her arm. 'I'll hire a car, though you'll have to drive it, because I'm still banned.' He put out his hand, as if to squeeze her arm again, then withdrew it awkwardly and smiled. 'I'm really sorry about the other night. I need a chance to make it up to you.'

<><><>

The hired Golf was a sweetheart to drive, incomparably better than Sophie's late, unlamented 2CV. She felt she was handling it with elegance and panache. She had found Radio Three, which was pouring out a silver tenor voice – as lovely and effortless as Keats' nightingale, she thought; singing of summer with full-throated ease. By rushing to Gatwick to fetch her, Octavius had finally, finally acknowledged that the pair of them had arrived at the state called Love.

And this sense of freedom and glamour, that came from being alone with the one right person in the world, was happiness. Only now did she realise how long she had lived without it. She began to sing along with the radio:

'*Im wunderschönen monat Mai – als alle knospe sprangen – der ist, in meine hertzen –*'

Octavius watched her, amused. 'What is that?'

'One of Schumann's *Dichterliebe* – sorry, I was murdering it. It's meant to be very soft and poignant.'

'Do you know what it means?'

'*Natürlich*. I'm half-German, for godsake.'

'So you are. I keep forgetting.'

'Because you want to, I daresay,' Sophie said. 'It's not a

220

popular nationality.'

Disconcertingly, Octavius did not contradict her. After a silence, he said: 'I suppose not. But surely that's all in the past. People don't still hate Germans on principle.'

Sophie had heard this many times. Without rancour, but firmly, she said: 'Deep down they do. And it really is difficult, when you meet Gerda and she's got numbers on her arm from Buchenwald.'

'Do you take responsibility for that?'

'Not exactly.' She frowned, grappling for the words. 'It just sort of hangs about in the air, like a smell. And you'd be amazed how many people start talking about Nazis when they hear. Or they make jokes, and quote that episode of *Fawlty Towers* – "I mentioned it once, but I think I got away with it".'

Octavius observed her seriously, then smiled. 'Tell me what the song means.'

She took her eyes off the road, just long enough to see the glow of the gold flecks in his hazel eyes. At this stage, she no longer had to defend herself against the effects of his beauty. 'It's about the buds bursting in May, and love blossoming in people's hearts.'

'Pretty,' said Octavius.

She laughed. 'Shut up. I'm not doing it justice.'

He took a bag of toffees from the glove compartment. 'How did your phone call go?'

Like prisoners, they had each been allowed one call home before they left.

'I was lucky,' Sophie said. 'I got Dad. I could hear Mum and Primrose making a fuss in the background, but Dad just gave me a mild ticking-off and wished me merry Christmas. You?'

His smile was still there, but the light had died out of his face, as it always did when he talked about his family. 'I was quite lucky, too. In that I got Ilse.' Ilse was his cousin, daughter of Bruno and Gerda. 'I think she was only too relieved I was bunking off. There'll be fewer fights without me.'

Sophie longed to know about the fights, but knew that

221

asking about them would have been a very bad conversational move indeed.

'Of course,' he went on, 'it was worse when I brought Caroline. None of them liked her. Maybe that's why she decided Christmas was the time to dump me.'

'God, she didn't!' Sophie was fascinated. He had never talked to her about his wife. His face had cleared, which showed – intriguingly – that she was not such a sore subject as his family.

He was almost cheerful. 'Wasn't it awful? On a par with leaving a puppy on the hard shoulder. I crawled home to the farm, and they found me sobbing on the doorstep.'

'Poor you,' Sophie said. 'You get tired of all that crying, though, eventually. Didn't you find?'

'Yes. I wouldn't like to think I'd got harder hearted. But where that particular subject was concerned, I just ran out of tears. I nearly bloody drowned in them. Fancy a toffee?'

'No thanks. I like having teeth.'

He unwrapped one, and bit into it. 'Gerda took me to the Tate Gallery yesterday. She wanted me to see the Leary painting.'

'Ah, my grandmother in the flesh – and in so much of it. What did you think?'

Sophie had tossed the remark out lightly, expecting him to make a joke of it.

But Octavius, after a long pause, said: 'She's beautiful. And she looks like you.'

Instantly, the atmosphere inside the car changed. They both tensed and stiffened, suddenly acutely aware of their journey's purpose.

For the rest of the drive, Octavius had the air of a man nerving himself for a terrible ordeal – not exactly flattering to Sophie, or conducive to romance. She began to feel oppressed, and to wish there was some way she could get out of it. If he failed this time, there would be no escape. They would be stuck together in a country hotel, wearing the failure around their necks like an albatross.

They arrived in the indigo dusk of a clear winter's afternoon, at a charming seventeenth-century manor house. One of the owners, a tweedy middle-aged lady with a lacquered helmet of grey hair, was on the steps to meet them. A labrador frisked picturesquely at her heels, and the hall was full of conspicuous antiques. Sophie, roasting in front of an aggressive log fire, realised where she was. Oakeshott Hall was one of those places you read about in *Vogue*. It had a famous chef, a matchless cellar, and it cost a fortune. Sophie thanked Providence that she had packed her red velvet dress.

The woman showed them to a large, white-panelled bedroom, dominated – rather embarrassingly, in the circumstances – by a large four-poster bed. Another log fire crackled in the fireplace. There was a blinding smell of pot-pourri. Through an open door, a bathroom could be seen, gleaming white and strewn with tiny, exquisite soaps and sewing-kits. Half a bottle of champagne was politely cooling in an ice-bucket. In the exact centre of each pillow reposed a packet of Bendicks Sporting and Military Chocolate.

'Dinner is at eight,' the woman said. 'Shall I send up some tea?'

Octavius, visibly relieved, said: 'Yes.'

'Just a pot, or the full afternoon tea?'

Sophie realised, in a rush, that she was ravenous, and would never last till eight. 'Afternoon tea, please.'

When they were alone – standing on opposite sides of the room, both as far as possible from the bed – she said: 'Hope you don't mind. It probably costs the earth.'

'Of course I don't mind.' Octavius said it testily, and she cursed herself for mentioning money.

He picked up the bottle of champagne, and suddenly grinned at her. 'Bloody perfect, isn't it? See if there's a Sporting and Military condom under the chocolate.'

The tension between them snapped. They both howled with laughter, and were still giggling when the waiter arrived with their tea. They ate egg-and-cress sandwiches and mince pies lying companionably on the bed, fully clothed. When they had finished, Octavius opened the champagne.

'Merry Christmas.' He clinked their glasses together, adding: 'And did you ever see flutier champagne flutes? My God, it's like drinking out of a test tube.'

'Merry Christmas,' Sophie said. 'This is heaven.'

He rolled closer, so she could feel the heat striking out of his body. He propped himself on one elbow, and looked down into her face with an expression that made her want to cry. 'I'm going to say it now, in case you have any reason to doubt it later on. Or – or ever. I love you.'

'Thank God for that,' Sophie said. 'I thought it was just me, and I was going batty.'

What reason could there be to doubt him? They kissed again, for a long time. They shed their clothes, clumsy with physical hunger. It was many, many months since Sophie had had sex, and years since she had done it with anyone but Gus. She had been afraid she had forgotten the language, but discovered that with Octavius, there was no question of doing something wrong. The instructions were written in every cell – compulsory, imperative. His scent was of musk, soap, sap, new grass; so delicious it made her giddy. The orgasm tore from her almost against her will, and she bucked and twitched madly under his thin, long-limbed body.

She would recall, when she thought about it later, that through the chaos and wild relief of coming, she was conscious of a peculiar look on his face – resignation, bordering on despair, as if he had been forced to surrender. As he hurtled unmistakably towards his own orgasm, the expression changed to panic.

He roared: 'No! No!'

His eyes scrunched, as if he were in severe pain. He rolled off Sophie and clapped his hands across his forehead. His body jack-knifed into a foetal curl, and he began to moan like an animal in a trap.

'Octavius?' Sophie crash-landed back to earth, and sat up, trying to subdue the crazed thumping of her heart. He really was in severe pain. She was frightened. 'What is it?'

Between moans, which he was trying to muffle in a pillow, Octavius gasped: 'Headache – migraine –'

'What can I do? Should I call someone?'

She watched – feeling particularly stupid, naked and helpless – while Octavius staggered off the bed to the gleaming bathroom. She heard him retching, as if turning inside-out from the soles of his feet.

This should have been a nightmare, but Sophie found herself unexpectedly confident. She had given herself permission to be in love, so she was allowed to express tenderness, compassion, protectiveness, without fear of being thought possessive or grasping.

She pulled her old towelling dressing gown out of her bag and followed Octavius into the bathroom. He lay on the varnished cork floor, his face pulled into a grimace of agony. When he saw her, he cried: 'Sorry, sorry, sorry, sorry–', sure he had lost her. She felt his despair, and his deep, inexplicable inner hurt.

He was trying to explain. 'Comes suddenly – can't stop it –'

'Octavius, listen, shall I get them to call a doctor?'

'No, God, no! Got some stuff.'

'Where? Your suitcase?'

'Front.'

Sophie rootled through the litter of maps and paperbacks in the front pocket of his scuffed leather suitcase, and found a brown plastic bottle of formidable pills stamped with the name of a Tiverton chemist. 'O. Randall. One as needed. Do not exceed stated dose.' God, they were the size of torpedoes. 'These?'

'Mmmm–'

Sophie opened various cupboards, until she found a genteel bottle of mineral water. She poured a glassful, crouched on the bed beside him, and gently pulled his hands away. He swallowed the enormous pill, and she held him in her arms.

He fell asleep almost immediately. The look of anguish faded from his face, leaving it blank with exhaustion. She held him until one arm went numb. Her bloody stomach was rumbling again. What time was it? Very, very carefully, terrified of waking him, she disentangled herself.

She need not have worried. Octavius's naked body lay across the bed, still as a corpse. Covering him as best she could, she hunted for her watch, found it tangled in her tights, and saw that it was nearly eight o'clock.

Noiselessly, she dressed in her new red velvet – her only decent outfit, because she had packed for a week on a pig farm. She did not want to risk disturbing him by ringing for room service, and would not mind eating alone. She wrote a note to Octavius, in case he woke: 'Gone down to dinner. Call me any time. I love you. S.' This she left on the pillow beside him, where he could not fail to see it if he opened his eyes.

On impulse, just before leaving the room, she looked through his suitcase, to see what books he had brought with him. Conrad, *Heart of Darkness* – not bad. Tolkein, *The Hobbit* – oh God, terrible; worse than woodland mammals. Dickens, *The Pickwick Papers* – brilliant, there was hope for him yet. She added a PS to her note: 'Taken Pickwick,' and stole out of the room.

The dining room was hushed and splendid, each snowy table decorated with a wreath of holly. Extremely smart people, in extremely expensive clothes, murmured over the chink of thin glass, and plates that a breath could break. Sophie, trying not to feel shy, but wishing she had replenished her make-up, endured a Frenchman in a dinner jacket making a mild fuss about her being alone. The owner, now upholstered in velvet, materialised, to express just the right level of concern about Octavius.

She settled Sophie at a sequestered corner table ('So I don't depress anyone,' Sophie thought wryly, 'sitting here with a book,') and provided her with another glass of champagne. Anxious as she was about Octavius, Sophie began to relax. It was shamingly hard to be anxious about anything, in the face of such physical comfort. She ordered wild mushroom risotto and duck, and fell to considering what had happened. This time, her judgement was less clouded with panic.

Octavius, she gathered, was struck down by tearing pain, every time he made love. Fear of that pain explained his fear of sex, which fought constantly with his desire for it. I should be flattered, she thought; he's been through agonies for me. She remembered Bruno telling her that Octavius's wife had said he was sick and needed therapy. So the

226

problem predated the death of his marriage – might even have caused it. There was something else, working away inside Octavius to tear him apart. What?

Eating the exquisite breast of duck, soothed and comforted by the adventures of the Olympian Pickwickians, Sophie decided it had to be his family. She had only met Bruno and Gerda. They were charming, but what the hell were the others like? Surely, if they were as bad as all that, Bruno would have dropped her a few hints?

Sophie ended the meal with a blissful chocolate mousse, downed a cup of coffee, and decided she could return to the room. She took off her shoes to creep in.

Octavius murmured: 'Sophie?'

'You made me jump. I thought you'd be asleep.'

His voice was husky, and his lids were swollen, but it was obvious the pain had lost its edge. 'You've eaten.'

She sat down on the bed, turning the lamp away from his eyes. 'Yes, and it was divine. Mrs Whatsername says she'll send some up, if you're hungry.'

'No. I'd like some tea, though.'

'I'll make some. I found a kettle and a tea tray in one of the cupboards.'

The corners of his mouth lifted in a cautious smile. 'Sophie, you are clever.'

'I tell you, this place has got everything, it's a temple of bodily comforts.'

He looked dazed, then chuckled. 'Glad you like it.'

She was so relieved he felt better, she felt absurdly happy. 'I'm glad you like Mr Pickwick. I can work with a man who likes Dickens.'

'Sorry about the Hobbit.'

'Rome wasn't built in a day.'

'What's wrong with it, anyway?'

'Octavius, I pity you. If you own a poster of Gandalf, I'm afraid it's all off.'

'Sophie, I do love you.'

'It's ridiculously mutual.' She kissed his forehead, and got up to make the tea. Octavius watched her luxuriously. She undressed, put on her dressing gown, and got into bed beside him. They drank tea, limp with contentment.

'Do you honestly feel better?'

'Miles better. And Sophie, I'm so desperately –'

'Don't you dare apologise.' She ran her hand through his hair, as she had often wanted to do. 'I just wish to God you'd told me.'

'I hoped it wouldn't happen this time,' he said.

'Doesn't it always?'

He lowered his eyes. 'Maybe I expected a miracle, because it's you. I really should have known it doesn't have anything to do with my feelings for you. And I do think I should apologise. I've dumped a burden on you now.'

'And dragged me to this penal hell-hole, where I'm forced at gunpoint to drink vintage champagne.'

He smiled. 'You are being nice about this.'

'Rubbish.'

'Now you see why I've taken so long to get to bed with you. I held out until I couldn't bear it any more.'

Love, Sophie discovered, made one furiously hungry. She opened the Sporting chocolate. 'Does it happen every time you come? When you wank, for instance?'

Octavius gave a snort of laughter. 'I don't want to risk it, so I don't wank. I have copious rude dreams, since we're being so frank, and it never happens then.'

She made her voice as gentle as she could. 'Do you know why it happens?'

He frowned unhappily. 'Of course not.' She reached out, and smoothed the lines in his forehead. He sighed. 'I mean I sort of do. I saw a therapist, a friend of Gerda's, who reckoned I was expressing all the unresolved tensions in my family.'

'Why would they express themselves in your sex-life?'

She was stroking his forehead, with hypnotic rhythm. He shut his eyes wearily. After a silence, he said: 'You've seen that picture of them, at Bruno's. The photo of all seven of them, during the war.'

'Yes.'

'My grandfather, my father, my uncles. The whole Randall tribe.'

228

'You've never said – which one is your father?'

Under her fingertips, she felt the hard ridges in his forehead as he frowned. He had the inward look again. 'Guess,' he said.

Sophie tried to recall the group in the photograph. 'God, I don't know.'

Octavius opened his eyes. 'That's just the trouble,' he said. 'Neither do I.'

Chapter Two

1941

——◆◆◆◆◆——

'It's a girl! Stop it, Kit – you'll frighten her.'

The awful bandaged face was pushed aside, and replaced by a smiling one. A young man, wearing disordered khaki battledress and smelling of alcohol, crouched beside her.

Lily rubbed her eyes, and stared over the officer's pips on his shoulder, trying to marshal her stunned senses. This was stranger than a dream. The farmhouse kitchen was full of enormous men. Six fair heads, coloured across the Saxon spectrum from pale flaxen to light brown, and one of iron-grey, brushed the low rafters. Seven pairs of bright eyes stared down at her. A muddy, bedraggled red setter wove around their feet.

'What on earth is she doing here?'

'Bloody hell, the place is clean! Actually clean!'

'What's she done with my pellets?'

One of them whistled, and murmured: 'Either I'm very tight, or she's very gorgeous.'

The smiling one said: 'Hello. Are you all right?'

His hands were on her shoulders, warm through the thin fabric of her dress. Lily shrugged them off, and stood up. The men looked less enormous, but she still had to tilt back her head to address their faces. She made an effort to appear self-possessed. 'I'm terribly sorry, I didn't mean to fall asleep. I was waiting for you.'

The ring of eyes stared and stared. There was a silence, broken only by the grunts and scutterings of the owls, and the hypnotic ticking of the clock in the hall.

She rushed into the speech she had rehearsed, hoping her voice would not wobble. 'My name is Lily-Josephine Gallant. I cleaned up while you were out, because I wanted you to let me stay.' She was conscious of her dust-streaked velvet dress, and how daft it must look beside the practical, dishevelled clothes of the men. 'I've – I've run away from home. I daresay I could find somewhere else. But I thought you might need me.'

There was another spell of silence. The eyes stared on, as if trying to pierce through to the marrow of her bones.

One of the men was much older than the others. His tall figure was straight and vigorous, but his hair was a chaotic puff of dark grey, and a ragged grey moustache meandered across his lined brown face. 'All is explained,' he said. 'I asked the bees, and they have obliged.'

A rumble of suppressed laughter.

'You barmy old coot,' growled Bandages.

'That advertisement has been in the Post Office window so long, it's probably turned yellow,' the barmy old coot said imperturbably. 'I asked the bees as a last resort. I should have done it months ago.'

A young copy of him, with equally chaotic, overgrown hair and thick spectacles, stepped forward. 'Did you come because of the advertisement?'

The spectacles made his eyes naked and huge. There was no mistaking their cordiality. Lily smiled at him. 'No. What were you advertising for?'

The smile made a sensation in the room like a scream. All the young men braced their bodies against it.

'A housekeeper, actually,' said the bespectacled one.

'I don't have to ask if the post is still vacant,' Lily said. 'I've never seen such a mess.'

They all laughed at this. Lily, without knowing why, sensed a sudden sweetness and rightness in the atmosphere, as if the final piece had been slotted into a jigsaw.

Someone said: 'It's incredibly vacant.'

'Then I'll take the job. I have no experience, and no references. Mrs Gladys Tufton, at Lake Farm near Fairy Cross, will tell you I'm all right and won't pinch the silver.'

'We're not fussy,' said the old one. 'God knows, we can't afford to be. If you can find any silver, you're welcome to it.'

'This is ludicrous,' said Bandages. 'What will Bruno's people say, if we let in a total stranger? She might be a spy.'

231

Lily said: 'I'm not a spy.'

'Of course she's not,' the old one said. 'And there are seven of us against one of her. We ought to be able to defend ourselves against this little thing. Start tomorrow. Thirty bob a week. And please don't sweep away the owl-pellets in future.'

'Pa!' Bandages thumped the wall angrily. When Lily looked towards him, he ducked his head away. 'We don't know who the hell she is, or where she comes from. Look at that bloody dress. She's some spoilt little runaway heiress. She doesn't want to work for us – and it's glaringly obvious she doesn't know a damn about housework.'

'I can't know less about it than you do.'

The others roared with laughter. One of them said: 'She's right there.'

The smiling soldier said: 'Bugger off, Kit. If you send her away, I'll kill you.'

Kit banged the wall again, with a strangled shout of frustration, and stalked away to sulk on the long wooden settle. The others took a step nearer. Lily was hemmed in by strange men, all staring their eyes out of their heads. She wondered why this did not alarm her.

Too confused and tired to single out individual faces, she was nevertheless aware that some of these young men were very handsome. She had never seen such handsome men. She addressed herself to the one in spectacles – the least handsome and the kindest-looking. 'Please let me stay.'

'How did you get here?' he asked. 'Where's your luggage?'

'In the lane–'

'Good God!' the old one interrupted, 'that ruined vehicle is yours, is it? Well, it can't stay there.'

'I ran out of petrol,' Lily said.

'Oh. One of the boys can get it in the morning.'

'Where were you going?' the one in spectacles asked. Unlike the others, he seemed more concerned about Lily's welfare than the getting of a housekeeper. 'Is anyone expecting you?'

'Not a soul,' Lily said firmly. 'If you don't want me, I haven't anywhere else to go. Please let me stay.'

The soldier, kindly and rather patronisingly, said: 'But it's a horrid job, Miss Lily-Josephine. We're all so filthy. Those dear little hands of yours don't seem cut out for hard labour.'

'These dear little hands must earn their bread,' said Lily.

The bespectacled one considered her anxiously. 'It is a lot of work, I'm afraid. Even though we're not all here all the time. This is rather a special occasion.'

'That's why we were out when you arrived,' the solder said. 'We were in the pub. The landlord produced a bottle of Scotch, because the seven Randalls are together again.'

The old one drew his head out of the bread oven, oblivious to the fact that his wild hair was now powdered with soot. 'Introductions. I am Gerard Randall. These louts are my sons. This heap of inconvenience is my ancestral pile. I'm a naturalist. The owls are my work. Do they worry you?'

'Not at all. I rather like them.'

The ragged moustache stretched into a broad smile. 'Good. The large ones are *Tyto alba*, the common barn owl. The small chaps are Little Owls – *Athene nocta*. I'm also watching a pair of Tawnies out in the copse, and some Short-Eareds down by the river. But these are the two breeds that consent to live together indoors. You mustn't shut the scullery window, and please don't discourage the mice – they eat them.'

'I saw,' Lily said. 'Whose are the babies?'

'Owlets, please. They belong to my Tytos. I was thrilled to get a second clutch, this late in the season. None of my correspondents will believe it.'

There was a shifting and coughing among the young men. The old one suddenly rounded on them. 'If I can find a way of telling them! That's the tiresome thing about this stupid war.'

The one called Kit said: 'It's not a stupid war.'

'All wars are stupid. The ridiculous things I've had to endure, merely because I receive letters in German!' By the bored, resigned faces around him, Lily guessed this was a well-worn rant.

'For God's sake, Pa!' snapped Kit, 'I wish you'd stop

writing to that fucking Nazi Gauleiter. No wonder they've got you down as a fifth columnist. You practically are one.'

'My owls are above such considerations. My owls symbolise something eternal, important . . .' Pa was working up to a shout.

'Shut up, both of you,' Spectacles cut in, with surprising firmness. 'We've already had the great owl-debate, and it almost got us chucked out of the pub. I think she'd better hear about the humans, don't you?' He indicated Bandages. 'That's Kit, he's the eldest.'

Judging by the youth of the others, Lily placed him in his late twenties. Framed by the grubby stockinette bandage, his large, thickly-lashed hazel eyes looked almost childlike. These hazel eyes were a recurring theme. All the brothers, except the one in spectacles, had them.

'Kit's a Squadron Leader in the RAF,' said Spectacles. 'At least – he's home on sick leave.' He hurried on. 'I'm Bruno, Number Two. I'm too blind for the services. You won't see much of me, because I'm mostly away at my job – which is profoundly secret, so you mustn't ask. Number Three –' he thumped the shoulder of the soldier, '– Lieutenant Oscar Randall. Who thinks he's the family lady-killer.'

'Because I am,' Oscar said. He did not swagger, like Charlie, but smiled at Lily with sublime assurance. He certainly was very good-looking. His Randall eyes came with luxuriant, golden-brown hair and strong, rather rugged features. 'I've only got short leave, Lily-Josephine. I'm awfully glad you turned up at the beginning–' His brothers booed him off the stage, with laughter and catcalls.

'She might prefer sailors,' Bruno said. 'Numbers Four and Five – the twins, Jack and Quin. Jack's in the Navy, like the good Devon-man he is. Quin's got asthma, so he stays at home to run the farm.'

The twins were identical, and beautiful. There was nothing ethereal about their muscular figures, but Lily had an impression of seraphic otherworldliness – possibly because of the likeness between them, which was uncanny. Their hair was white-blond, contrasting strangely with their hazel eyes.

Bruno was dragging out a gangling boy, who had been hiding behind the twins. He cuffed the rough brown head affectionately. 'And this is Paddy, who doesn't do anything except lessons and gardening, because he's only fourteen. I hope you can cook – he eats like a horse.'

Paddy was very thin and very tall, with huge feet, and hands he didn't know what to do with. His hazel eyes were full of alarm, and he hid again the moment Bruno released him. His shyness clanged around him like a suit of armour. The others kindly ignored him, leaving him to wrestle down his blushes alone.

Finally, Bruno patted the red setter. 'This is Custard.'

Lily smiled round at them all. 'You'll have to be patient with me at first, and show me what to do. But I'm a fast learner. I won't make mistakes more than once.'

Kit stood up suddenly. He was slender and graceful, and moved with quick fluidity. 'You've all gone mad. She can't stay here – not unless you want to face an angry father with a horsewhip.'

'Nobody will come after me, Kit,' Lily said. Her use of his name made him flinch. 'I'll tell you the whole story – after I've made some tea, if you don't mind, because I'm parched.'

At least four voices clamoured: 'Let me – sit down – I'll do it –' and there was a scuffle over the kettle.

Lily leapt forward, grabbed it, and smacked away their hands. 'Don't be silly, making tea is my job. That's the whole point.' She glanced pleadingly towards Kit. 'If you'll let me stay.'

He dropped back down on the settle. Pa, with one of the Little Owls perched on his hand, sat down at the table. The others watched, fascinated, as Lily made a pot of tea. If she asked a question, five voices answered in unison. Five bodies fought to help with the cups – exclaiming loudly over their cleanliness – and cannoned together in their eagerness when she mildly asked for some milk.

Eventually, when the tea was poured, and they had resolved a whispered squabble about who was to sit next to her, they were all gathered around the large table. Except

Kit, who stayed on the settle, in the shadows.

Lily told her story – hesitantly at first, then speaking freely, encouraged by the sympathy in the radiant hazel eyes. It was impossible not to expand, before such an attentive audience. When she told about Charlie, they scowled and muttered. When she faltered her way through the final terrible disillusion with Ralph, they were silent and stricken. Lily was trying hard not to cry.

'I had to leave then – I knew I couldn't live there any more. Sidonia made him wicked. And if I'd stayed, I'd be wicked too.' She bowed her head. A large tear splashed onto the table. She felt them all tussling, in a male way, with compassion that longed to express itself in anger.

Finally, Oscar said: 'Of course you can stay here. Can't she, Kit?'

Lily looked up hopefully.

From his corner, Kit said: 'I suppose so. None of you are going to listen to me after that.' He had been sitting unnaturally still, and spoke with a harshness Lily interpreted as scepticism.

'It's all true,' she said.

'Oh, I believe you.'

She wondered what she had said, to make him so angry. The bandage made it impossible to read his expression fully, but his eyes looked as if he were chewing barbed wire.

The others, however, seemed eager to protect her from Kit. Or was it the other way round?

Jack and Quin went out to fetch her suitcase. Bruno gave her a Wee-Willie-Winkie candle, and led her up shallow, uneven stairs to a spare room which was to be hers. In the leaping shadows, Lily made out heavy wooden furniture, faded chintz and threadbare rugs. The walls were panelled, and there was a faint, wistful scent of lavender, beeswax and mould.

'You'll be all right here, won't you?' Bruno asked.

Lily had opened her suitcase on the high bed. She was examining the articles she had stuffed into it only a few hours before, as if they were ancient relics of another life. 'It's lovely. You are kind. All of you.'

236

Bruno hovered beside the door. 'Sorry about Kit. He hates strangers. His face was very badly burned when he was shot down, and he's touchy about being looked at.'

'God, the poor thing!'

'Don't show you're sorry for him, whatever you do. He'll take it as a fearful insult.'

'Can't they – I don't know. Isn't there an operation, or something?'

'He's had hundreds of operations,' Bruno said. 'They patched him up with bits and pieces of skin, like a quilt. But it must look pretty dreadful.'

Lily asked: 'Don't you know how it looks?'

'I've never seen Kit's face without the bandage. He doesn't need it any more, but he refuses to take it off. The hell of it is, he used to be the best-looking of us all.' Bruno's huge, wavering eyes were full of pain for his brother. Then he smiled. 'I'm glad you came, Lily-Josephine. I hope you like it here.'

<hr />

Lily could not sleep. Apart from her childhood holidays with Gladys, she had never slept in a strange house. She gave up trying when the first light bled through the faded curtains, and got out of the squashy feather bed to watch the dawn.

Then she dressed, and ran down the staircase – revealed by daylight as a massive, carved thing, ponderous as the prow of an old ship. The kitchen, in the first spears of sunshine, looked more dirty and cluttered, and also more appealing. The owls were huddled into the carved ends of the beams, looking like carved images themselves.

Lily foraged for food, wondering how on earth to conjure up an adequate breakfast for seven men. There were plentiful eggs, packets of Scott's Porage Oats and a stale loaf, which would do for toast. Just as she was casting around for milk, the first Randall appeared. He put down a churn of frothing new milk. 'Morning.'

'Good morning – er – are you Jack or Quin?'

'Quin.'

Lily had begun to saw the loaf into thick slices. 'It's an odd name.'

237

'Short for Quintus, because I'm Number Five. I think it stinks.'

'Well, I like it. Will there be any butter?'

Quin put his hands in his pockets. He was shy, and seemed somehow lopsided without his twin. 'Yes. We keep a small herd, and make it ourselves.'

'I can already milk a cow and churn butter. You should have woken me in time to help you.'

He smiled. 'Not on your first day.'

The impressions crowded into that first day set Lily's head whirling. All the young Randalls (except Kit) wanted to help, and ended up giving her totally conflicting information. They followed her around, until she felt as if she were on show at a fairground. Fortunately, they eventually lost interest. Lily was left with Bruno, who turned out to be an ideal guide.

It was Bruno who showed her the house. Randalls was a fine Tudor building of soft red brick, flanked by wings added haphazardly in the seventeenth and eighteenth centuries. Bruno said the place was an architectural nightmare, but had charm. He took her to the old still-room, where Pa catalogued and analysed his owl-pellets. Thanks to Bruno, Lily located the lamp-oil, candles and meat-safe.

'Perhaps, now you're here, we'll get ourselves into order,' he said. 'There hasn't been a woman here for years.'

Lily asked: 'What about your mother?'

'She died when Paddy was a baby. We've tried to get housekeepers, but they've seldom lasted more than a day. It's the mice and the owls, I think. And Pa wandering about in his combinations. We're absolutely notorious now, for our inability to keep help.' He frowned anxiously. 'But look here, are you sure you're up to it?'

'Perfectly. Could you tell me where I can find a telephone? I really must speak to Gladys.'

To her surprise, there was a telephone at Randalls. Bruno explained that it had been put in because of his job, about which she must not ask.

Ten minutes later, she was at the desk in Bruno's bedroom, waiting while Iris Driver ran for Gladys.

'Lily?' Gladys came on the line, gasping for breath.

'Hello.'

'You naughty girl – getting me worried out of my mind – my precious – are you all right?'

'Fine. How's Peter?'

'Never you mind about him. Where are you?'

Lily said: 'I'm afraid I'm not going to tell you. It's better that you don't know, if they come asking questions.'

Gladys's voice was softer. 'What happened, love? Can you tell me?'

'No.' Lily gamely swallowed the lump in her throat, suddenly longing to hurl herself into Gladys's arms.

'But you're truly all right?'

'Yes, I swear. I've got myself a job.'

'Get off,' said Gladys.

'Promise you won't laugh? I'm a housekeeper. I've got to feed seven men tonight, and you wouldn't believe how much they eat. Is macaroni cheese very difficult?'

'Oh, my God,' Gladys said. 'You're at the Randalls.'

Lily was dismayed that her mystery was so transparent, but could not help laughing. 'How did you know?'

'Everyone knows about those Randalls.' Gladys was grim. 'They're a byword for miles around. No housekeeper has lasted there for more than a week, and neither will you.'

'Honestly, Glad – I'm loving it. Everyone's so kind.'

'Kind! I'll just bet they are. It's not decent, love. Come back here and stay with me.'

'Gladys, I swear, I'm totally and completely fine.'

'Come straight home, if there's the least sign of trouble.'

'Darling, there won't be any. Now, tell me how to make macaroni cheese.'

Lily's debut supper took hours of sweaty preparation, and was liberally salted with tears of panic, but was declared a great success. The younger Randalls would have eaten old socks if Lily had cooked them. They ate with their eyes pinned to her, and nearly came to blows for the privilege of doing the washing-up. Even Kit was grudgingly complimentary.

Oscar took one of her hands, while she was clearing the

table. 'God, what a yawn, you poor duck.'

'Sorry.'

'Go to bed. You're exhausted.'

She was exhausted. Her limbs were lead, and her head was a chaos of blurred images. She wanted to sleep for a month. The five youngest Randalls clustered at the foot of the stairs, watching her.

'Good night –' they called up to her.

'Sleep well –'

'Sweet dreams, Lily –'

It was funny, she thought, how Gladys assumed she must be in constant danger. She had never felt so safe and warm in her life. Nothing bad could happen in this house. She wrapped her old merino dressing gown around her naked body.

What Bruno had told her, about the anguish Kit had suffered over his burned face, made Lily yearn for him to trust her. He had kept in the background all day, seldom speaking, but she had always sensed him watching her, sizing her up. She had already decided that his dislike and suspicion were not personal. The fact that she was female had activated some deep, private uneasiness – obviously, she thought, connected to his ruined face.

She padded barefoot to the bathroom. It was on a landing at the top of a crazy servants' staircase. All the doors were open to the still, summer night, and she heard them talking on the back step.

Oscar's voice: 'I keep thinking she'll vanish.'

The twins, speaking together: 'Isn't she pretty?'

Bruno's voice was emphatic, almost stern. 'She's beautiful. I've never seen such a beautiful woman. And she's a nice kid, too.'

'Listen to you all,' Kit said sourly. 'It's disgusting. She's turned you all to jelly. Pa was wrong – seven men are obviously completely powerless against her.'

Up in the shadows, Lily smiled to herself. Her yearning for Kit's approval hardened to absolute determination.

Chapter Three

'The Necks have left,' Lady Violet said. 'I saw Tom Neck in the Post Office, and he told me his wife wouldn't stay at the Prospect with Miss Lily gone.'

In accordance with ancient custom, she had summoned Charlie to talk to her in her bedroom while she dressed for dinner. Lady Violet was decking herself in formal velvet, not remotely bothered by the fact that the dinner would be meagre and meatless, owing to the small matter of a world war – she knew how she liked things done.

Nor did she care that Charlie lay slumped across an armchair, reading the *Sporting Life*. He might look as if he wasn't listening, but of course, he was. And she had ways of making sure he did as he was told.

'Neck wouldn't go into details, but something very funny is going on at that house. I never trusted Captain Gallant.' She was powdering her face at the dressing table, but watched Charlie intently in the mirror. 'I must say, I'm disappointed with Lily-Josephine. Her stepmother may be a ghastly woman, but running away like that was just silly and hysterical. And I had such hopes.'

Charlie turned a page, yawning noisily.

Lady Violet said: 'I thought, at one time, that you were rather keen on her.'

He turned another page.

'Well, thank goodness you spared me a daughter-in-law given to bolting.'

Very audibly, Charlie farted.

His mother's thin lips tensed angrily. Her voice, however, remained light and conversational. 'I heard quite an interesting piece of intelligence today. It seems that one of Mrs Gallant's girls is a Rumage. Why on earth didn't you tell me?'

Charlie said: 'What's for dinner?'

His mother turned round smartly, and he made the mistake of looking up. Though he tried to seem sullen, he was trapped in her steely blue gaze like a sparrow with a cobra. 'One of the Sussex Rumages; very nice people indeed. I was presented with Anthea Rumage. The girl must be her niece. Very pretty, I thought.'

She turned back to her reflection in the glass, and smiled. 'It really is high time you married, Charles.'

<hr>

The pain was relentless. Nothing eased it. Primrose had been living in dread of the postwoman, bracing herself for the news of Guy's death. She had not been able to imagine anything worse. Until now.

> Dearest Prim,
>
> Please don't hate me. I wish there was a better way, but the only decent thing is to let you have it straight. I have met a girl. Her name is Anita, and we are engaged.
>
> I know I have treated you very badly. But darling, darling, one day you'll be glad it ended this way. We both knew what we were doing was wrong, and felt awful about it. You deserve better. You had no hope of any future happiness with me.
>
> I'll never stop loving you, but the kind of love will be different, as it was supposed to be. Anita is a wonderful person. I pray like anything you'll meet someone wonderful of your own,
>
> Guy

Primrose leaned her head against the rock, and gazed out at the dull, lead-coloured sea. She had opened the letter at breakfast – her senses leaping at the sight of Guy's handwriting, God help her – and the effort of not breaking down in front of them all had nearly killed her. The moment she could escape, she had carried the hateful thing down to the beach; the place where they had first declared their love. Here, she could groan and howl like a wild animal in the first agonies of betrayal, with no one to see except the wheeling gulls.

It had never occurred to her that she could lose Guy to anyone except Death. And now she found herself half-wishing he had died. At least she would have kept the image of their love, preserved in amber, to ease the pain of life without him. Guy's death could not have hurt like this. He would marry his bloody Anita, and she would have to bear him being alive and on earth, and not thinking of her.

She had cried herself half-blind. Now, with tears still oozing painfully between her swollen lids, she made herself face the future. They had made plans, she and Guy – idle, canoodling, lovers' plans, as it turned out. They would buy a small farm after the war, and live together in sweet companionship, as man and wife.

All these dreams lay flattened and in ruins. This was the bitter reality: he would build a respectable home with Anita, and she would be stuck with Sidonia. In her desolation, Primrose could no longer ignore the fact that she was suffocating inside the enchanted circle.

Sidonia doesn't give a damn about me, was her first clear thought, after the tempest of grief. I'm nothing but a slave.

It had taken her all this time to realise that compliments about her housekeeping skills were not compliments at all. They were offered cynically, as payment for clean sheets, edible meals and sordid daily battles with rationing and austerity. No one else in the house would have dreamt of tackling all this.

And the burden was heavier, since the terrible, mysterious departure of Lily-Josephine. It had deprived Primrose of three useful pairs of hands, since Mr and Mrs Neck had left soon afterwards.

Somehow, in ways she did not begin to understand, the house had become dark and cursed. Why else would faithful Daphne Wadsworth write all those beastly letters, telling Sidonia she was a poisonous bitch? Primrose found the letters, left carelessly on sofas and tables, and guiltily read their hysterical tirades against her mother. She guessed that Sidonia pretended not to care, because she was so furious with Daphne for taking the side of her stepdaughter.

Sidonia had got rid of Lily, but she had not forgiven her

for whatever it was she had done. Her hatred was intense, and she watched Primrose suspiciously, for signs of sympathy. Primrose listened, in silent misery, while Sidonia plotted to cut Lily out of her inheritance.

Primrose had assumed that Ralph would try to bring his daughter home, or at least make an effort to find out where she was. She could not understand why he did absolutely nothing. Outwardly, at least, he expressed nothing except relief, at having a source of conflict removed. Within a few weeks of Lily's disappearance however, he looked like a man struck by lightning – greyer and more stooping, with a bitter drag to his mouth. But he was hectically cheerful, and drinking quarts. He and Charlie would drink anything, from priceless black market spirits, to the terrible elderflower hooch Mrs Dove made, and kept for cleaning the windows.

Sitting in the wreck of her dreams, Primrose wondered when Ralph would manage to drink himself to death, and whether she would care. If she had to stay in this life, she would go mad. She ripped Guy's letter to shreds, and wished she could talk to Lily.

Chapter Four

1981

❖❖❖

It was a strange and unsatisfactory state of being-in-love. Since Christmas, Sophie and Octavius had had an unwritten agreement not to attempt sex. By the end of January, it was becoming clear to them both that this was next to impossible. The physical force-field between them had been activated, and could not be ignored or wished away. As any amateur psychologist could have told them, their unmentionable mutual desire was all the stronger for being pushed underground.

What are you supposed to do, Sophie wondered, when you want to spend every waking and sleeping moment with a person, but must not allow your meetings to reach their inevitable third-act curtain? On three occasions, the agreement had been broken because Octavius could not help it, and Sophie lacked the strength of mind to resist him. Each time, Octavius had suffered a shattering, terrifying headache, and Sophie had blamed herself. The situation was heartbreaking, and perfectly absurd.

She found some distraction in the demands of her work. Thanks to the shamelessly nepotistic manoeuvrings of Sir Bruno, Sophie had been taken off nature books, and put in charge of a new MacTavish imprint, Classic Translations. This was a small-scale affair, run on a shoestring, but Sophie did not miss the denizens of coot and hern. As she corrected proofs of Fairfax's *Tasso*, or Chapman's *Homer*, or trawled the common rooms of obscure universities in search of cheap scholars to write introductions, she rediscovered some of her old delight in the making of books.

Besides – the fact remained, in spite of everything – she was in love. The whole desert landscape of her life had bloomed, because it contained Octavius Randall. What he laughingly called the 'smut embargo' had at least given them space to develop their friendship.

'Not an exciting concept,' Octavius said, 'but warm and durable. Like one of those indestructible blankets people give you as wedding presents.'

Quite apart from being beautiful, he was a good cook, great fun, and endlessly, quietly supportive. Simply being with him was bliss. Sturdily, while aching for him to make love to her, Sophie told herself that sex was not everything.

This counting of blessings was difficult, however, when Octavius was struggling with the weight of his unwanted inheritance. In the second week of February, Sophie came home expecting to find him, and found only a message on the answering machine.

'Sorry about this, I'm off to Devon. We're having a family argument, and they need to rant at me in person. If you don't hear from me, it's because I've been sectioned under the Mental Health Act. I love you.'

The peculiar connection between their two families meant that Sophie soon heard what the argument was about. Isobel telephoned, late that same evening.

'Mum? Hi –' Sophie answered croakily. She had been asleep on the sofa.

'I'm sorry it's so late, but I had to tell you. The shock of it fairly knocked me off my feet.'

Sophie struggled into a sitting position, causing the galley proofs of Carlyle's translation of *Wilhelm Meister* to cascade off her stomach onto the floor. 'What's happened?'

'Oh darling, I didn't mean to frighten you – nothing dreadful.' Isobel was breathless with excitement. She loved relaying news, and very rarely had anything to tell. 'Brace yourself.'

'I'm braced.'

'It's Juana. She's contesting Sidonia's will.'

This was fascinating. Sophie was instantly awake. 'On what grounds, for God's sake?'

'It's really Edgar.'

'Oh.' Sophie relaxed a fraction. 'I wouldn't put anything past him.'

246

'He's saying he has a right to Lily's money because it was legally Ralph's money – and he's Ralph's son.'

'But that's impossible!'

From the distant pig farm came an impatient sigh. 'Don't you see? It explains everything! This is why Lily was so furious with Ralph, and why she ran away that night. She must have caught him at it with Juana.'

Sophie settled herself against the cushions, and absently rummaged in a tatty paper bag for the last couple of jelly beans – all resolutions about healthy eating collapsed when Octavius was away. 'I always thought she ran off because of Sidonia.'

'So did I,' Isobel said. 'But I'm sure Sidonia knew. She knew, because Juana always told her everything, and she said she'd leave Edgar the money on the strength of it. No wonder Juana was so horrified, to find out how she'd lied.'

'So he reckons he's Lily's half-brother,' Sophie said. 'Does he look like her?'

This aspect of the affair did not seem to have occurred to Isobel. There was a silence, as she turned it over. 'Well – a bit. A tiny bit.' Her voice firmed with conviction. 'Actually, Edgar has a distinct look of Ralph. Don't you think?'

'Mum, I met Ralph once, when I was two. I've no idea.'

'No, no, I was forgetting. But he does, you know. Primrose believes every word of it, and she's furious. I had her on the phone for nearly an hour, going over and over what a tart Juana was. She says it makes her feel a lot less sorry for Ralph – he probably deserved Sidonia.'

'There's not much to base a case on, though.' Sophie was wondering why the Randalls were arguing. Even if Octavius cared about the money, this historic tittle-tattle would surely never stand up in a court of law. She decided not to say any of this to Isobel, who was already sniffing round Sophie's relationship with Octavius like a truffle-hound. 'I don't see how on earth Edgar expects to prove it. Unless he's planning to pick Ralph's ashes off the cliffs with tweezers, and analyse the DNA.'

'Ah, but Juana has a letter,' Isobel said, with a showbiz

flourish. 'A letter from Ralph, in which he apparently admits paternity.'

'So what? Honestly, Mum. This whole thing is completely silly – just one of Edgar's stupid projects, like his plan to turn canal-barges into floating conference centres. It's obviously doomed from the start. I refuse to lose any sleep over it.'

'I'm sorry, I know it's the middle of the night.' Unburdened, Isobel could now relent. 'How are you, anyway? How's the new list coming?'

'Everyone except me thinks it's the most boring thing on earth. Octavius forbids me to talk about it, unless I'm prepared to hear about his arse-numbing woodland beasties.'

Damn, she had mentioned Octavius.

Isobel swooped. 'I thought you should know what's going on. I mean, Octavius's inheritance obviously affects you.'

In ways you cannot imagine, Sophie thought wryly. Her mother was talking about the difference between marrying a nature writer or a millionaire. Firstly, this had nothing to do with her love for Octavius – had Isobel forgotten marrying for pure love herself? Secondly, the word 'marriage' had not been mentioned.

Firmly, she said good night to her mother, heaved herself off the sofa, and went into the kitchen for tea and Liquorice Allsorts. While waiting for the kettle to boil, she fingered the antique sapphire ring she wore on a chain round her neck. Octavius had slipped it into her hand – not onto her finger - after one of their hectic, suppressed, candlelit dinners, muttering that it had belonged to his Randall grandmother. It was not, she understood, an engagement ring; more a pledge for the future. And there could be no future, until Octavius and his family addressed the complications of the past.

Oh, Lily-Josephine, Sophie thought; did you have any idea what a burden you were leaving to your only child?

The following day, she found another message on the machine.

'Hi, I tried the office, but you'd gone. I came back before I killed someone. God, I've missed you. Can you come round to Hampstead for dinner?'

Sophie had just come from work, and had to dash from Crouch End to Hampstead with barely time to put down her briefcase.

'Ah, Sophie.' Gerda pulled her into the house and kissed her cheek resoundingly. 'What a relief – someone else who was not born a Randall.'

'Hello, Gerda. What drama, eh?'

'You've heard about the court case, then. A total waste of everyone's time and money, as far as I can see.'

'I just wish I knew why it got Octavius agitated enough to dash down to Devon.'

Gerda's small, slanted brown eyes were full of shrewd amusement. 'It's not Octavius. It's those silly old men.'

'Bruno too?'

'Even Bruno. I'd like to bang their heads together.'

Sophie unwound her scarf and peeled off her gloves, enjoying the fuggy warmth of the house. It smelt deliciously of goulash. Gerda's talent for creating solid bodily comfort reminded her that she had not had a proper meal in two days. Octavius was trying to wean her off her diet of sugar, nicotine and caffeine – and the minute he went away, she slid straight back into her bad old habits. Her stomach rumbled loudly.

'The place is full of food,' Gerda said, over her shoulder, as she led the way downstairs. 'Family crises bring out the Yiddisher Momma in me – feed them till they beg for mercy.'

'My Irish Momma does colcannon and soda bread in a crisis,' Sophie said, 'but the principle's exactly the same.'

In the kitchen, the French windows were misted with steam. A coal fire glowed above a grate full of cigarette ends.

Gerda examined various seething pans. 'Freud never knew what to do about the families of his patients. I wonder what he'd have thought of the Randalls – every single one of them crying out for a padded cell.' She handed Sophie a thick glass goblet of wine and sat down at the table opposite her, lighting the inevitable cigarette. Sophie, though rather half-heartedly trying to cut down, also lit a cigarette.

She asked: 'Where's Octavius?'

'Upstairs, arguing on the phone. Bruno's on the extension, trying to calm things down.'

'Listen, Gerda.' Sophie had had a long day, and wanted things to be spelt out simply, for a change. 'What is the bloody problem? Octavius doesn't care about his mother's money.'

'That, dear girl, is the bloody problem.'

'Do his uncles want the money? Is that it?'

Gerda eyed her speculatively, through a veil of smoke. 'He hasn't told you much, has he?'

'He never talks about his family. The Devon lot, I mean. I can't decide whether he loathes them, or absolutely adores them. I think it's probably both. He minds terribly what they think of him.' She could not help glancing over at the sideboard, where the old photographs of Lily-Josephine and the seven Randalls tantalised her with their secrets.

Gerda was wary, perhaps wondering how far Sophie could be trusted. 'If you want to understand anything about them, you must turn the clock back forty years. They are still living in ancient history. The old fools – very unwisely, in my opinion – refuse to let Octavius into the game. So he becomes more and more frightened of what he'll find, if he digs into the past.'

'What might he find?'

'The important thing is what he imagines he will find.'

Sophie said: 'The important thing is that you're not answering the question.'

Gerda let out a shout of laughter, as if Sophie had made an unexpectedly clever move at chess. 'All right. But anything to do with his mother is sacred ground. I learned to leave them to it years ago. Even dear old Bru, who has made a whole career out of being rational, cannot be rational about Lily.'

'Did you know her?'

'No. She died before I came on the scene.'

Sophie could not resist. 'Do you know which one of them

is Octavius's father?'

Disconcertingly, Gerda laughed again. 'Don't you think I'd have told the poor boy, if I did?'

'I suppose so.'

'It might be Bruno. When I helped to bring up Octavius, it was always at the back of my mind that he could be my Ilse's half-brother. But I've no idea.' Gerda bent, to take her goulash out of the oven. 'Now, before they come down, do tell me about your cousin Edgar. What's he like?'

'In a word, ghastly.'

'Is that family legend, or your own independent observation?'

Sophie smiled ruefully. 'A bit of both. I only know him slightly – but I do assure you, slightly is enough. I was brought up on stories about how much money he was chiselling out of Sidonia, for his stupid business ideas and his daily ton or so of cocaine. Basically, he's a nightmare. Spiteful, vengeful, bitchy – thinks the world owes him a living.'

'He sounds as if he needs help.'

'Oh, he's had help, from whole armies of shrinks. Unfortunately, none of them had a cure for a spoilt, hysterical arsehole. When he loses this stupid case, I expect he'll attempt suicide again.'

'Sophie!' Gerda, the unshockable, was genuinely shocked.

'Well, I know that sounds nasty. You'd probably say we all ought to have more compassion. But when there's a reptile like him actually in your family, you only think about self-protection. Mum stopped visiting Juana after she caught him feeding me eye-drops when I was a baby.'

'You know,' Gerda faced her deliberately, her wooden spoon dripping scarlet juice on the lino, 'my family was destroyed by the Nazis. We were not perfect, but we liked each other, and we wanted to be together. When I hear of families like yours, apparently working so hard to destroy themselves, without a Nazi in sight, I simply cannot understand. It's as if they had spent the war saying: Don't bother to invade us and tear us apart! We'll do it for you!'

Gerda's experience of the war was well-known and

minutely documented. You could not meet her without being aware of it, however remotely. But she had never spoken of it directly to Sophie. For a moment, Sophie was humbled by the familiar burden of history. And for a moment, she understood why the older Randalls had bottled their past and carried it into the present, refusing to accept there was such a thing as time.

Heavy footsteps sounded on the creaking stairs. Octavius came in, followed by Bruno. Sophie hastily stubbed out her cigarette, and jumped up to kiss Octavius.

He wrapped his arms around her, and held her close. He was very angry, but eager to assure Sophie that he was not angry with her. 'Hello, you. Had a good time eating rubbish?'

'Nothing but healthy salads, I swear.'

Gerda dumped a pile of plates and cutlery on the table. 'I take it that was Kit again?'

'Actually,' Bruno said, 'it was Quin.'

Octavius released Sophie. 'All the way from Umbria, telling me what to think. But you're right, it might as well have been Kit.'

'He's on your side,' Bruno began.

'No he's not. He expects me to do as I'm told, according to the unwritten book of Randall law. Could you ask him to let me grow up, do you think?'

Sophie had a strong sense of division in the room, as Bruno took the side of his absent family, and Gerda silently supported Octavius. He was, evidently, an old issue between them.

'I meant it,' Octavius told Bruno. 'I'm not going to lift a finger to save my so-called inheritance. If this man wins his case, good luck to him.'

'The point is,' Bruno murmured, pained but persevering, 'it's gone beyond you and your feelings.'

'Well, excuse me. I think my feelings are rather fucking important.'

'All we're saying is, there are other considerations.'

'Yes, yes, you mean I owe it to my mother.' Octavius pushed away Gerda's hand, trying to give him a glass of

252

wine. 'I'd like to remind you all that my mother is dead.'

Sophie and Gerda caught each other making identical agonised faces. This was no way to speak of Lily being dead. Octavius appeared to be calm, but was mentally bristling and bare-fanged.

Sir Bruno, known as one of the finest brains in Europe, did not have the sense to back away. Very quietly, he said: 'Don't – don't betray her memory.'

Gerda shut her eyes wearily. 'Oh, God.'

'What memory? I don't remember her! So get off my case!' Octavius was shouting. 'I'm sick of the sound of her name!'

This heresy, suppressed for years, came rushing out like a wild beast. Octavius walked out of the room and up the stairs. A moment later, they heard the front door slamming.

There was a tense, breathless silence, during which Sophie stared at the floor.

Bruno broke it, with a long, whinnying sigh. 'I know what you're going to say. I handled that in the worst possible way.'

'Yes, you did.' Gerda, her face calm but pitiless, put a battered, cast-iron casserole on the table.

Sophie began: 'I suppose I ought to –'

'Don't you dare go after him. You have to stick it out now, or we'll all curl up with embarrassment.'

'Please stay,' Bruno said. 'Do, please. I'm sorry you had to witness that. I'm afraid poor old Octavius –'

'Enough!' Gerda held up the dripping spoon to silence him. 'Stop apologising for Octavius, pushing him into the wrong.'

Bruno, rather shamefacedly, glanced at Sophie. 'I'm afraid he is wrong. He won't even try to understand.'

'You don't want him to understand. You only want him to do as he's told. This isn't a little boy we're talking about.'

'He's behaving like one,' Bruno murmured.

Gerda whipped the lid off her goulash, filling the kitchen with the smell of paprika. 'And how are you behaving, all of you? God, you bloody old fools. You won't get Octavius on your side, until you tell him the truth.'

Bruno winced, but did not protest.

His wife went on: 'You can start by giving him the diary.'

'Whose diary?' The plot was thickening, and Sophie was anxious not to lose it.

'Lily's,' Bruno said unhappily.

'She kept a diary? Does Octavius know?'

'Yes, but there's never been a right time to show it to him. And he swears he's not interested, anyway.'

'Bollocks and rubbish,' Gerda said. 'You've got the thing, but you daren't make a move without consulting Kit. Just because he was the one who married her – the keeper of the flame.'

'Just a minute,' Sophie protested. 'Octavius never told me Lily was married –'

Gerda sighed. 'Typical. This is ridiculous. Bruno will give you the diary, and you can take it to Octavius. I'm sure you'll be seeing him before we do – I'd be amazed if he ever speaks to us again.'

Bruno turned to Sophie. 'I ought to make it clear, the diary doesn't contain any staggering revelations.'

'Yes it does,' Gerda said. 'It doesn't say which one is Octavius's father, but it's staggering enough. To any normal person.'

For the first time, Bruno sounded cross. 'Why are you so obsessed with identifying his father? What does it matter? He's never lacked affection. He's had more love around him than most people. He's always belonged to all of us.'

'And none of you,' Sophie could not help saying.

Bruno's eyes, huge and vulnerable behind his thick spectacles, widened in dismay.

'Told you,' said Gerda.

He sat down, and began mechanically spooning out goulash. 'I suppose it is hard for us to keep in mind that he never knew Lily, and has no notion of – of –' most uncharacteristically, he was grappling for the right words '– of the essence of her. How does one describe a taste, or a smell, when it cannot be compared with anything else?' He was trying to explain, and possibly defend himself, to Sophie. 'How on earth does one breathe life back into a dead girl, when she exists only in the memories of a clutch of old men?'

Sophie found herself drawn back to the photograph of Lily, smiling amidst the alien corn. Perhaps, she thought, if Octavius read her diary, he would be admitted into the secret of her magic.

More to the point, perhaps these besotted old men would admit him, instead of shutting him out.

—◆◇◆—

Sophie got home just before midnight, and was disappointed not to find Octavius. He had a key to her flat, and she could not think where else he would take refuge. She was longing to give him the diary, which Bruno had reluctantly put into her hand when she left. Nobody had forbidden her to read it, but she had told herself she must not, until Octavius had seen it first.

She changed into her dressing gown, made a pot of coffee, and settled on the sofa to wait, with some work to pass the time – the galleys of Dryden's *Aeneid*. Predictably, despite the coffee, this knocked her out like a blackjack.

A sense of delicious unease threaded into her sleep. The scent of Octavius was around her, and she woke to find him leaning over her. His gold-flecked eyes stared down into hers. He opened her dressing gown, and lightly touched her clitoris with the tip of one finger.

She mumbled: 'Should we?'

'I don't care,' he said. 'If I don't fuck you now, I'll explode.'

After this, there was no question of control. Very distantly, Sophie was miserably aware that she could not have stopped him, if she knew he would die of it. With a groan of surrender, she pulled his mouth down to hers.

The love-making was sharp and fierce. The edge of desperation made them both frantic. Octavius plunged inside her, thrusting with a kind of deliberate concentration, as if working his way through an obstacle-course. Sophie was hurtled through two racking orgasms.

While the spasms of the second were still dying away, she saw the signs of Octavius's punishment. She knew this was their last chance to stop, but could not let him go. His shout of release, as he came, seamlessly turned into a howl of pain.

The session ended, as the last three had ended, with Octavius retching and Sophie in tears. Drearily, she went into what was becoming a routine – finding his tablets, tucking him into her bed, holding him in her arms until he slept.

Then she made herself another pot of coffee. She was too unsettled to sleep now. To finish this way left her wretchedly unsatisfied. It had happened often enough for her to know she would get no rest, until she had reasoned herself out of being angry with Octavius.

She would crawl into work tomorrow, shaking and yellow from too much caffeine, cured of the resentment but inconveniently inclined to weep. Pandora, her shared secretary, would tell all the other secretaries that Sophie's new boyfriend was a closet gay, and they would all pity her for being a bitter old bag unable to sustain a normal relationship.

At around eleven, Octavius would send her a beautiful, extravagant bunch of flowers. She had not had the heart to tell him how embarrassing this was – they doubled in size each time, causing Pandora to spend the rest of the morning hunting for vases. By lunchtime, her office would look like a chapel of rest. Some people had decided Octavius sent the flowers as an apology for acts of deep kinkiness. Nobody meant to be unkind, but the place was a rumour-factory. If it had been happening to someone else, she would probably have gossiped with the rest, and found the whole situation madly funny.

She took a gulp of coffee, and reached for the brown paper bag Bruno had given her. There was enough anger lingering in her bloodstream to override any guilt about reading Lily's diary before Octavius. Bugger it. She was dying to hear the girl's voice. And didn't Lily's history now concern her, too?

The diary was a large, oblong black account-book, with a shabby cardboard cover. She opened it with a thrashing pulse, and was crestfallen to find the first pages covered with lists of household expenses – Sunlight Soap, National Wholemeal Flour, Scott's Porage Oats, black treacle, darning wool.

Still, it was curiously touching to see Lily's round, school-girlish handwriting, and the pencilled doodles of animals. Sophie turned the pages impatiently, until she came face to face with the diary.

She had written her name, and underlined it with a flourish. 'Lily-Josephine Gallant. Strictly private. If anyone reads this book they will DIE!' Sophie had written something very similar herself, in the diary she had kept in the fourth form. How young she was, this poor little Lily – a teenager, with a perfect right to be hopeful, naive and silly. Sophie had warmed to her already.

The first words leapt off the page, as if they had been scribbled the day before:

'28 July 1941. I think I am in love with Oscar.'

Chapter Five
LILY'S DIARY

❖◆❖

28 July 1941. I think I am in love with Oscar.

I don't want to go to sleep while my body remembers the touch of his hands and lips. So I am sitting in bed, writing this by the light of a candle, because there is no one else I can talk to.

Charlie laughed at me for talking about love, and he was right – what experience do I have? Except that I now think this is something you must learn by yourself. At last, I understand what Daphne W. goes on about in her books.

Ever since I came here, I have known that I would find my destiny. There is so much love washing about inside me – until tonight not knowing where to go - that it overflows in all directions. Not in a romantic way. I have, for instance, got tremendously fond of the owls. Especially Mr Tyto alba, who sometimes deigns to land on my shoulder of an evening. The grip of his claws makes me shiver, and he has that owly pong, but I am aware of the honour. Pa calls me 'Pallas Athene'.

In the same sort of way, I am very fond of Pa. He shouts and blusters, and comes out with some astonishing rants. But you feel the goodness of him, down to your backbone. There is a framed sampler in my bedroom, which his grandmother stitched, when she was a little girl. It says: 'Except the Lord build a house, their labour is in vain that build it.' This sums up the peculiar but lovely atmosphere around Pa.

I love the boys, too. But romance was always going to come in here.

Altogether, this has been the most peculiar day, at the end of a peculiar two weeks. It is the last day of Oscar's leave. Quin was out of sorts when we did the milking this morning. He was wheezing, which is a bad sign. Sometimes, it fills the whole room, like a phantom bagpiper.

He said he was sad about Oscar, but really minded about

losing Jack. We heard, the day before yesterday, that Jack's indefinite leave is over. He is to join his new ship at Plymouth, in ten days. His old ship went down at Crete. (Paddy told me this, Jack never mentions it.)

Jack is quite philosophical, and pleased to have the ten days, due to the ship having to come from somewhere else. He says he's glad not to have had a 'pierhead jump', which means you have to join the ship as soon as you get the telegram. But they are twins, and I know they hate being parted.

Bruno is off soon, too. So today is the last day the Randalls will have together for ages.

After milking, breakfast. Usual tremendous pan of porridge. Treacle finished, but plenty of less popular gooseberry jam. I was tackling the washing-up, when Pa came in for more tea. He often does this. He likes the black, stewed stuff at the bottom of the pot. He hadn't got round to shaving, but was wearing trousers over his combinations. Bruno says I am to take this as a huge compliment, the equivalent of Pa rigging up in evening dress.

He was ranting about rationing, censorship, the war giving nosey parkers a licence to pry. But of course, what really bothered him was losing Oscar. He kept wandering to the back door, to watch him playing with Custard in the yard.

I watched, too. Oscar was wearing his ancient sports jacket, more darn than tweed. The sun made his hair rich and glossy. This may have been the first moment I realised Oscar was the one.

Pa said: 'We play this charade, that it's only like sending them off to school. Poor Kit is a living reminder of the magnitude of that lie. We pretend not to know or care that they're returning to that stupid, evil war.'

I couldn't help reminding him of the polite lecture Bruno gave us the other night, when we were all complaining. He can't talk about his secret job, but begged us to believe the war was necessary.

Pa said: 'Bruno's young. He doesn't know what it is, to fling your children into its ravening maw, like the Mother of the Maccabees.' Then he sighed, and said it would be nice if I could cook something other than macaroni cheese for dinner.

Did he imagine I hadn't planned it? Quin had promised to kill

Gert and *Daisy*, oldest inhabitants of the hen-house. *Gladys* had written me detailed instructions about how to cook the poor creatures. So I could assure him everything was 'in hand', like an efficient housekeeper. I often wish *Primrose* were here, though. I rather miss her. And I feel slightly guilty about scooting off and leaving her with her hands full at home. But she says she finds housework comforting. And I suppose I can see how it might be, if you don't want to think or feel.

When *Pa* had gone back to the still-room, I started on the spuds for lunch. I have now realised (after some painful scenes, and one near-rebellion) that these must be dealt with as soon as the greedy swine have finished their breakfast. Seven men eat such a lot.

I was so distracted, stealing looks at *Oscar*, that I stupidly cut my finger. It left a dramatic trail of blood across the table, and I had to wash the spuds again. I thought there might be a plaster in the middle drawer of the dresser. This drawer is a sort of *Fortunatus'* purse – the boys pull all kinds of things out of it, and it is never empty.

I was distracted by the museum of *Randall* junk I found inside. Single gloves, broken china, hairy cough-sweets. And – ugh! – a dead vole. It had gone hard and didn't smell, but still. It must have flung itself in to escape from the owls. I took it outside on the coal-shovel. As *Pa* is always saying, *the iniquity of oblivion blindly scattereth her poppy*.

Then I came back, and found something so interesting, I still don't quite know how it makes me feel. I found long pieces of broken glass, like daggers. There was a framed photo underneath. I was staring at a picture of Squadron Leader *Kit Randall*. He is in full flying gear, like the men in Picture Post, sitting in a basket chair outside a hut on an airfield. He is smiling, and holding a magazine. *Kit*, before the flames consumed him. Thick, light brown hair, darker eyebrows, perfectly arched – like bridges of sighs, as *Daph* would say. Nose and mouth like a Greek statue.

Here I was, enchanted with a face that no longer existed. The cruelty of it breaks my heart – no wonder *Pa* hates the war. Whatever *Kit* keeps under those horrid bandages, the man in the picture will never come back. I was looking at the part of him *that had died.*

I knew why the picture lay smashed in the drawer, and who had smashed it. How can he bear to be reminded of what he used to be? Saddest of all, he seems to have lost more than beauty. This Kit was not the growling sulker, whose moods I spend my days dodging. He is only the blackened shell of the Kit who was burned. Poor, poor Kit.

They swallowed their lunch (potatoes, corned beef, new carrots) at record speed. Thank heaven they live on a farm. It was then time to work on the dinner.

Jack and Quin kindly plucked and jointed the birds for me, knowing I could never do it myself in a million years. They left them in a big pan, under a weighted lid, to protect them from the owls, mice, foxes, etc., who treat this house like a canteen.

Gladys said fresh tarragon would distract from Gert and Daisy's age. So round I went to the Sleeping Garden, where Paddy was heeling in some of his cuttings. That boy has the greenest fingers in the world. Bruno says he could grow the hanging gardens of Babylon on a flannel. When he first showed me his herbs, I told him he was a Wizard. Now, inside the Sleeping Garden, I have to address him as 'Wiz'.

'Have you any tarragon, O Wiz?'

Paddy is terribly shy, and couldn't even look at me at first, without blushing and falling over his feet. He isn't used to girls. But now he knows I won't bite, we are great friends, and have all kinds of silly games.

I love the Sleeping Garden. It is an old, walled plot beside the small pasture, which has run wild. The wall is of red brick, so old it looks soft to the touch. Inside, it is the most peaceful place I know. On my third day here, Paddy plucked up the courage to tell me about his dream of restoring it – once, it was a physic garden, which means herbs for healing. I named it the Sleeping Garden, and he was so pleased, he gave me half his Mars bar.

He did have some tarragon, in the small bed of soft velvety soil he has cleared. His plants have names like poems. Vervain, feverfew, camomile. He finds them in hedges and ditches, or pinches them from people's back yards.

On my way out, I ran into Kit. He wanted to give me a great bouquet of shallots from the vegetable patch. He was wearing a wide hat, pushed down low over his nose. This, with the grubby stockinette bandage, made me think of Claude Rains in The Invisible Man. *Remembering the photo, I thanked him a bit too much. He walked off in the middle.*

My dinner took a hell of a lot of work, but was a howling success. Thanks to Gladys, my chicken stew was truly delicious. Though Oscar clutched his throat, and pretended to be poisoned. But he drank my health afterwards. We were all drinking cider, from some big stone bottles Pa brought up from the cellar.

The boys banged their tankards on the table so loudly, the owlets got excited, and filled the bread oven with squeals. Mr Tyto sauntered around our feet and across the table, as if he owned the place. Pa tries to stop him taking snacks of human food – some hope. Kit fooled around, making Mr T snatch chicken off his fork. I've never seen him so jolly.

After pudding (apricot crumble) Oscar dashed upstairs, and came down again with my banjolele. Damn cheek, snooping in my room. This diary is only just begun, but I'm going to hide it under the floorboards.

I haven't played my banjo for ages. Sidonia thought it was boring and vulgar, and generally the enemy of vamping, so Dad stopped liking it as well. I brought it with me to protect it, I think.

Oscar went down on his knees to beg for a song. 'Sweet Lily, it's my last night. You can't deny me.'

No, I couldn't. It is quite a thing, to have a handsome soldier with beautiful hazel eyes kneeling at your feet. Not bad, for a little country girl – Sidonia couldn't do better. I asked him what he fancied.

He said: 'You,' and then had to duck under the table, to shield himself from the things the others were throwing at him.

I tuned up the banjo as best I could (in other words, not very well) and sang 'Swanee'. Pa said he approved of Al Jolson, because he expressed 'the very essence of exuberant vulgarity, unsullied by shame'. So next, at his request, I did 'Toot-Toot-Tootsie'. He joined in, and we nearly died of laughing – I wish I could describe the grave way he droned 'If you don't get a letter then you'll know I'm in jail'. Even Kit, behind the bandage, was chuckling.

I have never had an audience like this – not even when I was tiny, and Dorothy and I gave concerts in the servants' parlour. But my success was followed by a brush with disaster, which still turns me hot and cold when I think of it.

Paddy demanded some George Formby. I must know all his songs – so why did I choose 'I Wonder Who's Under Her Balcony Tonight'?

There was a deathly silence. I noticed that everyone was looking appalled, and stealing anxious looks at Kit. I could see I'd somehow put my foot in it, but didn't dare to stop in case I made it worse. I thought, is the song too coarse? Kit says 'fuck' all the time in front of me, and pees with the door open, but you never can tell.

Then Kit suddenly made the most extraordinary noise; a sort of strangled yelp. Pa and the boys froze. Then he let out a shout – and it turned out he was laughing!

He laughed and laughed, and so did the others. It made me absolutely giddy with happiness and pride. When our party broke up, Kit said 'good night' to me quite kindly, and briefly touched my shoulder, and the honour has completely turned my head.

People who are very rude and surly and difficult to please always get the best that is going, I've noticed. Sidonia works in the same way. I refuse to fall into that trap. I shall ignore my instinct to reward Kit's tiny bit of civility.

All the same, I shall be as patient with him as possible. Under cover of everyone going to bed, I asked Bruno what had happened, and he said: 'To tell the truth, your choice of song could have been more tactful.' He explained that poor Kit had been desperately in love with a girl, before he was shot down. When she saw his burnt face, she dumped him for someone else.

I was mortified – Kit must have wanted to kill me. But Bruno smiled, and assured me that he hadn't seen Kit laugh like that for ages. Poor thing. What a cow that girl must be.

And now I come to it – the whole reason I started this diary. It is two in the morning, and I have to be up for the milking in a few hours, but I must write this.

All through the evening, I had been aware of feeling excited, and this feeling seemed to centre around Oscar. We were left alone downstairs. He helped me carry the dirty dishes into the scullery. He wasn't teasing any more. In the semi-darkness, his eyes glittered down at mine, with such obvious longing I could hardly breathe. I have never been on the other end of a look like that in my life.

He asked: 'Will you miss me?'

I said, 'Yes.'

'More than you'll miss the others? No, forget I said that.'

I was glad, because I honestly couldn't say, just then, that I wouldn't miss Jack and Bruno just as much. For the sake of saying something, I said: 'It'll be awfully dull, without you to torment me.'

Oscar said: 'I do it because you torment me. Not on purpose – by being so staggeringly gorgeous.'

His arms went around my waist. He pulled me against his body – I could feel his heart beating. He kissed me, and my blood turned to champagne. I had the feeling that I was dissolving – melting into him as if we were about to become one.

We drew apart. I felt that I had just arrived in a new body. Or that I had arrived in an unknown country. My head is still spinning.

It must be Oscar, or I couldn't feel this way. I do love him. But I had the strangest idea, even at that moment, that something was incomplete. It's not that I want Oscar to be different. He is quite perfect as he is. They all are.

He whispered: 'There, I've bagged you. My mark's on you now. I won't ask you for any promises, except one. Please be here when I get back.'

That was a promise I knew I could keep. 'I'll be here,' I said. 'I'll always be here.'

Chapter Six

1941

In the still, sunlit house, someone was crying. Lily, who had thought herself alone, followed the desolate sound along the crazy, uneven corridors, to the foot of the narrow attic stairs.

The fierce sobs stopped as soon as the first step creaked under her foot. She pushed open the attic door. In the stifling space under the steep, pitched ceiling, beside a tiny window with a giddy view of the Sleeping Garden, Jack was hunched defensively on an old iron bed with a bare mattress.

'Oh, it's you,' he said. He made a sketchy attempt at wiping his wet face on his shirtsleeves.

Lily did her best not to show her surprise. Poor Jack, he was trying to scowl at her, but could not push his face into any expression except poignant, childlike misery. Obviously, he hated her seeing him like this – but she had seen him, and there was no loophole left for pride-saving pretence.

'Jack, darling –' She felt in her pocket and found a handkerchief.

'Go away.'

She sat down on the bed beside him, folded her arms around him, and pulled his head down to her shoulder. With a sigh of defeat, he leant his full weight upon her. She felt his warm tears soaking through the fabric of her washed-out cotton dress. His head lay heavy on her collarbone.

Lily listened to the house, creaking like a galleon around them; to the moans and judders of the cistern in the corner, and the steady, thrumming call of the pigeons roosting on the leads above them. With the warm weight of Jack's body in her arms, she felt a great strength and serenity, as if another piece of a puzzle had fallen into place. Bars of August sunlight lay across them. Jack's fair hair blazed white-gold in the heat. Lily kissed the back of his head, dreamily inhaling its sweet, musky scent.

He drew himself out of her arms and sat upright, blinking. Lily's handkerchief was in his hand. He stared at it, as if trying to work out what it was, then blew his nose violently.

'Sorry. You won't want it back now.'

'Keep it.'

'Thanks. You're really awfully sweet.' His hazel eyes, so like those of Oscar and Kit, studied her cautiously. He was trying to step back to the usual distance, but this was now impossible. Enormous intimacy had occurred. He must either die of embarrassment, or fight through it. 'Don't take it too seriously. Sometimes, I have to let it out, that's all. I can't show the others. They'd feel they had to do something. And they'd have to work at not despising me.'

'They'd never do that.'

'Not despise, exactly. They'd hate having to think less of me.' Hesitantly, he reached for Lily's hand. 'Did anyone else hear? I thought you were all out.'

'Everyone else is,' Lily assured him. 'Pa's taken Paddy to the dentist and I think Quin went fishing with Kit.' This accounted for everyone. Two days after the departure of Oscar, Bruno had vanished back into his secret job. The place was rather disturbingly quiet. Lily found she particularly missed affable, untidy Bruno.

Jack blew his nose again. 'I'm messing up your work, aren't I?'

'The world won't end. It's nice to be out of that kitchen.'

With his free hand, Jack took his cigarettes out of his pocket. He smiled ruefully. 'That bloody picture.' He held up the packet of Navy Cut, showing Lily the picture of the cheerful, bearded sailor on the front. 'Jolly Jack Tar, eh? Only he's not very jolly, just at the moment.'

There was a spell of breathless silence, before Lily dared to whisper: 'What is it? What's the matter?'

He murmured: 'I'm dreading joining the new ship. I thought the Navy was my life – there's never been anything else I wanted to do. And now I don't want to go back. It's all wrong.'

'Why?'

'I could put it whimsically, and say my heart went down with the *Audacious*. That I left it at the bottom of the sea, somewhere south of Crete, with the three-quarters of the ship's company who didn't come home.'

'For God's sake, don't be ashamed of crying for them.'

'I'm not ashamed. I'll cry for them as long as I live. They were as brave as they could be, and they fought like tigers. It wasn't their fault. They were coming at us from the air, and there's bugger-all a destroyer can do against a swarm of planes. Even when she's the *Audacious*, fit to hold her own against anything in the water. I can't bear that she died so horribly, and so – so unfairly, that's all.'

Lily twined her fingers round his. 'Didn't you say any of this to Pa? Or Quin?'

He shrugged, and shook his head. 'I didn't go into detail. I don't terribly want them to know what it's really like.'

'Darling Jack. You've been carrying the whole nightmare alone.'

'When we were hit,' he said, 'I thought I'd died. When you abandon ship, you can't imagine how far you plummet into the water – down, down, down. When I came up, there was oil everywhere. And they –' Jack drew a breath, forcing himself to say it in the same even tone, '– they fired on us in the water, while we were swimming for the float. Blood and oil. Choking black smoke, screams, confusion. Blood – or did I already say that? And the awful loneliness, helplessness, of watching the *Audacious* being swallowed into the depths, with my Captain aboard and one gun still firing.' He wiped his eyes. 'There'll never be another ship like her, that's all. And I can't help wondering why I wasn't with them at the end – why should I come home, when better men didn't?'

Lily had her arms around his neck, before she knew what she was doing. He clasped her to him desperately; a drowning man clinging to a spar. She wanted to wrap her whole self around him, to take the sting from his awful, secretive male sorrow. She did not love Oscar less – the image of his face only blurred in her mind for a moment.

Their lips met, and any doubts were blown to atoms. Jack was the only man in the world. His breathing quickened; his heart galloped against hers. None of it felt strange. Lily wrenched up Jack's shirt, to feel the muscles moving on his back. They were hard and taut under her palms.

His hand plucked at the buttons down the front of her dress. Because of the heat, she was wearing nothing underneath. His fingers brushed her nipple, and he let out a great, shuddering sigh. His touch shot sparks of longing across her body. They were writhing and struggling together now, simultaneously resisting the final barrier, and rushing towards it. Lily's centre of gravity had shifted. All her consciousness centred on the ache between her legs.

Jack groaned, and levered himself away from her, one hand clutching his swollen flies. 'Maybe we should – mustn't get carried away –'

This was a formality. His other hand was cupped around her breast.

Lily cried: 'Oh please don't stop!', with a passion that surprised them both.

The very last hint of strain melted from his eyes. His face moved towards hers. 'You want to?'

'Yes –'

'Oh, God –'

'Oh, please –'

This exchange was mumbled, with incoherent urgency, into each other's lips. Jack's hand moved from her breast, to the damp silk covering her vagina. Reflexively, she arched her hips towards his hand. He shuddered again, made a visible effort to control himself.

'Not here. Let's go down to my room.'

She asked: 'Why not here?'

This made him laugh nervously. 'Haven't got a johnny up here.'

'A what?'

'Oh, my God. You haven't done this before, have you? I mean, of course not – what a cheek, I'm so sorry. Look, do you still want to?'

'Yes.' She was impatient, and beginning to be annoyed.

As he gazed down at her, the longing in his face was tinged with doubt.

Slowly, the expression of his gold-flecked eyes softened, until they seemed to glow with tenderness. He picked up her hand, and kissed it reverently. 'Please trust me, Lily.'

Jack's room was full of framed photographs of groups of sailors under looming, bosomy figureheads. There was a lifebelt, inscribed HMS *Euterpe*, hanging on one wall, beside a yellowed poster showing various knots. Brushes and combs were laid out in orderly ranks, on dustless surfaces. The scrupulous neatness of the room was wildly at odds with the rest of the house, and suggested a man whose life was governed by whistles and bells, and made to fit into small spaces with beautiful compactness.

Lily was aware, even as she unfastened her dress with trembling fingers, that the loss of the *Audacious* had been all the harder for Jack because it outraged his love of order. How cruel it must have been, she thought, to watch that perfectly ordered fighting vessel, upon which such care had been lavished, coarsely destroyed by a dropped bomb in a matter of minutes.

All this was driven from her mind when Jack stood before her, naked and erect. Almost sick with longing for his touch, she forgot to worry that she was doing something wrong. Conventional scruples were simply irrelevant. She could not connect the veiled warnings of Gladys with something so profoundly beautiful.

She lay down on the bed. The eiderdown was cool and delicious against her flesh. In a trance, she watched Jack extract the item he had called a 'johnny' from a drawer, and fit it over his erection.

She drew in her breath sharply when he entered her, driving through her virginity. Gentle as he was, it hurt fiercely, and made her feel gored and helpless. As he moved inside her, however – biting his lower lip in an effort to keep control – she felt herself moistening and expanding around him.

And his body, above hers, felt more awesomely wonderful than she could have imagined – his weight, smell, texture.

269

Lily's overheated sex, already ripe and swollen, twitched with the intimation of a great, ultimate delight. She gave herself to him totally, and took his orgasm as the sublimest of gifts.

Jack rolled off her, gasping, and her smarting body registered his withdrawal as a loss. She lay with her cheek upon his tanned chest, stupid with happiness.

He stroked her hair. 'Lovely Lily. Sweet Lily. That was – that was bloody marvellous. I hope you liked it.'

She tucked a hand between his hard thighs. 'I don't think it's a question of liking "it" all by itself. I think I liked it because I love you.'

He eased her off him, so he could see her face. 'Really?'

'Darling Jack – I wouldn't do it with you if I didn't. There's no point at all, without love.'

He was moved to the core by this, but cautious about believing it. 'I thought you had a sort of thing for Oscar.'

Lily considered this. Did she now love Oscar less? Should she feel guilty about what she had done with Jack? She found that she did not. She found that she was a wicked girl, because she knew she would do exactly the same thing with Oscar like a shot.

'I do have a bit of a thing for him. Do you mind?'

'No. Not if you've got a thing for me, too – my God, never in my wildest dreams – but Oscar might mind.'

'Why?'

'Oh, Lily!' He was laughing. 'He told us to keep our hands off.'

'Well, he had a sauce. I didn't promise anything, except that I'd be here when he came back. That's all.'

'And will you? When I come back, too?'

She was touched that he asked so little. 'Of course. I'll tell you what I told him. I'll always be here. I'll never, never leave. And whatever I get up to, you must remember that there's a bit of me that's always yours.'

'You angel.' His hand moved down to her clitoris, and idly massaged the ridge of swollen flesh. 'Can I have this bit?'

She discovered then that she was throbbing with desire. Suddenly, she recognised the focus of years of confused yearnings. It was like knowing a new language. She put her hand over his, and guided his finger with surer, firmer strokes, until she came with a great sob of release, and clung to his hand until she had driven out each hard spasm.

Jack found another condom. They made love, slowly and deeply – and 'making love' was exactly what Lily felt she was doing. Making the most precious commodity on earth or in heaven, tasting the air of angels.

Lily thought: Now that I've found this place, I'll never come down again.

———⋘⋙———

Nobody said anything, but the brothers silently acknowledged the shift in relationships. They could hardly do otherwise. Jack shone with contentment, and sex made Lily's beauty glorious.

Pa, Quin and Paddy were relieved to see Jack's old, unshadowed self. His underground pain, and his stubborn refusal to let them sympathise, had made them miserable.

Kit had suffered for him, too, but regarded the affair with deep mistrust. Just when Lily had begun to think he was thawing, all his old surliness rushed back with interest.

'It's a game,' he told Quin. 'How can you watch her using Jack for her stupid games? When she dumps him, he'll be worse off than ever. It'll just about kill the poor bastard.'

Lily accidentally overheard this through the air-vent in the cellar, and wanted to bash him over the head with the frying pan. How dared he assume she would dump her handsome Jack? Because some girl had dumped him, of course. Thinking of this – repeating it like a prayer – stopped her anger, and helped her to bear his carps and snubs with the valour of a saint.

Jack said: 'I wish Kit would lay off. I hate the way he insults you, and I hate the way he treats me like a loony. He must think it's an act of charity to sleep with me.'

They were in his bed, in the syrupy heat of the early afternoon, on the day before he joined his new ship.

'He has a broken heart,' Lily murmured. She was lying on Jack's chest, dreamily inhaling the smell of his skin.

'He's lucky you take such a romantic view of things.'

'Mmmm. Do I?'

She felt the rumbling of his laughter. 'Oh, Lily, you're an incurable romantic. Or you wouldn't give Kit-the-shit such a lot of rope.' He caressed her hair. 'And you probably wouldn't be so sweet to me.'

'I'm a nice girl,' Lily said, 'and every nice girl loves a sailor.'

Below them, the clock struck three. They sighed, and moved apart as a first step to getting dressed. Both were reckoning how many more times they would be able to make love, before Jack left. His leaving loomed larger as the hours passed.

'I wish you'd let me come to Plymouth with you,' Lily said.

'No. I need to be alone with Quin. We sort of plug into each other's brains, and I haven't seen enough of him this leave.'

She was penitent. 'Because of me. I'm sorry.'

'Partly. But it was tough before you came. Our lives are so bloody different. I sometimes think I have the easier time, right out in the thick of it, than Quin does, stuck here on the farm.' He rolled off the bed, and pulled a shirt over his fair head. 'Will you do something for me?'

'Anything!'

'I'm serious.' He sat down on the bed beside her, and took her hand. 'Will you take care of Quin when I've gone?'

Lily ran her fingers through his thick hair. 'Of course. Though I don't see what I'll be able to do for him.'

'Well, the thing is – what I really mean is – if anything happens to me.'

She did not mean to cry. The tears gushed out before she could blink them away. 'Oh, this is ridiculous – I'm being silly – ignore it –'

Jack's eyes filled in sympathy, but he was radiant. He gathered her in his arms. 'Darling. I love your tears. I'll wear them like a lifebelt. I can bear anything now.'

<hr />

Pa found Lily sobbing next morning, as she scraped the remains of the porridge into the pig-bucket. Jack, already half a stranger to her in his uniform, with his eyes focused somewhere in the distance, had gone.

'Well, well,' Pa said. This was meant to be vaguely consoling. He poured himself the black dregs of the teapot.

Lily blew her nose vigorously, on the dish-towel. 'Sorry. But I didn't do this in front of him.'

'Miss Lily,' Pa said, 'do you mean to make an honest man of my Jack?'

This brought out a watery smile. 'What can you mean, Pa?'

'Call me old-fashioned, but I don't seem to have heard the word "marriage" yet. I feel I should mention it, because my room adjoins yours, and I've heard everything else.'

'We never got round to it,' Lily said. 'I'll marry him if you like. Do you think we should?'

Pa snorted with laughter. 'It's usual.'

'I'll say yes if he asks me. Though I don't see how it could make us happier than we are.'

He was still grinning, but eyeing her keenly. 'It would be one good way of pinning you down and keeping you here.'

'I'm not going anywhere.'

'I shouldn't have to go on paying you thirty bob a week.'

'Ha! I haven't seen a penny of it yet.'

'My God, I should have guessed when I took you in – the virtue of my sons isn't safe with you.'

'Pa, darling, I'm not playing fast and loose with Jack's affections, I swear. If I've ruined him, I'll do the decent thing.'

He laughed again, shaking his head. 'I can't make you out at all. I'm sure I ought to disapprove.'

'Why?' Lily asked gently. 'Does he seem unhappy? Does anyone?'

'No, no, what I mean is –' with an effort, Pa expressed a rusty tenderness '– what about you? Love's all very fine, but when I come in and find my housekeeper weeping –'

She dropped a kiss on his wild thatch of hair. 'Don't you see? It's because I've never been happier in my life.'

Chapter Seven

1981

———◆◆◆———

In dreams and fantasies, it is possible to wake up and find everything changed, for better or worse, as if by magic. Sophie's life took a small but significant leap forward, the day after she took possession of Lily-Josephine's diary.

She emerged from a long meeting, to find message-slips blooming all over her desk, in place of the usual penitential flowers. Pandora was hovering, in a high state of gleeful curiosity.

'He's been calling at ten-minute intervals all morning. I think it's urgent.'

Sophie sank into her chair. She felt frail and convalescent, after a night of too little sleep and too much coffee.

'He's at Sir Bruno's,' Pandora said. 'The number's on the blotter.'

'I know the number, thanks. Could you dash down to the machine, and get me a black coffee?'

And keep your dear, well-bred little nose out of my love-life, while you're about it.

Octavius answered the telephone after one ring – it barely had time to draw a deep breath. 'Sophie? Thank God. I have to go back to Devon. My grandfather's ill.'

More drama. 'Oh, darling, I'm so sorry. What's wrong with him? When did this happen?'

'He's broken his leg falling out of a tree, and claims to be dying. We've all been summoned.'

'Is he very ill?'

'He always says he's dying, when he's after something,' Octavius said. 'My guess is, he wants to stop us fighting over that fucking court case. But he is nearly ninety. We have to humour him.'

'Well, of course –'

'There's certainly nothing wrong with his tongue. I spoke to him this morning.'

'Bruno's taking you, I suppose,' Sophie said. 'When are you leaving?'

'He's stuck in Oxford until tomorrow. We'll hire a car, and you can drive me down this afternoon.'

'What?' She shifted the receiver to her other ear, as if this could improve her comprehension.

He sounded brisk, almost combative. 'Go home first, for some warm clothes. Randalls is always freezing.'

'Ground control to Major Randall,' Sophie said. 'You seem to have forgotten the little matter of my job. God, you've got a nerve. If I just waltz out, I'll be sacked.'

There was a significant pause. Octavius said, 'I'm doing this all wrong. Of course I don't just expect you to act as my chauffeur. Pa asked me to bring you. He wants to meet you.'

'Me?'

'The thing is, I told him about you.'

Another pause, this time stretching on and on.

'Told him what?' Sophie demanded irritably. 'That I'm good at Scrabble? That I do a striptease act with a python? You're up to something – you're doing your guilty, belligerent voice.'

Octavius said: 'I told him I'm madly in love with you, and that we're getting married.'

'Are we? You haven't actually asked me. You gave me the ring, with the romantic words: "Let's not make it public just yet." Have we suddenly gone public, or are you deliberately trying to confuse me? Is it going to be like this all the bloody time? God, you're an annoying man sometimes.'

He was laughing softly. 'Is over the phone all right? I'm down on one knee, by the way. Sophie, light of my life, will you marry me? I have nothing to offer but these empty hands, this full heart –'

'Yes, I get the idea, thanks.'

'I'm tired of secrets,' Octavius said seriously. 'You're the only thing in my life worth fighting for. I want to show them all how much I love you.'

He could strum her heartstrings like a harp. His

declarations of love made her want to weep, sing, dance, yell to the heavens. Sophie had just enough sense left, however, to read the small print.

'You want to use me as an offensive weapon against your uncles.'

Octavius was silent long enough to tell her that she was right. He never lied to her, and had to grapple for an acceptable version of the truth. 'As an amulet,' he said. 'A shield, a good-luck charm.' Quietly, he produced the three clinching words. 'I need you.'

Short and strange as their relationship had been, they had become two people who needed each other, to make themselves complete. Sophie knew that she would love Octavius if he never had sex with her again – so perhaps he was right to make their engagement public. In which case, it was time she saw Randalls for herself.

'All right. Just don't make me go for walks. I grew up in the country, and I hate any walk that doesn't have a shop or a pub at the end of it.'

It was decided. She found herself promising to leave the building, pack a case of warm, waterproof clothes, and follow him to the ends of the earth. 'Or Devon – whichever's nearest.'

She was dazedly wondering how to achieve this, when Pandora burst in, bearing a fragrant cup of real coffee from Richard's office.

'I told Richard it was Sir Bruno who asked for you. He says that's fine, stay as long as you like, and he hopes the old gent gets better soon. I've ordered a taxi for you, on the firm's account. It'll be here in ten minutes, so drink up.'

It was simply incredible. This beguiling little Sloane knew more about her affairs than she did. Sophie was about to be angry at the interference, when it occurred to her that it sprang from kindness. She had forgotten that people mostly wished to be kind.

'And you're not going to like this,' Pandora went on, 'but I told Richard about you and Octavius being engaged. I thought it would soften him up.'

'How did you –?' Sophie began feebly.

'The ring round your neck, silly. We all noticed.'

Sophie opened her mouth to protest, and surprised herself by laughing until her mascara ran. She had sense enough not to make her working life impossible, by apologising to her shared secretary for being a cross old bitch, but risked: 'Pandora, you're not as thick as you make out.'

'Oh, I am,' Pandora said serenely. 'But I do know about engagement rings – and that's the best one I've seen, since my sister bagged her earl.'

<hr />

'Not long now. About ten minutes. I'm not going to give you any instructions. If they love me, they'll love you.'

'Blackmail,' Sophie observed.

Octavius was driving the hired Rover. Just beyond Exeter, he had insisted that she stop at a service station and change places. 'I know I'm breaking the law, I know I'll lose my licence if I get caught, and I don't care. It's pissing with rain, it's pitch-dark, and Randalls is hellish to find.'

So here she was, driving illegally in pelting rain, in a labyrinth of narrow country roads, with a man who was as nervous as a bagful of ferrets. Octavius sped through the murk with the terrible, kamikaze confidence of the rural motorist. But he knew where he was going. This was a journey he could have made in his sleep.

The leaden February sky had deepened to black. Through the rhythmic swish-swish-swish of the windscreen wipers, Sophie watched the Catseyes, glinting in the headlights like a string of watery jewels. She was intensely curious to see Randalls, and also apprehensive. They were not about to step into a time machine, she reminded herself. Lily-Josephine was dead, and the young men she had described so lovingly in her diary were sliding into old age.

The past was more than a memory to them, however, and she wondered uneasily what kind of welcome they would have, for the granddaughter of Sidonia. Bruno's off-the-cuff remark about the Montagues and the Capulets no longer seemed amusing. In the Land of the Randalls, anything was possible.

Sophie asked: 'Did you find your mother's diary?'

'I did.'

'I'm afraid I read a bit of it, last night.'

She saw him in profile, watching the road sternly. 'Feel free. I left it on your desk.'

'Don't you want it first?'

'No. I might get round to it eventually. You can mark the good bits for me, if you like.'

The car made a sudden swerve, and the necklace of Catseyes ended.

'Darkness on the face of the waters,' said Octavius, wincing as the hired exhaust-pipe scraped the road. 'Hold tight.' They lurched and juddered across the craters, while the rain hammered on the roof.

Through the two fan-shaped openings made by the wind-screen wipers, Sophie saw the black bulk of a large building, studded here and there with squares of yellow light. Octavius skirted round the side, and before he switched off the headlights, she saw silver lances of rain, dancing on uneven cobblestones.

Octavius grabbed their bags from the back seat, and hurried Sophie out of the downpour. She found herself in a big, warm room, full of golden light.

A beautiful room. It was dominated by a handsome blue Aga, the only new article. Everything else was softened and worn, and seemed to have sprung naturally out of the stone flags in perfect harmony. The panelled walls were darkened by centuries of woodsmoke. A huge wooden dresser ran along one entire side, filled with old blue-and-white china. An open door revealed a modern kitchen, with a washing machine, tumble dryer and double sink. A red setter, the colour of an autumn leaf, lay huffing on a patchwork cushion beside the Aga. It jumped up, to lick Octavius's hand.

A tall, thickset man, with a high colour and startling, red-gold hair, was writing something at the big table. He glanced up, and smiled.

'Octavius. Good to see you.'

'Hi, Pete. Sophie, this is Peter Tufton, Pa's GP. Sophie Gently.'

Peter Tufton stood, and briefly clasped Sophie's hand.

'Your intended, I take it? Congratulations.'

'How's Pa?'

Unhurriedly, the doctor replaced the top of his pen, and tucked it into his breast pocket. 'Well, a broken leg's no joke at his age, but your grandfather never ceases to astonish me. He says he's fine, and I believe him.'

'Thank God,' Octavius said.

'Yes, indeed. Let's hope the plaster will keep him out of trees for a month or so.'

Octavius took a bottle of whisky from the dresser. 'You'll be lucky. Like a drink?'

'Not for me, thanks.'

'Soph?'

'Yes, please.' She did not really want a whisky, but thought it might help to induce ease. Despite the warmth of the big kitchen, she was freezing into a rigor of shyness. This was the first time she had seen Octavius on his own territory. He moved around the room with the blind assurance born of total familiarity. His attitude to his family may have been ambivalent and strained, but he slotted into this setting with an ease that made him a stranger. She perched on the carver's chair, while the doctor pulled on a battered wax jacket and took his leave.

'Tell Paddy the nurse will be here in the morning. He's stuffed with drugs, so he shouldn't be too much trouble tonight. Ring me, if there's a problem. I'll look in tomorrow.'

'Okay. Give my love to Gladys.'

'Of course. Do run over to see her, while you're down here.'

He left, and Octavius put a glass of whisky into Sophie's hand. 'Are you all right?'

'Fine. I wasn't prepared to be hailed as your "intended", though. Does the whole countryside know?'

'I don't care if they do, but Pete's not the whole countryside. He's practically family – his mother looked after me, when I was little.'

She began to see how past and present meshed in this place. On the chimneypiece were the same photographs she had seen at Bruno's – the clan of men, the girl in the field.

Octavius stroked the smooth auburn head of the dog. 'This is Custard, by the way.'

'The same as –? No, of course not.'

'There's always a Custard.'

'So – how many Randalls will I see?'

He leant against the rail of the Aga. 'We're a shifting population. Kit and Paddy live here with Pa. The others – well, we come and we go.' He was suddenly reticent, wary. 'Nobody really leaves.'

Sophie took a slug of whisky, to suppress the rising shudder along her spine. 'Stop being so weird.'

'Sorry. I want you to understand what I'm up against,' Octavius said, with one of his rueful, lopsided smiles. 'I was born in a house where the past hangs about like the smell of gas.'

'You're trying to frighten me.'

'Don't be silly.' He put down his drink, knelt in front of her chair, and wrapped his arms around her. His body felt reassuringly warm and solid. The soft light, from the shaded lamps at either end of the dresser, drew out the seams of gold in his rich brown hair and hazel eyes. Sophie, gazing down into his face, saw for the first time the impress of the girl in the photograph – something in the set of his cheekbones and the line of his sharply incised upper lip, gone as soon as noticed.

A door opened in the panelling – Sophie was quickly to learn that the design of the house lent itself to sudden, pantomime entrances. A tall man, brown and seamed, as if he had been left out in the rain for years, came into the kitchen.

Octavius sprang up. 'Paddy.'

'You're here,' Paddy said, unnecessarily. 'And this must be Sophie.'

She stood, and took his dry, sinewy hand. 'Hello.'

He stared down at her solemnly, with hooded hazel eyes.

'Patrick Randall. I've heard about you. From your aunt.'

'Primrose? Yes, she sent me one of your books for Christmas. She never stops going on about you.'

A transient gleam in the hooded eyes suggested pleasure.

'I've been helping her with the new garden.'

'Is the old man awake?' Octavius asked.

'Wide awake. Agitating to see you.'

'And Sophie, I'm sure.' He turned to her. 'Would you mind?'

'I'd love to meet him,' Sophie said carefully, 'if it wouldn't tire him too much.'

Both men grunted sardonically. For a moment, they were eerily alike.

'We're the tired ones,' Paddy said.

Octavius topped up the glasses of whisky, and poured one for Paddy. Tenderly, but with determination, he unhooked the chain from Sophie's neck, slipped off the no-longer-secret engagement ring, and slid it onto her left hand. Paddy watched the ceremony impassively.

'I'd better tell my parents,' Sophie said, 'now that we're official.' And to make the whole thing less peculiar.

'Come on,' Octavius said. He steered her out of the hidden door, and up a polished mountain of staircase. There was not one straight line here. The walls bulged and curved, the ceiling dipped, the floors sloped crazily. Yet Sophie had an impression of mass as immoveable as Stonehenge. Every whorl and knot of the ancient wood suggested stubborn, enduring strength.

'Is that the boy?' The voice was as old and strong as the timbers of the house. 'Number Eight, is that you?'

'Yes, Pa.' Octavius and Paddy led Sophie into a large, panelled room, with a wood fire snapping in a stone fireplace. It was a jumble of stuffed birds, flat glass cases full of labelled skulls and feathers, and teetering piles of books.

The old man, wrinkled as a piece of parchment, lay propped on pillows in the high brass bed. One leg, in a plaster cast, jutted out over the eiderdown. Another man stood at the window, with his back to them. Octavius shot a wary glance at him, before bending to kiss Pa's wild white hair.

Was this Kit? The famous Kit, who had accused little Lily of playing games and who ended up married to her? His back appeared to express disapproval. Of me, Sophie thought.

Suddenly, she was sure she had been brought here mainly to be inspected by Kit.

'You silly old fart,' Octavius said to Pa. 'What the hell were you doing up a tree?'

'Trying to get a look at a clutch of eggs. If you'd been here, I could've sent you up instead, and saved myself all this trouble.'

'No, you couldn't – I like my bones unbroken.' Octavius put his arm around Sophie's waist. 'This is Sophie.'

'Come into the light,' Pa ordered.

Sophie took a step nearer the bed, and submitted to the sweep of his eyes, disconcertingly keen and penetrating in his shrivelled face.

'Ah, you're lovely. What fun it's going to be, having a lovely young woman to look at.'

'We can't stay long,' Octavius said.

'That's what you think. We're in for snow.'

A deep, harsh voice said: 'Bollocks. He's been babbling about that snow all day.'

Sophie felt Octavius's hand tensing in the small of her back. 'This is Kit.'

Kit strode across the room, to present himself formally to Sophie. He shook her hand, and stayed very close to her, staring down into her face.

She did not allow her polite smile to waver, but the shock of Kit's appearance winded her like a blow. He was extraordinary. For the first fraction of a second, Sophie thought him hideous. His brow was set in a scowl and his mouth in a snarl, like a Japanese Noh mask. Beneath his thick mat of brown hair, his hazel eyes had a ferocious glitter. His skin was unnaturally smooth, but crazed all over with fine lines, like an old piece of glazed leather.

It took her only a moment to realise that he was, in a curious way, handsome. He was a man of bog-oak, wondrously hewn and weathered to a shine. He was vivid and magnificent, a man shaped by bolts of lightning. A Renaissance painter would have cast him as Vulcan at his forge. Sophie thought: When he was young and unblemished, he must have been quite amazingly beautiful.

When she arrived at this thought, Kit released her from his baleful stare, as if he had been waiting for it. He touched Octavius's shoulder. 'Congratulations. Both of you.'

This was not what Octavius had expected. Sophie felt him bristle defensively, braced for a blow. It did not come. Amazement took the place of suspicion.

Pa's loud voice swept away the tension. 'Now, perhaps Sophie will know – what can I do with a single pyjama-leg? Peter cut it off, when he did the cast. Perfectly decent pair of pyjamas ruined.' He gestured towards the orphaned blue cotton leg, hanging over the end of the bed. 'Seems a pity to chuck it away.'

He had noticed the silent drama being played out by Kit and Octavius, Sophie felt sure. 'A windsock, for an airfield?' she hazarded.

He chuckled. 'I like that. Brains, as well as beauty.'

'My father,' said Kit, 'is not in the final, tragic stages of senile dementia. He's been completely barmy for at least sixty years.'

'Disrespectful – insubordinate – what's Paddy drinking? Whisky? Yes, I'll have some.'

'Sorry, Pa,' Paddy said. 'No booze. Doctor's orders.'

'Go to sleep,' said Kit, making for the door. 'You can have some supper later, when we've finished ours.'

'I might not want the same as you. Someone tell me what's in the fridge.'

'Go to fucking sleep.' Kit motioned them all out of the room.

Pa's voice floated after them. 'You'll miss me when I die!'

'Take no notice.' Kit addressed Sophie, with a kind of rusty cordiality. 'He'll see us all out.'

He carefully left the kitchen door open, so they would be sure to hear if Pa called. Sophie sensed the deep love behind the ritualistic insults.

Paddy opened the oven door. 'Good supper tonight. Peter's wife sent over one of her casseroles.' He placed it on the table, and took four plates from the dresser. Kit noisily threw down a litter of cutlery.

'No champagne,' he said. 'There ought to be champagne.'

He wrenched the cork from a bottle of red wine. 'We'll have to make do with this. Get the glasses, Number Eight.'

Octavius fetched glasses from the dresser. He was still unbelieving, but with the beginnings of radiance.

Paddy spooned out the lamb casserole, and Kit poured the wine. They all began to eat. Sophie looked from one solemn Randall face to another. This was like a dream.

Kit cleared his throat portentously. 'You ought to have told us about this earlier. It changes everything.'

'Does it?' Octavius was cautious.

Kit addressed Sophie. 'You're so like Sidonia. I hoped you would be. Your coming has enormous meaning for us. When I heard, I admit I did feel angry at first.' His scowl deepened momentarily, making his face almost comically horrifying. 'But I realised I was wrong. And Octavius was right. She'd never have cared a damn about her father's house, or the money.'

'God almighty,' said Octavius, 'does this mean you're going to stop nagging me about the court case?'

'Yes. None of our business what you do. We see that now.'

What Kit thought mattered desperately to Octavius. Sophie felt his relief.

Paddy said: 'It's as if she'd arranged it herself. You marrying Sophie is exactly what she'd want.'

'I could almost hear her voice,' said Kit. 'Reminding us you're hers, as well as ours.'

Several things struck Sophie as peculiar. First, the assumption that the love between herself and Octavius was a move in some heavenly game; second the assumption that Octavius 'belonged' to his dead mother and his uncles, but not, apparently, to himself.

Her flesh crawled. These mad old men, she thought. She saw herself arriving at their ridiculously spooky house like Janet Leigh driving into the Bates Motel – a cinema audience would have said she had only herself to blame.

Strangest of all, Octavius reacted as a man unbound from heavy chains. She watched, fascinated, as he went round to Kit's side of the table and put his arms around his unyielding neck.

Kit submitted to this embrace, but did not return it. He dismissed his nephew with a curt pat on the shoulder. Octavius returned to his place beside Sophie, all tension ironed out of his face. Both then exchanged cautious half-smiles, as if communicating in some secret, telepathic language.

She found herself sympathising with Octavius's wife. None of them had liked her, he had said. It must have been hell for her here.

Once the announcement had been made, the conversation became general. Sophie listened to Kit and Paddy filling their nephew in on the local news. She ate the casserole, oppressed by the strong likeness between the three men – their brown skins, golden eyes and deep voices. Their shared habit of speaking in gulps and snatches, barely moving their lips.

Paddy assembled a tray of supper for Pa.

Kit said: 'You two will want to sleep together, I suppose. We've put you in Lily's room.'

❖❖❖

'My old room's full of kids things, and only has a single bed.' Octavius spoke just above a whisper, mindful of being next door to Pa, whose stentorian snores could be heard through the wall. 'They couldn't have put us in there.'

Sophie was sitting on the bed, still fully clothed. 'Where did you sleep with Caroline?'

'Upstairs, in one of the attics. It's madly uncomfortable. Look, this is a sign of how much they like you.'

'But they don't know me. Am I supposed to be pleased, because they've graciously approved the idea of me? I'm sorry. This is weird. Your mother's sacred room.'

The bed sagged, as Octavius sat beside her and pulled her into his arms. 'You're tired, my love. Don't read too much into it. It only seems weird because Kit and Paddy are so barking. Honestly, they're trying to be hospitable.'

She rested her cheek against his shoulder. 'You're pleased, aren't you?'

'Yes. I was dreading that attic. The mattress is like concrete. We stand a chance of actually sleeping in here.'

From the shelter of his arm, Sophie surveyed Lily's room – the room in which the black-eyed teenager had scribbled her diary, and dreamed of love. She could not feel easy about lying next to Octavius, upon the spot where – for all she knew – he had been conceived.

He stroked her hair. 'Get your clothes off, and don't worry. I'll take care of you.'

It was cold. The system that heated the rest of the house did not operate in here. Too tired to protest any further, when Octavius refused to understand, Sophie hurried out of her clothes. She wrapped her naked body in her dressing gown, and climbed between the old-fashioned linen sheets.

Octavius had an erection.

Great, Sophie thought sourly, just what I need. She burrowed her face into the chilly pillow, pretending not to notice. Please, please, no repeat of last night. No more retching and anguish and aching frustration – please.

She turned her back on him. He got into bed, and curled himself around her. Her flesh unwillingly acknowledged that the warmth of his body felt delicious. His erection dug into the base of her spine.

His breathing deepened into sighs. She felt his hand slowly pulling up the back of her dressing gown. Still lying on his side, he placed his hands on either side of her hips, and slid into her from behind.

Sophie was determined to take none of the responsibility for this, and none of the blame. She lay like a corpse, biting her lip to stop herself crying out with longing when he began to move inside her. She sensed him rushing towards his climax, and tensed miserably.

His lips against her ear, he murmured: 'I want to see you.' He withdrew, just long enough to turn her over on her back and re-enter with new urgency. He came. Tears spurted from his eyes, dropping down into Sophie's face. He came and came, in blissful, diminishing spasms, then collapsed on top of her, with a great sigh of release.

This was unbelievable. He had done it. Sophie held him in her arms. Both were oozing silent tears. At the very back of her consciousness, she knew she should be disturbed by the deep strangeness of the miracle, but the thought was pushed away by the force of all her pent-up desire for him.

He kissed her mouth, her breasts, her belly. He parted her legs and lapped at her clitoris with his tongue. Just before her orgasm possessed her, he entered her again. They came together, ploughing the sheets beneath them, and stifling their moans in each other's shoulders.

Sophie tingled and glowed, from her crown to the soles of her feet, as if her body had just returned to life after a long sleep.

———◆◇◆———

The rain stopped overnight, and a hard frost slammed down upon the countryside. By mid-morning, a few papery flakes of snow were meandering from a solid grey sky.

Pa was triumphant. 'I told them. It'll be a foot deep by nightfall. You'll be snowed in.'

Sophie smiled at him, warmed by the radioactive after-glow of the night before. 'I shan't mind.'

She was sitting with Pa, while the nurse took her coffee break downstairs. The painkillers made him loquacious, and he had expressed an urgent desire to talk to Sophie.

'I won't ask if you're comfortable here,' he said. 'You're in love, and love makes everything seem perfect. I'm glad Octavius found you.'

'Thanks. So am I.'

'And you're Sidonia's granddaughter. Most fitting.'

'Is it? I hardly knew her. I was usually away, at school or college, when she visited my mother.'

'Doesn't matter,' Pa said. 'You look so like that shocking, bosomy painting of her in the Tate. That's the thing. If I were a god, given to shaping the affairs of mortals, I'd have bred you up specially to love Octavius. It makes such a perfect finale.'

Love did make everything seem perfect, Sophie thought. Last night, she had deeply disliked being treated like a pawn in some supernatural family game. The uncles' solemn talk about her symbolic value had brought her out in goose pimples. This morning, however, she found she did not care. At home in Crouch End, it would probably seem rather endearing.

She was warming her back at the fire, and examining the dense clutter of objects on the broad stone chimneypiece – the souvenirs that had been left in the sand as nearly ninety years receded.

Bills, letters, penknives, broken old box cameras, bottles of pills. Photographs, of course. Loving families recorded everything.

She picked up a sepia wedding photograph. Here was Pa, nearly unrecognisable as a bright-eyed, dark-haired young stripling in antiquated morning dress. The bride on his arm, though she had been dead for more than fifty years, bore such a close resemblance to Octavius, Sophie could have picked her out in a crowd of strangers. Here was the source of the curling hair and luminous hazel eyes, reproduced down the generations. The grandchildren of Bruno and Gerda, snapped in the Hampstead garden, had them. So did the three curly-headed children pictured on a Mediterranean hillside – belonging to Quin, Sophie guessed. He had married an Italian, and grew olives in Umbria.

'You've had a look at the diary,' Pa said.

'Yes.'

'Quite a document. We found it about ten years ago, when we took the floorboards up in her room. What did you think?'

'I only got to the part where she fell in love with Jack.'

Pa smiled, and his sharp eyes blurred, as he contemplated the long ladder of years stretching behind him. So near the summit, the past had no more bitterness for him.

'That's our Jack,' he said. 'Behind the candlestick.'

Sophie found the framed studio portrait of the young naval officer, and brought it over to the bed. Pa barely glanced at the boy's poignant, smiling face.

'Now, Jack,' he said, smiling with the satisfaction of pulling out a pristine memory, 'Jack was an innocent creature. Very sweet and affectionate, in a childish sort of way. As sailors often are. Poor Tom Bowling, the darling of our

288

crew.' He sighed wheezily. 'His Captain wrote that he said his prayers at the end like a child at his mother's knee.'

She sat on the chair beside the bed. 'When did Jack die?'

'In the spring of forty-two. If you'd read any further in the diary, you'd have come to the bit about the telegram. This is how they told me my boy was dead. That my boy's grave was the bottom of the sea. A few curt words from the War Office. He lay dying of his wounds for four days, in an open boat – God, how that haunted me.'

Pa was miles away. He caressed the frame of the photograph with a shaking, claw-like hand. 'And I held Lily in my arms while she cried for him. I was glad she cried, because I couldn't. I was too angry. But I stroked her soft hair, and her tears soaked right through my shirt. Well, I'm glad Jack had those tears.'

Sophie, in her unbearably tender state, had tears prickling in her own eyes. They sat in silence, listening to voices and footsteps downstairs, and the icy stillness outside.

'Well,' Pa said again, more cheerfully. 'It's good that you should hear. I want you to know us all. Every single one. People you have loved only leave if you want them to, I find.' He smiled knowingly. 'How many are you, then, said I,/If they two are in heaven? Quick was the little maid's reply–'

Sophie finished the quotation. 'O Master! we are seven.'

Chapter Eight

LILY'S DIARY
1942

<><><>

How can he be gone? Nothing has changed here. He is as present as he ever was. His room still smells of him. I often wake up in the middle of the night, sure I have heard his voice. Then I remember, and the terrible, useless crying starts again. In my worst moments, I even think I would have loved him less, if I had known it was going to hurt this much.

Pa says I must accept the fact of death. He says young people are outraged, when they discover they are not immortal. He served in the last war, and tells me it taught him about the fragility of life. Which is why he now thinks all wars are stupid.

He grew his moustache because of the last war. An accident with a bayonet nearly severed his upper lip, and left him with a huge scar. I told him about Tufton and Daddy, and he said:

'Doesn't that make you feel more forgiving?'

Briefly, it did. I remembered Tufton saying that if a man did just one brave action like that, you had to call him basically all right. But the way he looked at me, and spoke to me, that last night – no, I can't forgive him yet.

Pa said, 'Feel sorry for him then, because he's a fool. He turned his back upon his child, and a man's children are his riches.'

I spend a lot of time talking to Pa these days. He has been my great friend and comforter. Today, while he was helping me hang up the sheets, he asked me to call him 'Gerard'. He says nobody has called him by his Christian name since his wife died, and that he's not the father of the whole world. It must be depressing, and I promised to try, though it will be difficult at first.

As usual, he – Gerard – really wanted to talk about Quin. What on earth can we do about him? How can we help him? We always end up fretting over Quin. Pa – Gerard, told me that when his wife knew she was dying, she kept murmuring 'Poor twins, poor twins,' and now he knew what she meant. He is afraid this parting will kill them both.

He is convinced I can help. I only wish I had a clue what to do, and I swore to Jack I'd take care of him.

Pa says, 'We can't sit beside Jack in that open boat, but we can and must stop Quin sinking with him.' He shouts: 'I can't spare any more sons!'

Like some Biblical curse, the telegram had smitten Quin to silence. Never a talkative man, he was now utterly mute. He trudged through his work on the small home farm, but if anyone addressed him expecting a reply, he stubbornly turned his face away.

After two months of this, Pa was frantic. He stopped hinting and requesting, and began absolutely begging Quin to speak.

'I don't care what you say! Pass the salt – or Fuck off the lot of you – show me you're still in possession of a tongue, and I'll leave you alone!'

Still, he remained in his self-imposed prison of silence.

In the village, it was the general opinion that poor Quin Randall had finally gone off his head, after years of being Not All There. When Lily cycled over to get the rations, she felt the whispers around her like a cloud of mosquitos. Eventually, as it was bound to do, despite Lily's efforts to shield him, the local gossip reached the ears of Pa.

He marched in from the pub one evening and pounced on Quin, roaring: 'Do you know what those ignorant swine are saying about you? Do you realise, if I dropped dead, they'd have you carted away to the asylum? Speak! For God's sake, speak!'

Quin sat himself down at the kitchen table. He looked at Pa, and Pa winced angrily away from the expression in his eyes. He was almost dancing with fury.

'Do you think this amuses me? Do you think I enjoy going down on my knees to you? Is this some kind of revenge against me, because I let poor Jack go to sea? You're doing it to punish me for my boy's death – doesn't it occur to you that I've been punished enough?'

Lily rushed in from the scullery, and seized Pa's arm with dripping hands. 'Gerard, for God's sake – what are you doing to him?'

He shook her off. 'I've had enough. This is a charade – a game – he's as stubborn as a bloody mule and as deep as Australia – he won't budge an inch until I shake it out of him!'

'Pa –'

'No, Kit, no! I've done kindness, I've done consideration. I will be listened to, and I will be answered!'

It was one of the great rants of Pa's career. He raved at Quin, he shouted imprecations at heaven, he swore to bomb the War Office, the Admiralty, Winston Churchill and the Royal Family.

Quin sat perfectly immobile, staring down at the surface of the table. Paddy whisked away upstairs like a wild animal. Custard sprang out into the night. The owls battered at the walls and ceiling with their great wings. Kit and Lily stoically sat out the tempest.

The grandfather clock struck the hour. Pa paused for breath.

Quin said: 'Stop.' This single word, uttered in a hoarse whisper, dropped in amongst them like a thunderclap. Quin's head sank down on the table. They all waited – Pa panting, as if he had been running. The minutes ticked past, and Quin did not move.

'Well done, Pa,' Kit snapped. 'He'll be a complete basket case when they cart him away – but at least he'll be able to talk.'

'Oh God, God –' Pa's face creased in anguish. He stormed blindly into the scullery. Lily followed, and found him with his face buried in a dish-towel, racked with silent sobs. She put her arms round him, as he had put his arms around her when the telegram came.

He comforted me, she thought; nobody has comforted him.

Pa clung to her, sinking his heavy head on her shoulder. 'I

can't bear it. I want to help him, and I end up torturing him instead.'

'He knows you don't mean to. You can't help it.'

'What should I do? What?'

'Talk to him, include him, whether he answers or not. Give him time.'

'I suppose you're right.' He sniffed, and pulled his head away. 'I haven't the patience, Lily, that's the truth. He frightens me. Then I start imagining he's doing it on purpose.'

'Let me try. It's time I did something. I promised Jack.'

She began her campaign the next morning, in the cowshed. Ignoring Quin's silence, she talked to him as if they were both engaged in a lively conversation. She felt monstrously stupid at first, describing the plots of films or reciting recipes sent by Gladys. After a couple of days, however, she grew used to thinking aloud, and even found it comforting – babbling to Quin was like scribbling in her diary, and she revealed more than she intended.

'This is very unselfish of me,' she told him. 'When you start talking, I hope you're discreet. You know me better than God does.'

Gradually, Quin showed that he was paying attention. At first, he stole glances at Lily, when he thought she was not looking. Next, he openly followed her with his eyes, then he progressed to trailing round the house after her, whenever he had a moment to spare. Occasionally, something she said brought out the ghost of a smile.

Lily wrote in her diary: 'I make gigantic efforts to be cheerful, but he breaks my heart – he is so like Jack, and so not like him.'

She caught herself staring at the fair hairs on his forearm, when they worked together in the dairy. She heard her voice faltering, when he leaned over her to help her and his scent made her heart lurch. She had several disturbingly delicious dreams about making love to Jack, and suddenly realising he was Quin. Her nipples hardened and her vagina moistened when he stood close to her, even as she prayed not to ruin everything by wanting him.

'I should never have done sex,' she sadly told her diary. 'I need it far too much. Some days in the month, the most disgraceful fantasies fill my head, and I can't fight them off. If only I didn't love them all so. Why can't I just love Q with my mind? My body is a distraction and a nuisance. I don't think Jack meant me to betray him.'

As far as Pa could see, she was having tremendous success. Delighted by Quin's fleeting smiles, he urged her to get out her banjolele again. Lily did so, feeling a fool but hoping George Formby's repertoire of boisterous, anodyne smut would keep her desire under control.

The routine of the house continued along its well-worn grooves. Pa studied his owls. Paddy worked in his Sleeping Garden, and cycled to and from the private school where he was a day boy. Kit skulked and lounged, vanishing on long fishing trips and helping on the farm when the fancy took him. Lily laboured on the domestic front, exhausting herself with the daily cleaning of the Augean stables.

Sometimes, the post brought a letter from Oscar or Bruno, which Pa read out in the kitchen, by the light of the oil lamp. Sometimes, he turned on the wireless for the news. They heard of the fall of Tobruk or the bloody Nazi advances in Russia, while Paddy did his homework and Lily sat darning what she called The Eternal Sock.

Ten weeks or so after Jack's death – soon enough for them to be still counting – Pa received a letter with a black border.

'Badger's dead,' he announced, over supper.

'Shame,' said Kit.

Lily, shovelling out potatoes, asked: 'Who's Badger?'

'My godfather,' said Pa.

'Oh, I'm sorry. But he must have been awfully old.'

'Seventy-three.' Pa frowned at her. 'Which is not "awfully old" in my book. How bloody old do you think I am? Badger was only seventy-three, and I am a mere fifty.'

'Fifty-four,' Kit put in.

'And last time I checked, I was still breathing. When I'm ready for the scrapheap, I'll let you all know. I'll put an announcement in *The Times*.'

Recently, Pa had begun to be sensitive about seeming old.

'I keep telling you,' Lily said, 'people assume you're older, because you go out of your way to look like an old man.'

'She wants you reeking of scent and greased up,' said Kit, his mouth full, 'like a pox-doctor's clerk.'

'Shut up, Kit. I do not. I'm just saying a haircut wouldn't go amiss. And shaving every day, instead of once a week. And holding up your trousers with a proper belt, instead of string –'

'Stop her, someone,' Pa grumbled, over the laughter of Kit and Paddy. Quin was smiling, and this made Pa more forgiving than usual about being nagged. 'I'll smarten up when I get to London. All right?'

Three voices chorused 'London?'

'Badger's left me some money.' Pa was enjoying their astonishment. 'Naturally, I shall attend his funeral.'

'But you never go anywhere!' protested Paddy. 'If you leave this farm, you'll probably crumble into ash, like Boris Karloff in *The Mummy*.'

Even Quin laughed outright at this. The sound made Pa's eyes gleam. 'Lily can drive me to the station, in that shocking old van of hers.'

He left early the next morning, with a mouldy black suit done up in a brown paper parcel. Lily ransacked the heaps of clutter in the bedroom and still-room for his unused clothes coupons, and made him take them with him.

'You never know,' she said.

Kit gave one of his barks of savage laughter. 'If you can get Pa into new clothes, I'll sing the German National Anthem.'

'Hope you know the words,' said Lily.

⚬≪◇≫⚬

Pa was away for a week and a half. He sent a postcard of Westminster Abbey, saying simply: 'I am well. Saw a *Strix aluco* in Regent's Park. Pa.'

'Brief but mysterious,' Kit remarked. 'I bet that kept the censors busy.'

Amazingly, Pa was staying, among sandbags and ancient servants, at his bomb-damaged club in St James'. Lily wondered what they thought, when the grizzled hillbilly turned up with his parcel, demanding a room. She missed him severely. His absence made her realise how heavily she had come to rely upon his company, his advice, his conversation. Kit, Quin and Paddy were no substitutes for Pa. Meals with them were like seances.

Late one afternoon Lily stood slicing tomatoes in the kitchen, with the scullery door standing open to the pale summer twilight. Custard, worn out by a long day chasing rabbits, lay in the last, fading square of sunlight on the stone-flagged floor.

A deep voice suddenly said: 'Where is everyone?'

Lily spun round, a welcome on her lips, and saw a total stranger.

The man was tall, slight and rather graceful, in a dark, double-breasted suit. He had iron-grey hair, cut close to his skull. His lean, handsome face was clean-shaven, with a thick, white scar curving across the upper lip. He smiled, showing perfect teeth. The smile crinkled his eyes, and Lily gasped:

'Holy cow, I don't believe it! Gerard!'

'Yes, it's me. How are you, my dear?'

Lily leaned forward to kiss his cheek, then hesitated. It had been easy to kiss Pa, when he appeared in the character of a crotchety old man. Kissing this elegant stranger was an altogether different matter. His cheek was smooth, and smelt of lemon verbena soap. His grey eyes crinkled again – her hesitation had pleased him.

'Custard recognises me, anyway.' He stooped, to slap the dog's flank affectionately. 'Disgraceful old hound – I smell the blood of blameless rabbits.'

Lily recovered her voice. 'I'll get you some tea, and fetch the boys –'

'No, no. Give me a minute before the barrage, there's a good girl.' He dropped into a chair. 'I got a lift with the milk, and he kept calling me "sir", so I must look a sight.'

'You look lovely.' Their eyes met properly, and Lily found the old, familiar Pa, alive and well inside the stranger.

'You approve, then?'

'Yes, I think so. It's rather strange, that's all. You go away looking like a scarecrow, and come back the handsomest of the lot.'

'I say. Draw it mild.' He rubbed the scar on his lip with his forefinger, where he had once had a habit of rubbing his lost moustache. 'Is everything all right? I feel as if I'd been away for decades.'

'We're all fine,' Lily said, turning to take the kettle off the range. She found it easiest to talk with her back to him. 'Quin's fine. That's what you really want to know.'

'Of course.'

'He's started saying the odd word, but don't get excited.'

'Why not?' Pa sat up. 'What does he say?'

'Things like "ouch" and "sorry". I didn't tell you straight away, because I didn't want you to make a song and dance about it.'

Pa sighed. 'You're right, I daresay.'

Lily made a pot of tea the way he liked it, spooning extra tea on top of the old, bloated leaves, and adding more hot water. 'Tell me about London. You look as if you spent the whole time being kitted out by dentists and tailors and barbers, like Mother Hubbard's dog.'

'London is a mess,' Pa said. 'Bloody great holes everywhere – St Paul's standing alone in a desert of rubble, no Eros in Piccadilly Circus, heaps of sandbags. I spent two nights playing bridge in the shelter, and kept forgetting my gas mask.' He began to eat the sliced tomatoes. 'The food was unspeakable. Badger's funeral was a bore, but one doesn't attend such affairs for fun. Went to the Windmill Theatre, and saw a lot of nude girls, holding Greek urns behind gauze curtains. God, I'm glad to be home. Mind if I loosen my tie?'

'Of course not. Fancy you asking.'

'Poor dear Badger left me fifteen thousand pounds. You could have knocked me down with the proverbial feather.'

From the back door, Kit's voice bayed: 'Bugger me!'

'Language, Kit,' Pa said, grinning. 'I thought we agreed not to swear in front of Lily. She being a lady, and all that.'

Kit advanced into the room, and walked round the table, surveying every transformed inch of his father.

'Well? Let me have it, boy, and get it over.'

Kit sang: '*Deutschland, Deutschland, über alles –*' and Lily collapsed into shrieks of laughter.

Paddy created a diversion, by entering in his school uniform and bicycle clips, and simply saying: 'H'lo, Pa. I got caught with a crib in Latin, and Mr Baxter gave me detention. You look smart.'

'Good old Wiz.' Lily wiped her eyes with the back of her hand.

'A master of understatement.' Pa cuffed him, warmly, using the cuff to cover a kiss.

Quin came in, and saw Pa. Both men, to Lily's sorrow, tensed defensively.

Pa hesitated for a second, then embraced him, with almost feminine delicacy. 'All right, Number Five?'

Quin responded with a half-smile, and shaped his lips into the word 'Yes'.

'I must love you for two now, eh?' Pa said.

He retreated, jerked a startlingly clean handkerchief from the pocket of his trousers, and blew his nose violently. 'Let money be no object. Kill the fatted tomato.'

Chapter Nine

Spring became summer, and Quin gradually, step by step, eased himself back into talking.

'You've been away from us,' Lily said. 'And now you're back.'

They were resting on a sunny bank after evening milking. The hedgerow behind them was spangled with fragile, quivering, scarlet poppies. From Paddy's Sleeping Garden poured the drowsy scents of bitter elder and sweet honeysuckle. Wood pigeons thrummed rhythmically into the silence.

Leaning on one elbow, Lily waited for a reply. This was the first time she had invited him to speak of Jack's death.

He was silent for a long time, frowning slightly and absently swatting at the midges, searching for words to express the inexpressible trauma of losing his identical twin.

'I think I knew, when it happened,' he said eventually. 'It was sort of like a light going out inside me. Or a little piece of my machinery suddenly breaking down. I was only running on one cylinder. Only half myself.'

'Lonely,' Lily said.

'Yes. And I was so bloody frightened. When the telegram came, and I knew he was dead, I was trying to hold on to him. Or follow him. Or maybe just wishing I could follow, or thinking I ought to.'

The revelation poured out from his heart, as if he had opened a vein. Lily sat up and put her arms around him.

'Oh, Quin.'

'I've been a complete pain in the arse, haven't I?'

She kissed his tanned neck. 'You certainly had us all worried.'

'Did Pa really think I'd have to be committed?'

'No, he was just getting into one of his states, because he felt so awful about Jack. And because he had no power to help you.'

Quin uncurled her arms and leaned back to watch her face. 'I must have been a nightmare. I'm so sorry. It's been tormenting me for weeks.'

'Stop it. I forbid you to apologise. We're all so glad to see you getting well again.'

'You – you –' his eyes watered, and the tops of his ears turned scarlet. 'You've been an angel to me.'

She laughed softly. 'Yes, I know. You'd better remember what I said about being discreet. You've had my life-story now. Not to mention the plots of every Marx brothers film in existence.'

'Honestly. Your sweetness, your kindness – I heard your voice, over the effort of trying to imagine his. You probably saved me from being carted away in a straitjacket.' His thin, asthmatic's voice was very low. 'I used to see Jack, dying in that boat, every time I closed my eyes. Now, when I close my eyes, I see – you.'

'My darling.' Lily tried to embrace him again, but he stiffened, and shifted away from her.

'The thing is,' he said in a rush, 'which you must have guessed by now – Lily, I've gone and fallen in love with you.'

The sun had whitened his hair, and tanned his skin. Lily thought how strange, and how beautiful, his tints of gold and bronze made him. He was slighter than Jack, with deeper hollows under his cheekbones, and flecks of green in his hazel eyes.

Impulsively, she said: 'You know, I've been blind. When I came here, I couldn't tell you two apart, and you're completely different.'

'We both fell in love with the same woman.'

'The same woman has fallen in love with both of you.' She placed her hand on his forearm. 'But Quin, I don't love you for being like Jack. You're another man, and I love you in another way.'

Quin said: 'Oh God, you're sorry for me.'

'No –'

'I'm like that owlet you nursed, with the broken wing.'

'No! Now, you listen to me.' Lily rolled up onto her knees, and took his face between her palms. 'When I fall in love, I do it with my whole heart, with my soul, with my spirit and my body. I don't go through all that for the sake of a man I feel sorry for. I love you, Quin – got that? I've fallen for you with the most sickening thud, and everyone in this house except you has watched me pining like Madame Butterfly.'

He pounced, roughly and clumsily, and his lips bit down desperately upon hers. His breath came in wheezing, shuddering gulps. His tongue invaded her mouth for a moment, before he forced his head away, and mumbled:

'No.'

He jumped up and stumbled blindly across the meadow. Lily was left sprawled on the warm grass, aching for his touch, and cursing herself for scaring him off.

⋘⋙

Pa chuckled softly, after Quin had pelted past them and crashed into the house. 'I sense a movement of troops,' he said to Kit. 'She's launched her offensive on his unguarded right flank. Now, she must dig herself in, while he regroups.'

The two of them were smoking out in the yard, on kitchen chairs. Custard dozed contentedly between Pa's feet.

'I suppose it's just as well,' Kit grunted. 'That girl will give Quin the seeing-to of his life, and he's crying out for a good fuck.'

Pa was annoyed. 'I wouldn't have put it quite like that.'

'However you'd put it, a bit of sex would be the making of him. We know for a certainty he's a virgin – unless he's been mucking about with the livestock.'

'Enough, Number One. A little more respect, if you please. He's your brother, and he's head over ears in love with that girl. I happen to think it's charming.'

'It's pathetic,' Kit said. 'He's practically dribbling over her, and every time she smiles at him, he wets himself. She must get a real kick out of it.'

Pa observed him shrewdly. 'Kit, it really is time you stopped this sniping at Lily. Or we shall all start to wonder if you fancy her for yourself.'

'Well, what if I do?' Kit was sullen. 'Of course I do. I've still got eyes, and a cock, even if I haven't got a face. But that doesn't mean I can't see through her.'

'There you go again. Lily's no player of deep games, boy. She's not stringing Quin along. She dragged him out of a nervous breakdown, when none of us could do a thing for him.'

'Look, I'm not denying she's been good for him,' Kit said. 'But how do you think Jack would feel, seeing how quickly she manages to switch her affections? It makes her love look like rather a cheap article, Pa – definitely not rationed.'

'Jack would be proud of her,' Pa snapped, 'and so am I.'

Kit leaned forward, resting his elbows on his knees. 'Do you know what they're saying in the village?'

'Nothing, thanks to Lily. No more of that rubbish about Quin being off his rocker.'

'Not about Quin. About you.'

'What? What?' Pa roared furiously. 'Spit it out, boy!'

'They reckon you're all cleaned up and youthful because you've decided to marry Miss Lily yourself.'

Pa looked thunderous, then bewildered. Then he surprised his eldest son, by letting out a shout of laughter. 'Do they, by God! And do they think she'd ever have me? Let's nip down to the pub and ask them.'

<hr>

The hot weather broke, suddenly and spectacularly. The smiling heliotrope sky turned livid charcoal, and a furious wind tore across the valley. Isolated, warning drops of rain fell heavily in the dust.

Lily cried, 'Hell, my washing!', and threw down the cucumber she was slicing for supper. 'Paddy! Gerard! Quin!'

Pa emerged from his still-room, and the pair of them fought their way across the yard to the long washing line. The wind hurled scraps of soiled hay into their faces, and Lily had to hold down her skirt, to stop it blowing up over her face.

The sheets, which she had spent nearly the whole day boiling in the copper, thrashed and cracked on the line like the great sails of a schooner. Lily and Pa jumped to grip them, starting to laugh as the damp hems smacked back in their faces.

One large sheet, as skittish and wayward as an unbroken colt, billowed off the line and over their heads. Pa grabbed Lily's waist, to steady her, and they fell awkwardly together on the cobbles.

The wind lashed and moaned around them, but Lily and Pa were protected by their tent of white linen. His face had an extraordinary clarity to her, as if illuminated by lightning – the muscles beneath the taut brown skin, the marbled grey of his eyes, the thick scar indenting his upper lip.

He said, 'Lily, my darling.'

He kissed her hard and with confidence, as if he had rehearsed this scene in his mind's eye for ages.

Lily's flesh surrendered to the hands of an expert. Her body lay passive, while her mind reeled with the shock of meeting this new Gerard Randall.

Over the wind, Quin's voice shouted: 'You comedians!'

He uncovered them, laughing. Pa and Lily scrambled up, studiously avoiding each other's eyes. With the help of Quin, they snatched up the washing, just as the sky burst in a solid summer downpour.

They ran into the scullery. Quin was between Lily and Pa. He stroked drops of water from the short, spiralling curls around her forehead, and looked down at the heaps of mud-stained sheets they had dumped on the floor.

'We made a mess of that – you'll have to do it all again.'

'I don't mind,' Lily said.

'You're not hurt are you, Pa? You took a hell of a fall.'

'Yes,' Pa said. 'A hell of a fall.' He risked a glance at Lily. 'I just hope it didn't hurt you.'

She said, 'I'm fine. Really.'

'You should do it more often,' Quin joked innocently.

'Poor Lily,' Pa said, rather grimly, 'I should think she'd hate that.'

Lily, trying to smile, murmured: 'I'd forgive you.'

The black eyes and the grey eyes met for a long, breathless moment, before Pa and Lily looked away. Quin neither registered nor understood their expressions of mingled shame and exultation. Lily was sorry he could be so easily deceived. Kit, always suspicious of Lily, was more observant. Pa worked all evening at distracting him. After supper, while Lily did the washing-up, he played chess with his eldest son as if for his life. Kit was too caught up in the game to pay much attention, when Lily muttered her good-nights and ran upstairs to her room.

She sat on her bed, fully clothed, waiting. The grey, disappearing light blurred every object in the room.

There was one brisk, furtive knock on her door.

'Yes,' she said cautiously.

Pa had removed his shoes. He stole in noiselessly, and gathered Lily in his arms. They made love with silent intensity. With his hands and his mouth, he explored her throat, her breasts, her vagina. He entered her, and nothing existed for Lily, beyond the immense relief of being fucked, expertly and urgently, until the tears rained down her cheeks.

He came twice, his face twisted with the effort of keeping silent. Afterwards, they lay a little way apart, listening as night fell upon the house. Outside, the howling of the wind had subsided to a muted keening.

The mattress rocked, as he leaned over to kiss her breast. 'My love,' he whispered, 'I must go.'

'Stay.'

'God, what have I done? I ought to be shot. You're young and lovely, and I'm a bloody old crock. It's obscene.'

'You're not a crock, Gerard.'

'I'm nearly sixty.'

'You were only fifty-four this morning.'

'Let me go, darling. I can't think properly here, and I must think.'

She sat up. 'So must I. D'you want some tea?'

'Tea? My dear heart – I'm about to unbury my sole pre-war bottle of brandy. You're welcome to join me.'

'All right.'

Creeping across the noisy floorboards, Pa retrieved the clothes he had shed in the fury of lovemaking, and covered himself in a pair of corduroys and an old sweater. Lily simply put on her washed-out linen frock, with nothing underneath, and they stole downstairs.

In the kitchen, Pa relit the oil lamp, and picked it up. 'Come on. We can talk in the still-room without disturbing the boys.'

Lily was forbidden to clean the still-room. A thick sheet of dust lay across its spartan furnishings and stacks of glass cases. A long bench ran the length of the room, under the window. Pa shifted a microscope, a heap of owl-pellets, a large pair of binoculars and three dirty teacups.

'I wondered where those had got to,' Lily said.

'Sorry.' From behind one of the glass cases, he took a bottle, half-full and furred with dust. 'But they can serve as vessels for my brandy, if you don't mind the lack of ceremony.'

Lily sat down in one of the two deal chairs. 'You know I don't.'

The brandy was pale gold, and very fine. Pa poured two generous measures into the teacups, and its rich, vinous scent filled the room, overriding the permanent reek of formaldehyde.

'Your health,' Pa said, staring intently down into her face. 'Your health for ever.' He smiled. 'What a gorgeous little gypsy you look, barefoot and wild-haired. I don't think you quite know how gloriously beautiful you are, Lily-Josephine. Let that be said in my defence, when I stand at the bar of heaven.'

She took a sip of the brandy. It was like swallowing sunlight. 'Are you sorry?'

He perched on the edge of the bench. 'I'm not, but I wish I could be. I had intended to be noble, and leave you to Quin. I mean – oh, God, I'm putting it all wrong –' He rubbed fretfully at his hair, forgetting it had been cut. 'Quin is in love with you, and I didn't feel I had any right to complicate matters with my feelings.'

Lily's bright dark eyes were sober. 'I'm glad you did. I needed it. I must be more like my father than I thought. Now you think I'm the most appalling tart.'

'No –'

305

'Don't you?'

'Lily, I've been wearing you like a hair shirt, ever since you came here. You upset fifteen years of dutiful sexlessness, which I felt I owed my boys. I could not find another woman good enough to put in their mother's place. She was an angel, and they were all so young. Six boys under twelve – she loved them so passionately, and trusted me to take care of them.' He poured more brandy into his cup. 'Sometimes, it occurs to me that a stepmother might not have been such a bad idea. You saw how we gradually turned into seven wild men, like a pack of feral dogs. Perhaps a woman would have civilised us. Perhaps she could have made up to little Paddy, for the mother's kisses he never knew. But until you came, there never was a woman to compare.'

'Julia Randall,' Lily said. 'Bruno showed me her picture.'

'Yes, Julia. Love of my life, bone of my bone, mother of my boys. She was a cheerful soul – she would have liked you.' He picked up Lily's hand. 'When she died, all the light left us. I would wake in the night, almost dying of longing, and hear my little boys sobbing for her.'

His eyes were wistful, but dry. His tears had been shed a long time ago. Lily was the one who wept.

'They had you,' she whispered.

He smiled down at her, with a tenderness that made his lean face beautiful. 'I did my best. And I like to think I'll be able to look her in the eye, if ever we meet again.'

'You will. Don't you believe it?'

'God, I don't know what I believe. But I take a superstitious comfort in thinking that she has Jack now. I suppose eternity passes in the blink of an eye, but she would feel her arms had been empty for too long – oh, Lily, I didn't mean to make you cry.'

'She must have loved you very much. She must have adored you. If I had to die, I'd be so glad to know my children were with a man like you.'

Pa set down his cup, and gently stroked her hair. 'You see why I didn't go out searching for romance. At first, I was too full of sorrow, and too anxious about the boys. Later, I went through tortures of physical deprivation, but one can learn to live with practically anything. When I got too desperate, I visited prostitutes and rogered myself into submission. By the time you came here, I had decided to be old, as if that would help me to live without sex. But your beauty has nearly driven me off my head – I have no right to call you a tart, God knows. I started it. You trusted me, and I jumped on you.'

'But I liked it,' Lily whispered, 'because I love you.'

He bent his grizzled, shorn head over her hand, and kissed it. 'I don't deserve such grace.'

'Gerard, I mean it. If I asked you to make love to me again, would you turn me down?'

He did not need to reply. His answer was in his eyes.

'And would that mean I had to stop loving Quin?' She was frowning, intensely serious.

'Wouldn't it?' he asked.

'I don't know. I can't choose. And even though you'll definitely think me a tart for saying it, I really don't see why I should.'

Pa was silent, unable to see what she was driving at.

'The awful, tarty fact is that I love you both. In different ways, of course, but equal amounts. I'm not going to let you give up something we both want and need. And I'm not going to give up Quin.'

'Do you –' Pa was cautious and wary, 'can you possibly mean that you want to sleep with us both?'

'It sounds horrible,' Lily said, 'and anyone who heard about me would think me very wicked. But yes. If it makes three people happy, instead of only two.'

'Would it make you happy?' Pa took both her hands, and studied her face. 'Think about what you're saying. The conventions exist, whether or not you approve of them. Flouting convention can be very uncomfortable. The locals are already gossiping about us. Do you really want to confirm their worst suspicions?'

'I don't care. We don't need those people, and what we do for the sake of our own hearts is none of their business. If you and Quin want me to choose between you, that's different. But you'd be doing it for your sakes – not mine.'

Reluctantly, Pa smiled. 'You make it sound so reasonable. And you know perfectly well, I never cared a straw for convention, or for the cretins who surround us. I would give you up, for Quin's sake. But I'd obviously rather not. After tonight, it'd be agony. I'm in love with you, and knowing I could never touch you again would make me absolutely bloody desperate.'

'Could you share me with Quin?'

He dropped her hands, and reached for his brandy. 'I don't mind, and I don't think he will, either. The seven of us have always been good at sharing. And quite frankly, if you can get poor Quin into bed, I'd be delighted. I'm surprised you didn't do it weeks ago.'

'Well, I've tried,' Lily said, with a sigh. 'But he must be the shyest man in the world. He told me he loved me, then avoided me like the plague.'

'My dear, it's no use dropping gentle hints. He needs a bomb under him – take it from one who's spent the last twenty years applying the boot to his behind. Quin dips his toe in the water for ever, unless someone pushes him in.' Pa let out a yelp of laughter. 'My God, I'm giving you hints about seducing my son! This is madness. You'd better marry one of us, at least.'

'Sorry, but I can't make those vows, unless I make them to both of you.'

'Then you are a wicked little tart, and you'll definitely go straight to hell. I just hope you won't mind frying next to me.'

'We'll make a lovely blaze,' Lily said, smiling serenely.

'My God, my God,' Pa shook his head. 'We take a pretty orphan-child into our home to scrub for us, and before you know it, we're knee-deep in smashed commandments. I really ought to go to confession, and give the priest a treat.'

Lily said, 'I didn't know you were a Catholic.'

'I was once, though I don't believe a word of it, and I haven't darkened a church since Julia died. Bless me, Father, I've committed a gigantic sin.' He stopped laughing. 'Which somehow doesn't feel sinful.'

They were silent, taking in the implications of what they

were about to do.

Lily whispered: 'If we don't hurt each other, how can we be hurting God?'

He wound a strand of hair around his finger, smiling apologetically over the sudden huskiness of his voice. 'Her sins, which are many, are forgiven,' he said, 'for she loved much.'

Chapter Ten

LILY'S DIARY
10 September 1942

◆◆◆

I can't possibly tell Gerard or Quin what Kit said. That would only make trouble, and make Kit right about me breaking up his family. But I was so doubtful, I had to check they really were happy with what Gerard calls our 'arrangement'.

I know I am happy. I never knew such happiness was possible. I am in love, and my days are spent anticipating the nights. Sex is divine. Gerard says I have a particular gift for it, because I have a kind heart and no shame.

Kit made me ashamed, though. By the time he had finished with me, I felt as cheap, mean and selfish as Sidonia. Are we so different? Q and G have been very kind and reassuring. I'm sure they would have been even more so, if I had sneaked on Kit.

They know, of course, that he has been in a monstrous great sulk for weeks, because he hates our arrangement, and hates the gossip about us in the village. But he is always in a sulk, and we didn't expect him to approve.

This afternoon, he appeared in the old orchard (six huge old trees, weighed down with thick clusters of fruit; we eat baked apples and apple crumble incessantly). I was halfway up the ladder, and Kit simply stood at the bottom, openly gawking up my skirt – smiling in a sinister sort of way, like Sidney Greenstreet.

I asked: 'Have you come to help me?' rather pointedly, because Kit never does a stroke if he can help it.

'You have quite enough help, it seems to me,' says Kit.

We get a lot of little barbs like this – for instance, that I must be exhausted by my 'extra duties'.

'I've finished anyway,' I said. I hooked the basket over my arm, and tried to descend in a dignified, haughty manner. Unfortunately, I was wearing Paddy's wellingtons, which are

310

miles too big. I tripped on the bottom rung, and Kit's arm shot out, to stop me falling. It was an automatic action, but at least he still has a few decent reflexes.

Then he wouldn't take his arm away. He stood there, squeezing me and grinning behind that bloody bandage.

I sensed a hostility in him, which made me very unhappy, and very furious. I struggled free, upsetting my basket in the long grass. The apples rolled everywhere. Afterwards, when I picked them up, I was so agitated, half were waspy, squashy windfalls.

He laughed, and said it was too late to fight for my virtue – that horse had well and truly bolted. He said it was obvious I was anybody's, that my services were on offer to make up for my dreadful cooking, and that it was his turn.

I lost my temper then, he had made me feel so despised and humiliated. I said he'd never liked me, he didn't want G and Q to be happy, and a lot of other stuff about what a dog in the manger he was. How his moods make us all miserable. I also – very meanly and I'm now sorry – told him Jack thought he was a shit for always sniping at me.

Kit said I was a slut and a scheming trollop, and I didn't have a clue what real love meant – I had taken advantage of two sex-starved backwoodsmen, who would have fucked anything in a skirt. Oh yes, I remember every word of it, and probably will till the day I die. He said the whole family had been at loggerheads since I came, and I wouldn't be satisfied until I had torn them all apart.

I said Kit was the only person at loggerheads with anyone. Unforgivably, I mentioned the cow who dumped him, and said I refused to be tarred with the same brush. We parted horribly, both seething, and have not exchanged a word since.

His accusations filled me with doubt about my situation here. I wanted to hear Quin and Gerard actually saying they loved me – I thought if they didn't love me as much as I love them, it would break my heart.

Sweet, unworldly Quin said he was enormously happy, and didn't in the least mind sharing. He brought me a lovely bunch of harebells, to prove it. Gerard was very busy, writing an article on kingfishers for a nature journal. But he is very sharp, and asked what brought this on – had anyone been annoying me? He

311

meant Mrs Blunt at the Post Office, who certainly is very annoying, but I could see he also suspected Kit.

I said, 'Nobody, I just wanted to be sure.'

Gerard kissed me, and said, 'Of course I'm happy, you silly girl.'

So here, despite Kit's claims, are the facts: I am happy, they are happy. Paddy, who has accepted the arrangement easily, seems perfectly happy. When Bruno was here last month, he was worried about it, but only because he thought the generosity was all on my side. Once I had convinced him nobody was taking advantage of me, Bruno was happy. Does this sound like a family tearing itself apart?

Admittedly, I've no idea what Oscar will think. I haven't mentioned anything in my letters, on account of the censors. But in this house, Kit is the only person who thinks we are doing wrong.

Just before I went to bed (alone), I remembered Glad saying 'let not the sun go down on your wrath', and would have loved to make it up with him. I was ashamed that I had said a lot of nasty things to a fighter pilot with a burnt face. But Kit looked straight through me, and we parted in a state of armed truce. The sun has long gone down.

I wish to heaven he could simply leave us all alone. I suppose it's too much to wish for his blessing. Life would be absolutely blissful, if he'd only stop being my enemy, and change himself into my friend.

Summer warmth lingered in the sheltered valley, and only a tang of woodsmoke in the air heralded the coming of autumn. Lily sat out in the yard, laboriously and rather painfully stripping the hips from branches of dog rose, which would be collected to make National Rosehip Syrup. Mrs Parminter, wife of a landowner on the other side of the village, was the local co-ordinator of the County Herb Committee, and she was willing to overlook the amazing rumours about the Randalls because their farm was famously abundant in hips. Quin left his hedgerows extravagantly untrimmed, and they had been a riot of wild pink roses all summer.

Now, the berries had blushed red; the point at which their precious vitamin C for the nation's children was at its highest. Mrs Parminter had sent out urgent pleas to all the farmers' wives. Quin, Paddy and Pa had dumped a great, prickly bale of branches down on the cobbles, and Lily was doing her bit by getting her fingers covered in scratches.

Gladys had written that she and Iris were making their own syrup, following instructions from the Ministry of Food. It was, she reported, 'a blooming lot of trouble', but little Peter loved the stuff, and was 'bonny'.

Her letters gave Lily her only moments of homesickness – not for the Prospect, which had been ruined for ever, but for Gladys herself. As she picked off the red berries, she pictured Gladys doing exactly the same, in her cottage on the Drivers' farm. She pictured her bonny little godson, now 'fat as a barrel', Gladys said, and running about. She knew the expression on Gladys's face as she watched him; the expression that was her own earliest memory.

Fortunately, Gladys lived too far from Randalls to hear the rumours. She would have been outraged – Lily wished she could talk to her, to make her understand. On the surface, her moral rectitude made the Prayer Book seem lax and permissive, but she would relent once she saw Lily's happiness with her own eyes.

Because she was thinking of Gladys and Peter, Lily's dark eyes were soft and wistful when she glanced up at the man who had come quietly into the yard.

'Hello, Lily-girl. Surprise, eh? I heard a description of a certain young lady at your charming Post Office, and knew it must be you.'

Charlie relished her surprise, and her involuntary horror. He was dressed in riding boots, breeches and tweed hacking jacket, though there was no sign of a horse. He had materialised, like an unwelcome spirit, behind the ragged tangle of thorns. For the fragment of a second, Lily refused to believe he was real, and willed the phantom to vanish back into her past.

He was, however, defiantly solid. His dead hand, tucked into his pocket, added to his air of arrogant nonchalance.

Lily noticed how sleek and smooth he looked, compared with the roughness of the Randalls and their habitat. He was a messenger from a forgotten world, in which everyone was polished and expensive. It was a shock, and not a pleasant one, to be reminded that this world still existed.

Her mouth tasted bile, as she came face to face with the memory of the last time she had seen him. He had almost tricked her into liking him – at any rate, into feeling sorry for him – until the ghastly scene with Sidonia. Now, as she stared at this handsome knight, in his armour of burnished riding clothes, all she saw was the coarse idiot who had found his true level with Sidonia.

'Shocked into silence!' Charlie crowed. 'I never thought it possible. Don't I get a "hello"?'

'Hello, Charlie. What on earth are you doing here?' He had violated her sanctuary, and she was afraid.

'That's exactly the same question I was going to ask you – what the hell are you doing here, in this broken–down barn-yard?'

Lily could not help sounding sulky. 'How did you find me?'

'Oh, I wasn't looking for you,' Charlie said airily. 'It was pure luck. I'm staying with some people called Parminter. I left the nag they lent me at the bottom of the lane – as you see, I'm riding again. Don't you think that's clever of me? But I still can't drive, and I miss our jaunts to the pictures. We could get up to some sizzling stuff in the back row.' He took in the yard, and the litter around the back of the house. 'Ye Gods, what a dump.'

'No it isn't.'

'Look at you, little wild–girl – are your legs bare all the way up?'

She rose, and said – trying to mask her desperation – 'I wish you'd go away now.'

'Charming. I expected you to be thrilled. You used to be so bucked to see me. Have you been hiding here since you bolted?'

'I work here. I'm the housekeeper, and they're going to get me registered as a land girl.'

'They? Who are "they"?'

'Please go away, Charlie.'

'No fear. Not without a look at the house you swapped for the Prospect.'

'Stop –'

The back door stood open. Charlie stepped into the scullery, chuckling over her distress. He glanced contemptuously round the cluttered kitchen. 'Where are they? I wanted to meet the family.'

'Well, you can't. They're all out.' As soon as she said it, Lily wished she had not told him she was alone. Paddy and Pa were in Exeter. Kit and Quin were out in the fields, and would not return until evening.

'Left you on your own, eh? God,' he looked down at the floor, 'this place is crawling with mice. So everything I've heard about this farm must be true.'

'Did you come here to tease me?' She must not show him she was nervous.

'No! I came to be nice, and give you all the news from home.'

'I don't want to hear it.'

With the deftness that now seemed sinister and repulsive, Charlie extracted and lit a cigarette with his good hand. The silver case snapped shut, like a bite. He smiled and smiled, but Lily read threat and aggression in his every gesture – and he knew she did.

'Sidonia never mentions you, but I think Ralphie would like to know where you are.'

'Really? Go on and tell him, if you like. He hasn't made the slightest effort to find me.'

He laughed. 'Perhaps it's just as well.'

Lily, unbending her pride with an effort, asked: 'How is he, anyway?'

'Oh, same as ever. I'm sure you know what I mean.'

Charlie's eyes travelled over her body, with an insolence that made her flesh creep.

She hurried on. 'I wouldn't mind you giving my love to Primrose and Isobel. How are they?'

'You haven't heard? Of course not. Primrose and I are

getting married.'

'What? You're joking!'

He perched on the edge of the table, delighted to have got a reaction from her at last. 'Next month. Isn't it thrilling?'

'Are you – in love with her?'

'Course I am,' Charlie drawled lazily, willing her to challenge him. 'She'll make a wizard squiress, don't you think?'

Lily was certain Primrose did not love Charlie – not the Primrose she had seen with Guy. But it had to be admitted, she would indeed make an irreproachable squire's lady, tramping round tenants' cottages and county shows in a Burberry and sensible shoes. Lily made a mental note to write to Gladys for the truth. For the moment, she needed all her concentration to watch Charlie.

'Congratulations,' she said. 'Your mother must be pleased.'

'Rather – it was all her idea. Sidonia's pleased, too. She likes the notion of tying me up with someone very obedient, who never notices anything.' He drove the point home with one of his braying laughs, so Lily would be sure to understand that the affair with Sidonia continued. 'Aren't you sorry you missed your chance?' He stood up. 'If you'd stuck around, I'd have married you.'

'You'd have had to bind and gag me first,' Lily said.

His smile did not waver, but the expression in his shallow blue eyes hardened. 'I couldn't marry you now, of course. Despard brides are supposed to wear white and keep their knickers on. But we can still be – friends, you know.'

Lily winced angrily at the insult, and the humiliation of being accused of cheapness by such a man.

He dropped his cigarette, and crushed it under his heel. 'I was slow to cotton on, but when you cut off your plaits, I had the most major hots for you. We've got some unfinished business to settle, haven't we?'

'Oh no we haven't.'

'Nobody needs to know what's going on here. Not if I don't tell them.'

'Please – please just go away!'

'Feel this.' He grabbed her hand, and pressed it against

his erection. 'I'm hard for you. Doesn't that make you all hot and wet for me?'

Quietly, her voice shaking, Lily said: 'Let go.'

'Don't you want any? You're lying.' Charlie's smile, without wavering, had become fanged and nasty. 'You're dying for it.'

She felt sick. 'Please, Charlie. Let me go.'

'No, I bloody won't. Why should I?'

She had forgotten how cleverly he could use his one good arm. He grasped her throat with his hand, slammed her against the wall, and pinned her there with his body. She had to struggle to breathe. His hand pounced up her skirt, and his fingers pushed into her.

'Lovely, lovely –' He forced his tongue into her mouth.

Lily sank her teeth into it. Charlie jerked away his head, and smacked her hard across the cheek – so hard, that she staggered and cracked her forehead against the corner of the dresser.

The room swooped and spun around her. Stomach churning with shock and pain, she put her hand to the wet trickle on her forehead, and gawped stupidly at the scarlet smear of blood.

'Naughty,' Charlie said. 'You're no fun at all.'

Lily swallowed hard, trying to beat back her nausea. She could not think. Everything kept sinking into twilight. When Kit crashed into the kitchen, it took her stunned eyes a few seconds to send the message to her brain.

Kit stood, blocking the light from the doorway, his shotgun broken over one arm, and four dead rabbits swinging from his hand. His head was bare. He wore his RAF tunic over a patched guernsey.

He said: 'What's going on?'

Charlie, thrown off balance by this extraordinary apparition – half decayed squadron leader, half bandaged mummy – attempted to laugh it off. 'Just a bit of fun. Lily and I are old friends.' He had decided the apparition was not dangerous.

Kit spat out each word distinctly, like bullets. 'What have you done to her?'

'Nothing. Bugger off and mind your own,' Charlie said testily. 'Tell him, Lily-girl.'

The rabbits thumped to the floor, and Kit's hand rolled into a fist. 'Get out of my house.'

'Oh, you're one of her employers, are you? Beg pardon for poaching on your preserve, old boy. I was going to leave half a crown on the table.'

'Get out.'

'Look, why are you bothering to defend her honour? Rather pointless, under the circs.'

Kit, in the same measured voice, said: 'You're not fit to clean shit off her shoes.' His mouth barely moved, behind the thick, discoloured mask of stockinette.

Charlie was rallying, pink with annoyance at the interruption. 'Well, what are you going to do about it? Thump a cripple with only one arm?'

'I like thumping cripples,' Kit said. 'And if you so much as look at Lily again, I'll break your other arm.'

Lily, her head swirling with pain, managed to collapse into the carver's chair before her knees gave way underneath her. From a great distance, she was aware of Charlie's fist, wearing a gold signet ring, near Kit's face. Disjointed images came and went – of Kit hitting Charlie, of Kit shouting and dragging him from the room, of animalistic noises outside, and Custard barking. Of Kit blueing the sweet afternoon air with a torrent of Anglo-Saxon.

She rested her head on her arms. Tears oozed from her eyes. God, the relief of seeing Kit. And he did care, after all. She was safe.

He came back into the room, breathing heavily, and holding his wrist against a red patch that had bled through his bandage. 'He's gone, and he won't be coming back. Not if he likes having bollocks. I'll warn Pa and the boys.' He knelt down beside her, and gently put his finger under her chin, to tilt her face towards him. 'Let's see what he's done to you.'

His voice had suddenly changed. It had an unfamiliar coaxing sweetness.

'I'm so sorry –' Lily mumbled. Her cheek was swelling, and

it hurt to move her lips. 'So sorry – but he tried to – to –'

'Yes, I can just bloody well guess what he tried. You were daft, to let him in when you were alone here.'

'But Kit, I didn't – he just came in by himself –'

'I'm not ticking you off, sweetheart. It wasn't your fault. Let's just thank God I came back when I did. Shit, I wish I'd killed the bastard.'

Lily tried to smile, screwing up her eyes against the pain. 'Thanks for defending my honour.'

His eyes were huge and naked-looking, and full of a kind of outraged tenderness. He felt in his jacket pockets, and unearthed a crumpled handkerchief, which he pressed to the cut on her head. 'I accused you of not having any, didn't I? And I didn't mean a word of it. I hope you believe that now. Look, I'm desperately sorry I was such an arse to you, the other day. Will you forgive me? Please, Lily. If you don't, I'm not much better than he is, am I?'

'Oh Kit, you're so much better – so much finer – I can't bear to hear you mentioned in the same breath –'

He put his arms around her, and she found she was sobbing into his blue shoulder. The bulk of that shoulder was inexpressibly comforting.

'You poor kid,' he said, 'you've taken one hell of a belt. You ought to see a doctor.'

She clung to him. 'No, don't be silly, I'll be fine. If I can just rest for a minute or two –'

'You'll rest for more than a minute, my girl.'

'But the supper!' Her face was now so swollen, this came out as 'shupper'.

The new Kit chuckled. 'D'you really think I'm going to let you fanny about making supper? Pa would murder me. Come on.' He hoisted her in his arms, and carried her up to her room, laughing amiably at her giddy, rambling protests.

The next thing she knew, she was lying on her bed. Kit was removing her sandals, and covering her with the quilt. A space of blankness, and he was giving her a glass of Pa's brandy and two aspirins. She whirled away into sleep, as peaceful and safe as a ship that has reached harbour.

Downstairs, while Lily slept, the four Randall men sat grim-faced, each with one hand clasped in the middle of the table, as if they had just taken an oath.

'It's understood, then,' Kit said. 'We're going to put it round, until every man, woman and child knows it – if anyone insults Lily, or hurts one hair of her head, the Randalls will beat them to a bloody pulp.'

Chapter Eleven

To Miss Primrose Rumage
  The Prospect
  Vere's Mills,
  N. Devon

UTTERLY PRIVATE

Dear Primrose
This is a terrible cheek, and I can't give you a reason, but please, please don't marry Charlie Despard. He is not good enough for you, and will never make you happy.

I don't know what happened between you and you-know-who, but I am sure Charlie is the last man on earth he would want to see you with.

Honestly, I am not being mean. If there is anything I can do for you, please write to me care of Gladys Tufton,
  Your friend,
    Lily-Josephine

Don't show this to anyone.

To Miss Lily-Josephine Gallant,
  c/o Mrs G. Tufton
  Lake Farm
  Nr Fairy Cross
  N. Devon

1 October 1942

Dear Lily,
  I was very pleased to get your letter, and do not

suspect you of being mean. However, unless you can give me some solid reasons why not, I shall go ahead and marry Charlie – you must see, I can hardly change my mind without a proper reason.

As for 'you-know-who', he is no longer in the picture. He is probably married himself by now. He wrote to tell me of his engagement, and that was that. I shall never forget how kind you were to us last summer, but I try to forget everything else.

Of course, I can never love Charlie as I loved Guy. I don't think I will ever love like that again. So I feel I should tolerate any small flaws in Charlie. The worst I know of him is that he can be rather an ass. But we are tremendous friends, and I am very fond of him.

And, between ourselves, I am looking forward to living at Despard Court. For the last few weeks, Mummy and Juana have made the atmosphere here absolutely unbearable and hellish. They have had a dreadful row about something. Mummy told me Juana had betrayed her, and stolen her most precious jewel – whatever that might mean. Lady Violet will suit me very well after this, I do assure you. She is extremely kind to me.

I know you always joked about the dullness of Despard Court, but I am not like you. Charlie needs a suitable wife, and I am happy that I can be suitable. The other sort of happiness is no longer possible for me, after Guy.

And that is quite enough about me. How are you? I hope you are well. Isobel and I have missed you. Isobel is a land girl on Mr Driver's farm. We don't see much of her, as she has chosen to lodge on the farm with the two other girls. She seems to love the work.

Mrs Dove has gone to Exeter, to live with her daughter. We have a girl from the village (Joyce Hopper, perhaps you remember her) working for us at the moment. She will stay until she is called up.

I will send you, via Mrs Tufton, a piece of my wedding cake. Lady Violet has shamelessly begged the sugar for it right and left, so it ought to be good,

Your affectionate stepsister,
Primrose Rumage

Primrose's wedding dress was of grey-blue wool, not new, but impeccably made over by a London dressmaker. It hung on a hook at the back of the bedroom door. All Primrose's other possessions, except her lipstick, hairbrush and dressing gown, were neatly packed in the set of leather suitcases Granny had given her, for the aborted voyage to India. After the wedding, she and Charlie were going straight to Scotland, for their honeymoon.

Primrose looked forward to this quite calmly – even with mild pleasure. Charlie was, after all, very good-looking, and she did not expect the business of consummation to be an ordeal. Perhaps there would be a pang or two of regret, but the great thing about Charlie was that he was so emphatically unlike Guy.

Her one real regret was that the war had cheated her of a proper, traditional wedding – bouquets, bridesmaids, Mendelssohn, champagne and speeches. Primrose had always assumed she would be married in white satin, with a filmy silk veil and her Rumage grandmother's tiara, and knew she had been born to look her best in such an ensemble.

Never mind. It was enough to be escaping from Sidonia. Charlie had presented living with his mother as rather a drawback, but Primrose felt she understood Lady Violet perfectly. Yes, she was demanding and inclined to interfere. She was, however, beautifully predictable and immoveable. You could guess, well in advance, her reaction to any person or situation. After the fairground-ride of living with Sidonia, this would be bliss.

Lady Violet's house ran on oiled wheels. Her servants, all too old to be called up, were respectful and competent. There would be no Forces Programme blaring out on their kitchen wireless all day, as there was at the Prospect. They would not question orders, nor need to be instructed in basic domestic skills, like the tiresome Joyce Hopper. On the whole, Primrose was looking forward to the quiet, correct and well-run life she would lead as Mrs Charles Despard.

The letter from Lily, arriving like a message from another world, had disturbed her at first. It had made her hold Charlie up to the light, and looking at the man rather than his outward circumstances awakened her buried sense that something was not quite right.

Primrose did not enjoy dealing with airy things like doubts or suspicions. She had decided, very soon after reading the mysterious letter, to accentuate the positive. Marriage to Charlie meant a life of Rumage-ish respectability. Weren't all her father's family delighted? Hadn't Grandmama sent her that glorious triple strand of pearls, as the seal and symbol of her approval?

She tightened the belt of her quilted dressing gown, and went downstairs, to check the details of a Prospect entertainment for the last time.

And a good thing, too. Isobel, wearing one of her cast-off dresses, was setting the arrangements of autumn leaves on the long table as if flinging dung across a barnyard.

'Prim! What on earth are you doing down here? Charlie's due any minute. He's not supposed to see you.'

'I think that's only for brides in new dresses,' Primrose said, adjusting the vases. 'He's seen my wedding dress a thousand times.'

Mellowed by the nearness of escape, she thought how pretty little Isobel looked these days. The work on the farm had fined down her plumpness, and given her soft brown curls a healthy gloss, like caramel.

Isobel asked: 'Is there anything else I can do?'

'Yes, you can entertain Charlie's best man, when the car arrives from Despard Court. He's rather shy, and Lady Violet never takes any notice of him.'

'Okay.'

Primrose made a noble effort not to show her distaste for her sister's casual, slangy manner. A farm in wartime was not, after all, a finishing school. 'Offer him a sherry.'

'Righty-ho,' Isobel said.

'I must find Mummy. Have you seen her?'

'In the kitchen, I think.'

Primrose hurried to the kitchen. Sidonia had promised

not to wear anything too outlandish, but their interpretations of this word were vastly different. Was it remotely possible for her mother to spend one day dressed as an ordinary human being?

'My darling, you should be in your chamber, thinking virginal thoughts before you unfold the white wings of your maidenhood!'

It could have been worse. Sidonia wore her long robe of old-gold, with medieval slippers dyed to match. Her emerald eyes sparkled becomingly with unshed tears, and she kissed her eldest daughter with real tenderness.

Primrose was deeply touched to see Sidonia so happy for her, so generous with her precious approval – too happy to listen to the internal voice asking: Why?

'I suddenly felt fidgety,' she said. 'Joyce, you can go to the drawing room now.' Her shoulders squared as she turned to the cheerful, seventeen-year-old village girl, who wore her black parlourmaid's frock with a jaunty and wholly unsuitable air of being in fancy dress. 'And while we're in church, don't forget to watch the joint.'

'No fear, Miss Rumage. Good luck.'

'Thank you, Joyce,' Primrose said, smiling and regal. At Despard Court, the servants would address her as 'Mrs Charlie', the treasured daughter-in-law elect. She would be housekeeping in her own establishment, instead of slaving here as her mother's unpaid drudge.

The satisfaction was a little spoiled when Sidonia suddenly burst out with: 'God, how strange it is, to be going to a wedding that isn't mine!', and Joyce scuttled out unmistakably giggling.

The time of the service was creeping closer. Soon, Charlie, his mother and best man would assemble in the drawing room, before walking to the small, damp church, in which Ralph had married Helena. Primrose and Ralph – who was giving her away – would follow after a decorous interval of ten minutes. Primrose knew she should return to her room to dress, but was reluctant to break this rare moment of intimacy with her mother. Surely, on her wedding day, she could allow herself to bask in Sidonia's full attention.

'When I married your father,' Sidonia said, focusing her memory with a vague, puzzled expression, 'Granny kept giving me screeds of advice.'

Primrose laughed. 'Which you ignored.'

'Well, darling, it was absolutely useless.' She kissed Primrose, and added a new coda to the old saw. 'My sweet firstborn, I had such fun conceiving you. I adored the pagan splendour of being pregnant, and thought you were the prettiest babe in the world. The marriage went under, but you have been nothing but a blessing to me.'

Here was a tribute beyond Primrose's dreams. She clung to Sidonia, her eyes swimming. The reward for which she had striven all her life was hers at last; the crown of her mother's love, the acknowledgement of years of devotion. She had never wanted more than this.

The moment did not last, and Primrose knew it would not. But she sealed it in a timeless, golden bubble, to store in her memory. Later, she would return to the moment obsessively, as a consolation for what happened immediately afterwards.

It happened like something in a film, and Primrose always remembered it in slow motion. Ralph came into the kitchen, dressed for the wedding in his pre-war morning suit. He was shaking, and holding a flimsy sheet of paper in a way that loaded it with significance.

Sidonia asked: 'Have they come? Is Charlie here?'

He did not seem to see Primrose, standing pink and transfigured, with the tears still spiking her lashes. Wordlessly, he handed Sidonia the sheet of paper.

Sidonia read it. She froze. A bereft whimper began in her chest, and swelled into a shriek: 'No – no, no, no –'

Ralph said: 'We're a fine pair of fucking great fools.'

'No!' screamed Sidonia, flinging the paper onto the table. 'It's not true! She couldn't do this to me – she couldn't be such a bitch.'

'She could,' Ralph said, in the same, dull voice. 'You'd better believe it.'

Sidonia had begun to thrash and rampage around the room, like a horse with a burr stuck under its saddle. 'I

326

adored her, I gave her everything – and in return she betrays me, she breaks my heart – she pretended to be sorry she stole Diego – she wants to rob me, destroy me, turn them all against me – she couldn't be satisfied until she'd taken everything I had in the whole world –'

And a great deal more, in the same strain. Sidonia picked up pieces of crockery at random, and punctuated her tirade by smashing them on the floor. Isobel and Joyce appeared at the door, to watch open-mouthed.

Primrose felt, at the pit of her churning gut, a dreadful foreboding. This was not one of Sidonia's usual storms. It had a sickening edge of fear and desperation. While everyone else gaped, mesmerised, at Sidonia, she picked up the piece of paper.

It was in Juana's angular handwriting, and said that she and Charlie had gone to London, to be married.

PART FIVE

Chapter One

1981

◆◆◆

The only thing Primrose disliked about her cottage was its name, 'The Puckle'. Octavius, when he visited with Sophie, had been unable to help muttering: 'What the Fuckle is a Puckle?' Primrose forgave him. Nothing and nobody could dim the glowing pleasure she took in creating, for the first time in her life, a home of her own.

It was a squat, two-storey, thatched cottage, set in a verdant spur of land on the edge of Exmoor. The rooms were small, with deep fireplaces and low ceilings. Primrose had decorated them in whites and off-whites. Simplicity was a luxury, after forty years among the antlers and Benares brasses of the Prospect.

'I'm sure it's ungrateful of me,' she told Isobel, during one of their telephone conversations, 'but I'm delighted to be shot of the place. It was a nightmare to run, and nothing one did to it made any difference. Here, I can stick a bunch of bluebells in a jug, and transform a whole room.'

'Sophie says it's as pretty as a picture-postcard,' Isobel said. 'I can't wait to see it.'

'So you shall. Now, can you talk? I'm dying to know how it's going.' It was the end of March, and Sophie had brought Octavius over to Ireland, to meet her parents and their pigs.

Isobel responded with one of her oddly girlish laughs. 'I can talk, and it's going famously. Why on earth did you say Octavius was surly? He's charming.'

'Transformed by love,' Primrose said. 'According to Patrick, he's a different man these days. And I've never seen Sophie so beautiful.'

Isobel's mouth moved nearer to the receiver, surrounding her voice with a gale of whispery breath. 'I'm down on my knees, thanking heaven for him. Sometimes, I watch them, and my eyes just fill with tears.'

'You always were appallingly sentimental.'

'Ah, but they're so beautiful, and she's so happy. Isn't it strange, to think that she's Sidonia's grandchild, and he's Lily's son?'

'Poetic justice,' Primrose declared. 'We might have guessed Lily would win the last round.'

'So much happiness makes me frightened.'

'Now, Isobel, get a grip,' Primrose said indulgently. 'Tell your mystical Irish blood to mind its own business. Don't borrow trouble, as Granny would say.'

'I find myself worrying about what Edgar will do, if he loses his case,' whispered Isobel.

'Well, what could he do?'

'I don't know. Find some way to ruin Octavius's career –'

Primrose was laughing. 'Plenty of scope for that, in the cut-throat world of forestry.'

Isobel joined in, evidently rather relieved to have cold water poured on her fears. 'You're right, I'm being daft. I'd better go.'

'So had I. Patrick's coming, and the place is a mess.'

Primrose's friendship with Patrick Randall had been prospering finely through the winter. Octavius had said something about Paddy being 'difficult to know', and Primrose had been unable to imagine what he meant. From their first meeting, they had effortlessly vaulted the barriers of his prickly shyness and her bossiness, and struck a rich seam of mutual understanding.

Patrick was helping her clear her acre of garden, and raise it again as a bower beyond her dreams. The bower mostly existed in theory at the moment, but spring was coming, to coax Patrick's inspirations off the paper and into blooming life. He sensed, without being told, what it meant to her.

After she had finished talking to Isobel, Primrose made one or two small adjustments to her appearance. Obviously, she was not going to dress up for an afternoon outdoors, but she put on the newer of her khaki sleeveless jackets, and pulled a comb through her hair. In her warm, cheerful kitchen, she checked her supplies of Assam tea and chocolate biscuits, and took a venison casserole out of the freezer for supper. One never knew.

Bunter suddenly jumped up from his basket beside the radiator, eager and alert.

Primrose bent to kiss the top of his head. 'You're always first to hear him, clever boy.' No less eagerly, she went to the sitting room window, to watch Patrick's Land-Rover pulling up in the lane.

A fierce wind parted Patrick's thick pelt of brown hair. He looked up at the sky, and as he did so, the first stair-rods of rain slapped against the lattice. By the time he got to the door, it was a downpour.

Gardening was out of the question. Primrose was surprised to discover that she regarded staying inside with him as a greater treat. She made a pot of tea, and laid the biscuits out on a plate, while Patrick built a log fire. They ended up sitting in front of it, bathing their faces in its warmth, and talking amiably about Sophie and Octavius. Just as an uncle and an aunt should, Primrose thought. Privately, she could not imagine the lovers' relationship being nearly as interesting as this one.

'I was rather brutal to Isobel, about her "feeling",' she told Patrick, 'because I've had a feeling or two about Edgar Despard myself. Nothing whatever to do with second sight. I know how relentless he can be, when he wants to spoil something. I used to get so fed up with the way Sidonia and Juana pretended there was nothing the matter with him.'

'What do you mean?'

'Well, I always thought he was rather seriously bonkers.' She replenished their teacups. 'Nobody ever told me the real version of things, but I couldn't help hearing about some of his adventures. For instance, he had a row with some boy, when he was at Oxford. The boy had to go to hospital, and Edgar vanished into a private clinic – too expensive to be called a loony-bin, but that's what it was. And Juana had to pay out some hefty fines for drugs. Sidonia took it all as evidence of Latin passion. She wanted him to be like Juana's father. Have another biscuit.' She pushed the plate towards him. 'Search me why. Diego Menendez beat her up, seduced their daughter and ended his days under a train in the Paris Metro. He wasn't even a good sculptor.'

Patrick let out a brief grunt of laughter. 'To add insult to injury.'

'Precisely. Sidonia did have rather a thing for beasts. To this day, I can't imagine what she saw in my poor old father. His second wife couldn't have been more of a contrast – followed him round the world, retired with him to Cheltenham, died very tidily, six months after he did. Fitting Sidonia into that sort of life would have been like – I don't know – putting a parakeet in a dovecote.' Primrose stretched. 'How about some scones and jam?'

'Yes, if you made them.' It was the sort of thing the curate said, but Patrick made it sound solemn and chivalric.

'The scones are mine, but the jam comes from the WI.'

'I'll risk it.'

In the kitchen, Primrose assembled a tray of scones, butter and raspberry jam, and made a fresh pot of tea. The window rattled, as the storm howled outside. She looked out at it benignly, enjoying the contrast with the comfort within.

'I'm probably being mean about Edgar,' she said, laying the tray down on the hearthrug. She had lost more weight, and no longer puffed when she bent over. 'Juana would say I was prejudiced against him, because of what she did to me.'

Patrick said: 'Leaving you at the altar.' She had blurted out the story at a very early stage of their friendship.

'The humiliation still makes me catch my breath. It hurts like a stitch. To his dying day, I couldn't look at Charlie's face, without wanting to slap it.' She peeled the disc of waxed paper off the top of the jam. 'I can't decide whether bearing a grudge makes you old before your time, or keeps you young.'

'Hasn't done you any harm,' Patrick said gravely.

This piece of gallantry brought a rush of warmth to Primrose's cheeks. She went to draw the curtains. 'It's a filthy afternoon, but it might clear up later. Why don't you stay for supper?' She was straining to sound casual, longing for him to say yes.

'Don't want to put you out.'

334

'Not in the least. There's oodles.' She darted back to the kitchen to put the casserole in the oven.

'Shall I open the wine?' Patrick called. He had arrived for his afternoon's gardening bearing a bottle of burgundy.

Primrose snatched up a corkscrew and two glasses. 'Why not?'

The bright fire made a tent of shadows in the darkened room. Something about a wood fire – its seductive, wintry perfume, or the hypnotic effect of watching the orange and blue arrows of flame – inspired confidences, Primrose thought.

The light made jewels of their wine glasses.

Patrick said: 'To your garden.'

'It's yours too. I'd never have been so ambitious, if you hadn't egged me on.'

He cleared his throat. 'I haven't finished. There's something else you positively must have.'

'What?'

'The rose Lily sent you.' He was looking at her levelly, under his heavy brows. 'The Light Perpetual.'

'Oh, Patrick, I'd love to have it.'

'I'll bring you one. You could put it against your west wall.'

'You're an angel. You know what it means to me.'

'Lily often told me the story,' Patrick said. 'You became a sort of legend to me. When I met you, that first time, it was like meeting a character in a story. You were the beautiful girl who had lost her true love, and been jilted by her false one.'

Primrose laughed softly. 'How kind of her, to make me sound romantic. Though I'm afraid there was nothing remotely romantic about the business with Charlie. I was a laughing stock for miles around.'

'What did you do afterwards?'

'If I'd been in a romantic story, I would have gone into a decline. Since I wasn't, I joined the Wrens.'

He chuckled. 'You must have looked tremendous in the uniform.'

'I did. And I rather enjoyed the whole experience. They

335

gave me a commission, and posted me to Italy. I lived in a villa painted with goddesses, and saw the sun setting over the Leaning Tower. I also did a lot of typing, and flirted with a lot of officers.'

'I'm surprised you weren't snapped up by one of them.'

'That was impossible. I was still carrying a torch a mile high.'

'Not for Charlie?'

'God, no. For Guy. My true love.'

They were silent, listening to the snapping of the logs in the grate, and the drumming of the rain outside.

Patrick said: 'Gladys Tufton told Lily that he'd been killed, and you'd come home. Lily said we must send you my rose.'

'I'm so very glad you did. It was the only comfort I had.' Her voice dropped, almost to a whisper. 'Because my true love was my half-brother. I couldn't be seen to mourn him in the wrong way. I felt like a criminal. Even Sidonia never committed incest.'

'Lily didn't think you were a criminal.'

'Lily believed in love.' Primrose exhaled years of guilt and grieving in a long sigh. 'I wish she'd known the whole story. I'm sure she guessed I only wanted to marry Charlie because I couldn't have Guy. Then, towards the end of the war, Guy wrote me another letter.' Her eyes smarted painfully. 'There isn't another living soul who knows this – he said he'd tried to stop loving me, but he couldn't. After the war, he wanted us to live together, just as we'd planned. And then he was killed. Sorry.' Primrose scrabbled in the pockets of her cardigan, found a tissue, and blew her nose briskly. 'I had a sort of breakdown, though nobody used words like that in those days. They sent me home from Italy, and none of my family appeared to notice I was completely out of my mind. Lily's letter, and the rose, reminded me I wasn't quite the loneliest person in the world.'

She was sitting on the hearthrug, looking into the fire, and watching the flames dance. Patrick, behind her on the sofa, leaned forward and placed his hand on her shoulder.

The gesture conveyed infinite sympathy. Primrose,

hollowed out by her confession, felt peace stealing into her bones. 'Anyway,' she said, 'you can see why this place is so important. It's exactly the sort of house Guy and I planned to have.'

Patrick said: 'I'd love to know what the letter said.'

'Lily's letter?' Primrose struggled up from the rug, and went to the slender walnut tallboy, which had been dragged from the rubble of Granny's bombed house. 'I still have it, in my pathetic, spinster's museum of souvenirs.'

From the top drawer, she took a small, faded cardboard folder. She extracted a yellowed piece of paper, and handed it to Patrick.

His face expressionless, he read it; hearing the echo of Lily's voice.

Dear Primrose,
I was terribly sorry to hear about Guy's death. I liked him very much. There is nothing I can say to comfort you. But do remember, he loved you, and love is stronger than death. I don't believe people you have loved ever really leave you, unless you want them to.

I am sending you a rose, grown by a great friend of mine, who says you must dead-head it religiously all through the season, prune it early in the autumn, and be ruthless when you do it. Give it plenty of manure.

It is called 'Light Perpetual'. You must think that when you are standing in the light, you will have Guy beside you – as part of him is beside you now, if only you could see him.
All my love,
Lily-Josephine

Patrick pored over this for a long time. He said 'Well,' and handed the letter gravely back to Primrose, keeping his eyes on it as she stowed it back in the tallboy. A single tear was threading its way down his lined cheek.

'And the "great friend" was you,' Primrose said. 'You wondered about me for all those years, and I wondered about you. I thought you might have been her lover.'

Patrick did not touch the tear on his face, but wore it with stern pride. 'Guy was your true love, and Lily was mine. The rose came from the Sleeping Garden. It grows there still.'

'Sleeping Garden?'

'My herb garden, at Randalls.' He leaned towards her. 'I should very much like you to see it.'

Primrose sensed this was a great honour. 'I should love to.'

'Yes. Good.' He was in retreat, panicking slightly because he had come so near the brink of revelation.

Bunter, like a fat, furry Cupid, healed the awkwardness by bustling into the room and bagging the warmest place on the rug. He settled across Primrose's knees, with a lazy sigh, and the barrier vanished. Primrose and Patrick smiled into one another's eyes.

In a freer voice, Patrick said: 'I hate to criticise, but you spoil this animal.'

'I know.'

'Thinks he's a lap-dog – don't you, Porky?'

He bent to stroke Bunter's back, and his hand covered hers. They both stared down at it.

Warmth pulsed through Primrose's blood, seeming to show her how cold and sluggish it had been, for too many years. She was almost afraid to look upon it, but the possibility of a new landscape spread out before her.

She felt she had to say something. 'Would you like some more wine?'

'I shouldn't. I have to drive home.'

Their eyes met again.

Primrose whispered: 'Don't –'

Chapter Two

LILY'S DIARY

19 December 1943

❖❖❖

Bruno is here, and we heard this morning that Oscar will be home for Christmas. Poor Gerard went horribly pale when the telegram came. I expect I did too – the last one told us Jack was dead. But Gerard ripped it open, and shouted: 'Oh, tidings of comfort and joy!' He rushed straight out to tell the boys.

Quin eyed the gander, and said: 'That's settled, then – it's curtains for you, mate.'

(NB Must ask Gladys best way to cook goose, and how to make stuffing.)

Later, in the still-room, Gerard cried a little. 'I was just remembering the time when we took being together for granted. And now we can never be all together again. The truth is, beloved Lily, loss does not get any less painful with the passing of time. One simply believes it more easily.'

We made love, deliciously, with me perched on the edge of the desk, my legs wrapped around his waist. I should think the whole house heard him.

He said: 'Sorry, my dear. But you make me come like the Wrath of Jehovah.'

After, I went to make mince pies, with the mincemeat Glad sent me. There was a lovely carol service on the radio, and I caterwauled along with 'Once in Royal' while I worked. I felt excited, wrapped in love, divinely happy. I daresay this is very selfish and wrong, to forget the war. But there you are. I don't think I've looked forward to Christmas this much since I was little, and Tufton used to nail one of Glad's stockings to my nursery chimneypiece.

Kit came stamping in out of the cold, wreathed in his own breath, just as I opened the oven door and filled the kitchen with a heavenly, pre-war smell of baking. He had bagged a couple of rabbits for tonight's dinner. He pretended to put his fingers in his ears when he heard me singing. Then he swore when he burned his hand on the tray of mince pies.

I said: 'Be it understood, Kit. If you touch one of these before I give you permission, you will die.'

'They're probably the only mince pies in England,' he said. 'They should be in a museum.'

After tea, Quin and I drove out, in the dark and the shivery cold, to the station. The train was late, of course. We put our arms around each other, to keep warm. The sky was absolutely clear blue, just like Stephens' ink, and jewelled with stars.

Mrs Parminter, who made me pick all those blasted rosehips, was on the platform, and when she passed us, she remarked that the only good thing about total blackout was the drama of the night sky – 'enough to make astronomers of us all'. She is not a bad old stick. I'm sure she knows I sleep with both Quin and Gerard, but she pretends not to; thus sparing herself the bother of disapproving.

I was worried that the cold would aggravate Quin's asthma. Also the general excitement. I said I'd keep some goose-fat, to rub on his chest.

He said: 'You must be kidding, you'll have to chloroform me first.'

At last, only twenty minutes late, in rattled the train, and disgorged a handful of squashed passengers. There was Bruno. Poor thing, he was pale with cold, and said he hadn't felt his feet since Bristol.

When we got him home, the kitchen was so warm and welcoming, I allowed myself to feel proud. A lot of the improvements are due to me, after all. However, I should give Gerard some credit this evening – he had warmed and spiced some of Quin's cider, and built up the fire so that Bruno's glasses fogged over.

Custard smelt Bru, and nearly barked himself to death. Gerard, though not so noisy, was just as pleased. Of all his sons, Bruno is the one most like him. And while G does not have a favourite, B occupies a very particular place in his heart. Gerard calls him the 'Affable Archangel' after the angel in Milton, who was so kind about giving Adam and Eve the gen on Paradise.

Bruno looks very like his father, but at the moment, Gerard is by far the smartest of the two — neat clothes and shorn hair, whereas dear old Bru is a scarecrow. Where on earth did he get that hideous pullover, and how can I find an excuse to chuck it away? There are cig burns in his grey flannels, which I may be able to darn. I certainly can't make them look any worse.

He is thin and exhausted. Whatever this secret job might be, it seems to be draining away his strength. Or is that simply because the men I see have tons of farm grub, and live out of doors? I suspect Bruno spends his days shut up in the dark, like a mushroom. And I'm sure he didn't have those tense lines around his mouth when we last saw him.

He sat in the carver's chair, with Custard lying on his (boggly and out-of-shape) shoes, and a pewter tankard of cider in his hand, beaming round at us all as if he had died and gone to heaven. Over supper, he made us laugh describing his landlady's cooking. When he had eaten (loads) he sat down at the jangly old piano in the parlour, and we sang carols.

Kit sings rather well. Quin can't really get up the wind to sing at all. Paddy is middling, and Gerard has no ear for music whatever — in the end, his singing made us laugh so much, we had to stop.

Bruno has a gift for happiness, and the pleasure of being at home made him radiant. But I still thought he looked pinched and cold, and wrapped a hot brick in a towel, to warm his feet in bed. Quin had built a wood fire in his bedroom.

'I'm overwhelmed,' Bru said. 'I've arrived in a land of plenty. Where I come from, everything is plastered with notices — switch it off, turn it down, save fuel, save water, save air.'

'If it grows, we've got it,' I said, busily turning down the bed. 'Though we've pushed the boat out for you, old thing.'

He lit a cigarette, and went to warm his backside at the fire. 'If you only knew what a relief it was, to see your face at the station, after that bloody journey. Oh, God — not that I believe in him — it's good to be home.'

'I know you're not supposed to say anything, Bru, but has it been ghastly?'

He blinked at me meaningfully, to show that it had. 'I've no right to complain. Just about every other soul in Europe would

341

say I had a very cushy number. This world sickens me, some-times. I wish I didn't know the half of it. Now that I do, I'm going to move mountains to build a better world, when this war is over.'

I asked: 'Will it ever be over?'

'Oh, yes,' he said, 'and we will win it.'

22 December

Oscar descended on us the day before yesterday. Bruno said it was like the arrival of the Queen of Sheba. An enormous and unnaturally clean Buick suddenly screeched to a halt in the yard, and out leapt Oscar – gorgeously handsome in his uniform, laden with cigs from the Naafi.

We were all dazzled. Once we got used to the dazzlement, we noticed the other man in the car – Oscar's friend, Lt John-Hugo Hennessy, known as 'JH'. He is short and stocky, with very black hair and very pale blue eyes. Not as handsome as Oscar, but nice-looking, and with a shy sort of smile which is very disarming.

He said: 'Didn't he tell you he was bringing me? How absolutely typical. Have you enough room?'

Gerard said: 'Yes, indeed, and you're most welcome. Especially if you're the JH he occasionally mentions in his very infrequent letters.'

JH produced, with an understandable flourish, a bottle of whisky.

Quin and Bruno whistled, and Gerard said: 'Now you're incredibly welcome. If I had a daughter, you could marry her.'

Since that moment, life has been one long party. Oscar is as wild and rackety as ever, and takes life as lightly as possible. His high spirits have woken us all up. This afternoon, he went out with Kit and Paddy, for holly and ivy to decorate the house.

JH stayed with me, and kindly peeled a mountain of potatoes. He told me he is an orphan, and that Oscar practically kidnapped him, in his determination to give him a family Christmas. He seems very fond of Oscar, and doesn't mind being the butt of nearly all his jokes. They were quite a double-act over dinner.

Oscar made me get out my banjo, as I knew he would, and

demanded George Formby's entire repertoire. I finished with the National Anthem at midnight, because Quin and I have to be up for milking. Quin is sleeping beside me at this moment.

How beautiful he is, with his eyelashes making spiked shadows under his eyes. And how like Jack. Perhaps I'm fanciful, owing to too much cider, but Jack doesn't feel so very far away.

25 December

It is two in the morning, but I am too keyed up to sleep. This has been an extraordinary day. There is something almost sickeningly exciting about Christmas Eve – a leftover from being a kid, I suppose.

Arthur Driver hoarded petrol to give me a very special present. He brought over Gladys, and my darling Peter. Glad has never been here before, and I instructed the Randalls to be on their best behaviour. I hugged her as if I'd never let her go, and gulped her nice, Gladys-ish smell, and probably shed a few tears on her best herringbone coat. Then I hugged my Peterkin, now grown into a plump little jug with Glad's red hair and blue, blue eyes and Tufton's air of gravity. He spent the whole visit playing with Oscar, JH and Custard.

Glad was a touch reserved, just at first. I've finally told her everything, and begged her to try to like the situation, for my sake, but she couldn't help being rather starchy when she met Gerard. With Quin, she was a little less wary. I think because he is so beautiful, and looks rather innocent.

She says she has heard they are all well at the Prospect, but never sees Daddy or Sidonia if she can help it. For the past couple of years, she has hinted that I'm being too strict with Ralph – but that is only because I didn't tell her the whole story. Primrose is still away, in the Wrens. I bet they love her, she's such a highly operational type.

Thank God, she didn't spoil her life by marrying Charlie. He is apparently back at Despard Court, with Juana, their little boy, and a troupe of peculiar servants. Probably, says Glad darkly, all with criminal records as long as your arm. Juana appears to have made it up with Sidonia, though I wonder how the old cow likes being a granny.

Isobel works on Arthur's farm, with two other land girls

*named Olive and Greta. It was nice, to hear Arthur and Gladys
singing her praises. Glad says she is the belle of all the dances at
the Army Camp. Arthur says Isobel is his right hand, and he
only wishes his son Denis had half the feel for farming. Since last
harvest, he has also been helped by some German Prisoners of
War.*

*'Makes your flesh creep,' Gladys says, 'to have them all
around you, not even guarded. Mind you, they're ever so polite,
always standing to attention and bowing – one of them clicks his
heels at Iris.'*

*Arthur was chuckling. 'And another does her hair. Them
saucy girls call him "Lili Marlene".'*

*Gladys tells me that Isobel is always begging to look after
Peter, and likes putting him to bed. She really is very sweet. How
Sidonia managed to produce two such decent daughters beats me.
I always liked Isobel, and I hope she bags herself a wonderful
man, to give her all the children she wants.*

*Through all of this, I was extremely proud of my menfolk.
They went out of their way to be charming. Gladys started off
rather on her best servant-behaviour. The manor may be falling
down, but it's still the manor. They soon made her drop her side,
however, and relax. She and Arthur made us roar with their
stories about the POWs. I suspect Arthur is fond of them. His life
was never this interesting, before the war. I can't help being glad,
for their mothers' sakes, that they have found a jailer as kind as
he is.*

*Just before they left, while Arthur was rounding up Peter,
Glad drew me aside.*

*'I don't like the set-up, and I never will. But they are very
nice, and real gentlemen. I'll go as far as that.'*

'Oh, Glad,' I said, 'I knew you'd like them.'

*'Hmmm.' She lowered her voice. 'This isn't what I wanted for
you, love – I didn't raise you to be a slave for a great pack of
men, no matter how nice they are. Isn't it time you thought of
moving on?'*

*I tried to make her understand there's no question of me
moving on. This is my home, I told her, and the Randalls are my
family. Gladys did not approve of me using the word 'family'.*

She said: 'I'm doing my best, but I can't understand it. You don't even like housework. It'd all be a lot more seemly if you could choose between the father and the son, and marry one of them. You can't really be in love with them both.'

I thought about this afterwards. All the rules I've ever heard say it is both impossible and forbidden to love more than one person at a time. It is not meant to be at all romantic, let alone decent. But if I feel I'm in love with them both, that is all that matters.

At this moment, I'm probably slightly in love with the whole pack of them. The fact is, Kit has been absolutely charming, and when Kit is charming, it sets the mood for the entire house. I am still reeling from the revelation he sprang on me after dinner. I must write it down, though Gerard, who is trying to sleep beside me, has asked me twice to put the light out.

We had a splendid Christmas Eve dinner (a cousin of Gerard's sent two brace of pheasants down from Scotland; G dealt with them because I couldn't stand the pong). When the hall clock struck midnight, we wished each other merry Christmas. Bruno played 'Christians, awake, and greet the happy morn' on the piano.

The boys stayed round the parlour fire while I cleared away. Full of exultation, I went outside to look at the stars. It was very cold, but knowing how warm and light it was inside made it quite easy to bear. I don't think I am religious, but I felt my prayer sort of lifting out of my chest and soaring to heaven – nothing in words, but an immense love for them all, and an overpowering wish that nothing should change.

Out of the darkness around me, someone whispered: 'Lily –'

'Here,' I said. I thought it was Gerard, and waited to feel his arm around me.

It was Kit. He murmured: 'I've got something for you. The others will see tomorrow, but I wanted you to be first, so you'd know it's really yours.'

He struck a match, and I had to stop myself yelling out.

He had taken off the bandage.

In the time it took for the match to burn out, the unmasked Kit printed himself on my mind, over the image of the old photo.

His skin is smooth and white, with a sheen like wax. The first impression you get is that he is growling, or laughing fiendishly.

345

*Where his eyebrows are supposed to be is moulded into a frown —
there is a sort of angry fold over the bridge of his nose.*

*There are folds, or puckers, around his eyes, as if they had
been pressed into a plate of porridge after it has formed a skin.
The same around his mouth. His upper lip is shorter than in the
photo, and has no indentation — his whole mouth seems unnaturally stretched, as if someone had nailed it firmly at either end.*

*His skin is achingly naked-looking, so that you almost feel a
breath would wither or bruise it. And for a fraction of a second,
before I had properly taken it in, I was afraid I was about to find
that he was very ugly.*

*What I actually found was a kind of power and character,
which makes words like ugly meaningless. And then the match
burnt out.*

*He asked — not at all in a nasty way — 'Well? Will I curdle
the milk?'*

*I said 'Light another match. I want to see again, because
you're beautiful.'*

That was the word that jumped off my tongue, and I meant it.

*He took my hand, planted a friendly kiss on my forehead, and
said: 'Anyway, happy Christmas.'*

Chapter Three

Above her head, Isobel heard the creaking of the floorboards, as Gladys moved around the cramped room under the eaves where Peter slept. It was Boxing Day. Isobel had volunteered to sit with the little boy while Gladys went up to the farmhouse, to listen to *The Mikado* on the wireless.

She had sat Isobel down in the armchair, and told her to relax. Isobel wished she could. Gladys's cottage was sublimely quiet, after the continual racket at the Drivers'. She had looked forward to putting her feet up – the only thing wrong with farming was that you never got enough rest, even at Christmas.

But the patient figure outside, sitting motionless at the farm's main gate, haunted her like a ghost. Gentlisch had stayed on after the other prisoners, to help Arthur Driver. The sow was farrowing, and Gentlisch was devoted to the creature. He had been grateful to Arthur, for allowing him to remain until he had seen the soft, speckled little piglets settled on their mother's teats.

He was now waiting for the truck to take him back to his camp. The soldiers who guarded him quietly bent the rules round Gentlisch, because he was so trustworthy. Nobody worried that he would make a dash for the coast, to signal some passing German submarine. He would not, in any case, have got far. The whole countryside knew the captive Germans. Gentlisch was extremely handy around the farm, and Arthur forgot, for long stretches, that he had ever been an enemy.

Isobel never forgot. Gentlisch's identity had been pressing on her uncomfortably, since the day the five POWs had been marched in to help with the harvest. Beneath his reserve, she sensed an immensity of wounded pride, which

347

made his captive status particularly painful to her. He did not swagger, or cringe. He accepted being a prisoner with a kind of stoical despair.

From their few conversations, Isobel had decided he could not be counted among the evil Nazis who tortured prisoners and abducted Jews. Such barbarism was utterly foreign to his grave, courteous nature, she was certain. Scholler, the fey Austrian who liked to do Iris Driver's hair, had told her that Gentlisch had quarrelled bitterly with an older brother who was a devoted party man. Yet he never tried to make excuses for himself, but seemed to take a stubborn pride in bearing the weight of his nation's sins.

The red coals shifted in the narrow iron grate. Isobel stretched her legs, clad in corduroy land girl's breeches, towards the glow. She felt awful about being warm, while poor Gentlisch froze outside.

Was it wicked, to think so much about the handsomeness of a German? Mrs Driver said 'handsome is as handsome does,' and took Gentlisch's conspicuous good looks as an insult. Deep down, she obviously felt the good looks of captured enemies should somehow be shared out among uglier but more deserving British troops.

Gentlisch was a textbook German, tall and stiff-backed, with hair so blond it was almost white, blue eyes and chiselled cheekbones. Isobel would look at him sometimes, and feel pleasure stirring in the very marrow of her bones. She had walked out with scores of the soldiers stationed nearby, and been vigorously kissed and groped by some half-dozen, after dances. Not one had conquered her like this defeated enemy.

On Christmas Eve, twenty POWs from the camp had driven round the farms, to sing carols. Arthur Driver had nagged his wife and sister to lay on tea and biscuits, and the captives had sung '*Stille Nacht*' like caged larks. Gentlisch had taken the solo, in his beautiful, soulful baritone. Isobel had wept to hear it; a sound that was the essence of peace and harmony.

Mrs Driver had said: 'I know they're inhuman beasts – but don't they sing lovely?'

Gentlisch's eyes had fastened upon Isobel, as they always did – he should be careful, someone was bound to notice – and as the POWs departed, his statuesque face had unexpectedly warmed into a smile. It had been like a hand reaching into her chest and squeezing her heart. Isobel had been counting the minutes until she could see him again, and feeling deeply guilty about it – but there it was. She was committing the treacherous act of falling in love with a German.

Gladys came downstairs. 'Fast asleep, bless him, clutching that wooden rabbit the prisoners gave him. He's tired out, so I doubt you'll hear a squeak from him.' She took her coat and hat from the peg behind the door. 'There's a little something for you, under that plate on the table.'

'Thanks, Mrs T.'

'I know you've eaten, but you girls are always ravenous.' Gladys chuckled as she buttoned her coat. 'Iris says she's no idea how you keep your figures, the amount you put away.'

'Mrs Tufton –' Isobel began desperately. She stood up. 'Couldn't I ask him in, until the truck comes from the camp?'

Gladys's eyes widened. 'Who? Gentlisch? He's not still out there, is he? Poor chap, he'd have been better off waiting with the pigs.'

Isobel suspected that Gladys liked Gentlisch, as far as one could like a German, and decided to play on her sympathy.

'I know it's wrong, and not allowed, but it is Christmas.'

'Christmas was yesterday. I can't help the rules.'

'It makes me so uncomfortable, being in here while he's out there.'

Gladys sighed gustily. This was a tough one. On the one hand, she did not want the poor young man to freeze. On the other hand, he was a young man, and a German young man. Nice enough, she was sure – but dare she risk leaving him alone with Isobel? She often suspected the girl had no real idea how pretty she was. Possibly, in the daily grind of ploughing, hedging and shovelling muck, she had forgotten.

'Well, I don't know, love. There'd be the most almighty fuss if the truck missed him. And he'd be the one to take the punishment.'

'Please, Mrs T – I'll hear the truck, and it's only for a minute.'

Gladys was visibly crumbling, in the light of Isobel's guileless, pleading blue eyes. Frowning and shaking her head, she jerked open the cottage door, and called out into the cold: 'Hey, you! Gentlisch! Come here. Quickly, now.'

Hesitant, with his woollen cap in his blue, ungloved hands, Gentlisch stepped into the cottage, bowing his head at the low door. 'Mrs Tufton?'

Gladys spoke scoldingly, cross with herself for giving in. 'You're to wait in here, till your lorry comes.'

'Thank you, Mrs Tufton. You are very kind.'

His English was heavily accented. He took enormous pains to speak it correctly.

'I'll be telling Mr Driver,' Gladys warned, 'so no funny business, do you hear?' On the threshold she paused, to say angrily to Isobel: 'Give him some cocoa. He looks perished.'

Forgetting Peter was asleep, she banged the door behind her.

Isobel and Gentlisch were left staring at each other, in a room that was suddenly, embarrassingly, too small. They had never been properly alone together.

He smiled shyly. 'What is "funny business"?'

His accent made Isobel giggle, and the smile made her head swim. 'She means you mustn't do anything naughty. Don't worry – she doesn't really think you will.'

'It was good of her, to ask me inside,' he said. 'But I think it was your idea.'

'You're right, it was. How's Maggie?'

Maggie was the sow.

'She is most well. As her eight little ones are also.'

'Eight? I bet Mr Driver's pleased.'

'Yes.'

'Sit down in the armchair, and I'll make the cocoa.'

His shining fair head turned, as he took in the small room. 'But where will you sit?'

'A kitchen chair will do me. Go on.'

Gentlisch lowered himself into the armchair. Isobel wondered how long it was, since he had sat on anything soft.

He rewarded her with another smile, and an 'Aaah' of pleasure, which made them both laugh. 'Thank you, Miss.'

Isobel hated him calling her 'Miss'. On his behalf, she hated his forced subservience to people who would have been his equals before the war.

'I'm Isobel,' she said firmly. 'Say it – nobody can hear.'

'Isobel.' He was obedient, but she was delighted to see that his eyes were full of laughter.

'You make it sound like a poem. Now, who are you? I mean, what's your name?'

'Marius.'

She repeated it carefully: 'Marius.'

'That is right. We are not all named Fritz.' Still smiling, he added: 'The guards call us all Fritz.' He was not bitter, but accepted this as he accepted everything.

Isobel put a pan of milk on the coals. 'What a cheek.'

'A cheek? No, I do not see this. They may call us what they wish. If "Fritz" is the worst, we are lucky.'

'I hope it is. I hope they're kind to you.'

Marius was surprised, and instantly cautious. 'You are asking, how we are treated?'

Isobel stirred cocoa powder into the milk, not looking at him. 'I suppose I am.'

He regarded her speculatively, as if trying to decide whether she really wanted to know.

'We are well treated,' he said. It sounded stiff.

'Of course,' Isobel said impulsively, 'I can't ask if you're happy, because you're obviously not. I often think it must be frightful, being treated like a criminal when you haven't committed any crime. I mean, have you?' The pan hissed. She turned back to it, blushing furiously.

Marius was startled. For the first time, it was possible to see the pain he hid behind his measured, tentative manner. 'I do not feel I have done a crime. I did not join the army of choose.'

'Choice.' Isobel handed him a cup of cocoa, and sat down opposite him. 'What did you do before the war?'

'I was a student of music.'

'Oh, how nice. No wonder you sing so beautifully.'

351

'Thank you.'

'And now you've ended up taking care of pigs.'

Marius smiled again, with the first glint of real humour. 'But I love pigs. This is not a pretend. They are so – *ach, wass ist "klug"?* – clever.'

'Mr Driver says they're more intelligent than people.'

'He is right,' Marius said. 'All round us, we see the stupidity of the human race. And *mit der Dummheit kämpfen Gotter selbst vergebens* – that means, with stupidity, even the gods must struggle. Pigs are not such dumb animals.'

'Perhaps you'll work with them again,' Isobel said, 'when the war's over.'

His face darkened. 'When the war is over, I will not be able to choice what I do. Germany will not win. I am of a defeated country. This is a very hurting thing.'

'Painful, you mean.'

'Yes, painful. I am not a Nazi, but I did not refuse to fight. I must take the punishing.'

Isobel was glad he had relaxed his self-restraint, and dismayed by the depth of sadness and anger he had revealed. She took a packet of Players from the pocket of her breeches, and held it out to him. 'Would you like one?'

'Please.' He leant towards her, bending his head over the lighted match in her hand.

Isobel longed to stroke his shorn hair. 'Have you had anything to eat?'

He exhaled a plume of smoke. 'I will eat at the camp. They do not starve us.'

'I'm sure they don't, but Mrs Tufton left me some food, and I've had my supper. I think you should have it.'

'I must not do this,' Marius said, with a wistful glance at the plate Isobel had taken from the table.

'Nonsense.' She uncovered it. 'Cold corned beef, cold sprouts, cold spuds. I wish there was time to warm it up.'

Unable to disguise the fact that he was starving, Marius attacked the food eagerly. Isobel felt the open wound in his dignity, caused by the continual small humiliations of being a stranger in a hostile country; forced to be grateful for every crumb of ordinary kindness.

She wanted passionately to know the real Marius, hidden beneath the defensive layers of shame and fear. She wished she could tell him she did not care that he had once worn a swastika, and tried to kill her countrymen.

With food inside him, a fire at his feet and a cigarette in his hand, he relaxed. Isobel asked him about his home, and he told her he came from Köln, where his father was a teacher of history. He never forgot their situation, but allowed himself to show glimmerings of enthusiasm and even – when describing the beauty of Cologne Cathedral – sentimentality. Their eyes filled in unison, and love hit Isobel like a lead-filled sock.

They heard the truck crawling up the lane outside. Marius jumped to his feet, eyes still swimming.

'Isobel, thank you.'

The dread of returning to the old formality made Isobel reckless. She flung her arms around his neck, and stood on tiptoe to brush her lips against his.

For a long moment, Marius stood very still. Then he swept her into his arms and, with a kind of angry desperation, kissed her hard on the mouth.

Chapter Four

❖❖❖

Towards the end of February, Arthur Driver dropped Gladys off at Randalls, on his way to collect a calf from a nearby farm. Gladys had not told Lily she was coming, and stood shivering in the littered yard, until she was seen by Bruno.

'Mrs Tufton, how terrific.' He ushered her into the kitchen, unfortunately not at its tidiest. 'I'll tell Lily you're here.' He tipped a pile of dirty socks and a sleeping mouse off a chair. 'Do sit down.'

Gladys perched on the extreme edge of the chair, watching the mouse as it nosed boldly among the crumbs under the table.

'Glad, you darling!' Lily came bounding in through the scullery door, wrapped in huge corduroy trousers and a grey school jersey, once the property of Paddy. 'Where's my Peter?'

'I left him with Iris.' Still keeping a sharp eye on the mouse, Gladys accepted a kiss. 'I'm sorry to burst in on you like this, but I wanted a word.'

'You two go into the parlour,' Bruno said. 'I'll bring you some tea.'

Lily peeled off the grey jersey, to reveal another, slightly smaller, underneath. 'No, you won't. Get back to your sofa.'

'Honestly, I'm feeling fine, and –'

'Bru, you're being very unpatriotic. What'll happen to the war effort, if you make yourself sick again?'

He smiled, in a way that suggested a dog rolling over on its back to have its stomach rubbed. 'Okay.'

When he had gone, Gladys whispered: 'He's sweet on you, that one. Don't order him about too much, or you'll make it worse.'

Lily slammed the kettle onto the range. 'I have to look after him. He's had influenza. They sent him home, more dead than alive, after he keeled over at his desk.'

'Well. I suppose you know what you're doing.' Gladys unwound her scarf, and folded it neatly on the cleanest part of the table. This was a sign that she was open for business. Hastily, Lily assembled the tea-things, and sat down beside her.

'Fire away. What's the news?'

Gladys was distracted by the jersey. 'Look at the state of you. Whatever are you wearing?'

'Never mind that – stop creating suspense.'

'It's the upset at the farm. Everybody's in a terrible state – Arthur in one of his rages, Iris taking it out on the land girls. And it's because of Isobel.'

'What's happened to her? Is she all right?'

Gladys shook her head portentously. 'No, she is not all right. She's gone and fallen in love with one of the German POWs.'

'No! How romantic.'

'It isn't at all, but I knew you'd see it that way. In fact, that's why I wanted to see you. I blame myself, because I left them alone together – that's how it started. And I thought she could do with some sympathy. I daren't show her any, with Arthur in such a fury.'

'Fury? That's a bit strong.'

'He caught them at it,' Gladys said. 'Canoodling, if you know what I mean. Arthur's trusted both of them a good deal – the German more than he should – and he reckons they betrayed him.'

'But one kiss doesn't count for much!'

Gladys's colour rose. 'I understand it was considerably more than one kiss. I'm glad you think it's so funny.'

Lily was laughing delightedly. 'Blimey, that naughty girl.'

'Chip off the old block, I can't help thinking,' Gladys said. 'Blood will out.'

This brought Lily back to earth. 'No, you mustn't say that, Isobel's nothing like Sidonia. She fell desperately in love, and got carried away, that's all.'

'Really, Lily!' Gladys banged down her teacup. 'Haven't you girls ever heard of waiting till you're married?'

'Not in wartime, when you might be separated any minute,' Lily said. 'What's he like, this German?'

'That's just it. If he wasn't a German, he'd be a nice boy. Hard-working, serious, thinks the world of Isobel. Arthur kicked up such a fuss, they're sending him off to another camp.'

'Gosh, poor Isobel. How's she taking it?'

'They've marched her back to the Prospect,' Gladys said. 'The night before she went, she sneaked down to see me. And I must admit, I couldn't be cross with her. She fairly broke my heart.' She sighed. 'Her face was all cried out of shape, poor little duck. She says to me: "We want to get married, Mrs Tufton, we love each other so awfully much; now we'll never be together again." I don't doubt for a minute she really does love him.'

Lily's black eyes were full of compassion. 'What d'you think will happen to her?'

'I expect the Land Army will find her another posting. I know she'll want to escape from the Prospect as fast as possible – the Captain made one hell of a row, apparently. Called her every name under the sun, and said she wasn't to set foot in the place again, if she had any more contact with the German.'

'He's got a nerve,' Lily said. 'It's always shocking types like him who take a high moral tone.'

'You can say that again, love. Mr Charlie was even nastier – told her she was worse than Lord Haw-Haw, and ought to go to jail for treason.'

'Pig,' said Lily. As Gladys had guessed, throwing Charlie into the scales weighted them totally in Isobel's favour.

'I don't know what you could do for her,' she said. 'But just a kind word would help. Right now, that girl hasn't a friend in all the world.'

———⋙⋘———

Lily told the story to Bruno, when she went into the parlour, in the quiet hour before supper, to build up the fire and give him some tea.

Bruno sat up against the arm of the sofa, an old tartan rug across his knees. His eyes were huge and vulnerable behind his thick glasses. He drank in every word hungrily, bewitched by the firelight reflected in Lily's eyes.

'From forth the fatal loins of these two foes, a pair of star-cross'd lovers,' he murmured, when she had finished. 'What a bloody unfortunate situation.'

'I wish I was her fairy godmother, and I could bring them together with a wave of my wand. But what can I do, short of finishing the war single-handed?'

Bruno stopped gazing wistfully, and applied his mind to the problem. 'The war will end eventually, of course. Looking at it coldly, they only have to wait a few years. But of course, love isn't like that. When one is in love, forced separation is torture.' As if realising the boldness of this declaration, he added: 'So I've heard. Every girl in love with a man in the army or navy has to grin and bear it, but it's undoubtedly harder for your stepsister. She has nobody to help her – and when she's trying to marry a defeated enemy, she'll need all the help she can get. Does she have any family, besides your wicked stepmother? For instance, a father?'

'Oh, yes,' Lily said, 'I think he's in London. His name's Colm Leary.'

Bruno was impressed. 'The painter? How fascinating. I went to a tremendous exhibition of his, before the war. Does he have much to do with his daughter?'

'No, as far as I could see. Primrose was constantly writing to her father, and I once asked Isobel why she didn't do the same. She said there was no point, because he never read letters. I don't know his address.'

'That ought to be easy enough to find.' Bruno lit a cigarette, forgetting that the doctor had forbidden him to smoke. 'The gallery would probably tell you.'

Lily sat bolt upright on the hearthrug. 'Then I'll go to London.'

'What? Don't be daft –'

'You'll all have to do without me for a few days. I'm going to find Colm Leary, and tell him he must help Isobel. If I meet him face to face, he can't refuse me.'

'No,' Bruno said softly, 'I can't imagine anyone refusing you. But Lily, do you know London at all?'

'I've only been once. Tufton and Gladys took me to see *Where The Rainbow Ends* when I was ten.'

'You can't possibly go alone. Let me come with you.'

'You're too ill.'

He threw off the blanket. 'Rubbish. I'm miles better.'

Lily held his face between her palms. 'Honestly? You're awfully pale and skinny.'

'Not much of a specimen,' Bruno said sadly. 'But I know I can be useful, if you don't mind my tagging along.'

She smiled and dropped a kiss on his nose, causing him to redden uncomfortably. 'You're an exquisite specimen, you Affable Archangel. I'd love to have you.'

They left early the next morning. Lily wore her one passable dress, a plain grey crepe Gladys had made for her, in the first winter of the war. The effect was rather spoiled by Paddy's outgrown tweed school coat, and unbecoming thick 'utility' shoes, but her eyes sparkled and her hair gleamed. Everything else was mere outline; the setting for the jewel.

Pa said to Bruno: 'Take care of our Lily, boy. Bring her home safely.'

He drove them to the station, in the muddy Randall Austin. On the long, chilly journey, they sat on either side of a packed compartment, foggy with cigarette smoke. Bruno rapidly fell asleep, over a copy of *Horizon*. Stray sprouts of his brown hair, which looked as if it had been cut with a scythe, stuck out above his collar and behind his ears. Being nearer in size to slender Pa than his burly brothers, he had borrowed the good dark suit. This, with a virgin, unspotted tie, belonging to Quin, made him unusually spruce. Lily, ostensibly reading a pamphlet Bruno had given her, about Leary's work, watched him thoughtfully.

At Paddington station, she had to shake him awake. He staggered drunkenly around the crowded platform, blinking owlishly at the racket.

'Of course I'm all right – absolutely first-class – never better –'

Lily had not asked. She tucked her hand into his arm.

'Come on. Let's find something to eat.'

For someone who did not know London, she attacked the city with remarkable confidence. In a shabby side street, next to a bomb-site overgrown with weeds, she found a café. One of its windows was boarded up; the other was dim and dripping with steam. Lily sat Bruno down at a bare wooden table, and bought what the café had – thick Spam sandwiches, and dark brown tea.

'Good old Spam,' Bruno said affectionately.

Each saucer contained one rather grubby cube of sugar, sitting in the tarnished spoon. Lily dropped both into Bruno's tea. 'You look better now. You had me worried.'

'Sorry. But I am better, you know. When I've finished this, and found somewhere to relieve myself, I'll be able to face your friend. I didn't have a chance to nip down the corridor on the train.'

'There's plenty of time,' Lily said. 'I'm not taking you anywhere until you've had a decent haircut.' She reached across the table, and pulled the knot of his tie straight. 'I've been dying to do that for hours.'

Bruno grinned at her ruefully. 'I must look pretty awful.'

'Pretty lovely, actually. But I can't resist adding a final touch or two. You're so handsome, Bru. I've never understood why you hide your light under a bushel.'

'I thought we were here for Isobel. Do you want to be my fairy godmother, too?' His pale, anxious face creased into a smile, which made him absurdly like his father. 'Well, I suppose I do neglect my appearance. I don't see the point of smartness.'

Lily blew on her tea. 'Why not?'

Hesitantly, staring down at his plate, he said: 'It doesn't seem to apply to me. I simply look like what I am – bespectacled, bookish, non-combative and generally weedy.'

'For someone so clever,' Lily said, 'you're pitifully dense. Why don't you want girls to find out how attractive you are? Assuming there are girls, where you work.'

He laughed. 'You're always fishing for information about my job.'

'Sorry.'

'As a matter of fact, there are one or two girls. But we're all far too busy to think about – well, you know – sex.'

'There's no such thing as too busy,' Lily declared. 'People can't help thinking about sex, whatever they're doing.'

'All right, I do think about it. Quite a lot, actually. But I try not to let it become a distraction. After all, what girl would look at me?' Though he threw this out lightly, his smile was forced. 'A man who's not in uniform has no right to dress up. If I were a girl, I wouldn't give the time of day to a chap like me. I'd go for someone big and handsome, like Kit or Oscar.'

Lily laid her hand on his. 'You'd find that loads of girls are looking at you like mad, if you bothered to look back. There's one doing it right now.'

'Where?'

'Me, you idiot!'

His eyes were full of alarm. He froze, as if scared to breathe. 'Oh, God –'

'I love you,' she whispered. 'I've loved you since I came to Randalls, and I think you're perfectly gorgeous.' Her voice firmed. 'I can see past your shreds and patches, but I'd prefer not to have to. I'm going to treat you to a haircut, so eat up your lovely Spam.'

Bruno stared down at the slab of bread on his plate. He was pale. He swallowed nervously several times. 'I can't eat it.'

'Are you feeling ill?'

He glanced up at her, with a timid smile. 'I think – I think I'm in love.'

⋘⋙

Lily knocked briskly on the door of Daphne Wadsworth's flat in Dover Street. 'I hope she's in. We haven't the cash for a decent hotel.' She kissed Bruno's cheek. 'And I'd like to show you off.'

He had emerged from the barber's looking, she thought, like a younger version of Pa; less spry and sinewy, intriguingly earnest. His floppy brown hair had been cut short, to set off the graceful shape and carriage of his head. His tie was straight, his collar without a crease. Lily could not take her eyes off him.

The door opened. Daphne, clad in her blue boiler suit, with an ARP armband, stood before them.

She gaped for a moment, then screamed: 'Lily! My Lily-Josephine!' and folded her in a bone-crushing embrace. 'Beloved child, what are you doing here? Why didn't you telephone? Where, where, where have you been? I've been out of my mind, since Gladys wrote to tell me.'

'Daph, this is Bruno Randall.'

Daphne released her, and swept her eyes over the astonished Bruno. 'You've been with him? How marvellous. I've known this Lily since she was a little thing of five, Bruno – it's a vast relief to me, to know she's safe and settled.'

'How do you do, Miss Wadsworth.'

'Oh, my dear. For God's sake, call me Daphne.' She pumped his hand, and yanked him inside. 'Come in, children, and sit down. You'll stay for supper – Audrey will be back directly, with the week's whale-meat, or cat-bum, or whatever she could get. The food situation in London is the absolute end.'

She wrenched the suitcases out of Bruno's hand, and motioned to them to sit down on the divan.

Lily said: 'I'm afraid we're after more than supper, Daph. We have some business in London, and we wondered if you could put us up for a couple of days.'

'Of course. You can have the spare room – well, you won't find anywhere else. Hotel beds are as rare as hens' teeth, I'm told.'

'We wouldn't be putting you out?'

'Not at all. Audrey keeps a few things in there, but she bunks with me.'

Lily had – fortunately – prepared Bruno for Daphne's outspoken Sapphism. In spite of this, however, he was amazed by her loud barrage of talk. He stared at her, open-mouthed, with a kind of uneasy fascination.

Daphne produced two small glasses of sherry. 'I warn you, I must have the whole story. I haven't been able to discover a thing about you, since I broke off relations with Sidonia and Ralph. Dear Gladys Tufton assured me you were safe, but she refused to reveal your whereabouts. I nearly hired a detective.'

Lily sketched in the details of the menage at Randalls. Daphne listened avidly, with many curious glances at Bruno. To his relief, before she could ask too many questions, a tall, stooping woman arrived with a shopping basket, and was introduced as Audrey Davis.

Audrey was an officer in the Wrens, who worked at the Admiralty. As soon as the introductions had been got through, Daphne's attention was focused on the contents of the basket.

'What the hell is this? A pound of captured enemy penises? Some of the creatures they're dragging out of the sea these days make me wonder seriously about God – what can he have been thinking of, when he made this? Thankfully, it's your turn to cook.'

Bruno asked: 'May we help at all?'

'No, dear,' Audrey said amiably, 'I have it all planned. I'm relying on you to distract Daphne and keep her out of my kitchen.'

The sound of his own voice encouraged Bruno to relax a little. While Audrey shut herself in the kitchen, he began to tell Daphne about Isobel and her German POW. Once again, Daphne poured her whole attention into the subject.

'I'm glad you came to me, because I know exactly where to find Leary, reprehensible old bog-trotter that he is. I'll telephone the latest concubine, and warn her not to let him out of the house till he's seen you. Don't forget to make him show you his work. The latest paintings are extraordinary.' Noticing the gleam of interest this had sparked in Bruno, she asked: 'Are you familiar with his work?'

He was, and they launched into an intense discussion about modern art. Lily, delighted to see Bruno thawing into animation and charm, nursed her sherry contentedly. Art carried them through to the cramped dining room, where Audrey had concocted a surprisingly toothsome pie from the unpromising fish.

'Right,' Daphne said, 'now we can get down to the nuts and bolts.' She looked at Lily and Bruno with mock severity, over the tops of her horn-rimmed spectacles. 'You're going to tell me what's really happening in your idyllic refuge.'

Lily told her, with such matter-of-fact honesty and ease that Bruno scarcely blushed.

'So,' Daphne said, between mouthfuls of pie, 'what a lovely family they must be. I always maintained you would have an immense capacity for romance. I'd love to put you all into one of my Phyllis Crewe novels, but the reading public is too dismally conventional. They treat sex like a strong cocktail, only one per customer. So mean.'

Audrey said: 'The war's changed things, surely.'

'Not the basic template of romance,' Daphne said briskly. 'That would take a revolution. Conventional romance exists to keep women in chains, by persuading them to love their fetters. Phyllis's novels are training manuals. Look how dear, conventional Gladys laps them up. Does she know about your antics with the entrancing Randalls?'

'She does,' Lily said. 'I know she'll come round, when she realises how wonderful they are. If I love them, and they love me, what can possibly be wrong?'

Daphne caught the involuntary look, crackling with electricity, which passed between Lily and Bruno. Her face was tender. 'Oh child, great is thy faith – and great is thy simplicity. But too much love is better than not enough.'

When supper was over, and coffee essence had been served in the drawing room, Audrey showed Bruno the spare bedroom, and went to remove the underwear that was drying in the unused servants' bathroom.

Daphne held Lily back. 'Wait, darling. Are you truly happy?'

'Everyone asks me that,' Lily said, laughing. 'Don't I look it?'

'If life really was as cut and dried as you make out,' Daphne said, 'I'd be living with a whole pack of Girl Guides, and telling any interested party that it was fine, because we were all in love.'

'You'd be getting love mixed up with sex.'

Daphne sighed, exasperated, and shut the door, so that Bruno would not hear them. 'Well, isn't that exactly what you're doing?'

'No! I'm deeply in love, passionately in love, to the marrow of my bones!' She seized Daphne's upper arms, alight with eagerness. 'Please, Daph – I trusted you to understand, and not moralise. Sex doesn't exist on its own. Since the moment I met them, I've known my destiny was tied up with the Randalls. It's as if we'd been waiting for each other, for years and years. Each one of them lives inside me in a particular way, as if he'd dropped into a him-shaped space there.'

Daphne gazed into Lily's face, with anxiety and helpless affection. 'Look at you,' she said, 'shining like a star, beautiful as the day, and burning to acquaint the whole world with your discovery.' Gently, she shook off Lily's hands. 'I need another sherry. Oh, how I wish it was gin.'

She held the bottle up to the light, then said: 'Fuck,' and poured herself half a tumbler-full. 'I bet those men can't believe their luck. Still, if they're all as nice as Bruno, I suppose you're safe enough.'

'You like him, don't you? I knew you would. He's so good, and so tremendously –'

'Yes, yes, darling, I like him. He's charming. And fancy you walking out with a chap who reads *Horizon*. But Lily –' She gulped back a large slug of sherry. 'Haven't you ever asked yourself, what exactly is the difference between you and your poor, idiotic father? Or, come to that, between you and Sidonia? Why is their incapacity for monogamy bad, and yours good?'

Lily flinched, as if Daphne had slapped her. 'The difference is that I'm not unfaithful. I don't do anything to hurt other people. Sidonia and Daddy don't give a damn about the feelings of other people – they're the ones who only care about sex. They don't know about kindness, or unselfishness, or the joy of making someone you love happy. Whereas I wouldn't hurt Gerard Randall and his sons for the whole world. I just want to live for them, not for myself.'

'You're an intelligent girl,' Daphne said. 'But Lord, so innocent, so naive. How do you know you're not hurting them? How much do those men go along with, simply because they know they'd lose you if they didn't? How do you know they're not waiting for a sign from you, to show which one you like best? If you showed a preference, they'd probably start fighting like dogs in a box, because that's how human beings are made.'

Before she was halfway through this speech, Lily had broken into a radiant smile, tears spangling her lashes. 'Writing your romances has turned you into a terrible cynic, Daph. I know they love each other as much as they love me.'

Daphne, her own eyes filling, gave Lily an irritable, sherry-tasting kiss. 'Then may they be blessed, and may you all live happily ever after. I'm not going to tell a sweet creature like you that spreading love in a world full of hate is wrong. Go off to bed. Your Randall awaits.'

'Good night, Daph. Thanks for letting us stay.' At the door, Lily turned back. 'Even though you disapprove – don't you?'

There was a silence, during which Daphne's lips worked, as she struggled to find the right words. 'Yes, I do,' she said eventually. 'Not because I'm a secret moralist. I've known you since you were a little thing, and I always saw how your heart raced out to embrace people. You have a talent for love. People must go to quite considerable trouble, to stop you loving them. So of course you love your Randalls, who showed you such chivalrous kindness. And of course, the fact they're all good-looking made you want to give your body, along with your heart – I don't doubt that you have the most extraordinary talent for sex, since ninety per cent of being good at it boils down to enthusiasm. Now, you're in a blissful state of satisfied body and heart, and you think it's the end of the story.'

'Isn't it?'

'At the risk of sounding like a superannuated old bore, you're awfully young, and you don't know how the world works. A girl like you – you're still waiting for the one, supreme lover, who'll burn through you like a fire, and turn you inside out. You live for all the others – but you'll die for him.'

There was another silence, this time stretching into

minutes. Lily stood motionless, her hand resting on the door, staring at Daphne in utter perplexity.

'I'm sorry I said your writing has turned you into a cynic,' she said. 'It hasn't at all.'

Daphne sighed. 'I give up. Maybe you're unlike the rest of the world. I hope so. Because for most people, love just isn't that easy.'

⸻◈⸻

Lily found Bruno pacing restlessly around Daphne's small spare bedroom, his hands in his pockets. He stood to attention when he saw Lily, and retreated defensively behind the double bed.

'You were a long time.' It was not an accusation. His forehead was corrugated with anxiety.

Lily, more rattled by Daphne's lecture than she cared to admit, studied him to reassure herself. Yes, this was Bruno, the Affable Archangel, who had always shown her such diffident, modest tenderness. She absolutely knew she loved him, and that love was quite distinct and separate from the love she bore Gerard, Jack and Quin. Her body, not given to debate, informed her of an immense, simple desire to tear down the final barrier between them. Together, the love and the desire combined to fill the pit of her stomach with the familiar urgency, and her eyes with tears.

She wanted to burst out with an extravagant declaration. Instead, she sniffed back the tears, and said: 'I was chatting to Daphne. Why aren't you in bed? You must be exhausted.'

He said: 'There's only one bed. If we both sleep in it, I can't guarantee that – I'm going to find it enormously difficult not to – perhaps I'd better take the divan.'

'Do you want to?'

'I really feel I ought to.'

'Oh.' She had not expected this. On top of Daphne's diatribe, it made her afraid.

'Is it – are you worried about Gerard and Quin? I was thinking of them, honestly I was.' The tears welled up painfully. 'I didn't think they'd mind, but if you do, then of course –'

Bruno hurried over to her, and took her into his arms.

366

'Oh, Lily, this is ridiculous, I've done it all wrong and made you cry. I was trying to consider you.' Very gently, he pushed her face from his shoulder, forcing her to look at him. 'All I meant was, I'm horribly in love with you, and if we share a bed, I won't be able to help betraying myself, in various untidy and embarrassing ways.'

She laughed shakily. 'Don't leave me, Bru. I want you so much.'

'Are you sure?'

'I'll put it in writing, if you like.'

Slowly, his anxious, speculative face melted into a smile. 'In that case, I'll happily make you a present of my virginity. But you'll have to tell me what to do. I haven't a clue about the details.'

'Just think of England,' Lily said. She tilted back her head, and he kissed her; tentatively at first, then fiercely, pressing his pelvis against hers.

She pulled away from him. He retreated immediately, afraid he had gone too far.

Lily said: 'Now we take all our clothes off.'

'Gosh, how rude. I don't know if I can –'

She took something from her pocket and closed it in her fist. Then she unfastened the hooks of the grey dress, and shrugged it to the floor. She kicked off her shoes, and stepped out of the faded pink silk step-ins. She took off her brassiere.

Bruno let out a high, involuntary groan, and pushed a finger into the top of her stocking. 'Oh, Jesus –'

Laughing, Lily worked loose the knot of his tie. He retreated again, and tore off his clothes with shaking, clumsy hands, staring as if to devour her with his eyes. His straining erection twitched towards his navel. When he was naked, he covered it protectively with his hand.

She turned back the covers of the bed, and lay down on her back. As it always did, her world contracted, until all that mattered was the sensation of his flesh upon hers.

Bruno knelt awkwardly between her legs. She opened her palm, revealing a condom. They were both trembling. Tears slid down the sides of her face.

She whispered: 'You have to wear this. Let me.' Deftly, she fitted on the condom, and guided him inside her. He lay still, his breathing shallow and apprehensive.

Lily reached out to take off his glasses. This reducing of his vision to mist and shadow seemed to help his surrender to the commands of his body.

He began to move inside her, murmuring: 'Please say, if this is in any way disagreeable –'

She wrapped her legs around him, and his movements gathered strength and speed. He came, with a shout of release, and an expression of enchanted disbelief, and collapsed on top of her.

Lily cradled his head against her breasts. She had not come, but he had quietened the clamour in her body, and left it glowing with repletion. This was real love, this warm peace and fulfilment; this almost unbearable ache of longing, only soothed by clasping his nakedness to hers, and feeling their hearts beating as one heart. Daphne had been wrong, to doubt the reality of her love.

Bruno rolled off her, panting, and fumbled for his glasses. 'I had no idea,' he said. 'The Elizabethans called it "a little death", and I never understood what they meant, until now. Death and rebirth.'

She laughed softly. 'It meets with your approval, then?'

'You meet with my approval. I refuse to consider the act in isolation.'

This was her own philosophy entirely, as she had tried to explain it to Daphne – the fusing of the body with the soul; sex as a sacred act of love, rather than a sordid, selfish recreation.

'Thank God we've done it,' she said fervently. 'I've been wishing for you, for absolutely years. I think I've been falling in love with you since my first day at Randalls, when you got all covered in soot, showing me how to work the kitchen range.'

Bruno propped himself on one elbow. 'And I've probably been besotted with you since we came in from the pub, and found you sleeping on the settle. Snow White, on the run from her wicked stepmother.'

'Except that you're not dwarfs.'

'No. Slightly better hung, I should hope.'

'You must admit, though,' Lily said, 'Grumpy is awfully like Kit used to be, before he decided to be nice to me.' She took his hand. 'Bru, do you think Kit will mind about me and you?'

'No. Number One takes things more lightly, these days. And I don't think you need worry too much about the others. I asked Pa yesterday if he minded your going off alone with me. He said it was all inside the magic circle.'

Lily liked this. 'The magic circle. Yes, there is a magic about you all. I wish I'd said that to Daphne.'

Bruno lifted her hand to his lips. 'And I wish I'd told her how you shot into the midst of my family like a silver bullet, transforming our lives, and making our hearth-fire and home-acre a perfect antidote to this war. No wonder we're all in love with you.'

'All of you? And yet you don't mind sharing me?'

'My father and my brother are not my rivals,' Bruno said. 'We want the same thing – to keep you.'

He slept, with his warm body curled around hers.

Lily lay awake, thinking of silver bullets and magic circles, and the happiness she had found in loving the Randalls. She refused to accept Daphne's warning that this was somehow the wrong sort of love; merely a rehearsal for the genuine article.

Chapter Five

◆◆◆◆◆

'He's right at the top,' Mrs Leary said, through the cigarette wedged between her lips. 'It's quite a hike.'

From the bowels of the tall house came a long, blood-curdling scream. Without removing the cigarette, Mrs Leary leaned over the banister, and yelled: 'Mickey! Leave Jane alone!'

The scream subsided into fretful wails. Mrs Leary resumed her puffing and plodding up the uncarpeted stairs. Behind her, Lily and Bruno exchanged uneasy grins. Daphne had warned them that Leary liked to live 'at the eye of the storm', but they had not expected chaos on this heroic scale.

The yellowed stucco of the house in Primrose Hill was peeling as if flayed. They had found the front path strewn with rubbish – squashed tins, cabbage leaves, cigarette ends – and a little girl was sitting in the empty dustbin, as if her parents had thrown her away.

They had waited for ages on the doorstep, until a small boy appeared, to inform them gravely that the bell did not work. Behind him, a hoarse female voice had shouted: 'Mickey! Who the hell are you talking to?' and Mrs Leary had fought her way past the pieces of broken bicycle choking the narrow hall.

Bruno had explained, with his usual amiable courtesy, that they wanted to see Colm Leary, concerning his daughter Isobel.

Mrs Leary had looked blank, then said: 'Oh, yes. The Wadsworth woman rang about you. I forgot to tell him.'

Two more children had appeared, while Lily and Bruno struggled through the bicycles. They were tiny, crusted with dirt, and staring like bushbabies. Mrs Leary ignored them.

'Come on, then. I'll take you up.'

She was a startling-looking woman, with a round, angry face and a heavy shock of dead straight, iron-grey hair. She was dressed in men's flannel trousers, a bright crimson jersey and a crossover pinafore. Lily and Bruno followed her upstairs. The house had no carpets. The walls were white, and plentifully blobbed with dirt at child-height. There was a strong smell of turpentine.

Bruno and Lily stole curious glances through open doors on the way up, catching glimpses of chairs heaped with ragged clothes, and crippled furniture that had recently been rather handsome and expensive. At Randalls, things took centuries to disintegrate. Here, it looked as if tables, beds and sofas were purposely destroyed, the minute they left the shop.

'He's rolling in money,' Daphne had said. 'Don't be put off by the mess.'

On the upper floors, the walls were lined with drawings and rough paintings, tacked carelessly above the dado. Bruno kept trying to stop and examine these. They were mainly portraits of Mrs Leary and the children, interwoven with surreal, unrelated images – fishes, suns, bits of bicycles. He made people into machines, and machines into people. Lily thought them hideous, but Bruno kept drawing in his breath sharply, and whispering: 'Remarkable – incredible –'

Mrs Leary knocked on a door at the top of the house. 'Leary!'

'Fuck off!'

'People to see you.'

'What do they want?'

'Ask them yourself.' She flicked the ash from the end of her cigarette, and began to plod downstairs, without a backward glance. Lily and Bruno were left outside the closed door.

Bruno was on the point of knocking again, when the door opened. Leary, bulky and potato-faced, was cleaning a brush with a reeking rag, and wreathed in a cloud of smoke.

'Mr Leary?' Bruno shook the hand that held the rag. 'My name is Bruno Randall; this is Lily Gallant. She doesn't know we're here, but we've come about your daughter, Isobel.'

Leary plucked the cigarette from his mouth. His eyes, round and blue like Isobel's, narrowed as he studied Bruno's face. 'Isobel? God, yes. Sidonia's little girl. Come on in.'

His studio was the two rooms of the top floor, knocked into one. The walls, and the dusty, splintery floorboards were crusted with layers and layers of paint. Paint hung from the windowsill in stalactites, and the two wooden chairs were speckled with it, like dirty Seurat landscapes. Portraits were propped round the walls, four and five deep. Looking at them, Lily realised what people meant, when they talked of a 'speaking likeness'. She knew none of the subjects, but they were shockingly, vividly alive, and seemed ready to speak at any moment.

Bruno was dazzled by them. Forgetting why they had come, he moved from canvas to canvas, with the innocent relish of a child in a sweetshop. Leary thoughtfully watched him, still scrutinising his face.

Lily touched his arm. 'She's not a little girl any more, you know. She's rather a big girl, in the Land Army.' She poured out the tale of Isobel and her German. She outlined, as heartrendingly as she knew how, the friendless state of the young couple, and begged Isobel's famous father to provide a refuge.

'Ah, you could draw blood from a turnip, so you could,' Leary said. Briefly, he brushed a hand across her hair. 'And you've the face of a little angel. Quite a stepdaughter for Sidonia. God's judgement on the old bag.'

'Mr Leary, if you could just tell Isobel she'd be welcome to come here —'

'No, she can't come here.' At last, he was businesslike.

'Would your wife object?'

'Rosie's not my wife. Mrs Leary lives in Hampstead, and wants nothing from me, except my signature on a cheque. When I'm late, she sends over a child or two – and frankly, Rosie's getting tired of finding my progeny on her doorstep.'

'Isobel's your firstborn, and you've never done a thing for her.'

Leary scowled. 'Are you sure Sidonia didn't put you up to this? I've never done anything because I won't deal with that woman.'

'You won't have to. In fact, now's your chance to go right over her head – she's been beastly about the whole thing.' Sure she was on to a winner here, seeing Leary's flash of interest, she added: 'Imagine how mad she'd be.'

'The question is,' Bruno said, 'what kind of help you can offer, and what use it could be to your daughter. Eventually, Isobel and her German will have to set up home together. You could promise a little financial support, once the war is over.'

'I never make promises,' Leary said. 'I can't think further ahead than dinner-time. But I am sorry for the child, by Jesus. Is she still pretty?'

'Extremely,' Lily said.

'Is she, now? None of my other kids are pretty. After Sidonia, I never went with another good-looking woman. Sid was the only beauty I could sling into paint.' He dropped his cigarette, and crushed it under his great navvy's boot. There was a spell of silence, as he paced across the room. He pounced back at them suddenly. 'Tell you what, I've been wondering what to do with a big house and farm of mine, in the West of Ireland. My mother made me buy it. She reckons it once belonged to some grand connection or other, but it's not worth a song and a pint of porter. She'll let me get rid of it, if I'm making it over to Isobel. Will that do, now?'

Lily stared at him, in stunned delight. This was a result beyond her dreams. 'You mean – you mean, just give it to her? When the war's over?'

'She can have it now,' Leary said impatiently. 'I don't want the fucking place – great white elephant.'

'Ireland's neutral, of course,' Bruno murmured. 'They're less likely to mind having a German for a neighbour when the war's over, and the POWs are released.' There was a slight tinge of disapproval in his mild voice, which made Leary glance at him beadily.

'Isobel loves farming, too,' Lily said. 'It's perfect.'

'There's a condition,' Leary announced. 'If I'm to make over Ballymunty, I want something in exchange. In the shape of a bit of modelling.'

'Modelling?' Lily echoed.

Bruno smiled at her. 'Obviously, he wants you to sit for him.'

'Her? What would I want with a little lovely like her?'

'Then who –'

'You!' roared Leary, nearly knocking him over with a slap on the back. 'I've been combing London for a face like yours! All angles and intellect – and I want your mouth all stitched up like an arse, as it was when you said Ireland was neutral. Consent to be painted by a wicked Irishman, who'd let Nazi warships sail right up the Liffey, and my girl Isobel gets Ballymunty.'

'I say – just a minute –'

Lily had been howling with laughter, since Leary's description of Bruno's mouth. 'Go on, Bru, it won't hurt. He'll be glad to do it, Mr Leary.'

'My agent,' Bruno said, with an unwilling smile. 'I suppose I should be honoured. I'm a huge admirer of your work. But I'm not sure what my superiors will think, if they see it. I happen to work in – in a rather sensitive area –'

'Oh, I shan't be exhibiting until you British have won your fucking war.'

'In that case, I'd consider it a privilege.'

Leary was already rummaging through a heap of blank canvases in a chair beside the window. 'Start this afternoon. And bring this little witcheen – I may not paint beauties, but I like to look at 'em.'

Bruno was destined to look back on his stay in London, in the early spring of 1944, as the most purely happy time of his life. Each morning, he and Lily took the underground from Green Park to Camden Town, then walked to Leary's house in Primrose Hill. There, they knocked and yelled until someone – usually Rosie, in her dressing gown – let them in.

Bruno went upstairs, to turf Leary out of bed. Lily went down to the basement kitchen, to brew coffee essence and cut jam sandwiches for the children. There were four of these cherubs, potato-faced like their father, and as dirty as possible. Rosie was constantly shouting at them and chasing them, and diving at them with damp flannels, to very little effect. After every effort with them, she collapsed into exhausted indifference. She told Lily she had just discovered she was expecting another, and that she couldn't get help, let alone keep it.

Rosie often ambushed Lily with startling pieces of information. 'He's an animal in bed,' she would suddenly announce, 'and he won't hear of birth control.' She was grateful to Lily, for taking the children up to the studio, to play while Leary painted and Bruno sat.

Leary liked having the children racketing around him, provided someone else stopped them eating his oils or jumping out of the window. He quickly became very friendly with Bruno. When Lily took his little ones out to play on Primrose Hill, he loved to embroil his sitter in intense political discussions.

Lily would return to find him bawling about Ireland, Socialism, or the perfidy of the British government, still painting furiously. Bruno, amused by his vehemence, aired his ideas for the new world to be built after the war. The debates continued until Lily had helped Rosie to put the children to bed. At around half past six, she put her head round the studio door, to tell Bruno it was time to go home.

Mid-shout ('Sell us all to the bloody Russians, would you?') Leary would break off, wish them a cheerful good evening, and go in search of alcohol. Lily and Bruno returned to Dover Street, sometimes fortifying themselves with a bag of chips on the way.

Daphne had taken one of her fancies to Bruno. Over supper, she talked to him about poetry or Victorian fiction, and like Leary, was apparently delighted when they disagreed: 'It's always the Russians, or the bloody French – you're forever turning up your nose at English novels, you cursed intellectual snob!'

Lily, who took little interest in literature and less in politics, listened serenely. The arguments did not sound harmonious – the man downstairs occasionally banged on his ceiling with a broom, if Daphne worked herself into a passion – but she had a sense of deep, underlying harmony and love; all she needed to make her happy. Her time came when they went to bed, and Bruno vented the desire that had been simmering between them for hours.

'This has been a time of great discoveries for me,' he told her, on their last night at Daphne's. 'The female orgasm, for instance, and the peculiar pleasure of engineering it. Seeing a great painter at work, and hearing his ridiculous opinions. Sharing a flat with two lesbians – which makes me feel embarrassingly but also rather reassuringly male. I feel as if I've travelled a thousand miles, and experienced a thousand lives. My only worry is that now I know more about sex, I'll mind more about not getting any.'

Lily lay on his chest, drowsy and contented. 'I've discovered things, too. About you, mainly – how clever you are, and how much you know.'

'That must make a change,' he said, 'from my wilfully anti-intellectual brothers and my owl-fixated father.'

'You're extremely sexy, as well,' Lily said, thinking she caught a note of sadness. 'I've had the most glorious time with you.'

'And now it's over. I have to go back to my job, and you to the farm.'

She kissed his bare chest. 'There'll be other glorious times.'

He said: 'Oh, of course.' He sighed, then smiled; then sighed again, as if deciding to settle something, or to put it behind him.

———⬥———

Leary had finished the painting, which was too bizarre to be called a portrait. Against a stark white background, Bruno's pale face glared, rather peevishly, above a body made of books and disjointed lines of print. Lily thought he looked 'as if you had a carrot up your bum', but Bruno, not a vain man, declared it brilliant.

They had bought toys for the children, and Bruno had chosen a present for Daphne; a tattered Victorian edition of a novel by Charlotte M. Yonge. Daphne, somewhat to Lily's surprise, was as thrilled as if Bruno had given her a Gutenburg Bible.

'You angel, I've been searching for this one for years.' She kissed him resoundingly on both cheeks, and added, in a stage whisper: 'I hope your wish comes true!'

To Lily, she said: 'Listen here, young lady, I'm not going to allow you to lose touch again. Bruno's given me your address, and if you don't answer my letters, by return, I'll have your lights and liver.' Her broad, beaming face crumpled. She hugged Lily fiercely. 'Oh, what a world this is. Keep safe and well, my Lily.'

They were seen off at Paddington by a whole committee of Learys – Colm, Rosie and all four children. Rosie was smiling, for once, because she had found a Polish refugee to help with the housework. 'She's tremendous – I don't even care if she sleeps with Leary.'

Leary embraced Bruno. 'When you're Prime Minister, don't forget old Ireland.' He gave Lily a beery kiss. 'I'll tell Isobel what a sweet thing you did, coming to London to seek her fortune for her.'

'It was completely selfish of me. I've had a whale of a time.'

'God bless you anyway, witcheen.'

The train was packed with sailors headed for Plymouth, all smoking furiously and staring, with naked admiration, at Lily. Perhaps because of this, Bruno was anxious and distracted. Lily, lighter-hearted with every mile that took her nearer home, did not understand what could be bothering him.

On the platform at Exeter, away from the audience of sailors, she asked: 'Is something the matter?'

'We've got a few minutes till our train,' he said. 'Let's have some tea.'

'Then will you answer my question?'

Bruno's mouth stretched into a smile, which did not reach his eyes. 'I'll do my best.' He was nervous, and kept looking at his watch as if imploring it for help.

They walked, through the steam and soot and milling

crowds of sailors, to the station buffet. Bruno sat Lily down with their bags, and bought two cups of scalding grey tea.

'Now you can tell me,' Lily said, leaning across the table. 'Have I done something wrong?'

'Oh, God, no.' He frowned down at his tea. 'But I do want – need – to talk to you, before we get back to the farm. And before you're swallowed up in ministering to the others.'

She heard the significant, hair's-breadth space he left, before the last sentence. 'Do you mind my being swallowed?'

'Not exactly. It's just that I want to make sure you know what this past week has meant to me, and I can't really say it in front of them. I said part of it last night – you have such a gift for living that being with you is like getting a new pair of spiritual or emotional spectacles. I see things so clearly, when you're beside me. I've felt magnificently – myself.'

'Well, good.' Lily was puzzled by his solemnity. 'I had a lovely time, too. A real holiday, even though I spent such a lot of it minding Leary's children.'

'I like the way he calls you "witcheen". It suits you. I think you are a sort of white witch.'

The solemnity was beginning to annoy her. 'Bru, is this leading to something?'

'Yes.' He looked up at her, and said: 'I want to marry you.'

Surprised and dismayed, Lily simply said: 'Oh.'

'Well? I mean – I ought to go down on one knee – will you?'

'No.'

He let out a long, tremulous sigh, like air escaping from a balloon. 'I didn't think you would.'

'Darling, it's not because I don't love you.' She did love him, and was desperate not to hurt him. 'If the others – if there were no other Randalls – I know you'd make me happy. But I can't marry any of you, because I love you all.'

His nervy, mobile face was relaxing back into its habitual expression of open affability, as if he were relieved to have got the proposal over with. 'Maybe I'd be the wrong husband for you, anyway. Those sailors on the train obviously thought you should be leading me on a string. Girls like you are never seen with chaps like me.'

'You know I think you're gorgeous. But it's probably more a case of me being the wrong sort of wife for you.'

Bruno was astonished. 'You'd be perfect – heavenly –'

'You need someone much cleverer, who reads the same books as you, and talks about politics. You don't want a wife who sits mute while you set the world straight, just waiting to take you to bed.'

In spite of himself, he smiled. 'Don't I?'

'You'll see I'm right some day. You don't notice my short-comings, because you share me with Quin and Gerard. Let's leave things as they are, while we're all happy.'

Bruno said: 'I'm glad you're happy.'

'Are you hinting that Gerard and Quin aren't?'

'I feel a brute,' he said, 'saying this in front of your great, candid eyes. Pa and Quin would pulverise me, if they knew. But Lily, have you thought at all about the future?'

'Not really. What's there to think about?' Lily heard a defensive note in her own voice, which made her wary of blurting out the wrong thing. Bruno's interrogations, though mild, were relentless.

'Pa's older, so it may not apply as much to him. Where Quin and I are concerned, though, do you think this "arrangement" can last for ever?'

Hearing an echo of Daphne's lecture about true love, Lily stubbornly fixed her mind on the present. 'I don't see why not.' Which, even in her own ears, sounded silly.

Very gently, seeing that she was listening, he pressed on. 'So, for years and years, you and I and Pa and Quin will all live together, like nesting doves. Never growing older, never thinking of settling down. If my life takes me away from the farm, I must be content to love you *in absentia*, with no rights that might impinge upon those of the others?'

This was harsh, though Bruno put it as kindly as possible. Lily had a breathless, frightening sense of being forced to confront something she had done her best to ignore. 'Do you mean you'd rather not be my lover, if you have to share me?'

He let out a comical sigh, that was half a groan. 'I only wish I were that strong-willed. Right now, I'll accept anything you care to give me, and be disgustingly grateful for it. I have no special claim, and I wouldn't dream of setting myself against Quin and Pa. You know how much I love them. But a wish to settle down – to have children, one's own home – is a basic human desire. What will happen, when one of us gives you the ultimatum? I mean, saying "choose only me, or I'll go and find someone else".'

Lily's eyes were swimming with tears. 'I'd never stop you loving someone else.'

'Give me strength,' Bruno groaned. 'As if we could! Don't you see? While you're on this earth, it's impossible to stop loving you!'

'You'd better kill me, then.'

'No, that wouldn't work, I'm afraid.' He whipped his handkerchief from his pocket, and gave it to Lily. 'Where is your logic? If death was a cure for unrequited love, we'd all be murderers. Film stars would be in constant danger – Franchot Tone and Clark Gable wouldn't dare to walk the streets.'

Lily could not help laughing. She mopped her eyes. 'Oh, Bruno – no wonder I love you.'

'All I'm saying is, if you chose just one of us, the rejected ones could call it a day, and begin the agonising process of getting over you. There's no possibility of that under the present arrangement. In the nicest possible way, your loving us all equally is a trap. Because we all love you so bloody much.'

There was a silence. Lily sipped her tea.

Bruno asked: 'You're not angry, are you? I'm not trying to hurt you – wouldn't hurt you for anything –'

'I was thinking of something Daphne said to me, on our first night,' she said slowly. 'She more or less told me that if I couldn't choose between you, it must mean I didn't love any of you enough. She says one day, I'll meet my true love, who blows the rest of you right out of the water. Apparently, that kind of love only ever belongs to one person.'

He smiled. 'For once, the cursed intellectual snob and the romantic novelist are in perfect agreement. Who was Daphne's one true love?'

'Sidonia,' Lily said. 'Poor Daph. What a waste of a good heart.'

'Yes, the unattainable object must be virtuous, or one's chivalric devotion is cheapened. Dantes must have stainless Beatrices.'

'But Bru, in my case, Daph was wrong. I do love you all. I swear to heaven. Couldn't we all stay as we are, just for a while? Please don't start getting over me, just yet. It'll be agonising for me, too.'

He stroked his finger down her cheek, following its soft curve. 'Oh, I'll never get over you.'

Chapter Six

1981

———◆◇◆———

Sophie found herself alone in the crowd, and experienced a giddy moment of dislocation.

Good grief, she thought, I'm married.

She was wearing a flattering but uncomfortable coat and skirt of cream taffeta, and still could not get over the unfamiliar appearance of Octavius in a grey suit. Two hours before, in a registry office near King's Cross, he had slid the ring onto her finger, officially ushering in a new era of happiness and good fortune. This was the final, crashing chord of a complicated piece of music; the bow that finished a formal dance. End with a wedding, tableau, curtain.

Except that marriage never was the end of the story. Both she and Octavius had the emotional battle-scars to prove that. Part of the strangeness of this occasion was that it negated the past, and made the memory of suffering seem irrelevant and nonsensical. Gus, now also remarried, had sent her a handsome Le Creuset casserole. Caroline had sent Octavius a postcard, saying: 'Hope she's nicer to you than I was.' Octavius had laughed, and said this would not be difficult. They were winners again, and everyone had to break the habit of feeling sorry for them.

The two families – two of Sidonia's daughters and five of Lily's Randalls – and their various attachments, were recovering from the ceremony in Bruno's Hampstead garden. Bollinger was being consumed. Vol-au-vents were circulating. Numerous feeble jokes were being made, about the forthcoming nuptials of the Prince of Wales. It could have been any wedding party, anywhere on this warm May afternoon. The men wore white carnations, and most of the women had broken out in hats.

Isobel, in one of the silly felt saucers popularised by Lady

Diana Spencer, was almost incoherent with happiness. She had settled her beloved only child, and was catching up with her past. She had exchanged memories with old Gladys Tufton, told Peter Tufton what a sweet baby he had been, and enquired minutely after all the Drivers. She and Bruno were now talking about Ballymunty.

'Oh yes, Leary kept his promises. It's a lovely old place, though it was in a shocking state when we got it. We moved there in forty-six, after they released Marius. Changing his name to 'Gently' was his idea. I didn't mind being Frau Gentlisch, but he got fed up with nobody being able to pronounce it.'

She had not known of Bruno's involvement, and the connection delighted her. Bruno, equally intrigued to think of the part he and Lily had played in the future of the unborn Octavius, was amiably explaining his 'secret job' during the war, as a code-breaker at Bletchley.

Marius and Gerda, across the gulf of history, were having an involved conversation in German.

Octavius put his arm round Sophie's waist, and murmured: 'What on earth are they talking about?'

'Dishwashers,' Sophie said.

'Oh, bless them.'

Primrose, in a wide hat of pale yellow straw, came up with a plate of prawn vol-au-vents. 'Have one of these.'

Being married meant endless thanking. Sophie said: 'Thanks so much for doing all this –'

Primrose laughed, and put the plate down on the wooden table. 'I dreamt last night about puff-pastry, but it was worth it. This is such a gorgeous occasion, I feel like dancing. But you shouldn't be together, you know – you have the rest of your lives, so stop canoodling and circulate.'

Octavius, keeping his arm around Sophie, said: 'All right, if you stop canoodling with Paddy.'

She smiled, and the colour deepened in her soft cheeks. Octavius could never resist teasing Primrose and Patrick about their autumnal love affair.

'Don't be disrespectful,' Primrose said happily. 'I want to know what Gerard meant, about you giving away all that lovely money.'

The problematical money was no longer a sore point. Octavius said: 'Perfectly true.'

She sighed comically. 'Don't tell me – owls? Badgers? The RSPB?'

'Near enough. A nice big lump of it is going on some important tracts of coastal woodland, for my charity.'

'Typical Randall – when you might have been whooping it up at the casino in Monte Carlo.'

'Come on, Primrose. I'm hardly the James Bond type.'

'It's heaven being solvent,' Sophie said. 'But I don't think it would suit us to be filthy rich. Apart from anything else, that money seems so unlucky. We want to escape the curse.'

'Pish and tush,' Primrose said gaily, 'you've been listening to your mother. She always was the most superstitious woman in christendom.' She held out her glass, as Quin Randall came past with the champagne. 'I suppose you're thinking about Edgar.'

After repeated advice, from dozens of lawyers, that contesting Sidonia's will would be a complete waste of time and money, Edgar had dropped his case. Immediately afterwards, perhaps thinking it would punish the victors, he had made one of his attempts at suicide. Only Juana took it seriously. She had used the fragility of Edgar as an excuse not to attend Sophie's wedding. She had been invited out of politeness, and nobody missed her.

'I know I ought to be kinder, and sorrier,' Sophie said. 'But talk about crying wolf – Edgar's constantly hurling himself in front of parked cars, and taking overdoses of Rennies.'

Primrose spluttered with laughter, spraying champagne. 'You're awful.'

'Aren't I? But cutting his wrists with a butter-knife, or whatever, was never going to make a blind bit of difference. The actions of Edgar no longer affect us. It's not our fault he's bonkers, and mean with it.'

'You're a cold, hard woman.' Octavius kissed her neck. 'I blame those tight shoes.'

'They do bring out my unforgiving side,' Sophie agreed.

'I'm going indoors, to take them off and make myself a cup of tea. Cover me.'

The long, cluttered kitchen was shaded and cool. A two-tiered wedding cake, ordered by Gerda from a Hampstead patisserie, stood on the table, surrounded by every mug, cup and saucer in the house. Sophie took off her high heels, with a groan of relief, made herself tea, and sank into a chair.

Left alone, able to wipe the bridal smile off her face, she found herself checking through the problems that needed settling, before she and Octavius could find a perfect balance to their life together. Their love was a many-splendoured thing, but there were one or two niggling little wrinkles.

For instance, where the two of them were to live. They had not yet worked out if Octavius disliked London more than Sophie disliked the country. She would walk through fire for him, but could she bear living at the Prospect, as he was now suggesting?

Sophie had visited the place only once, at the age of fifteen – rather bizarrely, because she was staying at Despard Court, which had been turned into an outward bound centre for schools. Mainly out of curiosity, she had visited her grandmother on her home territory, and found it uncomfortable and depressing. In the middle of nowhere, too.

Octavius had begun to drop hints about facilities for nature research and observation. They had not discussed it, but Sophie was haunted by hideous visions of herself in an Indian smock, serving communal lentil suppers to a lot of sociopathic nerds. She wanted to stay in London, and carry on working at her classic translations. Octavius went eerily quiet when she mentioned these, and got that terrible, shuttered Randall-look. They were obviously heading for a Pearl Harbour of a row. Sophie had already decided to follow Octavius to the ends of the earth, but she would not give in without a fight.

There was also the continued peculiarity of Octavius's relationship with his family. He had deliberately annoyed them all, by sending Lily's diary back to Bruno, unread and in a cheap brown envelope. He frequently said they were all dangerously mad, but he hated it when Sophie called

Randalls 'The Bates Motel'. Even he was locked into the family's romantic psychosis about his mother.

More and more, Sophie wondered what the dead, mythologised Lily-Josephine would think of the way the Randalls had brought up her baby.

A tall figure darkened the French windows. For a second, from the set of the shoulders, she thought it was Kit, then saw that it was Quin. He had flown over from Italy for the wedding, and Sophie had met him for the first time the previous day. His thick hair was silver and his face tanned olive from the Umbrian sun, but she would have known him anywhere as a Randall. The likeness between Quin and his brothers – particularly Kit and Patrick – was intriguing, and almost comical, when she had decided that Kit and Patrick were the most likely candidates for Octavius's father. It could just as easily have been Quin.

'Hello.' His arms were full of empty champagne bottles. 'Hiding, are you?'

'Just resting.'

'Hard work, these occasions.' Quin put the bottles on the floor, and dug his hands into the pockets of his distinctly un-Randallish Italian suit. 'I didn't get a chance to say it last night – I'm thrilled to see Octavius so happy, and I know it's all due to you.' His voice was thin, with a faint, surrounding hiss, like a badly tuned radio station. Several times, Sophie had seen him gulping at his inhaler. The official reason for his move to Italy was that the climate suited his asthma.

Sophie said: 'You don't have to thank me for loving him, you know. He saved me from going round the bend.'

Quin, relaxing a little, leaned against the kitchen counter. 'I suppose the change seems more dramatic to me, since I don't see him as often as I'd like. Last time I came over, he was as miserable as sin, and never stopped fighting with Kit. I'm glad they're getting on better, I must say. Those two have always been at odds.'

'I can't think why,' Sophie said. 'It's obvious they adore each other – to an outsider, anyway.'

Quin smiled. 'You're not an outsider. You're a Randall now, God help you. My wife's theory is that Kit and

Number Eight are too alike. There were endless rows when Octavius was growing up. Kit nearly criticised him to death.'

Sophie was interested to catch a tang of historic resentment. 'Really?'

Casually, as if reciting something well known, Quin went on: 'But he wouldn't hear of him coming to me in Italy. In the end, Gerda rescued him from Randalls, by persuading Kit and Pa to send him to school in London. We all knew she and Bru would make a decent job of bringing him up.' He opened the fridge, and took out two more bottles of champagne. 'Of course, the real irony of it all was that Lily loved Kit to bits and pieces.' Rapidly and expertly, he opened the champagne. 'Fancy a refill?'

'No thanks.' Sophie would have liked to hear more about Lily loving Kit 'to bits and pieces', but Octavius and Gerda came in, carrying piles of crumby plates.

'Cake-time,' Gerda said. 'Quin, are you sober enough to carry it outside? Then we can all see them cutting it together.'

Octavius said: 'Spare us. You made me do all that last time, and look what happened.'

'You've managed to get this far without being awkward,' Gerda said. 'Don't start now, darling.'

She and Quin carried the cake into the garden between them, eyes riveted nervously to the precarious top layer.

Octavius knelt at Sophie's feet, and put on her shoes.

'Come on, then. Let's humour them.' He pulled her out of her chair. While his arms were around her, he kissed her lips. 'Have I said how beautiful you look?'

Sophie laughed. 'Repeatedly. Wait till you see my rude silk underwear.'

He felt for the outline of her breasts, beneath the stiff carapace of taffeta. 'You're fabulously, outrageously beautiful. Little did I know, when you nearly broke my nose, that you'd end up nearly breaking my heart.'

Chapter Seven

Sophie's first coherent thought, beyond the numbing, Arctic shock, was: 'I knew it had to be a mistake; I knew my life wasn't meant to be this happy.' As if some angel, in charge of earthly affairs, had spotted the glaring error in her record, and exclaimed: 'Sophie Gently, happy? No, this must be rectified immediately.'

She entered the frozen zone of unreality at a quarter past one in the morning, when two police officers came to her door. Sophie had not called the police, but she had been about to. Octavius had left Bruno's house before six, ringing her just beforehand, to say he was on his way. He had not come home. Sophie had spent the evening telephoning anyone she could think of, vowing to wallop Octavius for putting her through this, and drinking enough black coffee to wake King Arthur.

The moment she saw the clichéd nightmare of the sympathetic police-persons at her door, she gagged with terror. Yet she heard it with amazing detachment – that a man walking his dog on Hampstead Heath had found Octavius lying in a ditch, with the contents of his wallet strewn around him, and his head smashed in like an egg.

The policeman did not say 'like an egg', but this was how Sophie imagined it.

She asked, in a voice that seemed to belong to someone else, 'Is he dead?'

She was braced to take the full impact all at once, but Octavius was not dead. He had been taken to the Royal Free Hospital nearby.

Sophie said: 'We only got back from our honeymoon the day before yesterday – we were in the Périgord.' She had a confused idea that this ought to make a difference, and could not understand why it only seemed to embarrass them.

They led her out to a squad car – which immediately made her feel guilty – and drove her through the dark, sleeping streets to Hampstead. The hospital was huge, modern and achingly bright. The WPC, whose name was Yvonne, sat her down on a plastic chair. A doctor came, and a lot of people asked her questions, which she answered as if confessing to something, and as if she might get a lighter sentence for being helpful.

The male officer said it looked like a classic mugging, for cash. The doctor, before he raced back to Casualty, told her she would be able to see her husband when he came out of surgery. Yvonne seemed very keen for Sophie to express her feelings. Sophie was afraid, because she had no feelings to express. All she could manage was anxiety, in case she was behaving wrongly – when Yvonne brought her a cup of tea, she nearly apologised for not being hysterical.

She stared at the mole on Yvonne's upper lip, thinking it was like an eighteenth-century beauty-patch. She wished she had something to read, and when they asked if there was anything she needed she was humbly mute, not daring to say she longed for a copy of *The Pickwick Papers*. She even imagined the police rousing some slumberous bookseller at the dead of night – Got any Dickens, sir? It's an emergency.

And all this time, she knew she was standing at the extreme edge of a great continent of dread. Nobody told her not to worry. At the end of that endless night, when Octavius had been wheeled out of theatre, Sophie sleepwalked into Intensive Care. It was very hot. She tried, and utterly failed, to connect the puppet, the robot, lashed to the bed by tubes and wires, with the man she loved.

Another doctor told her about head injuries, and bits of bone being tweezered out of brains. She tried hard to listen, while he explained the need to wait until Octavius regained consciousness, but was distracted by the inertia and false warmth of his hand when she held it.

Fearfully, she realised his absence. This still figure was not Octavius, but his effigy. Her mind rebelled against stepping further, and testing the theory of living without him.

She was beginning to accept, however, that nobody was going to tell her everything was fine.

Nothing was fine. Life, when it dropped its mask and stopped tricking you, revealed an obvious cruelty she was surprised she had missed. The ghastly loneliness and isolation, the severance from normality, were like death.

There was a sort of waiting area, with steel-framed windows looking out on the haggard dawn, and low chairs covered with orange tweed. Sophie was sitting here, stupid with shock, when Gerda arrived.

She dropped down beside Sophie, and folded her in her arms. Her warmth and softness suddenly thawed Sophie into shattering, shuddering sobs.

This was the last thing she remembered clearly, before everything fragmented into jerky, strobe-lit unreality; a disjointed silent film of panic.

<hr />

Gerda gave her something which made her sleep. She woke, late that afternoon, in Octavius's old bedroom at Downshire Hill. She found that while she slept, her world had shifted and rearranged itself around the horror. Bruno was watching at the hospital. Kit and Paddy were driving up from Devon. Pa, too frail to make another trip to London so soon after the wedding, had been left in the care of Primrose.

Heavy with despair, nauseated by a constant, dragging anxiety, Sophie fell into the routine that had been provided for her. After that first attack, she was – everyone kept telling her – splendid. She sat beside Octavius, clutching his copy of *The Pickwick Papers* like a talisman, hypnotised by the bleeps of the machines that kept his soul tethered to his battered body.

She spoke, with surprising calm, to her parents. She assured them she was fine, and they did not need to come over from Ireland. Only afterwards did she realise she had addressed them as 'Mummy' and 'Vati', for the first time since childhood.

The greatest surprise, however, was Kit. The moment he appeared beside her, Sophie was overwhelmingly conscious of his strength, and his fathomless kindness. Why had she ever been wary of him? He said: 'Don't worry, sweetheart – he'll be fine, everything will be fine,' with such confidence that she believed him. He was always near her, always gentle and reassuring. Kit told her when to eat and sleep, and when she needed fresh air. While Paddy, Bruno or Gerda took over the watching, he led her back into the real world, and there was no one else she trusted to listen to her formless ramblings.

It was Kit who broke the news, when the mugger was found, three days after the attack, with the blood of Octavius on his clothes. He was a heroin addict, with a long and detailed criminal record. He told the police Edgar Despard had paid him £500 to kill Octavius. Edgar silently verified this, by committing suicide. Juana found his body in the front seat of her Jaguar, full of exhaust-fumes and cocaine.

Sophie said: 'How awful for her. And how could I have laughed at him? If I'd taken him seriously, maybe Octavius would never –'

'Don't make it into an excuse to blame yourself,' Kit said. 'He's dead, and Octavius is alive.'

'When will he wake up, Kit?'

'Soon. You'll see.'

Kit sternly refused to accept any other possibility.

But the days stretched into a week, and the other possibility grew.

Gerda said: 'Bru, what on earth shall we do if he dies?'

She was in her kitchen, cutting cheese sandwiches. Sophie was upstairs, having a bath.

'Face it, I suppose,' Bruno said. 'No point thinking about it until it – unless it happens.'

'I disagree. I think we should be prepared.' Frowning, she put the sandwiches into a plastic box, for Sophie and Kit to eat at the hospital.

Bruno put his arm round her. 'Darling, you always want to assume the worst.'

'The worst happens.'

'Not always. Don't lose hope yet.'

Sophie came in, with damp hair. Gerda and Bruno sprang

apart guiltily, as if she might guess what they had been talking about.

'Do you want me to drive you?' Bruno asked.

Sophie smiled. She was colourless and angular, and the permanent anguish of anxiety made the tendons stand out in her neck. 'It's only round the corner. I'll walk.'

'Well, I'll come with you, as far as the newsagents,' Bruno said. 'We're running out of cigarettes again.'

The summer day was cloudy, but pleasantly fresh. Sophie and Bruno walked together past St John's church, and down Keats Grove towards South End Green.

Sophie said: 'Gerda thinks he's going to die, doesn't she?'

'She fears it,' Bruno said, 'and she's had too much experience of her worst fears being realised. When something really awful happens – for instance, when Ilse had pneumonia as a child – she tends to revert to being a girl again, with parents who were too hopeful to leave Vienna while they had the chance.'

'Poor Gerda.'

They slowed down, to look at Keats' house through the gate.

'People cannot escape their early lives,' Bruno murmured. 'The past is incredibly difficult to leave behind. I've been thinking about this a great deal, and wishing we had been more honest with Octavius.'

Sophie, crushed by anxiety, was thoroughly tired of the Randall parlour-game of hints and half-answers. She asked baldly: 'Who is his father?'

Before the question was out of her mouth, she felt Bruno sliding away into the territory of evasion.

'I'm tempted to borrow a joke from Dickens,' he said, 'and say "The Lord No Zoo".'

'Do you really not know? How many of you did his mother sleep with?'

Bruno grimaced unhappily. 'Oh dear, it sounds so awful, put like that. And I'm afraid I can't be absolutely precise. I know Paddy was in love with her, but I don't think they actually – he was very young, of course. The rest of us, however –'

'My God.' Sophie was amazed that this possibility had not occurred to her before. 'No wonder Octavius is so fucked up.'

'Yes, well. Fucked up – I suppose we deserve that.' His face was creased with distaste. 'But there's always more. That's why we wanted him to read her diary. I was rather cross with him, for his refusal to look at the emotions behind the facts. He might have understood why we made the promise to Lily.'

'You made a saint of her,' Sophie said, 'at his expense. You're always hinting – even you, Bruno – that he can never live up to her blessed memory.' She began to walk on, seething on Octavius's behalf. 'I'm not surprised he's ashamed of you. If Edgar hadn't tried to kill him first, he'd be dying of embarrassment.'

'Sophie, wait –' Bruno hurried to catch up with her, and took her arm. 'Ashamed of us?'

'I'm sorry. I shouldn't have said that.'

'You should, if that's how Octavius really feels. I wish I could show him his mother, in a way that would make him see her as we did. If he thinks badly of her, we have dishonoured her memory.'

He looked so pained and helpless that Sophie felt sorry for him. 'Don't take any notice of me. At the moment, most of what I say is complete rubbish.'

'My dear girl, you mustn't apologise. We know how it looks from the outside. That's why we're always searching for justification. For instance, there's a Bible story Pa likes to quote.' He frowned down at the pavement, trying to remember exactly. 'Some Pharisee asks Jesus about a woman who had married seven brothers, one after the other: "In the resurrection therefore, when they shall rise, whose wife shall she be of them? For the seven had her wife."'

He paused, glancing at Sophie's tense face, to make sure she was listening. 'And Jesus replies: "When they shall rise from the dead, they neither marry, nor are given in marriage, but are as the angels which are in heaven."'

Sophie digested this in silence. 'Stretching it somewhat, don't you think?' she asked, eventually. 'I seem to remember the woman in the Bible only married the brothers one at a time.'

Bruno sighed. 'True. I don't care to speculate about Jesus's possible opinion of our situation. But Pa uses it to illustrate his belief that our state, arising from love and harmony, was somehow exalted. That we are joined, like the angels, in a love which knew no possessiveness on earth, and shall know none when we all meet in heaven.'

'I didn't know Pa was religious.'

'Only when it suits him,' Bruno said. 'You've spotted the obvious flaw, of course. This is not heaven, and we are not angels. Down here on earth, the brothers are by no means equal.'

'Oh yes,' Sophie said. 'She must have had a favourite, because she married him. I always find it hard to remember that Lily got married.'

Bruno said: 'We don't.'

PART SIX

Chapter One
LILY'S DIARY
1 August 1944

*Kit asked me today, did I sleep with Oscar, when he came home
on leave?*
  He added: 'I won't be angry.'
  Whether or not Kit is angry, I had to say yes.

Lily found Oscar on the river bank, leaning against the trunk
of the weeping willow. He was blowing plumes of smoke,
and idly swiping at the columns of midges. There was a little
heap of cigarette ends, crushed into the soft soil beside him.
A few feet away lay a fishing rod and an unopened jar of bait.

'I'm not surprised you never catch anything,' Lily said.

Oscar started, as if recalled from an immense distance.
'You gave me a turn.'

'Gerard told me to bring you some sandwiches. You
missed lunch again.'

'Did I?' He glanced at his watch, without interest. 'Oh,
yes. I lose all track of time, when I'm out fishing.'

'So I see.'

He put his hand lightly on her bare, tanned calf. 'Don't
tell the others I'm not really fishing, there's a love. I need to
be alone sometimes, and I don't want them to take it personally. Solitude is a luxury, after the army.'

'All right.' Lily put the paper packet of sandwiches on the
ground beside him. Oscar had been preoccupied since his
return from Italy. He still had his moments of teasing and
creating mayhem. He still kept his father and brothers in the
pub until the dinner was cremated. During his periods of
retreat within himself, however, Lily had noticed he was
thinner, and seemed tired. He had aged, too. There were

unmistakable, sour lines around his mouth and eyes.

Oscar had changed. She did not have the heart to point this out to Pa, busy celebrating the hero's return. Pa, after the triumph of the Normandy landings, had decided the war was as good as over, and his sons safe for ever. He had forgotten that Oscar's war remained the principle business of his life.

'I'll leave you to it, then,' she said.

His fingers tightened round her leg. 'Stay a minute.'

Lily was glad he had asked. She sat down among the cool tongues of long grass. The river was low between the banks in the heat of early July. Minnows darted and browsed in the dim water around the reeds.

'I can't quite stomach their relentless optimism,' Oscar said, with an apologetic half-smile. 'The good news is rather academic, when you're in the thick of the bad news.' He lit another cigarette from the stub of the last, before extinguishing it in the dust. 'Maybe I'd see it differently, if I were marching through France, and gorgeous French girls were pelting me with roses. Where I've been, everything's just one noisy, ghastly mess.'

'You probably won't be going back there,' Lily pointed out. 'Not now you're going on that course. The war might be over before you've finished it.'

'Yes,' Oscar said.

'Gerard's so relieved. He thinks you'll be back at Cambridge next year.'

'I've no intention of going back to Cambridge. It'd be like going back into short trousers. I'm far too fucking old.'

Wincing over the pain in his voice, Lily tried to keep the tone light. 'He's counting on you getting your rowing blue.'

He managed a laugh, but his face was rueful. 'I've won blues in one or two other things now.'

'He'll understand,' Lily assured him. 'He only wants what will make you happy.'

'A job selling ladies' undies.' He opened the parcel of sandwiches, and blindly bit into one, scattering crumbs of boiled egg. His tense features relaxed, as he observed her. 'You know, Lily, you're more beautiful than ever.'

'Well, thanks.'

'I've kept meaning to tell you. I feel I should apologise, for not making a heavy pass.'

Lily laughed. 'I'm glad you haven't. You're a handsome beast, and that's just the trouble – you'd demand more time and energy than I've got.'

He joined in the laugh, and some of the anxiety lifted from his knotted brow. 'We've had a thing going for years, haven't we? Ever since I put my mark on you.'

'I'm afraid it must have rubbed off,' Lily said. 'In the hurly-burly.'

'That's what you call it, eh?' The cigarette was smouldering between his fingers while he ate. Lily plucked it out of his hand, and threw it into the river. He did not seem to notice.

'I do love you, of course,' she said. 'I'm as glad as any of them to see you at home.'

'When I did all that flirting with you,' Oscar said, 'I didn't know the first thing about love.'

'Neither did I. I certainly do now, though. Do you?'

He stared down at his hands. 'Oh, yes. I've been properly blooded. I went through the whole routine. Reckless infatuation, unbridled passion, rapture.' His voice thinned. He cleared his throat. 'Broken heart.'

'I'm sorry.' She thought she understood it all now. Oscar had met someone, and discovered that sex was no laughing matter. 'Did it end very badly?'

'As badly as possible, thanks.' He could not look at her. 'Don't tell the others. And don't say I'll get over it.'

'Some people do,' Lily murmured.

'You don't really think that. Everyone on earth – Nazi soldiers, Chinese chaps in paddy-fields – everyone has one major love affair they never get over. In they slip, easy as anything, then they're trapped before they know it.' He rubbed his sleeve across his eyes. 'And it stops being fun.'

Lily watched a dragonfly hovering near his rich, golden-brown hair, like a tiny V2. Here it was again, she thought; the theme of the one great love, that would not leave her in peace.

She stroked Oscar's knee. 'I wish you'd told us.'

'No, no, no. Out of the question. We had to keep it incredibly secret.'

'Was she married?'

'Worse,' he said. 'You've met my great love.'

'Have I?' Puzzled, Lily ran through all the women she could think of, trying to imagine one of them with Oscar's broken heart in her pocket. 'When?'

'Last Christmas.' He waited expectantly. There was a silence. They listened to the silky murmurings of the river. Oscar spoke very softly, as if breaking bad news. 'Darling, haven't you guessed? It was JH.'

Lily sat very still, trying to digest this information. She was stunned. The Oscar she assumed she knew – lady-killer, flirt, charmer – was reassembling himself in a new image she barely understood.

Cautiously, she said: 'I haven't really said how sorry I was. We all liked him.'

'He liked you.'

'You must miss him horribly. Anyone could see you were the most tremendous friends –'

'We were lovers,' he said. Her innocence amused him. 'Like you and your adorers here.'

'Are you saying that you – slept with him?'

'No, we never did anything as domesticated as sleeping. But we fucked like rabbits.'

'You loved a man?'

'Why not? You love lots of men, I can't help noticing.'

Once Lily had grasped the fact, her quick imagination started working. 'God, you poor thing,' she said impulsively, 'you must have been in agony when he was killed, and you couldn't tell a soul. The loneliness must have been awful.'

Her sympathy startled him. His eyes flooded. He drew his knees under his chin and buried his head in his folded arms. Three hard sobs shook his body. He wrestled them back angrily. When his wet, flushed face emerged, he was calm.

'Hell,' he said. 'It's been hell. He was beside me when the bullet got him. He died in my arms a few minutes later – not a word, not a sign. I couldn't make him look back, even for a second. One tiny bullet, and that was that.' He sniffed. 'You see why I couldn't possibly tell Pa and the boys.'

Lily wished she could disagree, but could not help recalling various careless, brutal remarks about men who did it with men. She understood enough now to picture their unbelieving horror, if they had to apply any of these to Oscar. She took out her handkerchief, and stuffed it into Oscar's fist.

'Thanks.' He blew his nose. 'You won't say anything, will you?'

'No,' Lily said. 'You can trust me.'

He scrubbed his streaming eyes. 'There's no need, because I won't be doing it again – changing my name to Mavis, and setting up with a chorus-boy in Maida Vale. JH was the one. And he'll be the only.'

'Talk about him, if you like.'

'Would you mind? I never get the chance. It's bad enough keeping a discreet silence when the person you love is alive. It's absolute murder when they're dead.' Fleetingly, he smiled. 'I got no end of a kick out of showing him off to you all. Sometimes, we were amazed you didn't notice.'

'Holy cow, did you do it while you were here?'

'Yes, and bloody cold it was, too.' He blew his nose again. 'I never thought I'd hear myself saying this, but the sex wasn't everything. It was so terrific just being with him. We moved heaven and earth, to spend an ordinary evening alone together. JH used to joke about me reading the paper while he did his knitting – really, all we wanted were those peaceful spaces other couples – normal couples – take for granted.'

Lily asked: 'And had you thought about the future?'

'Not really,' Oscar said. 'It was always going to be pretty grim, loving on the wrong side of the law.'

'You will have to think of your own future, sooner or later.'

He shrugged impatiently. 'No point, till the war's over. I don't even know that I have a future.'

'I won't let you talk like that,' Lily said sharply. 'You feel like death now, but one of these days, you'll find yourself

401

stubbornly alive and demobbed – what then?'

They sank back into silence, deep and uncomfortable. Lily watched him anxiously, trying to read his face.

Very quietly, he said: 'Don't count on my coming back.'

'What's that supposed to mean?'

Oscar shifted, so he was kneeling in front of her. He took her face between his palms. 'Will you promise me something?'

'You're a great one for extracting promises.' Lily spoke crossly, to cover her uneasiness.

His hands were cold on her cheeks. 'If you hear that anything's happened to me, please don't worry that you might have prevented it. Do you understand? Because there's nothing on earth anyone can say or do.'

Lily had never seen an expression of such fathomless desolation. They gazed into each other's eyes, all veils torn away, and a terrible chill gripped her; as if a part of his spirit had slipped inside her, and laid itself against her soul. For one moment, she experienced his despair as her own, and did not know how anyone could endure living with such pain.

The moment passed, and left her shivering. There was no need to tell him she understood. Oscar smiled, and whispered: 'How lovely and warm you are.'

She folded her arms around him, pulled his head down to her breast, and kissed his hair.

'What a nice girl you turned out to be,' he said. 'The proverbial tart with the heart of gold.'

Her eyes were full of sorrow, but he could not see this, and her voice was light. 'I'm not a tart.'

'Lily, will you do something else for me?'

'Practically anything.'

'Stay here for a bit. Let them all think I fucked you.'

'Honestly. Is your reputation as the Randall lady-killer really that important?'

'Go on,' he coaxed, laughing. 'There's more than one sort of love, and if you tell them I love you, you won't be lying. I love you enormously.'

'Hmmm. We'll see.'

He sighed and smiled, like a child settling down to sleep. He stayed clasped in her arms until they had watched the reflection of the sun setting, on the surface of the water.

⋘⋙

The anguish of Pa, when the news came only weeks later, was torture to Lily. The promise she had made to Oscar did not stop her endlessly revolving ways she might have saved him – for she did not believe a word of the official story.

'There is no God!' roared Pa. 'A just God would never give a man six sons and a world war!' The loss was all the more cruel to him, because he had allowed himself to hope.

'Bloody unfair,' Kit commented, with bitter irony. 'He comes through Monte Cassino without so much as a stubbed toe, only to be killed by a British tank during exercises on the South Downs.'

Pa went (alone, at his insistence) to the training camp where Oscar's mangled body lay. He would not hear of military ceremonies. He made such a sustained and effective fuss that they let him bring his son home to Devon. Oscar was buried, as simply as possible, next to his mother.

The Randalls assumed Lily was mourning a lover. They seemed to find comfort in this idea. Kit, when he asked her, point-blank, if she had slept with Oscar, said: 'I'm glad he went to his grave with something other than a war to remember.' He was kind, and she hated lying to him, even in a good cause.

On the other hand, she decided it would have been positively wicked not to lie to Pa. This second blast of the reaper's freezing breath had aged him. His lithe figure stooped, and his thick, close-cropped hair was more plentifully sprinkled with grey.

'They didn't want me to pull back the tarpaulin,' he told Lily, tears cascading down his cheeks. 'But I made them show me his face. I'm glad I did, or I would have conjured up all manner of grotesquery. As it was, his face was unmarked, and peaceful – remember that, my dear. He looked as if he was sleeping off a hangover, because his beard had gone on growing, after he – I wanted to shave him, but they treated me as if I were completely barmy.'

403

'Poor old bastard,' Kit said to Lily, 'he is fairly barmy. All we can do is pretend we don't notice.'

He took care of Pa with limitless patience; listening to his rantings and ramblings, sitting with him, in silence, for hours at a time. He was a rock, to which they all clung. Oscar's death had brought home to Lily how totally and irrevocably she belonged to the Randalls. Their suffering was hers now, and they all grieved together, huddled up, as Bruno said, 'like wet bantams in the rain'.

Oscar's secret, however, lay between Lily and her adopted brethren. She took desperate pride in keeping their conversation locked inside herself. It gave her sorrow a particularly bitter flavour. The worst of it was the recollection of the dreadful sadness, and she worried endlessly that Oscar had not managed to escape it.

As soon as she could bear to, Lily made herself go back to the willow tree beside the river. She sat underneath it, and wept until she was scoured out and exhausted. Then she leant against the trunk of the tree, as Oscar had done, and invited the sights and sounds around her to swamp her senses; plashings of the water creatures, the clean scent of the willow leaves.

She unclenched her hands, suddenly breathless with the powerful instinct that she could receive Oscar, if she concentrated hard enough. Very gradually, as the shadows lengthened around her, a velvet stillness took possession of her. It was like falling into a sleep, except that the deepest dreamlayer of her mind was alert and receptive.

The stillness warmed into a great, profound peace. It seemed to vaporise her body, and suspend her consciousness in bliss.

Just as gradually, the sensation faded. She came back to herself awe-struck, chasing the vanishing shadow of the sublime. She was convinced that Oscar had somehow been permitted to show her a glimpse of what he had become.

If this is death, she thought, there is no death – there is nothing to fear.

Though she was weeping silently, for the absence of Oscar and Jack, she knew she wept for herself, not for them.

Stalks snapped behind her, and she heard branches being pushed aside. Lily suddenly realised she was sitting in the twilight. Trees, river and meadows were glimmering and insubstantial, somewhere between this world and the next. The curtain of willow parted. A figure appeared, veiled in shadows.

'Lily? Thank God. We've been looking everywhere.'

'I forgot the time – the supper –'

Kit put out his hand, and helped her to her feet. She was surprised to find how stiff her limbs were, as if she had been asleep for hours. He gently brushed her cheek with the tip of his finger.

His voice was low and sweet. 'Poor kid, have you been crying all this time?'

His arms were round her. For several minutes, they stood in a silence embrace, with their hearts thudding out an uneven rhythm. His face moved towards hers. She knew, before their lips touched, that she had been made whole – it was like hearing the answer to an impossible question, and cursing because it turned out to be laughably obvious. There was no dramatic difference between the states of knowing and not knowing. Lily simply accepted, with massive relief, the truth. She had been in love with Kit Randall for five seconds – for three years – for all her life.

The Kit in the photograph and the real Kit merged into this one man, whose strength and goodness moved her to the core. She recalled and acknowledged Daphne's prophecy – 'You live for the others, but you'll die for him.'

Kit pulled his face away. His eyes had an unearthly glitter in the dusk. He knew, as she did, that they had crossed the barrier.

'You love me,' he said. 'It is me, isn't it?'

'Yes. Always.'

He kissed her again, with an urgent abandon that made her moan into his lips. Physical longing assaulted her, with frightening strength. Ravenous for the feel of him, she ran her hands across the sinews of his back. He bit into her face, her neck, her shoulders. His hot hand slipped inside her dress, and when his fingers found her nipple, she almost came.

With a long, shuddering sigh, he pushed her away, rested his hands on her shoulders, and held her at arm's-length.

'I could make quite a speech,' he said, 'about how I've wanted you and loved you and adored you, all this time – how I've done my damnedest to fight it, when I thought you couldn't possibly want a man like me –' He closed his eyes for a moment. 'It'd be the easiest thing in the world to rip your clothes off, and fuck the daylights out of you.' He released her. 'But I'm not going to do it. I won't worship at a crowded shrine. I love you too much to share you. It would kill me.'

She swallowed a sob. 'It'll kill me if you don't.'

'If you love me properly, I must be the only one.'

'Oh, but Kit – I love all the others so much – you wouldn't be so cruel to them!'

'Yes I would – out of sheer self-preservation. I can't make love to you, knowing a part of you belongs somewhere else. I simply do not dare to give into this thing, unless I can be sure I have all of you. Body and soul. Because that's what you'd have of me. I'd kill for you, I'd die for you – but I won't share you.'

Lily was dazzled, knowing the love he offered her would change the landscape of her life. The promise was on her tongue, begging to be made. But she forced herself to remember the others, and could not bear the appalling pain of hurting them – it would have been like ripping out her own heart.

'Don't you know what you're asking me to do? You're the one who's always accused me of playing games with their feelings.'

'Because it hurt me! I've been through agonies over you!' Kit reined back his voice, making an effort not to shout. 'You're ridiculously naive, Lily. You treat love like a toy. You think it's kind to sleep with a man, when you're fond of him – that's not real love. And it's not love like mine.'

Lily gathered up all her reserves of self-control, to stop herself surrendering, when she wanted to so desperately.

'I know you're different, but it's too late. I'm better than you seem to think, and I won't tear the family apart. I do love them all. I won't betray them.'

'In that case,' Kit said, 'you and I have nothing more to say.'

Chapter Two

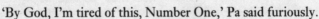

'By God, I'm tired of this, Number One,' Pa said furiously.

Kit did not look up from Bruno's day-old copy of the *Manchester Guardian*. He was stretched on the parlour sofa, beside a saucer full of cigarette ends. 'Tired of what?'

'You're an absolutely awful man when you're unhappy.'

'Who says I'm unhappy?'

Pa was simmering with the anxiety and irritation that had been building inside him for days. He had delayed saying anything, out of a desire to be tactful, and now it burst out in the least tactful manner possible. 'The entire house stinks of it. The foods tastes of it. Lily wanders about like a lost soul, burning dinners right and left, and blueing everybody's underwear in the wash. Custard's cowering under the scullery sink. The owls are moulting themselves bald. You haven't been this ghastly since you were shot down.'

Kit's face was stony. 'You'd better stay out of my way, then.'

'I wish it were that simple – put that fucking paper down!' Pa darted forward and swiped it out of Kit's hands. 'Why aren't you out in the fields with your brothers?'

'I'm not a farmer.'

'Bruno's not a farmer, and he's not lying about like a Victorian lady with the vapours.'

Slowly, Kit swung his legs off the sofa, and stood up to face his father. Behind his permanent frown, his eyes glittered dangerously. 'All I want is to be left alone.'

'Unfortunately, you're not alone. We have to live with you.' Pa let out a high groan of frustration. 'I'm doing this all wrong. I meant to be immensely sympathetic, and ask you if you were ill –'

'I'm not ill.'

'– but you do so annoy me. Something of moment has occurred. It has made you exceedingly miserable. It has also made you impossible to live with. This house is like a city after a thousand-bomber raid. We're all picking over the rubble, watching the sky for the next onslaught. Kit, this will not do. Whatever has happened, stop taking it out on the rest of us.'

There was a silence, during which the two men glared at one another balefully.

Kit put his hands in his pockets. 'Is the rant over?'

'Yes.'

'Best one you've done for ages.'

'Thank you. I'm thinking of setting some of my finer rants to music.' Pa sighed. 'I'm sorry, boy. There's something wrong, and I can't think what to do about it. Lily says the trouble with men is we get angry when we mean to be sympathetic, because we hate not having a solution.'

His bright, shrewd eyes took in Kit's involuntary twitch at the mention of Lily's name, as if he had prodded a bad tooth.

More gently, he asked: 'This is about Lily, isn't it?'

'Has she said anything?'

'She doesn't need to. She's exceedingly miserable too, though she shows it more poetically. I've never seen the poor little thing so woebegone. She hasn't said a word, but I guess either you turned her down, or she turned you down. Would I be near the truth?'

'Near enough,' Kit said stiffly.

'In which case, I'm baffled. How can one rejection add up to two suffering lovers?'

Kit sat down on the sofa. 'I have noticed she's unhappy. Don't imagine I like it.'

Pa dropped down beside him. 'You know, I've seen this coming for years. You don't deserve it, but she's fallen in love with you, that's what. Women often like the awkward bastards best.' He squeezed Kit's arm. 'You're madly in love with her, of course.'

'What if I am?'

'It puts me in a very delicate situation,' Pa said. 'I can hardly beg my son to sleep with my mistress. Yet that's what

409

a part of me wants to do – the part that would really do anything to make her happy. Meanwhile, the fatherly part of me rejoices, because my beloved firstborn – who thought no female would ever look at the face he fried for his country – has won the love of such an angel.'

Kit turned to him, in sudden desperation. His thin skin reddened. 'Would you give her up for me?'

'So that's it,' Pa said. With a visible effort, he made himself address the dilemma – a choice between the two central loves of his life. 'The important thing is what Lily wants most,' he said. 'But I wouldn't give her up for anyone else.'

'She won't let you go – any of you. She had to decide between hurting all of you, and only hurting me.' Kit scowled down at the threadbare Persian carpet, his voice hoarse with pain. 'She decided it would be fairer to hurt me. I don't believe she was thinking of herself. It was a typically democratic response to my selfish, fascistic demands.'

'Ah,' Pa said.

'It's destroying me, Pa. If there was a way of measuring hurt, I can't help thinking mine would add up to more than all of yours put together.'

'You're an all-or-nothing man.'

'Yes I am,' Kit said. 'Say I have a jealous nature. I can't even think of sharing her, without feeling sick. I wouldn't trust myself not to kill you all.'

'Dear, dear.' Pa was thoughtful, and there was a gleam of humour in his eyes. 'You do take things hard, Number One.'

'It's the way I'm made.'

'I do understand. I was originally made that way myself.' He smiled reminiscently. 'I once threw Badger – may he rest in peace – off a boat in Maidenhead, because I caught him kissing your mother.'

Kit looked up sharply. 'Good God, Pa.'

'Oh, I was desperately in love. I don't think your mother wanted Badger to kiss her, but the sight was like a dagger in my side. That was the day she heard the first of many rants. I told her I was dying for love of her, and I meant it.'

'What did she say?'

410

'Your eyes are just like hers. Full of disapproval, too – just as hers were. She said there was a very simple cure for my wretched condition.'

'What?'

Pa laughed. 'Marriage.'

'I wish to God Lily would marry me.'

'She's refused to marry the rest of us.' Pa was serious again. 'But I now see that was different. I always suspected she would end up loving one of us best. Cross-grained and bad-tempered as you are, you would appear to be the one – yes, boy, I truly believe it. The problem is her reluctance to hurt us poor others.' He put his arm around Kit's shoulders. 'Don't go into a decline, Number One. The time has come for the ultimate test of our love.'

Kit's shoulders were rigid. 'What are you saying?'

'Nothing, for the moment. Wait until I've exercised my authority – assuming I have any.'

⸺◆⸺

Lily stopped at the scullery sink, to splash her face with cold water. She patted it roughly dry with her cotton skirt, and stepped out into the yard, squinting against the low rays of evening sunlight. The air was still and warm, and full of harvest scents of ripeness and cut stalks.

She climbed over the low fence, crossed the meadow and made for the coppice, where she knew she would find him. She had cried herself half-blind, and her chest still heaved with the occasional leftover sob. Something had ended, but she was becoming conscious of the possibility – though not the certainty – of a new kind of happiness. In any case, whether she found joy or sorrow, the thing was done.

'This won't kill us,' Bruno had said. 'It's a change, and changes often hurt at first.'

They had turned the parlour into a courtroom, and called Lily in to hear the verdict. By then, whatever had gone on before, they were all in agreement. Solemnly, one by one, they had kissed her. The kisses felt like farewells. One by one, Lily had searched their eyes for any signs of rebellion. There were none.

Pa was the last. He was smiling broadly, but his eyes had

411

glistened with tears – which was when Lily had broken down. He held her tightly in his arms, stroking the back of her head, while she wept on his shoulder.

'What a fuss,' he had said. 'Let's have no more of it – no more burnt dinners and pining, do you hear? Go and be happy, you silly girl. None of us can be, until you are.'

The small beech coppice was old and neglected. The trees grew close together, filtering the strong light into dots and daubs. As Lily stepped into the cool shadows, she saw a curl of cigarette smoke unwinding from behind one of the trunks. Kit, in his faded blue shirt, was leaning against it. A book lay face-down in the spindly grass. He noticed Lily's arrival without a word.

She leaned against the opposite tree-trunk, suddenly oppressed by shyness. Kit was shy too, and it made him cross. He was also wary, ready to retreat.

Lily said: 'Hello.'

'Hello.'

'I'm here.'

'So I see.'

'Kit, I'm here. I've come.'

There was a breathless silence. Kit's eyes, riveted suspiciously to her face, slowly widened.

'My God,' he said, 'they've done it!'

She was embarrassed, and could see that he was too. 'Yes.'

'Anybody dead?'

'It wasn't like that – please don't joke.'

'You've been crying,' he observed. 'Your eyes look like a pair of cricket balls, and your nose has doubled in size. What did they do to you? You obviously hated it.'

He was not going to make this easy for her. Lily said, as evenly as she could: 'They made me admit how much I love you.' She swallowed. 'That I love you the most, and – and would rather have just you, being horrible to me, than all of them being nice.'

Kit dropped his cigarette and trampled it out. Behind the mask of permanent anger created by his surgeons, his eyes expressed pained vulnerability. The expression turned in Lily's ribs like the point of a dagger, as she felt how she had

412

hurt him.

After another spell of silence, he murmured, in a gentler voice, 'Doesn't it all strike you as peculiar? Being propelled into each other's arms?'

Lily said, 'It had to be like this. Because you were stubborn, and I was blind.'

'Did you want them to let you go – or were you simply being your usual, obliging self?'

'Kit, you can punish me as much as you like, but it won't change anything. I'm here, loving you. Whether you want me or not.'

'All right, stop it, of course I want you.' His eyes filmed over with tears. 'I want every atom of you.'

He pulled her into his arms, and held her against his hard, warm chest. They stood, locked together, for a long time, as if trying to end the unbearable separation by fusing their two bodies into one. Kit wound his arm around Lily's waist and clutched her to him, dropping silent tears into her hair.

He bent his head down to hers, and their mouths met. The moment his lips and tongue touched hers, Lily felt her blood dissolving with an overwhelming, almost frightening desire. They kissed with hungry desperation.

When they drew apart, breathless and dazzled, Kit took her hand and led her to the centre of the coppice, where the shadows were thickest. There was no question of waiting. The moves were inevitable, and they went into the dance like sleepwalkers.

With her whole body beating and pulsing, Lily unfastened the buttons of her dress, right down to the hem. She shrugged it off, stepped out of her underwear, and stood before him; a white, naked dryad in the dappled shade.

Kit's gold-flecked eyes devoured her rapturously. 'You're so ridiculously, outrageously beautiful,' he murmured, 'it's almost driven me out of my mind. I think I've dreamt about this moment every night since I first saw you.'

He put out his hand, to caress the warm triangle of hair between her legs. His touch was gentle, but it shot a charge of electricity through Lily's swollen clitoris, which made her cry out. When he withdrew his hand to take off his shirt, the

413

loss of contact made her frantic.

He spread his shirt on the ground. Lily cast herself down upon it, hypnotised by the gold hairs on his sinewy forearms. He knelt between her legs, trembling in an effort to restrain himself. Reverently, he bowed his head over her vagina, and the heat of his breath almost made her climax.

With agonising delicacy, he began flicking his tongue around her aching clitoris. Lily was faint with the longing to have him inside her, but his tongue went on probing the silken folds of flesh as lightly as the wing of a butterfly until, with exquisite slowness, he carried Lily to the very brink of orgasm.

Kit groaned, and without warning, his control snapped. He entered her, and began to thrust into her violently, his face flaming into ecstasy. They came together, in blissful spasms that rocked through them until they had driven out all the torturing urgency of the past few weeks.

Their cries had sent the birds wheeling out of the branches above them. The minutes passed. Peace stole into their bones. Lily lay in Kit's arms, amazed by this magical fusion of the emotional and the physical – love brought to a pitch of perfection she had never imagined. The act of making love with Kit was more, she realised, than the satis-fying of a bodily desire. She had seen and touched his soul.

She had not noticed that he was crushing her, until he levered himself up on his elbows. She had not noticed that she was still spilling tears, until he stroked her cheeks with the back of his hand.

She breathed: 'I love you,' knowing he would understand that the words had a new meaning for her now.

He smiled down into her face, and rolled off her. 'My God, I was possessed. You're an angel.'

'With eyes like cricket balls, and a fat nose?'

'Even so. Isn't love extraordinary?'

Lily struggled into a sitting position. 'It certainly is. Something's digging right into my bottom, and I've only just started to mind.' She felt under Kit's shirt, and pulled out a twisted scrap of metal. 'Ouch. I'll probably be scarred for life.' It was one of the tags Pa fixed to owls he was watching;

a narrow ring, attached to a flat disc.

Kit took it from her, and slipped it onto the fourth finger of her right hand. 'With this ring, I thee wed. You're mine now.'

She kissed him, smiling. 'Yours for all time, till death us do part.'

'I'm serious.' He held her left hand between both of his. 'I won't settle for anything less than eternity.'

'Darling Kit, you're building a fence round me, and you really don't have to.'

'What do you mean?'

'You're so busy rushing to get all of me, you don't see that you've got me already. What are you so afraid of? Don't you trust me?'

'Of course,' Kit said seriously. 'I must, because I've put my whole life into your hands.'

'I wish you wouldn't talk like that – it makes me feel I might sneeze and accidentally drop you.' Lily laid her free hand upon his bare chest, and felt his heart beating against her palm. 'But you'll never have any reason to doubt me. I couldn't stop loving you if I tried. You could open me up and saw my bones in half – and you'd find "Kit" stamped all through them, like sticks of Brighton rock.'

This made him smile. 'I suppose I'm afraid of the world. I've learned, in the last few years, how outside forces destroy the best-laid plans, and force people apart. But now that I've found you, my Lily, no power in the universe will make me let you go. So you'll have to live for ever.'

LILY'S DIARY

12 August 1944

Grouse shooting begins. Lily's diary ends. Kit is sleeping beside me. Too happy to write any more.

Chapter Three

❖❖❖

Smithson & Hardy
38 Furnivals Inn
London EC
15 October 1944

Dear Miss Gallant,

    My client, Captain Ralph Gallant, instructs me to advise you that he cannot enter into any manner of communication with you,

    Yours sincerely,

    M.G. Smithson

At the crossroads, a knot of curious locals had gathered in the clear autumnal cold, to observe the strange procession. The five wild men of the manor, unrecognisably immaculate, marched up the lane towards the church. Each wore a wedding-favour of white ribbon in his buttonhole, and a black armband for his dead brethren. In their midst walked the beautiful creature who had provided the village with such astounding and enjoyable scandal – finally, finally headed for the altar, before her neighbours wore out their tongues with wondering.

Lily, on the arm of Pa, who was giving her away, wore a simple, short dress of cream velvet. Gladys Tufton had cut it down from her own wedding dress. Between sniffs, she eyed the seams anxiously, not having had time to finish them to her satisfaction. Little Peter, singing madly to himself, rode on Quin's back. Custard, who had followed without being invited, trotted soberly at the heels of Paddy.

Kit, splendid in his RAF uniform, glanced at the watchers suspiciously, ready to pounce at the smallest suggestion of disrespect. He was rather taken aback to hear instead murmurs of 'Good luck, dear' and 'Doesn't she look a picture?'

'Kick me, if I blub,' Pa said. 'It wouldn't do at all.'

'I'll probably be too busy blubbing myself,' Lily said.

'You're very happy, aren't you, my darling?'

'Outrageously happy. I keep thinking I'll wake up.'

Pa said: 'Sacrifices don't usually bring any reward, except a sense of virtue. But this one has paid off handsomely. You've brought me back the old, pre-war Kit I thought I'd never see again.'

She laughed. 'It hasn't stopped you fighting. I thought I'd be ninety before I got to church.'

Lily had been wearing her owl-tag for months, while Kit and Pa wrangled over where the real marriage should take place. Belatedly remembering he was a Roman Catholic, Pa had wanted his son married in the dismal Catholic Church, some twenty miles away. Kit, a resolute unbeliever, argued for a civil ceremony. In the end, they had settled on the Church of England, into which Lily had been baptised, as a compromise; largely to spare the feelings of poor, prejudiced Gladys, to whom the registry office and the Catholic Church were equally scarlet.

It made no difference to Lily, who had felt irrevocably bound to Kit since the day she first fell into his arms. The two of them had been living in paradise, making love at all hours, constantly amazed by their own joy.

Through the keen, frost-spiked air, they walked into the village church. At the door, Kit turned his head to smile back at her, and she humbly wondered what she had done to deserve him. Kit happy and in love was a man transformed – or rather, a man restored, like the sun emerging from thick cloud. Lily had been saddened by Ralph's rejection of her olive branch, but could not feel his absence when she had Kit.

The unreality of it made her light-headed. She heard her own voice, from a long way off, saying:

'I, Lily-Josephine, take thee, Christopher Gerard –' And only properly returned to herself when she left the church

417

clinging to her husband's arm, as Mrs Randall.

The moment they were out of the porch, Gladys hugged her, oozing tears and wreathed in smiles.

'My precious girl – I saw your mother married – bless her, she'd be so happy - Peter, throw your rice, love –'

Peter gravely uncrumpled the brown paper bag he had been clutching in his fat fist. Laughing, Kit and Lily crouched down, so he could fling the hard grains of pudding-rice at their heads.

'C'mon, boys,' Paddy said. 'Time to kiss the bride. Stand aside, Kit.'

They each kissed her, with exaggerated decorum, which made Kit swipe at them in mock anger. 'Saucy bastards – leave my wife alone.'

Pa blew his nose resoundingly. 'Never, in the whole of my crowded life, have I longed for alcohol so desperately.'

Gladys hung back for a moment, clutching Peter's hand, to watch the laughing group of Randalls hurrying Lily through the churchyard.

'Well, Bert,' she whispered, 'it's all right now. We did it.'

<hr>

A wedding breakfast, of almost pre-war magnificence, was spread on the big table in the Randalls' kitchen. The ration books and larders of the Randalls, Gladys and the Drivers had been ransacked, so that the newlyweds could feast upon breaded roast ham, chicken pie and plain chocolate cake. There were stone jugs of Quin's farm-brewed cider, and Pa had paid out a king's ransom for a bottle of Scotch.

They settled round the table in a noisy group. Peter was perched on a pile of books, between Gladys and Pa. Custard, the small daylight owls and several bold, foolhardy mice nosed for scraps on the floor.

'Makes one recall one's own nuptials,' Pa remarked to Gladys, over the marmalade head of Peter.

'Doesn't it just?' Gladys sighed. 'That gown brought it all back to me. I was slimmer in those days, but I could have covered two Lilies in it, and still had some over.'

'Awfully decent of you,' Pa said, 'to cut it up.'

'Nonsense, Mr Randall – Gerard, that is.' All the Randalls

were working on Gladys, to make her drop the 'sirs' and 'misters'. 'I'd have cut up every scrap I owned, so my girl could go up the aisle in a decent dress. I've been planning her wedding since she was in her cradle.'

'This wasn't quite what you had in mind, was it?' Pa asked gently.

Gladys met his eye, and laughed. 'Not quite. When she was a little thing, me and her governess used to dream about St Margaret's, Westminster, and pictures in all the society papers. But over the past few years, I don't mind telling you, sir, I've worn my knees out praying she'd settle down with one of you Randalls.'

Pa was amused. 'I won't ask which one.'

'I wasn't fussy, sir – Gerard. Though I must say, I was surprised to hear she'd chosen the Squadron Leader. And pleased. From what I've seen of him, he's a very fine young man.'

'Indeed he is. I take great pride in my firstborn, Mrs Tufton. Thanks to Lily, he's grown into the man he was always meant to be, before this wretched war threatened to ruin all our lives. I wish my wife could know how well it is with our boy.'

His eyes were moist. Gladys, attended by her own dead, patted his hand sympathetically. 'I'm sure she does. And if I'm to call you "Gerard", you must call me "Gladys".'

'Sorry.' He laughed shakily. 'I was forgetting the orders of young Mrs Randall.'

'It doesn't do to disobey her. She's always been a one for getting her own way.'

Pa dropped his voice. 'Except with that father of hers. I could cheerfully have committed murder, when that solicitor's letter came. Is the man a total fool?'

'I know what the Bible says, about calling people fools,' Gladys replied tartly, 'but with the Captain, that's about the size of it. When he brought that woman into his house, anyone could have predicted she'd find a way to drive Lily out of doors. But he's been punished for it. I saw him the other week, in Barnstaple, and hardly knew him – grey as a badger, shuffling about like a broken-down old man.'

'That's what happens to people who cast off their children,' Pa said. 'I don't let go of mine, for anything less than death.'

'My husband would have been sorry for him,' Gladys said. 'But I say, he made his bed, and now he must lie in it. What really gets me in a stew is Lily's money.'

'She doesn't need money,' Pa said proudly. 'We have more than enough.'

'It's what they call the principle of the thing. If Lily had her rights –' Gladys broke off, to prevent Peter throwing a large slice of ham to Custard – 'if she had all her rights, she'd be one of the wealthiest women in England. Did you know that? Millions, her mother had.'

Pa looked across the table at Lily, and bayed with laughter. 'Good God, she never told us. What an odd girl she is, sometimes.'

Bruno, who had been elected best man because he was the second oldest, and could be trusted with the ring, banged the table for silence.

'Fill your glasses, everyone.' He stood up. 'I'm not going to inflict a speech on you. I'd just like to propose a toast – to Lily and Kit, the bride and groom.'

They all rose and echoed the toast – including Peter, who was lifted onto the table by Pa, and drank the healths of the bride and groom in rosehip syrup.

'Speech, Kit!' Quin shouted.

'Bugger off,' said Kit.

'Terse and pithy,' Pa said. 'You should go into Parliament, boy.'

Lily stood up. 'It's not the done thing, but I'd like to say something.' She was pale. She smiled mistily around the table. 'Gerard, Bruno, Quin, Wiz – I'm drinking my toast to all of you, because I love you so dearly. It might not be the sort of love it used to be. It's changed, but it's as strong as ever. You all helped to make my happiness today – I thank you for it, and I'll blame you whenever my husband gets into one of his tempers. You're the best men in the world.' Tears dimmed her black eyes. 'All seven of you. The other two are here, even though we didn't lay places for them.' Her face blanched to tallow. 'Jack and Oscar –'

With a trembling hand, she raised the glass to her lips. It crashed to the floor.

Gladys shrieked: 'Lily! Somebody – quick –'

Lily fainted into Kit's arms.

Gladys's voice cut through the panic-stricken babble. 'Out of the way, all of you – Kit, take her to the sofa. Peter, stay in here, lovey.' Unceremoniously grabbing collars and shoving aside shoulders, she beat her way through the crowd of Randalls around Lily.

Secretly, she was frightened by Lily's stillness, and the pallor of her lips, but knew it would be worse than useless to show it. Someone had to take charge, and the men looked terrified. Touchingly, they obeyed her orders like lambs, sure she would know what to do.

Kit, to her relief, had stayed calm. He carried Lily into the parlour and laid her on the sofa, just as she was opening her bewildered eyes.

'What –'

'Darling, take it easy.' He knelt beside her, cradling her hand in his.

Gladys took off Lily's shoes, and placed a cushion under her feet. 'Too much excitement, young lady. Did you get any sleep last night?'

Lily smiled into Kit's strained, anxious face. 'Not much.' Her colour was creeping back.

'You naughty girl.' Gladys dropped down on the end of the sofa. 'Giving us all a scare.'

'Sorry, Glad. Sorry, Kit.'

He kissed her fingers. 'How do you feel?'

'Fine, but terribly silly. I can't think what made me do it.'

'I'll get you some water.'

'I'd rather have something to eat – I haven't finished my cake.'

Kit relaxed enough to smile. 'Let me unfasten your dress, anyway. It's too tight.'

Gladys looked up sharply. 'Tight? Rubbish. She's been the same size since she was sixteen. That dress fits perfectly.'

'I'm getting fat,' Lily said comfortably. 'I always seem to be starving, these days.'

'Oh, my good lord.' Gladys rolled her eyes heavenward. 'I might have known. You didn't get to that altar a minute too soon, love.'

'Do you know what's the matter with her?' Kit demanded.

'I've a fairly good idea. Don't look so worried, dear. And excuse me – but Lily –' Gladys turned pink, 'when did you last have the curse?'

'Goodness,' Lily said vaguely, 'I can't remember.'

'Not since you've been with me.' Where Gladys was red, Kit's tender, scarred skin was white. 'That was in August. God almighty.'

'I must say, I like the way you men are always surprised,' Gladys remarked.

'Glad, what are you talking about?'

'It's a miracle it hasn't happened before. You're expecting.'

Lily's lips and eyes stretched into three Os of astonishment.

Kit glared down into her open, trusting, innocent face, dropped her hand, and began to laugh grimly. 'Well, well. A baby Randall,' he said. 'The question is – which Randall?'

Gladys gave a little shriek of horror, and hastily clapped a hand across her mouth, to stifle it.

'Kit –' Lily struggled upright. 'You're not angry?'

'I don't think so.' He looked angry. 'Not much point, is there? You'd better see a doctor.' He stood up, scowling. 'May I tell the others?'

'If I'm right,' Gladys said, 'they'll know soon enough.'

He left the room, slamming the door behind him. Gladys winced. She leant close to Lily.

'Think carefully. When did you last have your monthlies, and – and how long have you and Kit –'

'Been sleeping together?' Lily supplied helpfully. 'That's easy. August the twelfth – the Glorious Twelfth. And before you ask, he's been the only one since then.'

'Yes, yes, but what about just before?'

'Before Kit seems such ages ago.' It was not a time Lily

cared to remember, but she made herself look back at the weeks of dragging, relentless unhappiness, when she had been trying to teach herself not to want Kit. She had, she realised – with an unfamiliar pang of shame – used sex with the others to dull her misery. The fact that it had not worked was hardly relevant now.

Gladys read her silence perfectly, and groaned. 'So, it might be any one of them. Oh, Lord. I thought you were – you know. Taking precautions.'

'We did,' Lily said, 'mostly.'

'Mostly!'

Lily's lips twitched. 'Well, precautions aren't always easy to come by.'

'Oh, Lily,' Gladys said, more in sorrow than anger, 'you never did learn restraint. Do it first and think about it after – that's you.'

Yes, this was her. Lily had to admit, she was inclined to let passion overrule commonsense. The result had been inevitable.

It explained her recent gargantuan appetite, and sudden bouts of deathlike sleep. Biology, rather than true love, had made her breasts sore. At first, she felt stupid. Then, as it sank in, her world was overturned by a flash of extraordinary joy.

She grabbed Gladys's hand. 'A baby! An actual baby of my own!'

'Bless it.' Focusing on the child, instead of its embarrassing conception, melted Gladys's disapproval. 'You can't say you know what love is, until you've had a baby.'

The door opened, and the men filed solemnly into the parlour, Pa carrying Peter.

'Did he tell you?' Lily demanded. 'Isn't it wonderful?'

Pa placed Peter in the arms of his mother, and stood over Lily with his hands in his pockets. 'I feel a fool. I always knew when Julia was expecting – often before she did. Congratulations, my darling. When should I bring the cradle down from the attic?'

Gladys had been doing mental arithmetic. 'Early next summer, I should say. Round about my Peter's birthday.'

The younger Randalls were exchanging troubled glances, anxiously watching Kit.

He was staring at Lily, rather ominously meditative. 'Is there any way of telling whose it is?'

Bruno murmured: 'That doesn't matter now. Naturally, it will be yours.'

'You'll be the legal father, in any case,' Pa pointed out.

Kit said: 'I'm not sure I fancy being any sort of father.'

'My dear Number One, what else did you think marriage was for? This little chap will be the first of many, I hope and trust.'

'You make it sound like a litter.'

Lily sprang off the sofa. 'Kit, don't be cross.'

'I'm not cross with you for being pregnant,' Kit said. 'But I'm not sure I fancy taking responsibility for a baby that might not be mine. If I knew it was mine, I could accept it as the wages of sin. As things stand, I utterly refuse to let you others put the whole rap on me. Lily's mine, but the baby's different.'

'And what do you propose to do about it?' Bruno demanded, with unaccustomed sharpness. 'You can't marry Lily, and then tell us you only want the parts of marriage that happen to suit you.'

'That's not what I meant.' Kit turned towards Lily. 'I don't see why we have to pretend the past didn't happen, just because we turned respectable a couple of hours ago.'

She let out a laugh, which was half a groan, and took his arm. 'You impossible man – why the hell can't you accept the outward appearance of something, just this once, and behave as if this baby is yours? It probably is yours, after all.'

'You mean, you wish it was mine. Well, that's very nice. But I can't take wishes for reality.'

Quin, in a shadow of a voice, wheezed: 'You're not being fair – it's not kind –'

'What are you talking about?'

'I know what he means,' Lily said. 'Think how you'd feel, if Pa refused to be your father.'

'I'm not refusing. I'm saying we should share the father-hood.'

'Not possible –' Quin gasped, '– and unfair –'

Irritably, Pa said: 'Number Five, I absolutely forbid you to have an attack.'

'Don't snap at him, Gerard.' Lily released Kit, and steered Quin to the sofa. 'You know it makes him worse.' She made Quin sit upright, with two cushions wedged against his back.

Kit addressed Bruno. 'Admit it, you'd all love a share of the brat. You'll never be able to resist sticking your noses in. Especially you, Pa. We might just about keep up the fiction that it's mine to the outside world – but we know the truth, and pretending amongst ourselves would be sheer hypocrisy.'

There was a silence, during which Lily searched all their faces thoughtfully.

'Oh, God,' Pa said, 'we should have foreseen this.'

'He has a point,' Lily said. 'I love the idea of my baby being a part of you all, owned by you all. That's how it would feel in our hearts and our minds, whatever version we tell the world. Isn't that what you meant, Kit?'

He drew her towards him, wrapping a possessive arm around her waist. 'That's the general idea. I don't have to worry about making a hash of being a father, if I know the others are there to fill in the gaps.'

'Darling, you'll be a brilliant father.'

For the first time since the breaking of the news, Kit smiled. 'Come on, you know how cussed I am. This will be a lucky kid, if he has the rest of the firm to fall back on.'

Pa patted Quin's shoulder. 'A private arrangement, of course. But since when have we Randalls needed pieces of paper? We've already proved ourselves excellent at sharing – oh, I beg your pardon, Mrs Tufton –'

Gladys sighed. 'I've heard the lot, dear. You couldn't shock me any more if you tried.'

'Could you honestly bear it, Kit?' Bruno asked. 'Look, we'd try not to tread on your toes. But wait a while – you might change your mind later.'

'Kit never changes his mind,' Lily said.

'I'm just relieved he's not about to commit murder,'

Paddy said. 'I was ready to leave the country.'

There was a general exhalation of laughter, and a breeze of optimism lightened the room, as the Randalls tested the notion of shared paternity, and found it intriguing.

'Let's open a book,' Paddy said. 'Boy or girl?'

'Boy, of course,' said Pa. 'There hasn't been a female Randall in four generations.'

Kit had kept his arm round Lily. He spread one hand across her stomach. 'My son, my nephew or my brother. I suppose I'm bound to like him.'

Lily kissed her husband's neck. 'You'll be crazy about him. He'll be a prince, the eighth man in my family – I'm going to call him Octavius.'

Chapter Four

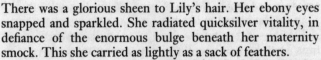

There was a glorious sheen to Lily's hair. Her ebony eyes snapped and sparkled. She radiated quicksilver vitality, in defiance of the enormous bulge beneath her maternity smock. This she carried as lightly as a sack of feathers.

'She certainly looks very well,' Bruno said. 'Blooming, in fact.'

Kit lit a cigarette. 'You cannot imagine what she looks like undressed.'

'I won't try.'

'Extraordinary, that's what. Sometimes, you can see the bump moving, all by itself. When she's in the bath, she puts the soap on her belly, and the boy kicks it off.'

'It might be a girl,' Bruno pointed out.

'Hope not,' Kit said. 'If it is, she'll be one of those mountainous, hockey-playing Girton types. It kicks all bloody night.'

They were leaning against the low stone wall, watching Lily hurl sticks for Custard in the meadow. It was an evening in May. Bruno had arrived at Randalls half an hour before, and had not lost his everyday expression of harried anxiety.

'This is so strange.'

Kit grinned. 'Of course, you haven't seen it growing. Must be quite a shock, finding her in full sail.'

'It is,' Bruno said. 'And so's the thought of having a baby around again. But what I really meant was – how strange it is to come home, and find you all completely cut off from the rest of the world. How the hell do you do it? On the planet I've just left, everyone's glued to the papers and the wireless reports, talking endlessly about the German surrender and Victory in Europe - dusting off the bunting, rolling out the barrel. And you lot manage to ignore it.'

'Aren't we clever?'

Bruno let out a long, tired sigh, and loosened his tie. 'Brilliant. I hope it rubs off on me. We've had a nasty few months – can't say any more, but take my word. Thinking of Lily, and the babe growing inside her, has probably saved me from going mad.'

'And us,' Kit said quietly. 'We don't talk about it, but we've had our war here, and fucking awful it was, too. We've lost Jack and Oscar. It doesn't seem like a victory.'

'Paddy's pretty safe now, thank God,' Bruno said. 'By the time he's called up, there won't be much left to do.'

'Yes, that's quite a comfort to poor old Pa.'

Bruno shot him a glance of appraisal. 'That and the baby, I should think.'

'Of course. You know the old man and babies.' Kit did not look at his brother, but frowned down at his hands. 'He's started acting as if Lily was dropped here by heaven, to replace his dead sons.'

'Well, I think I sympathise,' Bruno said, gazing at Lily. 'If I were superstitious, I'd be inclined to marvel at the way she arrived among us, and insulated us from the awfulness of losing Three and Four. I do wonder sometimes what on earth this family would have done without her.'

'Don't you start,' Kit said sharply. 'She's my wife now, and she's here for me. None of you even have the right to punch my head, if I make her unhappy.'

Bruno's tired face creased into a rather wistful smile. 'Obviously, you don't. Her letters are all rhapsodies about you, and how disgustingly marvellous, virtuous, wise and sexy you are. She's madly in love with you – lucky bastard.'

Kit asked: 'You don't really mind, do you?'

'I'm over her, pretty well. The baby makes it easier – the socialist collective baby, who belongs a bit to us all. Pa looks ten years younger for it.'

'He never stops talking about the brat,' Kit said. 'He keeps dragging our old baby whatsits out of the attic. He put the cradle in our bedroom weeks ago. I bark my shins on the bloody thing, when I get up to have a pee.' He sighed. 'I'm glad he's glad, but I can't match his enthusiasm, I'm afraid.

428

I've tried, but I'm not exactly looking forward to meeting the stranger Lily insists on calling "Octavius".'

'Because he might not be yours?' Bruno suggested gently.

Kit shrugged, as if trying to loosen something stubborn and constraining around his shoulders. 'I don't give a damn whose he is. Possession of the Lily is all that matters to me.'

<hr />

The approach of Victory in Europe, combined with the approach of the birth, gave the house a restless, pent-up atmosphere. Each day that slipped past without dramatic development seemed wasted and irksome. Bruno followed every news bulletin round the dial of the wireless, impatient for the end. His father and brothers watched Lily's belly, impatient for the beginning. She was the only serene person in the place, wholly and contentedly absorbed in her baby.

Pa had unfortunatley fallen out with the new doctor; an unbending plank of a woman, full of modern ideas. She had recently converted to Catholicism, and had said some rather personal things to lax, lapsed Pa. He had responded by persuading old Doc Bassett, who had delivered all his sons, out of retirement nearby. Doc said he'd be delighted. He was bored with sitting around at home, forced to listen to Mrs Bassett's conversation.

'I never should've sold the practice to that hideous woman. I can deliver a baby with my eyes shut.'

'And a good thing, too,' Kit commented later. 'They probably will be shut, the amount he drinks.' He did not care for Doc Bassett, who was red and tweedy, and boasted about delivering his calves and foals himself, to avoid shelling out for the vet.

Pa said: 'I promise you, he's the best medical man for miles. He saved your mother's life, when the twins were born.'

'That was twenty-five years ago! For God's sake, Pa. Just because Doctor Draper quoted "The Hound of Heaven" at you, doesn't mean she isn't capable of delivering a baby.'

'You've got first-time nerves,' Pa said, patting Kit's shoulder soothingly. 'Dear, dear – the night you popped out, Doc had to give me brandy-and-water, and put my head between my knees. But there's really nothing to worry about.'

Lily was not worried in the least. Gladys, who had spent the last three months of her own pregnancy in a state of miserable, bloated lethargy, said Lily was obviously one of the lucky types who breezed through the whole thing. All the same, a week before the baby was due, she left Peter in the care of her sister-in-law, and took up residence at Randalls.

Nobody had invited her, but nobody dared to question her presence. Kind and calm as she was, there was a tigerish glint in her eye, if anyone appeared to suggest that her rightful place was not beside her Lily. One more woman in the house seemed like a feminine invasion. Gladys, standing at the range in her flowered pinafore, was a large, undeniable symbol of the hidden female wisdom of the ages. Her cretonne knitting bag sat on the corner of the dresser, as if she had been running the house for years.

Though Lily laughed at her, and called her a fusspot, Gladys washed and aired enough tiny white garments for an army of infants. The male Randalls – except Kit – were awed and submissive before these flapping muslin squares and microscopic vests. All of them, including Kit, welcomed her superb cooking.

On the 13th of May, Gladys and the Randalls gathered around the wireless, clutching glasses of cider, to hear the Prime Minister's broadcast. With indrawn breath and thudding hearts, they listened as Churchill's voice filled the old house to the rafters.

'Advance Britannia! Long live the cause of freedom! God save the King!'

Officially, the war was to end at midnight. Unofficially, the nation had already exploded into frantic celebrations. Across the fields, they could hear distant screams and car horns. The indefatigable Mrs Parminter had organised a party, on her ploughed tennis court, for all the local children. Kit and Quin, the previous evening, had found an immense conga-line jigging through the pub.

Pa turned off the radio, and they stood in unbelieving silence.

430

He held up his glass solemnly, and murmured: 'Absent friends.'

They echoed the toast, choking on conflicting emotions – sadness, anger, pride. On the shelf above the range, the faces of Jack and Oscar smiled down, frozen into history.

'We won't forget them, will we?' Pa asked suddenly, his voice unsteady. 'We won't let the passing of time take them too far away?'

Gladys, dabbing her eyes and thinking of Bert, found herself rattled by the stern way his boys replied 'No, Pa,' and 'Never, Pa.'

'I'll put the kettle on,' she said. 'We need a good cup of tea.' Gladys could always find sustenance in the prospect, or even the abstract concept, of a cup of tea.

Lily gasped: 'Ow!' and jerked forward sharply, clutching Kit's arm.

They all stared at her in alarm.

She laughed. 'Perfect timing – Advance, Octavius!'

⊰⊱

Octavius Randall was pulled out of his mother at ten minutes past two, the following afternoon. He was long, with a large head, sturdy shoulders and a determined snuffle. Doc Bassett carried him down to the kitchen, at Lily's request, while Gladys cleared away the signs of his struggle into the world.

Pa and his sons were unshaven and hollow-eyed. They had sat through a horrible night of listening to Lily's screams. Three times, his brothers had forcibly restrained Kit from rushing upstairs – Doc considered fathers a nuisance, and had warned Kit that he would walk out if not left alone.

Kit was now pacing restlessly to and fro, mouth set and eyes blazing. Bruno, Quin, Paddy and Pa were round the table, which was strewn with dirty cups, smudged glasses and brimming ashtrays. When Doc came in, all the Randalls jumped as if electrified, and gaped, astonished, at the bleating bundle in his arms. The living force of this little thing was powerful and extraordinary. His personality changed the balance of the room.

431

In the crook of Doc's elbow, they could see a red scalp, covered with thick, waxy strands of black hair. All, except Pa, backed away cautiously, as if Doc were brandishing a weapon.

'How is she?' Kit demanded hoarsely. 'Is Lily all right?'

Doc's eyes were pouchy and bloodshot with exhaustion, but he spoke reassurance. 'Fine, Kit, fine. You can go up as soon as Mrs Tufton's settled her.' He did not think it necessary to tell them about the worrying amount of time it had taken to remove the afterbirth, and to staunch the bleeding.

Pa's bristled face slowly cracked into a smile. He approached Doc, and gingerly pulled aside a fold of flannel blanket, to expose the child's cross, squashed face.

'A boy, I presume?'

'Of course. Another strapping Randall boy.'

'Well, well,' Pa said softly. 'Hello, Number Eight. May I?' He held out his arms, and Doc gave him Octavius. 'He certainly feels like a Randall – I'm not surprised he gave Lily a bad time, the monster. Come on, boys – he won't bite.'

Bruno, Quin and Paddy sidled up to Pa, to stare at the incredible creature. Octavius stared back, with unfocused, greyish eyes. One tiny hand flapped around his face. Bruno experimentally placed a finger in the palm, and chuckled when the hand closed round it like a sea anemone.

'How d'you do, young man? I'm sorry about the outside world, but you'll get used to it.'

Quin wheezed: 'Let's put him in the scales, and see how much he weighs.'

Paddy asked: 'Who does he look like, Pa?'

Doc, who had no idea of the real situation, said: 'He's the image of his father. Don't you want to see your son, Kit?'

'I want to see Lily.'

'Yes, yes – but she'll be furious if you don't admire her work.'

Kit, visibly struggling for patience, strode over to Pa's side, and glared down at Octavius. 'I take it all babies are this ugly.'

'Nonsense, he's a marvel,' Doc said. 'Didn't you hear the

432

way he bellowed, when I slapped his bum? You could show him for money.'

From the top of the stairs, Gladys's voice called: 'Doctor!'

'Ah, the all-clear.' Doc took back the baby. 'Up you go.'

Kit was already charging up the shallow stairs three at a time. Gladys was waiting at the bedroom door. Lily's long, agonising labour had been more painful to her than her own. She looked ten years older. Her eyelids were swollen, and her plump cheeks sagged heavily. She was, however, smiling.

She kissed Kit. 'Congratulations, love. Keep her quiet, won't you?'

'Is she really all right?' he whispered urgently. 'Really?'

'Ever so tired, but I've never seen her so happy.'

Lily's face was chalk-white against the pillow. She lay very still. Her dark hair was pinned back, making her look absurdly young. There was a large bundle of dirty linen, wrapped in a sheet, in one corner. Gladys had changed Lily's sheets and nightgown, and removed the waterproof cover she had put over the mattress, but the room smelt of blood.

Kit, feeling a breath would blow his heart to pieces, knelt beside the bed and stroked her cheek. 'My darling.'

Her eyes opened. She smiled beatifically. 'Hello.'

Tears streamed down his face. He seized her hand. 'You poor angel, it's all over now.'

'Kit, isn't he wonderful?'

'Wonderful,' Kit said automatically.

'Have the others seen him? Are they pleased?'

He managed a shaky smile. 'In raptures.'

Doc Bassett came in with Octavius, whom he handed to Gladys. 'Nine pounds, three ounces.'

'Bless him.' Gladys tenderly kissed the baby's head. 'You'll have an appetite, won't you, clever big boy? I'd better make you a bottle right away.'

Lily said: 'I wanted to feed him myself. Like Julia did.'

'Certainly not,' Doc said. 'You haven't anything like enough strength.'

'Sleep now.' Kit put her hand to his lips.

'Gerard and the boys –'

'No, sleep first. They're not going anywhere.'

Her dark eyes were anxious. 'My baby –'

Gladys laid Octavius on the pillow, between Lily and Kit. He mewed fretfully, and light flooded into Lily's wan face, like the sun rising. Clinging to Kit's hand, she drifted into blissful sleep.

Kit, when he was sure nobody was looking, briefly placed his lips to Octavius's tufted head, and whispered:

'Be mine, little boy.'

Chapter Five

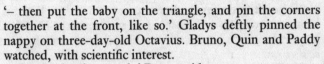

'– then put the baby on the triangle, and pin the corners together at the front, like so.' Gladys deftly pinned the nappy on three-day-old Octavius. Bruno, Quin and Paddy watched, with scientific interest.

'Looks simple enough,' Bruno said.

'I dunno,' Quin said doubtfully, 'I'd be scared stiff of sticking the pin into him.'

Gladys whisked down the baby's flannelette gown. 'I've known a few cack-handed Dads in my time – my brother Arthur springs to mind – but I never met one who managed to stick a pin into his baby. You'll soon pick it up.'

Paddy announced: 'I've never seen such peculiar shit.'

Bruno nudged him. 'Language.'

'Sorry.'

'But now that the subject has arisen, Mrs T, ought it to be dark green? I seem to recall Paddy's being sort of yellow.'

All the brothers laughed. Being with the baby distracted them from their gnawing anxiety.

Gladys joined in the laughter. She had surprised herself by becoming fond of the young Randalls, and found their company immensely comforting. 'It'll change to yellow in a day or so. You'll see enough of it, I promise you. Now, who wants to put him back in his basket? Come along, you mustn't be shy about picking him up.'

'I will,' Bruno said. His face, when he looked at Octavius, became boyish and dreamy; like a teenager's in the grip of a first infatuation. After only a few days, he could gather the child in his arms with ease and confidence. He laid Octavius over his shoulder. 'It must be nearly time for his grub.'

The bottle was warming beside the range. The brothers glanced at it hopefully, for they all loved feeding him.

435

Gladys, however, shook her head. 'Give it another half-hour, or he won't be hungry enough, and we'll have to start all over. Feeding in fits and starts makes them colicky.'

Reverently, Bruno placed Octavius on his back in the basket. Quin and Paddy pressed closer, to watch. The baby made effortful, drunken faces, flushed purple, then suddenly drew up his legs and farted.

They all laughed again, and stopped abruptly when Kit came into the room. It always annoyed him, to find his brothers cooing over the baby. Lily was not well. Far from helping him to forget his anxiety, Octavius was seen by him as its focus.

The exchange was always the same.

Bruno asked: 'How is she?'

Kit shrugged and sighed, and blindly accepted the cup of tea Gladys put into his hand. 'Sleeping again. Let's hope it does some good this time. Pa's with her now. You lot can come in later.'

'You should eat something,' Gladys said, eyeing him critically. 'You won't help her, unless you keep your strength up.'

'Not hungry, thanks.'

'Is she fretting for the baby much?'

'Not at the moment.'

Instead of recovering from her long labour, Lily seemed to sink further into exhaustion. She could not eat, and was spending more and more time in a dazed half-sleep. Doc Bassett, when he called late that afternoon, shook his head over her temperature, and looked annoyed when he listened to her heart.

'Plenty of rest,' he said. 'As much as she wants.'

'That's what you always say,' Kit muttered angrily. 'And it hasn't made any difference.'

Doc patted his shoulder, with clumsy concern. 'You could do with a spot of rest yourself, it seems to me.'

'Why does everybody keep prescribing for me?' Kit demanded.

The question hung on the air. Pa and Gladys, on the other side of the room, exchanged helpless glances. It was kinder,

they thought, for Kit to work the answer out for himself –
that they might be approaching a time when the love of his
life was beyond prescriptions, and he was the one who
needed healing.

Doc turned to Gladys. 'Little one all right, is he?'

'Yes, sir.'

'Good-oh. Let his mother see him when she asks, but
don't let him tire her.'

Lily had planned to keep Octavius in the huge, antique
wooden cradle beside her bed, never letting the angel out of
her sight. Instead, he spent most of his time in his basket on
the kitchen table. Pa, looking stricken, had banished the owls
to the old stable, set traps for the mice and closed the scullery
window. He had not told Lily, since changes distressed her.
When awake and lucid, she wanted to see all the faces she
loved around her, as if drawing nourishment from their
familiarity.

Kit was essential to her. If he left the room, she became
nervous and disoriented. She slept easier when he held her
hand, or laid his own hand over her forehead.

Octavius, though she was too weak to hold him, or feed
him, was her delight. Gladys saw those huge dark eyes fixed
adoringly on the little creature, and had to fight off a memory
of Helena, with a dreadful chill seeping into her soul.

After the boys had been in to say good night to Lily, and
she had left Octavius under the supervision of Bruno downstairs, Gladys held an urgent, whispered conference with Pa.
While Kit brooded over his still wife, she beckoned Pa over
to the open casement.

'I don't like it. This isn't my Lily. What shall we do?'

Kit heard, and raised his head. His face was bleak and
ashen. 'She's fading away,' he said, 'and I can't hold on to
her. It's – it's like trying to keep sand from running through
a glass. I think you should tell Doc to come back.'

'No,' Pa said. He scowled. 'I'm going to fetch Doctor
Draper.'

On his way out, he paused to embrace Kit, with a tenderness that made Gladys's eyes prickle, and brushed his lips
against Lily's white forehead.

From downstairs, they heard a piercing infant wail.

Lily's eyelids fluttered. She mumbled: 'My baby –'

Kit made his voice warm and reassuring; even humorous. 'You'll see him in a minute. He's being fed.'

'Who?'

'Paddy,' Kit said. 'It's his turn.'

The corners of her mouth twitched, in an attempt at a smile. 'Dear old Wiz.'

After a pause, during which her eyes seemed to show that she was labouring to express something important, she said: 'I want you all to share him. I want you all to be fathers to him. I don't ever want to know who his real father is.'

Kit gently kissed her lips. 'You don't have to worry. He already has an embarrassment of besotted fathers.'

She loved to hear about Octavius and his amateur nurses. Gladys wondered how on earth Kit could bear to go through the recital tonight, but he went on cheerfully: 'Bru gave him a bath today. And Quin took him for an airing round the farm.'

'Did he like it?'

'According to Quin, he's a born farmer's boy. Paddy says he's going to train him up as a gardener. Bru, on the other hand, thinks he's an intellectual, and wants him to be a philosopher.'

Drifting contentedly back into sleep, Lily whispered: 'What do you want for him, Kit?'

He waited until her heavy lids had closed. Then, with despair flooding back into his face, said:

'A mother.'

~≪≫~

Gladys held Paddy in her arms, as he cried and cried. His wrenching sobs, muffled in her shoulder, dropped into the awful stillness of the house like stones in a well.

He's only a boy, Gladys thought. Seventeen years old. How must the world appear to him?

From time to time, she raised her hand, to dab her own, streaming eyes. The smoky, earthy smell of Paddy's thick brown hair, and the feel of the bones on his skinny back, took the extreme edge off her pain.

438

Bruno seemed to be drawing similar comfort from Octavius. The baby had been sleeping peacefully for ages, but Bruno would not put him down. He sat in the carver's chair, cradling the warm bundle, and often rubbing his cheek against the velvet head.

Quin, wheezing alarmingly, had Custard across his knees on the settle. Gladys was sure the dog was bad for his asthma, and equally sure that this did not matter. They all needed something living to hold on to.

Doctor Draper had been kind, driving nearly ten miles at the dead of night. She made plain, however, what Doc Bassett should have made plain – that there was nothing more to be done. When she left, she told Gladys, apparently mistaking her for the monthly nurse, to telephone her when there was a change. It was obvious what she meant. They were headed for a change, all right.

Lily was very feeble now. Kit was with her, and Pa would not leave Kit. He fed his firstborn pieces of toast, putting them into his mouth like an owl feeding its young.

Kit did not cry. His voice never faltered, his eyes never moistened. He was pouring every atom of energy and concentration into a hand-to-hand battle with death. While she slept, scarcely breathing, he whispered to her:

'Don't leave me, Lily – we haven't had enough time –'

Pa, though he flinched away from the memory, thought of the night he had sat beside Julia, hoping he could keep her if he held on hard enough. He knew how it felt to be Kit at this hour. His own love had been so strong, he had refused to believe any power, on earth or in heaven, could be stronger.

By God, he thought, that boy's an even more stubborn fighter; he won't give up until the absolute end. This, of course, was how Kit had survived in a burning Spitfire – by sheer, furious force of will. It was another layer of torture to Pa, on top of seeing Lily so weak and wasted. His eldest son was burning again, and would emerge from this struggle with scars all the more hideous for being invisible.

And Lily, pretty Lily, bringer of hope and laughter – Lily who had enchanted them with her terrible cooking and tuneless singing –

Pa had lost all faith in the God of his fathers, but he almost prayed now, because he dreaded the idea of there being no heaven for Lily. Feeling that he had been turned to stone, Pa crept out of the room, to fetch the boys and Gladys.

He did not need to speak. When he appeared in the kitchen, they all stood without a word, and filed up the great staircase after him. They stole into her room. Paddy was still shamefacedly swallowing sobs. Gladys kept hold of his hand, irrelevantly thinking how hard she would hug Peter when she saw him. Bruno cuddled Octavius. The baby's plump cheek nestled against his neck.

Kit was on the bed, with Lily in his arms. She lay still as marble, occasionally dragging in a breath that made her chest crackle. Pa, Gladys and the boys watched her face intently. It was troubled and pallid.

It was still dark outside, but there were streaks of light on the horizon, and the breeze that gently ballooned the curtains over the sill had a morning freshness. A single thrush began to call.

Lily's eyes opened to narrow slits. Slowly and painfully, as if trying to find them in a fog, she took in each of the figures around her. Her mouth twitched. She was trying to smile.

Gladys suddenly hissed: 'The baby! Let her have the baby!'

Startled by her sharpness and urgency, Bruno gave her Octavius. Gladys, trembling, placed him on the pillow beside his mother. He was deeply, rosily asleep, but let out a comical little sigh when he was moved.

Lily's blurred eyes opened a little wider. For the fraction of a second, her lips formed the beginnings of a smile.

Quite distinctly, they shaped the word: 'Kit.'

Kit shifted her into the crook of his arm, so she could see his face. He bent his head, touched her lips with his, and held them there for a long time. Afterwards, he tightened his arms around her, protective and possessive, and still dry-eyed.

Gradually, the grey dawn became gold and blue, and the chorus of birds under the window mingled with scattered,

440

stifled sobs amongst the watchers. Pa, with infinite gentleness, picked up Lily's heavy arm, and felt her wrist.

'She's gone,' he said. 'Let her go, boy.'

Like a sleepwalker, Kit allowed Pa to unwind his arms, lay Lily back on the pillow and close her eyes.

Without warning, Octavius stiffened beside her, and let out a furious wail. Kit flinched, and shot the child a look of bitter, anguished hostility. Gladys, choking with sobs, scooped him up protectively and held him close.

She wanted to leave them. The beautiful effigy on the bed was not her Lily, and she had a powerful sense of the Randall family as a single unit, turning its collective back on all outsiders. She stumbled to the door, with Octavius screeching, as he had never screeched, in all his short life.

Just before she closed the door behind her, she glanced back, and saw, through a wavering miasma of tears, the crowd of Randalls around Lily's bed.

Only when she was downstairs, in the strange quietness and normality of the kitchen, did she realise what was printed on her memory. She began to shake, so violently that she placed the howling baby in the safety of his basket.

Seven Randalls. She had seen seven of them.

Chapter Six

Lily looked so beautiful, when Gladys had laid her out beneath a snowy, lavender-scented sheet, that none of the Randalls could bear to talk about her burial. The pale, exquisite face, gently smiling, belonged to their old Lily; worlds removed from the poor, fading, anguished creature of the past few days. How could they surrender something only just regained?

Doctor Draper had returned, to sign the death certificate, and none of them could connect her bald description of Lily's departure – respiratory failure, following postpartum infection – with the marble angel sleeping on the white bed.

Bruno said: 'I hate to think of her in the dark.'

Quin said: 'I hate to think of her boxed in.'

Kit, who had kept vigil beside Lily, day and night, brooding over her with tearless, implacable eyes, said:

'You're asking me to bury my soul.'

Gladys, who liked the largest events in life to run along conventional lines, according to tribal custom, was upset by the continued absence of undertakers and clergymen. Her vision of all seven Randalls, clustered around the deathbed of her beloved child, had rattled her more than she cared to admit. She sturdily dismissed it as a trick of the light, but was secretly afraid their madness might be contagious. This made her all the more anxious to do things properly. In her experience, a death in the house meant plates of sandwiches, extra chairs in the parlour, and a stream of whispering visitors. As far as she was concerned, the eccentric mourning of the Randalls was not decent. They saw nobody. When local people called, full of sympathy only faintly spiked with curiosity, Gladys had to turn them away, unable to answer their kind enquiries about the funeral.

Lily was destined, however, to defy convention in death, as she had done in life. She would have no decorous church-yard plot, marked by a slab of stone. Her monuments were to be larkspur and camomile, white poppies and aconite.

'We will lay her down in the Sleeping Garden,' Pa decreed. 'She always said it was a peaceful place.'

His sons seized on the idea, with the strange elation, not unlike happiness, that often accompanies the crisis of a death.

Only Kit seemed to accept, in the depths of his soul, that Lily was lost for ever. And even he found a kind of comfort in the Sleeping Garden.

'She wanted to stay with us,' he said. 'Now we'll have her for ever.'

Pa rediscovered his energy, and worked off the sharpest edge of his grief, in applying to the Vicar, the Parish Council and the Town Hall. On a May morning, with fitful sunlight glancing through the leaves, Lily's coffin was lowered into her grave, at the exact centre of the camomile lawn in the Sleeping Garden. The Vicar, who had married her, read the funeral service to the music of birdsong.

It was the simplest possible ceremony. The Randalls wore their rough, everyday clothes. The undertaker and the sexton kept a respectful distance at the garden door. Behind the Vicar's dry voice, there was a profound hush, broken by the sobs of Gladys, and the occasional bleats of Octavius, in her arms.

'Man that is born of woman hath but a short time to live; he cometh up and is cut down like a flower –'

Gladys found herself thinking: There is nothing to fear. Here, Death was only Sleep's near relation, who turned his kindest face towards the innocent and deserving.

And she was innocent, Gladys thought; I was wrong to worry that she was a sinner, there's no hell for the likes of Lily.

Kit turned away sharply, as soon as he had thrown his handful of soil into the grave. He came to Gladys, and held out his arms for the baby. Gladys was startled. He had never shown the smallest inclination to hold Octavius. She put the child in his arms. Octavius immediately began to howl. Kit, taking no notice, strode out of the garden. Bruno and Pa had to run, to catch up with him.

'Kit, what on earth are you doing? Where are you taking him?' Bruno jumped straight in front of Kit, forcing him to stop.

'Get out of my way.'

'No! Where are you going with Octavius?'

'I'm going to show him to her shit of a father,' Kit said. 'Let him feel proud of himself now.'

Pa put his arm across Kit's broad, rigid shoulders. 'You're not fit for anything, boy. Not till you've had a rest.'

'I can't rest. I want him to see, and realise what he's lost. I owe it to Lily.'

Gladys, tear-stained and breathless, caught the last of this. 'Take him to the Prospect? Put that baby in the back of the car? You can't let him – he don't know the first thing about taking care of him.'

Bruno firmly took the howling baby out of Kit's arms. The feel and smell of him were already familiar to Octavius. His shrieks subsided when he nestled his firm, fat cheek against Bruno's neck.

'If you really must,' Bruno said, 'I'll come with you.'

'Don't interfere.'

'Don't you be an arse, Kit. You know you can't look after Octavius in the car. Where do you propose to put him – in the glove compartment?'

Kit's scowl faded. He rubbed a hand across his bewildered, exhausted face. 'I'm probably crazy, of course I am. But it ought to have a proper ending. I can't rest, until I've seen his face when he hears.'

'You want to punish him,' Pa said quietly.

'Yes, Pa. I want to punish him.'

Quin and Paddy had joined the group. They all stood in silence, like a jury. Kit, momentarily stripped of his sustaining wrath, had allowed them to see the agony of his grief. For a long moment, it looked as if he might put his heavy head down on Pa's shoulder, and give himself up to a storm of crying.

Bruno said: 'Let us do it. He's right – just sending a letter isn't good enough. And you know Number Eight will be all right with me. Mrs T will tell me what to take.'

'Well –' Gladys said doubtfully. She hated letting the baby out of her sight, but had to admit she trusted Bruno. And soon enough, whether she liked it or not, she would have to leave Octavius to the care of his fathers. If they insisted on going through with this, she must help them, for Octavius's sake.

In her heart of hearts, she relished the notion of Ralph's punishment. At last, Bert's Captain would have a good use for his self-pity and his crocodile tears. Let him come face to face with the fact that his selfish weakness had driven away the one beautiful, redeeming thing in his life. Let him see Lily's child, and remember the adored child she had once been. Then let him look at his hard old strumpet of a wife, and remember the price he had paid for her.

She beckoned Bruno towards the back door. 'I'll give you his bottle, and another of boiled water, and don't you dare let another thing pass his lips. He can lie in his little basket on the back seat, if you ride beside him. I'll pack another basket with his things.'

Octavius's things were plentiful – nappies, pins, muslin squares, tins of talcum powder, jars of zinc and castor oil. Also a threadbare plush monkey, once the property of Jack, which Octavius appeared to find comforting and amusing.

Kit rattled the key of the Austin impatiently. 'How much does one baby need, for godsake?'

Bruno addressed the others, who were milling about in Gladys's way. 'He'll be fine, I swear.' He stroked the warm, bald head with such loving protectiveness that Gladys impulsively kissed him.

'I know he will.'

'Come on.' Kit went to the car, switched on the engine, and chafed while Octavius and Bruno were stowed into the back. He put his foot down, the second the door was shut. They lurched and swayed along the lane.

'Slow down!' Bruno complained, clutching Octavius's basket with both hands. 'You'll have him on the floor!'

Kit glanced into the rear-view mirror. 'Keep him quiet, can't you?'

Octavius was wailing, and cranking himself up to a roar. He kicked off his pale-blue knitted boots, and arched his back furiously. Bruno fitted the little boots, with difficulty, on the rigid feet. He picked the baby out of the basket, and cuddled him in his arms. He waggled the plush monkey before the purple face, in a half-hearted manner that fooled nobody. In desperation, he slipped his little finger into Octavius's mouth. Gladys had forbidden him to do this, on the grounds that it would give the baby thrush, but it worked. Sucking vigorously, soothed by the motion of the car, Octavius's yells suddenly stopped, as if someone had switched him off.

Both men sighed with relief.

'God, that sound goes through you,' Kit said.

'Nature is remarkable,' Bruno said. 'She makes infants scream in a way that cannot be ignored, and also makes them so beguiling that you generally don't kill them for it.'

'Beats me what you find beguiling about that awful little bag of wind.'

Bruno considered the tense set of Kit's shoulders, and the fury of the eyes in the mirror, and decided not to argue. It would be foolish to annoy him, when he was already driving at the extreme limits of his patience. He smacked the horn at hay-wagons and tractors, and swore when forced to stop for stately processions of cattle.

Quin and Paddy had begun to accuse Kit of hardness of heart towards Octavius. Bruno, being less like Kit than they were – a mild Randall, as their mother and poor Jack had been – thought he understood him better. Bruno saw a man suspended, by a thread, over a dark pit of absolute despair. Kit did not dare to let anything soften him into falling. He wound his grief around him like a spiked chain, as if his suffering could keep him sane.

Bruno's heart was broken too, but still generous enough to ache for his brother. While married to Lily, Kit had shown how happiness could transform him. Now that he had lost her, he could only survive by driving that powerful,

446

overwhelming love back underground. One day, he would be able to bear letting a little of it out for Octavius. It was unkind to expect it now.

Kit sniffed. 'What's that fucking awful smell?'

'What do you think?'

'Oh, God. Don't just sit there – do something about it.'

'You'll have to stop,' Bruno said calmly. 'I can hardly change him in a moving vehicle.'

'Why not?'

'I don't want us to arrive plastered in shit.'

Kit swerved angrily onto a sward of green at the side of the road, and pulled the handbrake. 'Don't take all day.'

Bruno had never changed a nappy without Gladys looking over his shoulder. Sweating with nerves, he removed his jacket and tie, and rolled up his sleeves. As if defusing a bomb, he laid Octavius on the back seat and unpinned the stinking nappy. Breathing through his mouth, he wiped away as much of the canary-coloured contents as he could, with two muslin squares and both their handkerchiefs. It was, he thought, one of the trickiest operations he had ever performed – breaking Enigma codes at Bletchley was duck soup, compared with this. Gingerly, he smeared cream, shook talc, and pinned on a clean square of towelling. He was sure he had folded it correctly, but it looked baggy and insecure. He put Octavius back in his basket, and bundled the soiled articles into a compact brick, disagreeably heavy and warm.

Then he leaned against the car and lit a cigarette. 'All clear,' he called. 'Well, clear-ish.'

Kit had been smoking beside a hedge, well out of range. He returned to the car. 'May we go?'

'Yes.' Bruno picked up the basket, and placed it on the back seat. As he did so, he was unable to resist tickling the soft folds of flesh under Octavius's chin. He stopped doing this when he intercepted a thunderous look from Kit.

Kit refused to have the dirty nappy in the car. Bruno left it, together with their handkerchiefs and the muslin squares, under the hedge. Gladys was not going to like this wanton waste, but she did not have to deal with Kit.

'There's still an almighty reek,' Kit said. 'All you've done is spread it about a bit.'

'Too bad.' Bruno was trying to fasten his tie, keeping the basket on the seat with his knees.

They raced over the few remaining miles to the Prospect, without another word. Bruno, when they passed through the weathered stone gateposts, felt his flesh crawling. Here were some of the unknown things Lily had carried in her head, all the time they had known her. Once again, he had to remind himself that this time was over.

The road between the gate and the house was steep, elaborately twisting between clumps of black shrubs. The Italianate chimneys were visible, now on their right, now on their left, for ages. Kit stopped the car at the flight of stone steps up to the front door.

'She loved this man once,' he said.

'He was her father,' Bruno pointed out.

'He chose the stepmother, over his own child.' Kit was talking to himself. 'If he hadn't, Lily would never have scarpered. She might never have met us. She'd probably still be alive now.'

'Kit, you are following all the signposts to Loony-Land.' Bruno tried to make his voice bracing. 'What on earth is the point of torturing yourself with what might have happened? You can't change the past. I often wish I'd had the foresight to shoot Adolf Hitler, when I visited Berlin in thirty-eight, but the fact that I didn't doesn't make the war my fault.'

For the first time since the birth of Octavius, Kit laughed. The pain did not leave his eyes, but they were full of affection for Bruno. 'I love the idea of you taking a pot at the *Führer*. He'd have to come up close, and stand awfully still.'

Bruno smiled, gamely swallowing one of his sudden rushes of acute longing for Lily. 'There you are, then. Useless to worry about it.'

He wrapped Octavius in his white shawl, and carefully carried him out of the car, up the stone steps.

The door was opened by a middle-aged woman in the black afternoon uniform of a parlourmaid. She took in the peculiar party on the doorstep, and her eyes narrowed suspiciously.

'Yes?'

'I want to see Captain Gallant,' Kit said. 'Is he in?'

She looked doubtful. 'I'll go and see.'

Kit stepped into the hall, before she could shut the door on them. She hurried away along a dark passage, cluttered with sullen paintings and brass trophies. As soon as she halted, Kit strode after her, pushed her aside, and stepped into the room.

'What? What is this?' A stooped man, with thick white hair, struggled out of an armchair. He stared, trembling and helpless, and openly horrified by Kit's scarred, ferocious face.

Kit's voice was very quiet. 'Ralph Gallant?'

'Yes. Who the hell are you?'

'My name is Kit Randall. I'm Lily's husband.'

Bruno came into the room. Kit had his back to him, but he saw Ralph, frozen and loose-mouthed, on the hearthrug. His wrecked face was all the more ghastly, because he bore such a marked resemblance to Lily. The eyes were pale and filmy, where hers were dark and sparkling. Otherwise, he was a grotesque mockery of the woman they had loved, and would love until they died. Bruno shivered, and raised his elbow to shelter the baby's face.

The parlourmaid said: 'I'm sorry, sir. He forced his way in, before I could stop him.'

Ralph, staring with naked fascination at Kit, said: 'That's all right. You can go.'

'Shall I tell Madam, sir?'

'Yes, by all means,' Kit said. 'We wouldn't want Madam to miss this.'

The woman left, and Ralph cleared his throat several times. Ducking irritably away from Kit's searchlight gaze, he shuffled to the sideboard, and poured himself a large glass of Scotch. He did not offer it round.

'Who's that?' He pointed at Bruno.

'My brother.'

'Oh. Well, I've been expecting something like this. You're after money.' He slugged back the Scotch. 'And you're not getting a farthing. Is Lily with you?'

449

'No,' said Kit, 'she is not.'

Bruno thought he saw a flicker of disappointment. 'Because if you've left her outside – if she's planning to crash in and make a scene, she's wasting her time. If she wanted my support, she should have stayed in my home, instead of flinging insults at myself and my wife.'

'Lily's dead,' Kit said. 'I came to tell you that your daughter is dead.'

'Eh? Dead?' Ralph was unable to let go of his indignation. 'This is some sort of trick, isn't it?'

'She died three days ago. We buried her this morning.'

There was a spell of silence. Ralph gaped. Bruno was the one who shed tears. The man who could not have shot Hitler could not help pitying Ralph, even knowing how cheaply he had treated Lily.

Kit, however, was merciless. 'She doesn't need your filthy money. She's where you can't hurt her any more. I hope you're pleased. I imagine you must be.'

Octavius sneezed two juddering, convulsive baby sneezes.

'That?' Ralph asked, pointing with a shaking hand.

'Her baby,' Kit said. 'I wanted you to see him. I hoped the sight of him would make you sorry for the way you treated her, and the bloody mess you nearly made of her life.'

The door opened. A deep, smoky female voice said: 'What the hell's going on? I couldn't get a word of sense out of that gormless Ivy.'

Bruno's first impressions of Sidonia were of an undulating, serpentine body, hair as blonde as a baby's, and extraordinary, slanted green eyes. He recalled the sensation made by Leary's painting, 'Sidonia-in-Emeralds-in-Sidonia'. This was the woman. A closer look showed him that her famous emerald eyes were netted in lines as fine as old lace. Her hair was beginning to tarnish, and middle age had thickened the siren's figure. There was an unattractive, sour drag to her mouth.

She flicked her eyes briefly over Bruno and the baby. Kit had his back to her.

He said: 'Hello, Sidonia,' and slowly turned around.

For a moment, she was startled, as people always were by

450

his appearance. Then her lips parted, and her pale face turned the colour of parchment. She looked, thought Bruno, as if she had seen a ghost. As soon as this occurred to him, he realised that she had. He would have known who she was, without Kit saying:

'You told everyone I was dead. That was sweet of you.' He smiled. 'The last time I saw you, I was lying in a hospital bed, and you were being escorted out between two nurses, yelling that you couldn't love a monster, and you wished I'd burnt to death.'

'Kit, this is extraordinary!' Sidonia's eyes were fixed to his face. She did not seem to have heard what he said. 'It's you – somehow intact, behind your mask. And you don't disgust me, not in the least.'

'You disgust me, though.'

Again, she failed to hear him. 'You have a kind of rugged splendour, which rather reflects the harsher aspects of your character. But oh, I miss that boy of mine; my carefree, loving boy. Perhaps I was cruel, walking out on you like that. I simply could not live without your beauty. My love for beauty rules me without mercy.'

Bruno, distractedly cuddling a fidgety Octavius, was astounded by vanity on such a spectacular scale.

'It was all for the best,' Kit said.

'Oh, I'm glad you think so.'

'I might have married you, before I realised what a silly old whore you are. As it was, you left me free to discover real love, with a proper woman.'

Sidonia's eyes narrowed. She had not been able to ignore this. 'Good for you. I always thought you lacked the stamina to love an artist. Is she terribly plain, and terribly dull?'

Ralph hissed: 'Shut up!'

'No,' Kit said, 'I married a beautiful woman, far lovelier than you ever were. I married your stepdaughter, Lily-Josephine.'

'Good God!' Ralph shouted, catching up at last, 'you're the Eagle!'

Sidonia turned to him furiously. 'Why didn't you tell me Lily was marrying a man named Kit Randall?'

'You didn't ask. You'd have known, if you'd read the letter she sent me.'

'I didn't want to. She hates me.'

'She's dead,' Ralph said.

They froze into silence. Bruno, to his embarrassment, started to cry. Nobody noticed.

Sidonia said: 'She hated me.'

Ralph was trembling. 'You were a bitch to her. Your lovers always did prefer her to you. Except me.' He was oozing spirituous tears. 'Except me.'

Bruno wanted to hit him, to make him stop. Witnessing the man's remorse made him feel unclean.

'She's dead,' Ralph said. 'Because I listened to you and your daughter. And nobody forced me. That's the incredible thing. It was all my own work.'

Sidonia visibly shrivelled into concentrated malice. 'You didn't give a damn about Lily. You congratulated yourself for getting her out of the way, so you could carry on your affair with Juana. It wasn't your daughter you cared about; it was mine.'

Ralph pressed a hand over his eyes. 'Her baby,' he said, 'what is it?'

'A boy,' Kit said.

'He won't – be forgotten. I shall remember him.'

'I hope so. You won't get another chance to see him.'

'Did she –' Ralph made an attempt to square his sagging shoulders. 'Did Lily mention me, at all?'

Kit suddenly turned on him, teeth bared. 'After that letter from your lawyer, I wouldn't let her dirty her mouth with your name.'

Ralph doubled up, as if Kit had punched him hard in the stomach.

'Oh, I know what this is about,' Sidonia said. 'She's leaving Charlie, leaving this backwater, leaving you. She doesn't want to see you again.'

Ralph cried: 'She does!'

Bruno shivered. Lily had faded out of their misshapen minds, and they had plunged into some eternal argument, like a pair of the doomed lovers in Dante's hell. He shot a

452

pleading glance towards Kit.

Kit nodded towards the door. They left without a word.

———◇◇◇———

'I wish we hadn't done that,' Bruno said. 'It's left a filthy taste in my mouth. Are you satisfied now?'

'No,' Kit said.

They were in a meadow, five miles or so from the Prospect. Octavius had screeched furiously in the car, and they had been forced to stop. Bruno sat cross-legged in the long grass, feeding him his cold bottle. Kit was huddled against the mossy stone wall, ashen with exhaustion.

Bruno asked: 'Why didn't you tell us it was Sidonia? Why didn't you tell Lily?'

'I was ashamed. I was afraid she'd despise me.'

'You know she never would.'

'I couldn't risk losing her. I thought I'd been punished enough for making an arse of myself over that woman.'

'You're doing her an injustice,' Bruno said. 'Lily wasn't the punishing kind. You were the love of her life. She told me so.'

Kit, since Lily's death, had been an image of rage carved in granite. As Bruno watched him, he cracked and crumbled. A sob tore through him, like an internal explosion. He bent his head, and gave himself up to a tempest of weeping.

God help you, Bruno thought.

He wanted to put his arms around his brother, to take some of the force of the racking sobs, but his arms were full of Octavius. He waited, in silence, until Kit had clawed back some self-control.

He muttered: 'Sorry.' He scrubbed at his face with his sleeve, ducking away from Bruno's sympathy.

'I'll drive back,' Bruno said, 'if you look after the babe.'

'No.'

'Honestly, there's nothing to it. He'll probably doze off, now he's full of grub.'

Kit, after a final bout of internal wrestling, forced out:

'He killed Lily.'

Bruno knew Kit had told him this because he trusted him not to fly off into recriminations. Paddy, Quin, even Pa,

453

would have seen red too soon to pick up the hidden message of self-loathing.

All he said was: 'Now that you've come out with it, I hope you can see it's nonsense.'

'Is it?' Kit looked at him sadly. 'If you could choose, Bru, which would you have? The baby or Lily?'

Bruno considered the question seriously. 'Lily, if I'd never seen Octavius. But I have seen him, and now I couldn't deny him life. Even to bring her back.'

'Perhaps I loved her more than you did.'

'Very possibly,' Bruno agreed.

'But she'd be furious, wouldn't she, if she could hear me? I promised I'd take care of the little bastard, and while I was doing it, I hated him for making her suffer.'

Bruno sighed. 'You don't hate Octavius.' He took the bottle from the baby's mouth, and slung him over his shoulder. 'You don't, you know.'

'I know,' Kit said. 'I love him so bloody much, it scares me.'

Chapter Seven

1981

—◆◆◆—

'Lily didn't want us to know which of us was his father,' Pa said, shaping each word carefully, 'for the same reason we never tried to find out. We were all terrified that it wouldn't be Kit.'

Sophie shifted in her chair, to get the sun out of her eyes. 'I know,' she assured him. 'I absolutely see it now.'

'Kit cannot love less than enormously,' Pa went on. 'There are no half-measures.'

'I know,' she repeated gently. 'So does Octavius.'

Pa really was remarkable, she thought, for a man past his ninetieth birthday. He looked almost transparently frail, his bird-bones hunched in his wheelchair, but his eyes were full of beady intelligence. He missed nothing. He could see how all the horror and dread had brought Sophie to a far clearer understanding of the family's obsession with Lily-Josephine, and their stubborn refusal to name Octavius's father. The key was Kit – put simply, they all adored him. It was ancient family policy, to protect the hidden vulnerability of this powerful man.

Sophie understood, because she had also come to love Kit. On the emotional roller-coaster, at the hospital, Kit had – metaphorically and actually – held her hand. Through despair, through the joy of Octavius regaining consciousness, through the tension of waiting to see if his recovery would be complete, Kit had stayed at her side. She had cried on his shoulder, and babbled her heart out to him, always with a sense that he could be trusted completely.

The thing about Kit was that you had to communicate with him using a kind of emotional ESP, slicing through all the layers of mistrust and reserve. These were protective walls, it turned out, around one of the tenderest souls in the world. He allowed very few people to know this – Octavius was only just learning, after a lifetime of being held at a distance.

Kit's voice shouted, through the open parlour casement: 'Bugger you!'

Sophie smiled, hearing Octavius's laughter. 'Royal flush beats two pairs – I didn't make the rules.'

The two of them played poker incessantly, though Octavius had progressed beyond invalidish pastimes. Neither could do anything by halves – if poker was to be played, they played it for dear life.

Octavius had woken up, quite naturally, on the tenth day of Sophie's vigil. He had been baffled and outraged to find himself bristling with needles and pinioned by plastic tubes, with fluids dripping into him and seeping out. He had been very weak and easily tired at first, and the left side of his body had been faintly out of synchronisation with the right side; but his doctors were confident that this would pass. They had told Kit, and nobody ever lied to Kit. It was obvious that he could take the truth.

As if to prove this, he had agreed to face the ultimate truth – a blood test, to determine the real father of Octavius. Incredibly simple, potentially devastating.

Kit was the calmest, while they waited for the result.

'Of course, I want it to be me,' he had said to Sophie. 'And I want him to know how much I want it. But it'll serve me right if it's not. I should have been a father to him in any case. I was too much of a coward to risk loving him properly, as my son – I didn't dare, without absolute possession. If he'd snuffed it, I'd never have had a chance to make it up to him.'

Sophie had filled in the rest – that he would have had longer with Lily, the love of his life, if he had not had this damaging yearning for absolute possession. She admired him, for trying to change.

Kit had insisted upon bringing Sophie and Octavius down to Devon, to recover at Randalls. With Bruno's assistance, he had weaselled extended paid leave out of Sophie's ghastly boss. She was constantly surprising herself with how little she minded being stuck out in the country. God, it was bliss. Octavius had been restored to her, and his family were spoiling her rotten. The summer days slipped by, like fat, bright beads on a necklace. She felt replete and languorous; ridiculously relaxed. Before I know it, she thought, I'll be dressed head to foot in Laura Ashley florals, and I won't even care.

'You might take a squint at the tea now,' Pa suggested.

'Okay. It must be black enough, even for you.'

Pa's broken leg was taking a long time to knit together. He could hobble short distances on his crutches, but had eventually allowed Peter Tufton to persuade him into the wheelchair. Sophie, who found him a very entertaining companion, had parked him in the yard outside the kitchen door this afternoon, so they could enjoy their tea in the warm sun.

He had always loved to sit out here, though the yard had changed out of recognition since Lily's day. The round grey cobbles had been reset, and severely weeded. There was a table and chairs of white-painted wrought iron, and wooden tubs filled with scarlet geraniums. Hens no longer pecked and browsed here. Kit kept his large and profitable flock of free-range birds in the big field beyond the orchard. Things change, Sophie thought, and time moves on. Kit and Paddy had turned the farm into a successful, modern concern. They were not as wedded to the past as Octavius assumed.

She poured Pa his stewed tea. 'Is this all right?'

'You're learning, my dear.'

'Peter said it was bad for you.'

'Peter thinks everything pleasant is bad for one. Poor old Gladys, he put her on a low-fat diet in his first year at medical school. If she buys a bit of streaky bacon, she feels like a drug-addict.'

The kitchen door banged. Kit and Octavius came out, for their share of tea and Primrose's shortbread biscuits.

'He won again,' Kit said. He set a chair for Octavius, and

pushed him into it, with a mixture of crossness and consideration.

Octavius laughed. 'That's about forty-two thousand pounds you owe me now, Kit.'

'Bugger off.'

'You're a terrible loser.'

Kit smiled reluctantly. 'And you're an insufferable winner.'

Octavius scratched the stubbled tonsure on one side of his scalp – he complained that the hair around his network of thick red scars was growing back very itchily – and poured himself some tea. 'All right, my Soph?'

'Never better. Nobody lets me lift a finger. I feel disgracefully lazy.'

'That's the German protestant coming out in you. Ignore it.' He smiled at her over the rim of his cup, in a way that suddenly reminded her of Pa. He was a mixture of them all, and she realised that the result of the blood test was anybody's guess. Was it Bill, or was it Ben? As Homer said, it's a wise man who knows his own father.

In the house, they heard the telephone. After three rings, someone answered it – probably Primrose, working in the kitchen. Since the attack, she had been spending more than half her time at Randalls.

Around the table, Kit, Sophie and Octavius studiously avoided each other's eyes. This could be the dreaded, the longed-for moment of truth. Each time the telephone rang, they mentally braced themselves.

Sophie murmured: 'It's probably Mum.'

With seeming irrelevance, Pa asked: 'Well, Number Eight? When are you and Sophie going to take a proper look at your house?'

'None of your business, you interfering old fart,' Kit said. 'Take no notice, you two. He's only doing it because he thinks you've dropped your guard.'

'I'm merely being practical.'

'You are merely grabbing another excuse to nag Sophie and Octavius. For the last time, they don't want to settle down in that white elephant. Do you, kids?'

Sophie laughed. 'Constant dripping will wear down a stone. I'm rather coming round to living in the country.'

'Really?' Octavius was so delighted, so hopeful, that Sophie could no longer go along with his pretence that he did not care where he lived. It had to be faced – he belonged in a rural setting. She could bear separation from London, but Octavius could not flourish without his native soil. His life, his work, his ambitions, were all in Devon. The great question was, could Sophie accept transplantation? The second she asked herself, she knew that she would.

She telegraphed a 'talk later' look, with a smile of encouragement. God knew, she had nearly lost him. She would make any sacrifice for him now, and this would not be a large one. Though she drew the line at cooking lentils for the nature-nerds in his research centre.

'Ta-dah!' sang the voice of Primrose, 'clear the table!'

She emerged from the house bearing a tray full of glasses. Paddy was behind her, with a bottle of champagne. Both were laughing.

'That was Bruno,' Paddy said. 'We have a result.'

He hurried on, to spare their suspense, but in the hair's-breadth pause between the sentences, they all held their breaths.

'Congratulations, Kit.' Paddy slapped his hand down on Kit's shoulder. 'You're a Dad.'

They sat in silence, letting the news sink in. Sophie saw the faces of Octavius and Kit flaming joyfully, then cautiously setting into scowls of stony embarrassment. She had thought she would feel nothing more than mild relief, and she had a ludicrous impulse to cry. She glanced at Pa, who sat very still, dazedly plucking at the blanket over his knees with gnarled, trembling fingers.

Kit reached over to squeeze Octavius's shoulder. 'That's wonderful. Hope you're pleased, boy.'

'Yes, but don't expect me to start calling you Dad.'

'Hmmm. I'll bloody murder you if you try.'

Primrose giggled. 'Why did you need a test? They're so alike!'

Slowly, Kit smiled. 'There you are, Sophie. When he behaves like an arse, you can blame me.'

'He never does,' Sophie said. 'He's an angel – and so are you.'

'Oh God, she's crying,' Octavius said. 'Dry up at once, my girl, or it's straight back to the divorce court for you.'

Primrose swooped down and gave Octavius a smacking kiss. 'Kit, aren't you proud of this beautiful, bouncing boy?'

'Lay off, Primrose.'

Kit was serious. 'Very proud,' he said quietly. 'I wish – I wish your mother could see you now, boy.'

The eyes of the father and the son, eerily alike in their shape and colour, met fully.

After a spell of tense silence, Octavius murmured: 'You've forgiven me.'

'For what?'

'I killed her, didn't I?'

Kit grimaced painfully. 'No –'

'I killed her,' Pa put in. 'I would insist on Bassett, when the Draper woman might have saved her. I must admit, you boys have been very good about not reproaching me.'

'Shut up!' Kit looked as if he were trying to swallow a mouthful of ground glass.

'Not with antibiotics,' Pa continued. 'It was probably too early. She might, however, have managed not to spread infection in the first place.' He had begun to drift. 'Very with it, that woman. She became a nun, you know. She went to Zaire.'

'Pa, nobody killed Lily.' Angrily, Kit wiped his eyes with the back of his wrist. 'If anyone deserves blame around here, it's me. I've been a bad father. I hope Octavius will forgive me. I suppose it's too late to start again.'

'Never too late,' Octavius said. 'Never.'

He stood up, swaying slightly, because he was still unsteady on his feet. Kit stood up. They faced one another, looking as if they were about to start fighting. Then their arms went round each other, and locked together in an unbreakable embrace.

Pa exhaled gustily. 'Lord,' he whispered to himself. 'Lord, lettest now thy servant depart in peace.'

Epilogue

1997

'There's nothing I love better than a gathering of the whole clan,' Primrose declared. She whipped the clingfilm off her quiches, so the hot sun would not turn them mouldy. 'Isn't it fun, being part of a clan? I can never get over it.'

'It's wonderful,' Isobel agreed. She flapped at a wasp, with the corner of a tea-towel. 'I think I should leave my Pavlova in the fridge, don't you? Cream goes so quickly.'

'Oh, you and that Pavlova,' Primrose said airily. 'Don't get into one of your states. Everything's going beautifully.'

They had placed the two trestle tables in the orchard, in the dappled shade of the ancient apple trees. Kit, totally unsentimental about the rest of his land, would not hear of having these cut down. Behind the tables, the wooden door to the Sleeping Garden stood open, allowing a glimpse of the jewelled serenity within.

Primrose, her pink lips curved into a smile of pride, patted the pile of glossy books she had insisted on putting out with the food – *The Sleeping Garden*, by Patrick Randall, with its loving dedication 'To my wife, Primrose'. The previous year, she had finally persuaded Paddy to open the famous garden to the public. Once a week, in the summer months, she gave reverent groups of twenty the guided tour, and fed them her home-baked cream tea afterwards. Five pounds each, all proceeds to the lifeboats.

Sophie, holding a glass of champagne, laughed when she saw the books. 'You're a shameless self-publicist, Prim.'

'Every little helps. The local paper's coming, you know. We might get them in the photograph.'

Isobel squinted over at the other table, where Octavius and Paddy were dispensing Marks & Spencer's champagne, orange juice and mineral water. 'Are the glasses holding out all right?'

'Fine, Mum,' Sophie said. 'Relax, and start enjoying yourself.'

'Just what I keep telling her,' Primrose gazed round at the groups of people under the trees. 'Wouldn't Pa have loved this?'

Kit had toasted the old man's memory, the moment they were all assembled. Primrose liked to think he could see them all, from whichever corner of paradise they kept for stubborn but decent atheists. These were, after all, his people. Quin and his wife had flown over from Italy, bringing their son, Marco, and his eldest son, seventeen-year-old Luciano. Bruno and Gerda were here, with Ilse, her husband, and their three offspring. Peter Tufton and his wife were here, too – Kit had insisted that Gladys should be represented, today of all days.

Most surprisingly, Juana had agreed to come, with her kind, deaf, doddering old husband – Primrose could never remember if he was number three or four. After a lifetime of digging for gold, Juana had settled for a smaller bank balance and a larger heart. Edgar's death, and its attendant agonies, had knocked the starch out of her. These days, she lived quietly in Knightsbridge, grazing peacefully in Harrods and telephoning her sisters once a month.

Primrose only laughed to herself now, when she thought that she had sworn never to forgive Juana. That historical scandal seemed absurd, when so many gallons of water had flowed under the bridge. Pa had been absolutely right to believe that family ties were of supreme importance; the only reliable earthly source of joy. His legacy was visible everywhere.

Octavius had left the drinks table. He was glancing crossly at his watch. 'Lily! Where is that bloody kid? I told her not to vanish at the last minute. Lily!'

Sophie, beside him, squeezed his arm. 'She can't hear you. She's got her Walkman in.'

Octavius scowled. He was fifty-two, and every year made him more like Kit. 'Who the hell gave her that ghastly thing?'

'Primrose, of course. Need you ask?'

'She spoils her disgustingly.'

'Look on the bright side,' Sophie said. 'It means we don't have to listen to U2 and Boyzone.'

'She'd better take those earphones off before the ceremony.'

'She knows what to do. You get everybody into the garden, and I'll fetch Lily.'

Sophie had spotted the golden-brown head behind the trunk of one of the trees. Smiling, she walked through the rich, juicy grass towards her daughter; the child she had thought she would never have. Lily's amazing arrival had blessed their first, chaotic, paint-smelling year at the Prospect. Sophie never stopped thanking Providence that Pa had lived to hold this miraculous great-grandchild in his arms.

All things considered, fifteen-year-old Lily had turned out surprisingly unspoilt. Primrose and Paddy were ruinously doting, Isobel and Marius would have pawned their underwear to please her; yet the focus of all this worship remained sunny and affectionate. The worst you could accuse her of was a propensity to snog young Luciano Randall – which Sophie had to keep from Octavius, because it would have made him hopping mad. Very like the other Lily who had grown up at the Prospect, this Lily-Josephine Randall was emerging as an enchanting, joyous, five-star trollop.

And she was beautiful enough to stop the heart – Sophie knew this was a fact, far beyond maternal pride. When Lily saw her mother standing over her, she shook her long, lustrous curls from her gold-flecked eyes, and smiled. Sometimes, at certain angles, she looked remarkably like the Lily in the old photograph.

'It's time,' Sophie said.

'What?'

Sophie leant down, and lifted the earphone out of one delicate ear. 'I said, it's time. Switch that thing off, before your father has apoplexy.'

'Okay.' Lily disentangled herself from the Walkman,

handed it to Sophie, and sprang to her feet. She had been surgically separated from her boot-cut jeans for this occasion, and wore a short dress of tomato-coloured silk, which made her long, bare, tanned legs look endless. Sophie made a mental note to discourage her from sunbathing in a bikini on the lawn, in full view of Octavius's salivating botanists. Her little girl was bursting into flower as extravagantly as an orchid. Pushing the thought away, Sophie slung an arm around the slender waist, to reconnect with the familiar feel of the baby inside.

Ahead of them, the others were filing into the Sleeping Garden. Paddy, Kit and Octavius moved among them, refilling their glasses with champagne. Primrose firmly banished the latest Custard, who was trying to sneak in after her, and took her camera out of its case. She had already positioned the reporter and photographer from the local paper where they would not get in the way.

At the centre of the camomile lawn was a shape covered in a dust-sheet. Everyone shuffled into a circle around this. Gradually, they sank into the deep peace and silence of the Sleeping Garden, as if the hundreds of scents, pouring from the densely planted herbs, really had the power to cast them into an enchanted slumber. The sun lay upon them, heavy as syrup. Bees hummed drowsily, and butterflies drifted like falling petals.

Lily glanced doubtfully at Sophie, self-conscious for the first time. Sophie nodded, and gestured her forward. With a sudden assumption of dignity, she stepped onto the mat of camomile. The sun turning her hair to caramel, she carefully pulled away the sheet.

Underneath, in the exact centre of the lawn, on a pedestal of grey granite, was a sundial of white marble. On one side, in gilded letters, were the words:

HERE
LILY-JOSEPHINE RANDALL
1922–1945
LIES SLEEPING

Lily bundled up the sheet in her arms, staring solemnly at the simple monument, exquisitely carved by a local sculptor. It made a perfect point of stillness in the living green. Kit kissed Lily's cheek, took the sheet from her, and handed her a glass of champagne. She smiled up into his face.

Raising her glass, she recited, in her fresh, clear voice: 'Joseph was so beautiful, the lilies of the Nile turned their faces towards him, mistaking him for the sun. My grandmother was named for both the Lily and the Joseph. We put this sundial here in her memory, to remind ourselves that people once mistook her for the sun. To the first Lily-Josephine.'

'The first Lily-Josephine.' The toast was echoed in a muted murmur. Isobel and Primrose met each other's tear-filled eyes, and exchanged grimaces of embarrassment. Sophie, struggling to swallow her own tears, noticed that Kit, Bruno, Quin and Paddy were standing in a tight group, frowning to subdue their emotion. There was a long silence, stretching into minutes, as the past surged into the present, and flavoured it poignantly with remembered happiness.

'Well done, my sweetheart,' Kit whispered to Lily. 'You were perfect.'

She put her arms around his neck and said, in her normal voice: 'You can have the food now.'

The shadows melted, in a scattering of laughter. Breaking the circle, the witnesses began to stroll away towards the orchard. Primrose, blowing her nose resoundingly, rushed to her buffet table and tied on a PVC apron. Isobel, also blowing her nose, dashed back to the house, to fetch her Pavlova. In twos and threes, people settled around the folding wooden tables Primrose had borrowed from the church hall. The warm afternoon air hummed with conversation.

Kit and Bruno were leaning against the weatherworn brick wall of the Sleeping Garden, on either side of the open door, watching Lily. The Walkman riveted to her ears, she was dancing round the sundial, tunelessly keening along with the inaudible music.

Bruno chuckled softly. 'I always knew she'd come back to us.'

Kit said: 'She never left us.'

WILD YOUNG BOHEMIANS

'A ride in the fast lane with a gang of modern-day Gothic hedonists . . .'
Vogue

Melissa Lamb and her cousin Ernestine are at the centre of the Wild Young Bohemians, an exclusive dining club at Oxford for the beautiful and ambitious. Melissa is in the grip of an obsession. Ernestine however, mild and practical, does not see through Melissa's ruthless determination to restore her derelict family mansion – a Gothic legacy of lust, greed and death, with a spectacular secret that has slept for a hundred years.

Melissa will let nothing stand in her way – until a vengeful stranger enters their magic circle. But he is only a catalyst: the seed of evil is already sown.

'Gripping and entertaining'
Sunday Telegraph

'Hugely enjoyable, glossy, sexy and wittily turned'
The Times

Also available in Arrow

A SONG FOR SUMMER

Eva Ibbotson

When Ellen Carr, daughter of a militant suffragette and raised to be an intellectual, takes a job in Austria as house-mother at the Hallendorf School of Music, Drama and the Dance she simply wants to cook beautiful food. What she finds when she reaches Schloss Hallendorf is an eccentrically magical world occupied by wild children, naked Harmony teachers, experimental dancers and a tortoise on wheels.

Life in Hallendorf seems idyllic, but outside the castle Hitler's Reich is already casting its menacing shadow over Europe and the persecutions have begun. Through her growing friendship with the mysterious groundsman Marek, Ellen encounters the dreadful reality of flight from Nazi Germany, and, on the brink of war, discovers a passion that will shape her life.

In this witty, touching and above all delightful novel, Eva Ibbotson combines an immensely satisfying love story with a gripping account of the gathering storm of war. *A Song for Summer* is a joy to read.

☐ Night Shall Overtake Us	Kate Saunders	£6.99
☐ Wild Young Bohemians	Kate Saunders	£5.99
☐ A Countess Below Stairs	Eva Ibbotson	£5.99
☐ Madensky Square	Eva Ibbotson	£5.99
☐ A Song For Summer	Eva Ibbotson	£5.99
☐ Hot Water Man	Deborah Moggach	£5.99
☐ Porky	Deborah Moggach	£5.99
☐ Driving in the Dark	Deborah Moggach	£5.99
☐ Smile and Other Stories	Deborah Moggach	£5.99
☐ The Stand-In	Deborah Moggach	£5.99
☐ The Ex-Wives	Deborah Moggach	£5.99
☐ Seesaw	Deborah Moggach	£5.99
☐ Close Relations	Deborah Moggach	£5.99
☐ Light a Penny Candle	Maeve Binchy	£6.99
☐ Echoes	Maeve Binchy	£6.99
☐ Dublin 4	Maeve Binchy	£4.99
☐ The Lilac Bus	Maeve Binchy	£4.99
☐ Silver Wedding	Maeve Binchy	£5.99

ALL ARROW BOOKS ARE AVAILABLE THROUGH MAIL ORDER OR FROM YOUR LOCAL BOOKSHOP AND NEWSAGENT
PLEASE SEND CHEQUE/EUROCHEQUE/POSTAL ORDER (STERLING ONLY) ACCESS, VISA, MASTERCARD, DINERS CARD, SWITCH OR AMEX.

EXPIRY DATE .... Signature ....
PLEASE ALLOW 75 PENCE PER BOOK FOR POST AND PACKING U.K.
OVERSEAS CUSTOMERS PLEASE ALLOW £1.00 PER COPY FOR POST AND PACKING.
ALL ORDERS TO:
ARROW BOOKS, BOOKS BY POST, TBS LIMITED, THE BOOK SERVICE, COLCHESTER ROAD, FRATING GREEN, COLCHESTER, ESSEX CO7 7DW.

NAME ....
ADDRESS ....
....
Please allow 28 days for delivery. Please tick box if you do not wish to receive any additional information ☐
Prices and availability subject to change without notice